Haunted by Your Soul

Marguerite Labbe

Dreamspinner Press

Published by
Dreamspinner Press
4760 Preston Road
Suite 244-149
Frisco, TX 75034
http://www.dreamspinnerpress.com/

Haunted by Your Soul

Cover Art by Dan Skinner/Cerberus Inc.   cerberusinc@hotmail.com
Cover Design by Mara McKennen

ISBN: 978-1-935192-72-5

Printed in the United States of America
First Edition
September, 2009

eBook edition available
eBook ISBN: 978-1-935192-73-2

For Suzane Ritch,
for all her years of support,
the brainstorming and beta reads, and
for providing me with an anchor back home.
I love you.

For her husband Wayne,
who probably heard much more
of my stories than he wanted to and
allowed me to steal his wife's time on many a night.

And for our muses, the Idjits and
Amber and Lasoe, who put up with us.

Chapter 1

A SENSATION. A thought. A dawning sense of individuality drew my notice and woke me up. I had been drifting, caught up in the swirl of mass consciousness for how long I didn't know. Time had no meaning here, or the Ascended existed outside of time, or all points of time at once. I knew not which.

Only now, terms such as I and me began to form in my psyche; words altogether foreign to the whole. Though we speak with many voices, the Ascended were of one mind; one being. Independence and individualism held no meaning for us; no importance. Instead of thinking in terms of we and us, this new possibility of existence including things such as I or me seemed new, yet somehow familiar. Words that made me separate from the whole, distinct in my own right.

Why was I different?

"Stay."

The whispering started again, pulled me back under, my brief moment of individuality swept under the weight of the hive mind. Other elements, other psyches left on occasion and came back. We changed in an endless ebb and flow of different minds, a kaleidoscope of personalities and souls, moving in shifting, myriad patterns. I allowed myself to be incorporated back into the whole without a fight. There was still so much left to learn and I wasn't ready to stand on my own.

At least, that was what they kept telling me.

Yet something else continued to tug at my mind, keeping me from sinking back into oblivion. I shifted, flitting over other distinct psyches searching for the tether that insisted on propelling me ever onward. My systematic hunt was interrupted again and again as I lost track of my bearings as other minds came or left, forcing me to start from the beginning.

Then I realized the compelling force wasn't coming from my companions. It was elsewhere; somewhere beyond the boundaries of my new world. Curious, I drifted. Sometimes old memories, strange desires darted through my mind before being forgotten again. I felt along the edges of the mass consciousness and realized there was yet another place that existed beyond my new life.

Somehow, I managed to find my way to the outer limits of the barrier and forced an opening to the other side. I wasn't sure how I accomplished the feat and it was as if my eyes opened again. Or maybe a more apt term might be that I had my mind reawakened. All of existence unfurled before me, other dimensions, universes, galaxies, whole civilizations being born and others dying.

I froze. The vastness of the beyond was frightening, terrifying in its breadth and weight. It was enormous, mind-numbing, unbelievable and unfathomable by any one individual. Out there was to be alone, while here inside my bubble there was constant companionship. No, I would stay here where it was safe. Where I was safe. I was but newly born and needed to be with my family.

Then the call came again. No words, no thought behind it, just pure emotion driving away my fears with an overwhelming sense of loss and despair.

I slipped through the barrier separating me from the rest of existence and stood alone. The call was stronger here, almost agonizing in its intensity. My psyche took shape into a form I recognized and I trembled. My mind whirled, trying to decipher what it all meant. I could hear the Ascended whispering, calling me back home. There was something about them and the unique sound they made that was significant and teased my memory. But the other plea was stronger, almost shrieking, drowning out the Ascended and my nascent understanding. Yet I didn't know how to find it or how to sever the connection.

As I struggled with the dilemma, another presence emerged next to me. Her semblance was as thin as mine. I knew her. Yet in the same moment I didn't. Why couldn't I remember? I had touched upon her once or twice in the mass, of that I was sure. But that wasn't where I knew her from. It was someplace else, long gone and forgotten. Her hair was dark golden, her eyes a serious brown. Somehow, she seemed to be more a part of me than the other Ascended, yet I knew not why.

"You shouldn't be here." Her voice was gentle and coaxing. "You aren't ready yet."

"I know," I replied and studied her face, searching for the elusive trigger that would cause everything to fall into place.

She held out her hand. "Come back with us. Come home."

I started toward her, the sweet song of the other minds swelling, beckoning me into their comfortable anonymity. Then I hesitated, drawing back as my fetter yanked toward the unknown call. Through the connection, I could sense agony, a desperate loneliness and rage. I cried out, my mind spinning from the brief contact.

"It's time to let him go," she said, moving closer. "Your old life is long past. It doesn't concern you now."

Her words made sense, but I found myself moving away from her again, evading her hand. I sensed that, if she touched me, the link between myself and my unknown puppet master would be shattered once the Ascended enveloped me again. Maybe it was foolish, but I didn't want to lose the part of myself that made me distinct from the rest.

"No… not yet."

"If you wish." She drew back, patience in her eyes. "In time it will become less on its own. We thought merely to ease your discomfort."

Two sides pulled at me. One offered solace, new knowledge, and constant companionship, the other confusion and pain. It was a ludicrous decision, yet still I found myself letting the outside one pull me along. It needed me more.

She disappeared in a flash of confused images, too quick for me to make out. A distant world of blue and swirling white appeared before me and I hurtled toward it. Then it changed to a jumbled maze of concrete and glass, scents and sounds that left me aching.

He called again.

He?

I struggled to make sense of it all, but the jigsaw puzzle refused to match up into a complete, sensible picture. He called me.

He who?

Too much information bombarded me; a whole world of sensation and memory and words. It was painful and I struggled to pull away again. Afraid, I wanted—no, needed—to go back to where I belonged. But he wouldn't let me.

Who?

The world fell still.

Jacob.

Chapter 2

THE sidewalk milled with costumed people in a curious mixture of horror and comic. Jigsaw in his distinctive white and red mask rubbed elbows with Jay and Silent Bob. Carrie's bloodstained prom dress stood out in the throng as she scampered down the street, her date sporting a very realistic-looking proton pack strapped on over his Ghostbuster uniform.

It was unreal. On this night, one year ago, I stood at this very spot when I recognized Kristair.

Lost in memory, indifferent to the people streaming around me, I remained frozen, cradling the rose I'd brought in my hand. Muttered curses followed after me as other students were forced to detour, but for the most part they were too intent on the promise of alcohol and a night of uninhibited celebration to notice. Last year I had been one of them.

It was part of a whole other life. This year, things were different. Different in so many ways it hurt my brain to try to process them all at once.

Tony was gone now. The last words I had said to him were full of hate and fury. It ate at me during the long, dark hours before dawn when I lay awake, my arms empty. I didn't know if my friend had survived his trip to Rome or how the Syndicate had greeted him. I wondered about it whenever I closed my eyes and heard Tony's screams for mercy. Or when his mom would call in the hope that maybe Steve or I had heard from him. Or every time I walked by our old, empty apartment. I would never know what had happened to him. I accepted it as part of the sentence to my own private hell.

Tony, Steve, and I had been the best of friends since the first day we'd been assigned the same dinky-ass dorm room as freshmen. Maybe two and a half years isn't a long time to some, and I know friendships come and go, but not for the three of us, or so I'd thought. We were more than friends; we were brothers. Sure, we'd had our share of blowups in the past, but in the end we were always there for one another. Until I had let Tony down. He'd been trying to protect me. Instead of recognizing that, I had lashed out at him in my own hurt and rage over Kristair's death. It didn't occur to me until much later that he had been acting on what little information I'd allowed him to have. Maybe if I'd been honest with him.... Fuck. It was the same loop: maybes, what-ifs, regrets. It was a wonder I was still sane.

God, please, I have no damned right to ask anything from you, but if you could grant one thing, please let Tony be okay. I don't care if he hates me for the rest of eternity or if I never know what happened to him, but please make it so I didn't send him to his death. That's all I ask.

Of course, maybe death was preferable to whatever life he might be living now. Sometimes I hated the way my brain enjoyed torturing the fuck outta me.

Steve was still around, in a way. He'd distanced himself from me. Not that I could blame him. Kristair had set him on edge from day one and with everything that happened afterward, how it all got so fucked up, it didn't help. I sighed and scrubbed a hand over my face. No, I couldn't blame him one bit.

I had always viewed Steve as the big brother I never had. Steve was the person I went to when I had a problem I couldn't tackle on my own. He'd listen, sometimes cuss me out a bit if I had been an idiot, but then helped me take care of it or offered suggestions in his abrupt kind of way.

Now Steve seemed almost afraid of me at times. I'd catch him looking my way out of the corner of his eye, the expression on his dusky face almost wary. It hurt like hell. Still, Steve stuck by me. If I called, he listened. If I came by his new place, he didn't kick me out, and, on occasion, I even got a visit from him. On a rare occasion.

He understood why I went nuts and thought Tony had fucked up. But despite all that, in his mind, there were still some things you didn't do and I had gone over the line. Big time.

The pedestrian light changed and I crossed the street, my eyes locked on the spot where Kristair had been standing last year. I wasn't even sure why I was doing this, why I was here. For some type of closure, I guess. That was a fucking laugh. Even now, after all of this time, Kristair was with me every damned moment, eternally haunting me. It was a constant torture.

Though our bond had shattered, my mind held all of Kristair's memories; I still carried his heart, which would start beating at odd times with no rhyme or reason. At first, it had given me hope that Kristair still lived and would somehow make his way back to me. Over the long months, hope had died. He had been gone far longer now than we had ever been together.

So yeah, Kristair and I may be as one, our souls bound when he completed the ritual that saved my life and allowed me to walk again, but I knew he was dead. I'd never forget the last expression on his face, the agony and ecstasy twisting his elegant features into an inhuman mask. I may have had his memories, his knowledge, but there was no emotion behind them. And though it rarely showed on his face, Kristair had held more emotion inside of him than most men did.

I'd never gotten used to his lingering presence. At times it had almost made me forget he was gone, most often when drifting off to sleep or upon first waking. I could pretend the feeling was real until I'd find myself reaching for him. Then it would come crashing down all over again and it would be as if I'd lost him all over.

I couldn't go on like this. Somehow, I had to let him go, to regain my sense of self. Kristair's personality was as strong as my own. However, the number of years I'd been alive weren't even measurable against his. I'd find myself saying things I'd never say, doing things in a certain way that had people looking at me sideways and whispering behind my back. My Ma thought I'd joined a cult and Coach Latimer thought I was on drugs. The only ones who took it in stride were Steve and Kayla, but they were also the only ones who knew the whole story. The true story.

Even then, it was hard for them to be around me at times. I'd see Kayla looking at me with her gray-blue eyes wide on the verge of tears and know I had done something that reminded her of her father. There was a certain amount of attraction between us; there always had been. Only now, I didn't know if she was reacting to me or to what she saw in me of the man who she'd always wanted to be more than her protector, and who had known of her feelings, but could never return them. It was more than weird.

God, it hurt.

Nothing in my life had ever prepared me for this constant aching emptiness, the continual depression I couldn't shake off. The worst was the fury. It simmered underneath everything else heaped up on me and the target kept changing—everybody from myself to Kristair to the goddamned geek in my class who thought he knew everything already. I got a perverse amusement out of using Kristair's knowledge and flair for words to knock him down hard during debates.

Yeah, there had been some good things that came from all the shit I'd encountered in the past year, but those times didn't hold a candle to the burning ache the rest had left inside of me.

Someone shoved up against me. "Get outta the way, asshole." I turned my head and gave him a cold glare, irrational rage bubbling up at the interruption. He paled and stumbled back, and then the crowd flowed around me creating a little pocket, leaving me alone once more.

I returned to my brooding.

I glanced back down at the spot I'd been drawn to, my eyes stinging. I hadn't cried since the night Kristair was killed and I wasn't gonna start now. Sometimes I wished I'd never caught his attention, never met him. Those moments didn't last long because at least I knew what it was like to love someone, truly love someone.

I'm sure most wouldn't get how I could have had such a deep connection with him when we'd only had such a short time together. When we were as different as two people could be.

Come off it. Pick up and move on. There were other guys out there, or girls; you liked girls too. At least they'd take your mind off him. Yeah, I'd heard it all. But when you'd held someone in your arms and heard every thought they had, the good and the bad, felt every damned emotion they experienced, that kind of relationship never came again. Nor would I want it to, not unless it was with him.

Kristair loved me, even with all of my pride and need for dominance. I loved him despite his own arrogance and knowing that no matter what I ever accomplished he'd always be stronger, wiser, and smarter than I was. We fought, made up, and fuck I missed him. I wanted to hold him again, make love to him. God, I just wanted to know if he could hear me, could still feel me.

A very wise woman once told me this: one day you'll meet someone who by their presence heals you. When you do, everything you've ever been through in your life, every ordeal, every trial will be worth it because they're there. Only she never told me how to handle it when they left you alone, and I was too chickenshit to ask her.

What screwed with me was the fact that I couldn't be sure I'd ever see Kristair again after I died. My deep-set beliefs in life, death, and the afterlife had been shaken to their core. Who's to say what happened? Maybe there wasn't a heaven. Maybe there was only emptiness, oblivion. Just maybe, except for those few short months, I was alone for the rest of eternity.

There was nowhere else I could go to say goodbye to him, so I returned to our beginning.

I refused to revisit the warehouse. Kristair's office had been gutted and rebuilt and now belonged to Kayla. It somehow seemed fitting to do it here under the streetlamp where I first saw him. I touched the griffin head torc around my throat. It was the only thing I had left of my lover. I brought the Baccara rose to my lips and then let it fall, the light shining down on its dark petals where it lay on the cold, impersonal cement.

Goodbye, Kristair.

My throat swelled shut. What else could I say? Blinking rapidly, I turned and strode into the crowd.

I hadn't pushed my way very far when some deep instinct made me pause. I continued at a slower pace, all the while scanning the streets, the crowds of drunks, until through the costumes I caught a glimpse of a man staring at me with the eyes and bearing of a predator. For a second, I swear my heart froze in my chest. No, not again.

Fury reared. Hell no, not ever again.

I shoved my way toward my watcher, ignoring the curses around me, but when I reached the spot there was no one in sight. Seething, I spun around, examining everyone and everything once again. My fellow students gave me a wide berth. I must've looked crazed.

Then doubt crept in, leeching away some of the anger. I was losing it. That's what I got for inviting old ghosts with my oh-so-emo ritual. I was seeing things, or wanting to see them. Either way, I was done with it.

Disgusted with myself, I turned to head back to the dorm. If I kept clinging to the past I'd never move forward. Lost in my internal lecture, it took me several minutes to realize I was still being watched.

This time my anger was cold. I'd get nothing accomplished by running off half-cocked again, chasing down shadows. With deliberate casualness, I turned up the collar of my jacket and used the red light at a cross-street to study my surroundings, forcing myself to look as unconcerned as possible. And with my mood at the moment, that was no small feat.

Nothing out of the ordinary. More students in costumes, but any one of those masks could hide a predator. Except that I'd learned predators rarely hid, especially when hunting. They were among us all the time. Kristair had introduced me to a whole new side of the world, one with its own strange rules and the constant edge of danger.

To top it off, Pittsburgh reminded me of Gotham, a place not quite sane, where the saviors were as terrifying as the villains. Skyscrapers reared up to claw at the sky, huge monstrosities of stone and steel. Some effort had been made to clean it up, to wipe up the detritus left by decades of steel mills and factories. Renovation had brought glass and chrome, but it just seemed to me it was kind of like a whore attempting to cover up the dirt and hopelessness on her face with an extra layer of makeup. Still, I loved the place. It had such character, and as much as I was a southern boy, this was the home I'd chosen.

The light turned green and as I stepped off the curb to cross, the nape of my neck prickled with predatory awareness. My watcher was still there and I became very aware of the gun I had been carrying next to my skin for months now.

"You're being followed," Kristair's voice whispered in my mind, stirring the old familiar rush of pain. It no longer stabbed, just felt more like a scab picked at one too many times. It still bled.

"No shit, Sherlock," I growled back.

Silence.

That was how I'd finally figured out it wasn't my lover trying to reach me. Kristair would have answered back, but this voice never did. It was merely his echo, the memories, instincts doling out advice whether I wanted it or not.

Instincts honed over thousands of years led me away from campus toward the maze of small side streets, interlocking alleys, and service doors. A perfect place for an ambush or for springing a trap. It might just be one of Ussier's men wanting to talk with me, but hadn't they heard of a goddamned phone? Or it might be a different kind of monster than a vampire. After all, if one legend existed, couldn't another?

My heart pounded, my senses sharpening. As I moved in deeper, I released the mental restraints I had laid on my body. The hunt was on, but I wasn't any damned unaware prey. At least not anymore. I sharpened my anger and held it close inside, letting it fuel me, giving me strength.

The attack came in a dark alley reeking of rotten garbage and stale piss. Thin light filtered down from a stuttering bulb farther down the alley. It was the kind of place where, if screams managed to escape, no one would bother to investigate. What little light the streetlamps provided barely pierced the gloom. Three of them flowed out of the night, fangs and claws bared, but I was ready.

I exploded into action, ducking under the arm of one and sending another slamming into the wall with a hard shove. They paused, surprised by my strength and speed. I spun and kicked the second one into the third, sending them sprawling. I wanted to follow up my attack, to pound them with my fists and my rage until there was nothing left of them. I wanted it so badly I could taste it, a hot sharp tang in my mouth. Instead, I gritted my teeth and yanked the gun out of my waistband, stepping back to cover all three of them.

"Your weapon can't kill us," one of them said, a woman seemingly in her mid-thirties, her hair a wild brown tangle hanging to her shoulders. Her smile would've chilled me to the bone a year ago, in a whole other life.

"Maybe not," I replied, smiling back just as cold and cocky, my hand steady on the gun. "Unless I hit your heart dead on. These bullets are more than enough to make it explode right in your scrawny fucking chest. Believe me, I've been practicing and I'm fast enough. See, I've learned a few things. There are two ways to kill a vamp: destroy their head or their heart. Even if I don't manage to kill you with one shot, it'll slow you down. You'll need blood to heal. Do you want to take the chance?"

"You're not a killer," another one said, his face a mask of scars, twisting his features into a grisly permanent scowl.

"Damn, you're an ugly one," I taunted. "Now tell me what you want." Goddamned vampires. Would I ever be free of them? It was bad enough knowing I shared a city with them, even worse knowing they weren't all bad despite what some had done to Kristair and me; after all, I'd fallen hard for one. But if I had never seen another one for the rest of my life I would've been cool with that.

"You know who we are, child," the woman said.

"And what we want," Scarface added.

The third remained ominously silent. Then they began moving outward, separating themselves so even if I shot, I'd have a hard time hitting all three before they attacked. Still I hesitated, my finger frozen on the trigger.

"Enlighten me," I snarled, my heart beating faster, adrenaline soaring.

"Don't allow them to distract you. Take them down now and ask questions of the survivor later," Kristair's ghost said.

"Shut up!" For fuck's sake, talk about distracting.

Mocking feminine laughter echoed off the brick walls. "The Ancient One's secrets are locked inside your head." Bitter bile rocketed up into my throat so fast I almost choked on it. "We're here to take you back to Rome, break open your mind like an egg and suck out everything you've been hiding."

Before my anger and fear overran my cursed conscience they attacked again, the silent one rushing at me from the side. I half-turned, firing, and the bullet grazed his temple. Then they were on me. The gun was wrenched out of my hand and skittered down the alley.

I shoved one off with a shoulder block to his ribs and punched another in the face, bone crunching under my fist. Then my feet were swept out from underneath me and I went down in a tangle of furious limbs.

"Yer getting nothing from me!" I snarled, struggling to get to my feet.

The Syndicate. Fuck, oh fuck, they were back, and if they managed to subdue me and take me to Rome, then Kristair would've died in vain. That thought alone was enough to send new strength surging through my veins.

"Kill them. Kill them all." I couldn't be sure if the thought was mine or Kristair's.

These were the ones responsible for Kristair's death. They were all going to pay. My blood seethed as I kicked. One of the vamps flew backward toward a new figure that had appeared in the alleyway. Fuck! I should've thought about the possibility of reinforcements.

The newcomer drew a sword as the female vamp jumped back up, turning her back on the fourth. There was a flash of silver and her head rolled away in another direction as her body crumpled to the ground in a heap.

My stomach heaved, sobering me as the rage and killing instinct fled. Suddenly, this wasn't a game any longer. The silent vampire scrambled off me to face the new threat, leaving me to contend with the scar-faced bastard.

My new ally laughed as he faced off with his opponent. "Going out and not being ready for a fight to the death. How short-sighted."

I shoved Scarface off me and scrambled to my feet as the silent one drew a sword of his own. It was like being in the middle of a damn *Highlander* episode. A burble of hysterical laughter rose in my throat as I dodged my attacker and dove for the gun. My fingers closed on it just as a foot grabbed my ankle and jerked me back.

"Never hesitate in war."

Instinct took over. I rolled onto my back and unloaded the clip in the vamp's chest. The sound of the gun was amplified, echoing off the close walls. My heart jerked with each report. The vamp fell back, his body pummeled, his chest a grotesque mess, each hollowed-out bullet destroying flesh and leaving gaping holes. My hand—hell, my entire body—shook, as I staggered to my feet and walked over to where Scarface lay. Did I get his heart?

The newcomer still fought with the silent one, dancing in the alley in a flurry of moves, nothing but whirling shadows out of the corner of my eye.

Scarface stared up at me, his gaze still aware, his fingers twitching. The wounds were starting to close, skin creeping over holes. I didn't have to look to know what was happening. I dug into my jacket for a spare clip. Fighting the urge to scream, I clenched my teeth. I'd never really thought I'd actually have to use this fucking thing. This was far different from the practice range.

The vampire's eyes widened as I pointed the muzzle right at his head. He tried to push himself up. I steeled myself.

"Never hesitate," my ever-present guardian goaded once again.

I unloaded the clip into his skull, forcing myself to watch the grisly results so I could be sure. Nausea crawled up the back of my throat. He wouldn't be able to heal from that.

I turned my attention to the two fighting and ran over to help. "Hey, fucknuts!" The silent one paused, jerking his eyes away to glance at me. There was another silver flash and his head went rolling in a spray of cold blood that misted over my face. I gagged. Leaning over and holding my stomach, I scrubbed at my face with shaking fingers. My skin crawled. Oh god, I was never gonna get the taste and scent off of me.

"You pulverized a man's head and now you're getting a tummy ache over some blood," the newcomer murmured. There was something about his voice that was strangely familiar.

"Fuck off! Sorry. I don't have a taste for it like some." I wiped the back of my mouth with my hand and forced myself to straighten. "Who are you? One of Ussier's friends?" I knew I was being rude—the guy had probably saved my ass—but my nerves were jangling. I squinted and tried to get a better look at his features, but the stranger was shrouded in gloom under the shadow of the wall and, quite frankly, I didn't want to get any closer to him or his damn sword unless I had to.

"I think Steve was right. You have the self-preservation instincts of a suicidal squirrel. Not to mention you're an ass on top of it. Didn't he always tell us never to pull a gun unless we were prepared to use it?"

I froze as he took something out of his pocket. A moment later, light flared from a Zippo as he crouched down and set fire to each body, one by one. They erupted into flames, lighting up the alley with flickering tongues. I swear my heart stopped as it fell into my stomach. I couldn't tear my eyes away from the man standing a few feet away from me long enough to blink or pinch myself to make sure I wasn't dreaming. Unless I had finally lost my mind. That wasn't a cheery thought either.

"You've got to be sure about them, Jake. I doubt this one has the strength to piece his skull back together, but you can't take the chance."

"Tony?"

Holy hell, it was him. Paler, his eyes harder, the goofy look he'd always had about him almost erased under something edgier. I had the completely asinine thought that he'd never again have any problems scoring with chicks.

"The one and only." He grinned, but it didn't touch his eyes.

"What are you doing here?" I flung up my hand, my heart twisting. I hadn't wanted for it to sound so confrontational. "Wait, that's not how I meant it."

"You mean, why am I here, saving your punk ass, after what you did to me in the warehouse?"

Damn if that didn't strike right at the sorest spot. "Tony, I—"

"No, don't say it. I don't want to hear it, Jake. I'm here 'cause I owe you, for the part I played that night."

I shut my mouth. The guilt came crushing back even as I smothered any further apologies.

"Consider yourself duly warned. The Syndicate thinks your friend left you his secrets and they want them. They'll stop at nothing, but I'm sure you know that already." Tony's jaw tightened and his eyes glittered in the light. "You owe me too. We can settle it right here and walk away and never have to deal with each other again."

A heavy weight settled over me, dragging at my shoulders. What had I expected, an "I'm sorry" and a hug and then everything would be smoothed over? Things didn't work that way, not in the real world. I raked a hand through my hair and only managed to keep from fisting it with an effort. My throat was so tight it took several moments before I could speak. "You're right. I owe ya big time. What do you need me to do?"

I couldn't believe this was happening. I couldn't believe I was here, talking to Tony after all of these months, after all of the worry and the heartache. Whatever it took, I'd do it and hope that in some small way it made up for me not helping him when he'd been packed into that coffin and then shipped off to my worst enemies.

"I need you to go to Ussier for me and request an audience on my behalf. He might listen to you because of your connection with Kristair."

How could he sound so damned calm and removed? There was no expression on his face. It was unnerving. Even hate would be better than this horrible blankness. I'd happily give my chance for a shot at the NFL for one of his old, goofy fucking smiles.

"Are you outta yer damn mind?" It suddenly hit me, how much Tony was risking being here in the city right now with a death sentence over his head. If he was spotted by any of the Pittsburgh vampires who answered to Ussier.... "Couldn't you have called instead and warned me? Asked me then?"

"I had to be sure you'd listen."

"It's a very convenient story. You're attacked; he saves you," Kristair whispered, centuries of survival instincts and paranoia kicking in.

My eyes narrowed as I took in the remnants of the bodies littering the ground around us. "You didn't stage this, did you?"

"Jesus Christ, Jake." For a second, Tony's mask slipped and showed a bit of his old exasperation, though he'd never showed it with quite the same flair Steve did. Just as quickly, the irritation was replaced with anger, and relief flowed through me. He wasn't some brainwashed robot. Tony was still there somewhere, dwelling beneath the new façade. He still had some feelings and that was enough to banish Kristair's instincts into silence.

"No, asshole. I did not set this up just to get on your good side. I don't give a damn whether you hate my guts, because you're not on my list of trustworthy people either. You owe me, Jake. Now are you going to set up the meeting or not?"

"Of course I am, and I don't hate your guts either. I'm sorry. I know you don't want to hear it, but I am. If I could go back—"

"You can't," Tony interrupted. "You can never go back."

And there it was, hanging between us. Regret and guilt. I sighed and checked my gun to make sure the safety was on before I stuffed it back in my waistband. "I'll try and talk with Ussier tonight. Kayla will know how to get a hold of him. Speaking of which, how the hell am I supposed to get in touch with you if he agrees?"

Tony dug a slip of paper out of his pocket and handed it to me. "That's my cell. Do me another favor. Don't tell Steve. At least not until I know how this is going to play out."

More guilt. Steve was going to be pissed if he knew I'd kept something like this from him. He'd been just as worried about Tony as I'd been, maybe even more. He'd always been the mother hen of the group. But a little hope glimmered too. Maybe this meant Tony was back for good and maybe, somehow, we'd find a way to repair our friendship. Hope springs eternal and all that bullshit. I couldn't help but want it.

"You've got it." I hesitated. "It's good to see ya, man."

Tony broke the awkward moment by walking away, the sword he'd carried tucked away hidden somewhere under his long jacket. I watched him go, my gut churning, hands stuffed in my pockets. I wanted to call him back. I wanted to apologize again, beg his forgiveness, but I remained silent.

At the corner, he paused and glanced back at me. "For the love of god, Jake. In the future, please stop trying to spring traps in alleyways."

Before I could respond, shadows coalesced around him and he was gone.

Chapter 3

STILL in a daze of misery and indecision, I found myself standing outside Kayla's dorm room. I scrubbed a hand through my disheveled hair, trying to straighten it some, and prayed to god there were no lingering traces of blood on my face. She'd freak. I'd washed up best I could in a fountain, tossed my T-shirt and about froze my nuts off in the process. At least my jacket was dark. I made a mental note to buy a new one and have this one burned. As long as I kept it buttoned, she wouldn't realize how ugly the fight had gotten.

I heard the sound of music playing through the door, soft and romantic as a woman sang about "no ordinary love" in a sultry voice. I hesitated; I should've called first instead of busting in on her like this. I had no other way of getting a hold of Ussier, though.

There was a long pause after my knock and I was about to turn away when Kayla opened the door, tucking a strand of honey-brown hair behind her ear. Her welcoming smile died on her lips. "Jake! What are you doing here? I didn't expect to see you tonight."

Tonight. My sort-of anniversary with Kristair. Yeah, I'd intended on avoiding everyone.

I gave her a halfhearted smile at the concern in her eyes, an almost paternal affection rising up. Seeing her was a shock to my system with Kristair's intuition so active right now.

"Little one."

Memories flooded my mind, of Kayla as a teenage girl, eyes filled with anger, all long limbs and sharp angles. Of her with defiance and fear in her eyes as she clutched a worn backpack to her skinny chest, and then another of her lying curled up on her bed with her fist pressed against her cheek as Kristair's hands covered her with a blanket.

"Stop it! I'm Jake, not Kristair. I'm myself. Just stop it," I raged, and the memories faded.

"You look like hell." Kayla stepped back to usher me into her tiny room revealing Steve, who sat on the edge of her bed with the air of someone long used to being there. He frowned and I knew him well enough to recognize the wariness in the tense set of his shoulders as well as the worry on his dark face.

Oh damn. I hadn't counted on Kayla having company, least of all him. Anybody else I could dismiss, but now it would be trickier with Steve around. What was she doing having company anyway? Somehow I managed to keep from asking what the hell he thought he was doing in her room so late.

Late? Jesus, it was barely ten. I really needed to get a grip on reality.

I didn't want to deal with Steve now, especially with Tony's secret hanging over my head. It was bad enough Kayla had to be involved, but I wanted to keep as many people out of this as I could. After what had happened last time, I'd become very overprotective of the friends I had left. It wasn't like I was inviting anyone new into my life.

I hesitated in the doorway. "Hey," I managed to acknowledge him, glancing away as guilt welled. Tony was in Pittsburgh and I couldn't say one damn word to Steve about him. It would be crowded in Kayla's room with the three of us, the space made even smaller by Steve's lanky legs, and though I may be short, I wasn't small. Too crowded. "I'm sorry. I can come back another time."

"Don't be stupid." Kayla dragged me inside, then plopped down on the bed next to Steve and folded her legs under her. "Tell me what's wrong."

Steve leaned forward, resting his elbows on his knees. "What happened? You look a mess."

I ran a hand through my hair, my thoughts racing as I tried to figure out what to say and what to leave out. Secrets. They were what caused so many problems last time. I hated secrets. They watched me as I hooked Kayla's computer chair with my foot and sat down before I popped right back up again to pace.

"Okay, I need you to hear me out. And I'm not going to be able to answer all of your questions, not tonight, because I made a promise, but I swear you'll get all your answers as soon as I can manage."

They exchanged glances and Steve's mouth tightened. I turned my gaze away, acid hitting my throat as I studied my hands, trying to focus on something else other than my friend's reaction.

I had killed again tonight. The thought of it, even in self-defense, made my stomach turn. I was no warrior like my lover had been, able to shrug it off and look forward to the next fight. I only wanted to be left in peace so I could pull my life back together. I wanted to play football and get my Ma a new house, not fight a war I never started in the first damn place. Sudden exhaustion dragged me down until Kayla's gentle voice drew me out of my dark thoughts like a caress.

"We're listening."

I gathered my thoughts and began before I could second-guess my decision to tell them even the smallest bit. "The Syndicate came looking for me tonight." Kayla gasped and Steve lurched to his feet with a string of muttered curses. "They want to take me back to Rome because they think I can give them the info they want. What they were trying to get out of Kristair."

"Never."

I paused, shaken, because I couldn't tell whose thought that had been. Would I ever get used to Kristair's constant presence? It was getting worse as the months wore on.

On top of that, I didn't even know what the hell the Syndicate was after. Not really. Kristair hadn't been exactly clear on that matter, just kept insisting he wasn't going to share.

"Oh my god, are you okay?" Kayla asked. "They didn't touch you, did they?"

Steve eyed me, searching for injuries, and demanded, "Where? What happened?"

"Yeah, I'm fine. I killed one of them." I somehow managed to say that without flinching. It shut the both of them up, which was good, because dodging questions was sure to piss Steve off. "Thanks for helping me get the gun, man, and taking me to the range. It saved my ass."

"I'd hoped you wouldn't have to use it." Steve hooked his thumbs in his jean pockets and his shoulders slumped.

Our eyes caught and held. For the first time in a long while, there wasn't a huge wall between us. "Me too, but I did." And I could still taste the metallic tang of blood, still feel it on my skin even though I couldn't see it. I rubbed my arms as gooseflesh rose and the crawling sensation faded. As much as I wanted the Syndicate to pay, the reality of killing someone, even a vamp, was hard to stomach.

I turned my attention to Kayla. "I need to see Ussier, tonight if possible, or at least talk to him on the phone, but I'd prefer in person. Do you think you can arrange it?"

Kayla's brows furrowed. "It shouldn't be a problem, especially considering this news. He's been wanting to see me anyway. I guess now's as good a time as another."

Steve and I exchanged a glance. I wasn't too keen on her accompanying me and it seemed like he wasn't too fond of the idea either. We didn't say a word, though, as Kayla dug out her cell phone. Neither of us dared suggest to her that she stay behind. There were some women you couldn't pull that off with, even if it was for her own good. Kristair's daughter was at the top of the list.

Steve crouched down in front of me as she talked. "So what happened exactly? How many of them were there?"

"Three. Look, you don't want the details. You'll kick my ass for being a moron."

"I might just kick your ass on general principle." Steve studied me, his face troubled. "Fine. Don't tell me if you're going to get all thickheaded about it, but promise me you won't take any more stupid risks."

"Me?" I tried to feign innocence, only my heart wasn't into it. "Okay, I swear. I'll be on my best behavior."

"That isn't saying much," Steve grumbled.

"We're on, Jake," Kayla said, stuffing the phone in the back pocket of her snug jeans. "He wants us to meet him at Deke's bar in an hour."

"Where's that?" I didn't like the thought of meeting in a bar, even if it was a public place and certainly preferable to whatever private location Ussier might pick. "There's not going to be only vamps at this place, is there?" Now that was a really scary thought: a vampire biker bar in Pittsburgh.

"Don't be ridiculous." Kayla laughed. "There aren't really that many vampires in town. It would start a territorial war. A vampire needs a large feeding area."

"Isn't that a pleasant thought?" Steve grimaced. "Vampires fighting over who gets to feed off humans."

A chill raced down my spine. How Kayla could sound so casual about it I didn't know. "Does the bus go by there?"

"It's off of Forbes Avenue. We can walk."

"We can take my ride," Steve said. "If you don't mind me tagging along."

I definitely minded, even if he'd be able to help me watch Kayla's back. It was going to be hard enough talking to Ussier without tipping her off; Steve would want to know everything. He'd insist on it. He was just biding his time before demanding answers.

"Actually, I thought it might be a better idea if I went by myself. I don't want to drag you two into another mess."

Kayla gave me a withering glance. "Don't even think about it, hotshot." She laid her hand on Steve's arm. "You can come. You're a part of our little hobbled-together family. There's nothing I wouldn't share with you and I know Jake feels the same."

I tugged on my earlobe and bit my tongue as suspicion crossed Steve's face. "Jake?"

I sure as hell was not interested in another fight. "Sure, man. Someone needs to help me keep *chica* out of trouble."

Steve laughed as Kayla glared. "More like to keep her from killing you."

I gave her a lopsided smile and kissed the back of her hand. Despite the seriousness of the night and everything weighing on me, it was good to be with the both of them. Maybe that was why I wasn't arguing more to keep them behind. It had been too long since the last time I had spent time with either one of them without sensing that I was still alone and that I couldn't cross over the chasm to be with them.

"Let's get this show on the road, kids," Steve said, gesturing to the door. "I'd like to get back home before the guy we're meeting with starts to get hungry."

Chapter 4

"YOU'VE got to be kidding me. This place is run by a vampire?" Steve asked as he parked his used SUV in a little parking lot next to a row of brownstones. Across the street sat an old red stone church with stained-glass windows. A neon-blue sign emblazoned with POOH CORNER was the only indication this was a bar and pool hall, not what the building had originally been erected for. I shook my head as I clambered out. The nuns back home would have a fit if they saw this.

"Pooh Corner?" I couldn't believe it. Oh, for chrissakes, I'd landed in a modern-day version of *Wizard of Oz* or maybe *Alice in Wonderland*, where reality met fantasy in a skewed and creepy way. A bar that used to be a church owned by a vampire and it was named Pooh fucking Corner.

"Deke's got a twisted sense of humor. At least that's what Kristair always said." Kayla grinned at the two of us and I had a sneaking suspicion that she was enjoying our reactions.

"Ya think?" Steve muttered.

I dug my hands in my pockets, rethinking the wisdom of coming here with them. If something went wrong, Kayla and Steve could get hurt. The side of me that held Kristair's memories told me to trust Ussier, but it was hard to think of doing that when the creature we were about to see face to face could kill us all in under a minute with his bare hands. Once again, I was conscious of the gun in my waistband. I doubted it would stop a vampire as powerful as Ghedi Ussier.

"You've been here before, haven't you?" Steve asked as we crossed the street. More than a dozen bikes crowded the sidewalk in front of the establishment.

Kayla laughed. "Once, for my twenty-first birthday." The smile slipped off her face. "Kristair hadn't been too keen on the idea, but I talked him into it."

"Oh, I'm sure he was thrilled." I could imagine only too well the expression on my lover's face. His lips pressed together with disapproval in that sometimes snooty way of his. It had probably taken her next to nothing to get him to agree though. Kristair would've denied it to the end, but Kayla had always had him right where she'd wanted him. He'd loved his daughter more than I had realized was possible. It made me understand more what my Ma had felt for me.

We climbed the steps and Steve opened the wooden door, gesturing for Kayla to precede us. The bar was about half-full, the pool tables to the left of the aisle and the place surprisingly well lit. I'd expected it to be dark, like something from a horror movie set. The right side of the aisle held a number of small tables, though the hard-looking men in leather and denim seemed to be more interested in the games than sitting and drinking. The few women who were with them didn't look all that safe either.

Kayla didn't pause, but walked right up the aisle to the bar with a little bounce in her step that had Steve rolling his eyes and me trying to hold back a snicker. If I ever met something that intimidated that girl, I'd probably run screaming in the other direction.

A tall, burly man stood on the dais where the altar used to be, replaced now with a bar. He watched us coming and didn't say a word as he continued to pour beers. His hair was grizzled and iron-gray with a Harley cap stuffed over it. His face was craggy, unwelcoming, and very familiar. At the sight of him, everything that happened the night Kristair died etched even deeper in my mind. Yeah, I remembered Deke. He was one of the vamps that ran close with Ussier, helped back up his decisions.

Quite a few of the patrons watched our progress, their eyes unfriendly and curious; a dangerous combination. "How come I get the feeling she's the only one of us who knows what the hell they're doing?" Steve muttered under his breath to me.

"Because you've got very good instincts."

"He's waiting for you in the back," Deke rumbled, pointing to an unobtrusive door behind the bar with a thick finger.

I nodded and took a deep breath. "This won't take long, guys. Stick by Deke."

"Wait just a minute, hotshot. We're going with you," Kayla said, moving around the bar before I could stop her.

"I certainly didn't drive your punk ass here to play a game of pool," Steve added. "We're all going together."

I nodded, unhappy with the whole situation. I hadn't thought keeping them out was going to work, but it had been worth a try. I followed Kayla to the back room, ignoring Deke's stare and Steve's glower. The room had once been the dressing area for priests and now it had been converted into an office. Empty storage crates supported a fax machine and printer. It was almost scary how normal it appeared, vampires as bartenders and librarians. Who would've thought it? Sure as hell not me; not 'til last year.

To my surprise Ussier was back there by himself, sitting on a rolling office chair, working on modifying some bullets lined up in a row on the table in front of him. When we entered he shut off the TV and rose to his feet. "Girl, you're looking good," he said, holding out his arms to Kayla.

"Uncle Ghedi." She kissed him on the cheek. "Have you been keeping out of trouble?"

"No. Did you really expect me to?"

She laughed. "Nope. It's good to see you again."

I swear my eyebrows just about shot up into my hair when she called Ussier Uncle Ghedi. Whether she'd known the man since she was a child or not, this particular vampire didn't seem like the uncle type for anyone. He should look friendly with his round, broad features, light gray eyes, and dimples. But more than any other vampire I'd met, this one carried all the grace and air of a dangerous, intelligent predator, which erased any hotness he might have had.

Steve caught my eyes and mouthed, "Uncle Ghedi?"

I shrugged and leaned in to whisper, "She adopted a vamp for a father when she was a kid. What else can you expect?"

"The cute ones carry all the weird baggage."

I almost laughed it was so much like old times. Except for the fact we were in the back room of a biker vampire bar, having a private meeting with the head guy himself. "Amen, brother."

"Boys, you're being rude," Kayla tsked, beckoning us in.

I came forward and shook Ussier's hand. He was not the kind of man you disrespected by crossing him, no matter how much he gave you the creeps. There was power in his gaze, in the way he carried himself. Kristair stirred in my memories. "Sir."

"Mr. Corvin." He nodded and turned his attention to Steve. "Mr. Teasia, welcome. Would you like a beer? Deke's got his own special brew. Don't tell him I shared though."

"No, I'm good." I had no wish to try Deke's "special brew." I should have been more relaxed. These guys saved my ass six months ago, but their world was too different from mine and a constant reminder of everything I was trying to let go.

Steve and Kayla declined as well and Ussier gestured to a small table. "Let's get down to business. What did you need to tell me, Mr. Corvin? Little Miss Trouble here said it was urgent."

My mind whirled as I sat down at the table. Kristair made several suggestions of how to speak with Ussier about Tony without giving him away to the others. "The one you banished to Rome last spring has returned with information." The ease with which the Latin came to my tongue surprised me despite how much I'd gotten used to having Kristair's knowledge locked in my brain.

Kayla's brows snapped together and Steve scowled, but if Ussier was surprised it didn't show on his smooth brown face. "Has he, despite the consequences he faces? What makes him risk it?" he asked, responding in Latin as well.

"He wishes to meet with you." The effort to appear calm and collected was wearing on me. It was like wearing a different skin, or someone speaking out of my mouth while I jumped and hollered in the background.

"Regarding the Syndicate?"

Kayla was staring at the table, a tiny frown between her brows. She appeared to be lost in thought. Steve's scowl deepened and I was struck with another pang of guilt. With any luck I'd be able to tell him everything soon.

"Yes, he wanted to warn me they were looking to take me back to Rome, but I don't think that's the only thing he wanted to meet with you about. I'm sure there is another reason. He was too insistent about it."

Ussier frowned in thought. "Why all the cloak-and-dagger melodrama? He doesn't wish your other friends to know he's survived?"

I didn't look at Steve, but I sure felt the weight of his presence. The tension in the room was so strong I could almost taste it, just like another predator. "He wouldn't want to get his hopes up, especially if it ended badly."

Ice cracked down my spine every time I thought about what Tony was risking. Ussier was more than capable of carrying through his threat and executing Tony for returning, warning or no warning. In fact, the only vampire who had shown some humanity that night was Artemise, now the eldest in the city after Kristair. Maybe that was what happened when a vampire became an Ancient; they received back some of the mercy and compassion they had lost. They had reached the top so they now had room in their hearts and minds for something other than survival.

"There's more, sir," I said, switching to English though it didn't appease Steve any, his glare remaining as it had been. Hell, it might even be worse. Quickly, I sketched in the details of the attack earlier in the evening, leaving out Tony's involvement. The way Ussier's light gray eyes studied me, I'm sure he guessed what I was not saying.

The room was silent when I finished. Kayla was shaking her head with an air of disbelief and Steve looked ready to throttle me. I swear his hands actually twitched. "You're right, Jake. I didn't want to know the details."

Ussier remained quiet, mulling it over and studying the three of us. "It's clear you know many of the old man's secrets. How much do you know?"

I hesitated and Kayla's head jerked up, her eyes darkening to blue. She guarded Kristair's secrets as closely as my lover had and I'm sure that extended to me. I smiled and reached over to squeeze her hand, once again having the urge to protect her and comfort her. I had to stop myself from tucking back her hair for her. It was so hard tonight to hold onto my own sense of self.

She gave me a barely perceptible nod and then I met Ussier's gaze. "All of it, sir. I have Kristair's memories, his knowledge, his experience." In fact, thinking about it, I wondered if I'd be able to manipulate my body the way my lover had, not that I wanted to. I wanted to be normal, but the possibility was there, wasn't it? It could be used if I needed it.

Ussier's sudden intent gaze pushed those dangerous thoughts out of my head as a whisper of foreboding slithered through me. Was Kristair wrong about trusting him? Kayla too? The stillness in him reminded me of a water moccasin hidden among the reeds of a bank in a bayou, waiting to strike. God help me, if he chose to do so I'd have better luck with the water moccasin.

"That is something we definitely do not want the Syndicate to have. Do you understand me, Mr. Corvin?"

"Hey, wait a minute," Steve broke in, his anger now directed at Ussier. "He came to you to warn you. What's with all the threats?"

"It's okay, Steve...," I began and he turned back to me, his expression indignant and oddly afraid. Did that mean he still cared more than he let on, that he was ready to let me back in, or was I grasping at futility? The hope was almost painful.

"No, it's not okay, man."

"Steve," Kayla said softly. He turned and met her eyes. I'm not sure what passed between them, but he quieted, the corners of his mouth turning down.

I sighed and leaned forward, trying to will Ussier to see how much I meant what I was saying. "I understand, sir, and I'm willing to do whatever it takes to keep it from happening. I have my own score to settle with them." Whatever it took. Ussier must've caught the underlying message because some of his tension eased. I grinned. "But, I do intend on coming out of this with my skin whole."

"You'd better." Kayla poked me in the side.

"Not funny, Jake." Steve stood up. "You'd better do anything this man says 'cause I'll be damned if I lose another friend." He looked away and then headed for the door. "I'm going to go play a game of pool. You don't need me to finish this up." The room fell silent again as he left and Kayla stared after him, half-rising to follow before turning to glare at me.

Kayla shoved her finger in my side. "I know Latin too, ass. You tell me why I shouldn't go tell Steve that Tony's alive."

Jesus fucking Christ, I should've known. "Because you want me to stay in one piece?"

"Stop joking. It's not funny. Why would you keep something like that from him?"

"Because I gave my word to Tony." I glared back at her, somehow managing to keep from shouting as my frustration boiled up. "I don't like it either, Kayla. Okay? It fucking sucks. But I promised him and how could I say no? After what I did to him and then he comes back and saves my ass!" I took a deep breath and rubbed my aching temples, fighting to get control again, cursing the fact that Ussier had witnessed that little outburst.

"Look, sir, I know he's on the level. Just let Tony meet with you, guarantee his safety in and out of the city for at least that long. Listen to what he has to say. Please." I hated sounding like I was begging, but if that was what it took I'd get down on my knees that very second.

As Ussier considered it, Kayla rose as well. "I'm going to go check on Steve."

I caught her hand and searched her face. Lord please, she couldn't go to Steve. Not now. "Kayla?" I gave her my best little-boy eyes, which always worked on my Ma. God help me if she said anything.

Her eyes softened slightly and she squeezed my hand. "I won't say a word… for now."

I grinned and brought her fingers to my lips. "Thank you, beautiful lady."

"Whatever, Jake. Figure it out quick."

"Wait a moment, girl." Ussier got up and went over to a backpack lying on the floor next to the couch. "I have something for you." Kayla watched him, her eyes wary as he retrieved a white envelope and brought it to her. Reluctance flickered over her elfin features as he held it out. "Please. He asked me to."

There was no need to say who and I was both grateful that Kristair had not left me some final words, yet envious that he had for Kayla. Her lips tightened and she took the envelope and stuffed it in her back pocket, then excused herself.

I watched her go, my conscience nagging at me. She shouldn't be alone when she read that, but damn, I didn't want to share it with her either. "That girl is more than a handful," Ussier said with a wolfish smile of appreciation that made his dimples flash. "She would make one dangerous vampire."

I sat up straight, bristling with protective outrage. "You wouldn't dare, Ussier," I growled, forgetting just who and what I was talking to. To my surprise he started laughing as he sat back at the table.

"No, I wouldn't. I made a promise and I keep them. Seems like that might be something we have in common. This is what I'm going to do. Tony can meet with me tomorrow night, here, at eleven. I'll make sure my people know he's not to be touched either coming or going and I promise to hear him out. But I'm not going to agree to lift the bounty on him until after I hear what he has to say."

"Fair enough," I said, letting out a long breath. It was both more than I had expected and less than I had hoped. "I want to be here as well."

"Don't you trust me?" Once again, he smiled and I got the feeling Ussier was at his most dangerous when those dimples appeared.

I thought about it long and hard before I answered. "Kayla calls you Uncle and Kristair trusted you. That's good enough for me, but I want to be here. Whatever Tony has to say concerns me too."

"That's not the real reason." Ussier's gaze was penetrating. "Let's have it. Why do you really want to be here?"

"No, it's not," I agreed, trying to ignore the little stabs of shame and remorse without much success. At least now I could do something about my guilt instead of wallowing in it. "I didn't stand up for Tony before and I should've. I know he'd never intentionally betray me."

"Let it go." The flash of kindness in Ussier's eyes was disconcerting. "Even if you had spoken up, it wouldn't have changed what happened to him. He's one of us now, not one of you. He still would've been sent to Rome as a warning. This isn't a kid's game and it sounds to me like he's learned the hard way how to survive. You don't last long as a vampire if you're soft."

I stared at my hands, wondering just what I was: not quite human, not quite vampire either. Where did I fall? "I know. Deep down I know all that. Doesn't make it any better."

"Listen, the truth is you're letting your guilt fuck with you. This guy, be he friend or enemy, is going to use that guilt. Whatever Kristair left you up there in that skull of yours, you'd better tap into it, boy. Because he knew that sentimentality is for victims. If you loved that man, protect what he left you. Fight for that motherfucker."

I closed my eyes. Ussier's words struck deep and hard. "You sure don't hold back, do you?" He was right though; I could see it too. Tony was manipulating me with my guilt, but it still didn't absolve me from trying to help him.

"Diplomacy is for pussies." Ussier clapped a hand on my shoulder. "Get out of here, Corvin, and take that nuisance daughter of Kristair's and her ugly friend too. I'm going to have someone escort you all home and keep an eye on you until things die down. Don't argue with me," he interrupted, his gaze suddenly flinty when I started to do just that. "They've already proven they can get to you through your friends and I'm not about to let them. I'll see you tomorrow night. Until then, stay out of trouble."

I recognized a dismissal when I saw one and reluctantly headed out, uneasy with so many conflicting emotions and thoughts running through my head.

"Mr. Corvin, you said he'd never intentionally betray you." I paused, tensing myself for what was coming, but it still didn't soften the blow. "You think that's still true?"

"I wish I knew."

Chapter 5

KAYLA was subdued the entire way back to campus. She'd wrapped her jacket tight around herself and stared out the window as Steve sped through the light traffic. She hadn't even commented on the guards Ussier had following us, and that was unlike her.

It was enough to distract Steve from asking all the questions that had to be burning in his mind. He didn't say a word, just kept casting Kayla little glances before reaching over to take her hand. Her fingers curled around his darker ones and I frowned at the little stab of jealousy that pricked me.

So what if they had something going on? I stuffed my fists into my jacket and ignored them, or at least tried to. Kayla was upset about the envelope and Steve was trying to comfort her. No biggie. Only it emphasized the empty space on the seat next to me, where Kristair should be sitting, and reminded me that I wasn't doing a very good job taking care of his daughter like I'd promised.

Steve pulled up in front of the dorms and shut off the engine. "Do you want me to come up with you?"

Kayla shook her head and withdrew her hand. "No, I want to be alone tonight." She gave him a smile, no less enchanting for the touch of sadness about it, and I noticed how it worked its magic on my friend. Oh boy.

He nodded. "Call me if you need to." Steve met my eyes in the rearview mirror. "Jake, I expect to see you tomorrow night."

I clasped the hand he held up with a surge of affection for my friend. Steve and his quiet strength were always there, whenever I needed it, whether I deserved it or not. "I'll be there."

He pointed a finger at me. "See that you do."

I stepped out of his SUV and nodded at the men Ussier had sent in the car following us. Several got out to escort Kayla and me to our rooms and the remaining two stayed to see Steve home. It occurred to me to wonder if Ussier had thought of the possibility the Syndicate might hire someone to attack me during the day. Knowing him, though, he probably had. Ussier was thorough, I'd give him that.

I walked a couple steps away to give Kayla and Steve some privacy. What would Kristair think of those two? He and Steve had been at odds from their very first meeting when Kristair had strolled right into our apartment, and it had gone to hell from there. He'd probably appreciate the irony of it. At least he'd recognized that Steve was a good guy; Kristair had just enjoyed antagonizing him.

The sound of the door opening alerted me and I turned to face Kayla. I loved the little minx, as Kristair had sometimes called her in his thoughts. She was a sister to me, a confidante unlike any other girl I'd ever met, and that compelled me to offer my company despite my reluctance. "You sure you don't want me to come up?"

She smiled and came over to kiss my cheek. "You're a sweet one, Jake, despite your insufferable stubbornness. I'll be fine. Thanks for offering."

Relief swept through me and I felt like a frickin coward for it, but it was there just the same. "Come on, trouble," I said, slinging an arm around her shoulders. "Let me walk you upstairs anyway and make sure you're tucked in."

"Walking upstairs I'll allow. As for the other, forget it."

I chuckled and shrugged a shoulder. "A man can try." I walked her up to her room and hesitated, strangely reluctant to be by myself, again. "You sure you don't want me to stay? I don't mind."

"Yes, you do." She smiled, trying to take away the sting of guilt. "Yeah, hotshot, I'm sure. There is something you can do for me though."

"Anything."

"I wish it were that easy. Sometimes you look at me and I see him and it's so hard." Kayla studied me for a moment, her eyes grave, and then her hand came up to cup my cheek. It would be so easy to give in to her comfort. If I were to kiss her, she'd let me. If I were to push her further, she'd probably let me as well, all because I sometimes reminded her of a man she'd loved for years. A man we both loved. And fuck, if it didn't feel like I was committing some kind of emotional incest, I'd fall into that desire, let her ease me. Who was I kidding? I couldn't use her that way.

She made a soft, sad little sound and leaned closer to me, her hand slipping into my hair, her forehead resting against my own. "Oh Jake, sometimes looking at you just breaks my heart."

Gee, thanks lady, I thought, but before I could respond, she pulled back again with a shake of her head. "You've got to stop holding it in. You're killing yourself. All that anger and grief... you've got to let it out."

Whatever I had expected her to say, that was not it, and the surprise cut through my spurt of rage. I raked a hand through my hair. Girls, I swear. They thought a good cry and a box of chocolates solved every problem.

"It's not going to bring him back. It's not going to solve anything."

"Jake, I swear that's something Kris would say, not you. The Jake I knew felt things, passionately and to the fullest. If he was pissed, you knew. If he was happy, or hurt, he expressed it and then let the storm blow over. You've been hanging onto it for months, letting it build, and that's so much like my father. In this one thing, at least, don't let him influence you."

"Kayla, I can't." Fuck, I hated seeing her face fall like that. "I don't know where to start." The very thought of letting it loose was terrifying and I closed right up inside at the notion. "I'm sorry."

I took a step away, turning my back. The sound of her door shutting was a lonely echo in the long hallway. *Good job, asswipe,* I snarled to myself. *Way to go helping her to feel better.*

My own room was just across the quad and ten minutes later I locked the door behind me after I'd checked to make sure no one was lurking inside. Ussier's men were somewhere outside watching and it was too reminiscent of those months Kristair had sat outside my window, watching and waiting for me to give in. So much for letting go tonight and making a clean break of it.

Sitting down in the window, I pulled out the number Tony had given me and hesitated. God, I hoped I knew what I was doing. Once again, I was running on pure instinct. Only this time, I hoped it wouldn't come back to bite me in the ass.

As the phone rang, I stared out over the city. Was Tony out there somewhere or was he lying low in one of the suburbs? I studied the shadows as well, seeking some sign of Ussier's men, but wherever they were, they were well hidden.

"Jake?" Tony's voice had changed, almost as much as the man had. He sounded... more sure of himself, I guess. He'd always kinda looked to me and Steve for guidance. Now, he was standing on his own with no hesitation. Perversely, I felt a little pride at that, not because I'd abandoned him and forced him to this point, but because Steve and I had always known he had it in him. The only one who hadn't known was Tony.

"Yeah, it's me. I talked with Ussier."

"And?"

I drew in a breath; it was too late to second-guess now. "He'll meet with ya, tomorrow night at Pooh Corner. It's a bar and pool hall in Oakland. He said to be there at eleven."

Tony was quiet for several moments. I wished I could see his face. Maybe it would tell me what he was thinking. "He promised me he'd hear you out. You're not to be touched coming or going," I tried to reassure him.

He laughed, sarcastic and sharp. "Excuse me if I have trouble having faith in either of your promises."

"Look, I did what ya asked." I drew my knees up to my chest and leaned my head against the wall, closing my eyes. "You wanted me to arrange a meeting and I did. Punk out if you want to, but Ussier is not a patient man. He might not agree to meet again if you pull a no-show. So if you want to say whatever you came here to say, now's your chance. You've got his curiosity up, but if you renege, he will come looking for you. Why don't you think on that?" It was something I wanted to avoid at all costs.

"Thanks for the warning. I say we're even now."

"Tony, wait…." But it was too late; he'd already hung up. I cussed under my breath and tried calling him back, but it went straight to voice mail. Dammit. I stared blindly out the window and tried to figure out what do next. I wanted to call Steve. Hell, what did Tony want? It was far from over. One little favor wasn't going to absolve my debt to him. Setting up a meeting didn't equate to Tony saving my life or the hell I'd put him through.

"He wants something else," Kristair reasoned.

It didn't take a genius to figure that one out. I sighed and scrubbed a hand through my hair. I'd see how tomorrow night played out. Whether or not Tony showed, I was talking to Steve afterward. I wasn't gonna let him continue stewing when Tony was kicking around town.

I puttered about my room to distract myself. I even pulled out my homework and tried to put a dent in it, but that only stirred up Kristair more. Even if it did succeed in driving back my guilt some, it wasn't worth the heartache. I was too tired to block him out. Even though we'd shared our thoughts for months, I never realized how much my lover enjoyed books, learning. He loved the scent of them, their weight in his hands. He loved arguing points for the sake of arguing, of challenging the mind.

I quickly gave up and shut off the light to stare up at my ceiling for what seemed like hours. Sleep crept in and I fought that too. I didn't want to dream tonight. I didn't want to dream of him and everything I'd lost, even if it was nice to pretend for a bit that nothing had changed. *"Kristair… god please, love, come home."*

There was an answering whisper in my mind, and this time, without fighting the call, I slipped into a dream.

KRISTAIR and I sat entwined on his overstuffed chair in the room behind his office. I remembered this night all too well. It was the night I'd first told Kristair I loved him. It was also the night those Syndicate bastards started their war. Some part of me knew I was dreaming and I shifted restlessly on the bed before sinking deeper, still struggling to return to consciousness.

I straddled Kristair, my mouth hungry on his. As we made out in his chair, in the back of my mind was the knowledge that the Syndicate was on their way to ruin our evening. Kristair would walk away from me to confront them and before the night was over two people would have died and my lover would have a bounty set on him.

It lent desperation to my kisses and my hands fisted into his shirt as if by doing so I could keep him with me. I wanted him to stay, to sink his teeth into me and make me feel alive again.

Kristair broke the kiss, his eyes more unreadable than ever. Then he smiled, a tender, loving one that made me ache inside. It lit me up, filled me with warmth. "Just ask me, *mo chroí*."

"Stay." I cupped his face in my hands and pressed my forehead to his. "Please stay."

"Always." He kissed me again before pulling back to strip my sweater off, revealing my tattoos, which were a perfect match to his, a mirror image my right to his left. Tattoos that he'd somehow painted on me permanently our first night together. There were several of various design, on my chest and back and one covering my side. Some I could make out as creatures; others I didn't understand. But what I did like about them was when we were pressed against each other, it was almost like fitting a puzzle piece together that fit as one.

He brushed his lips on the bare spot of skin between the two griffin heads on the torc. That didn't fit with my memory of the night either, because on that night in my dream I hadn't found it yet. If in fact my dream self turned around on the chair it would be lying somewhere on the bookshelf behind me. But I didn't move. I didn't want to think about how I'd last seen this room, gutted from the fire, all of Kristair's treasures lost but one. I didn't want to think about what was going to happen.

I kept waiting for Kristair to tense, to look at the door and announce the Syndicate's approach, but he remained warm and supple in my arms. If he sensed their arrival, he didn't mention it, and I pushed them from my mind. It was easy to do with him under me when I was touching him. I pushed away my internal war and surrendered to the dream.

"So, where were we, Kristair?" I slid his shirt down his shoulders, fisting the fabric in my hands so that it tightened around his arms and tugged him closer. I reveled in the power I held over him. He loved me enough to open himself up to me, to leave himself vulnerable. He'd showed me that time and again, and in my insecurities I hadn't noticed right away. Only, those were regrets for another time. Right then, I only wanted to be buried inside of him, with no interruptions.

"Stripping each other naked and about to fuck on the chair," Kristair replied, his thighs tensing as he kicked out of his shoes.

"Yeah, something like that." I grinned, utterly happy because somehow it seemed like I was getting my way. I knew I could be childish sometimes and prone to fits of selfishness. And yeah, maybe that was how I was acting now, but I didn't care.

I nipped at the tender skin just behind his earlobe, feeling the heat emanating from him, banishing the chill that had been in his flesh earlier. His head fell back, baring the elegance of his neck, and I dragged my tongue from his collarbone up to the hollow of his throat.

Kristair groaned, his fingertips stroking my forearms, though he made no attempt to rid himself from the tangle of his shirt while I continued to feast on his throat. His skin tasted clean, as if he had just bathed, and the image of him standing under a hot cascade of water made me weak. God damn, that was a fucking gorgeous thought.

I released him, standing up to get rid of my shoes and jeans. I loved the sensation of his eyes zealously hot on me, loved hearing the wicked whisper of his thoughts as he watched me. It added such spice.

"You're certainly inventive," I said, grinning. Then my voice turned teasing as I cocked my head and looked at him with his shirt half-hanging off him, sitting there still clothed before my own nakedness. "Get out of those damned clothes."

Kristair's eyes lit up, and as he rose, I knew he was going to indulge my need for dominance. Lord, he made me hungry for all kinds of naughty things I could do to him, knowing he'd let me with only a token protest. If that.

His shirt fell from around his elbows to drift onto the floor. His eyes were hooded and hot as his hands went to the button and zipper of his pants. Whatever he was thinking or feeling was lost to me as he drew the whispering fabric down his long legs. "Damn, Kristair." I would never get over just how elegantly sexy he was.

He smirked. "You don't seem to be half so mouthy now."

I looked up from my contemplation of the hard planes of his body, dusted with just a smattering of dark hair, and returned his smile. "I'm sure I'll make up for it later." I closed the distance between us and spun him around to face the chair. I wasn't interested in foreplay, or in being gentle, or in playing with him. All I wanted was to fuck him. I wanted him to still feel me inside of him when he went out to meet his guests, my scent heavy on his skin. If they ever arrived. Maybe they wouldn't; this was my fantasy, after all, and I was going to enjoy it to the fullest.

Kristair didn't say anything as he knelt on the cushions, moving forward so I would fit behind him without falling off the chair. The anticipation was so strong in him that I could almost taste it; it mirrored my own impatience. I spied his collage of candid pictures of me over his shoulder and turned my lips to his ear. "What is it you see when you look at those photos, my beautiful stalker?" I whispered.

He hesitated then turned his head toward me. "I see a smart-mouthed brat who's entirely too arrogant and used to getting his own way." Though his tone was acerbic, Kristair wasn't able to hide the surge of profound love that came with his words.

I chuckled and nipped at his shoulder in response. He had no room to talk. His own mouth put mine to shame. I slid my palms down his lean torso, over those hips that fit so right in my hands, and then rested them on his smooth thighs. "You're avoiding the question, love." Roughly, I pulled his thighs wider apart, reveling in his soft moan.

His head dropped back onto my shoulder and I pressed my lips against his neck. I slid my fingers down the cleft of his ass, sensing the way his anticipation fluttered through him. My other hand cradled his chin, forcing his head up so that he was looking directly at the pictures again as I slowly pushed my fingers into him.

"That right there, my love, those pictures are the actions of a stalker, and you sure as hell did hunt me down and hound me, just the way a stalker would." He tensed slightly at my words, then relaxed again as I pressed my fingers against his prostate, causing a sharp stab of pleasure to tear through him. I loved how our connection made it possible for me to feel everything he was feeling.

"However, I know that you aren't one. That bond you created between us let me know exactly how you felt about me. How much you loved me and wanted to take care of me. So shy and worried if I would accept you. And you tried so hard to keep me from realizing how deeply you cared. So tell me, Mr. Bad-ass Vampire, what do you see?"

Kristair twisted in my arms to give me a warning look, oddly mixed with intense desire. He caught my lower lip in his teeth and gave it a stinging nip before kissing me hard. My fingers kept up their ruthless rhythm, not even faltering when he bit my lip again and I tasted my blood as our tongues entwined.

"I see someone who wants to be more than he thinks he is, but doesn't yet realize that he's already there." He paused. *"I see the man I've loved since the first night he caught my eye."*

Damn him for always managing to get the last word in. I couldn't even begin to describe how he made me feel: loved, chastised, heated, and possessive, all at once. I grasped his hips, my cock finding his entrance, and slowly pushed deep inside him.

Kristair moaned, breaking the kiss to watch my face as I penetrated him. His tongue darted out to wipe the traces of my blood from his lips before doing the same to my own. The intimacy of us sharing blood was so damned erotic. I growled softly, my hands tightening without thought on his hips before I withdrew and drove into him again.

He was incredibly hot and so damned tight around my cock that it was an almost painful pleasure. Kristair's nails dug into the chair, scoring the smooth leather. I buried my face in his neck and slid my arm around his waist, breathing in his scent almost desperately even as I fucked him.

I couldn't get enough of the strangled sounds that caught in his throat or the way he moved his body so restlessly against my own. He rested his head against my shoulder again and his hand came up and back to wrap around the nape of my neck. I lost myself in his half-embrace. The physical pleasure paled in comparison to the soul-deep joy we shared at our renewed connection.

If I could just capture this feeling, this moment, and keep it inside me forever, I might remember what it was like to be happy.

There was just one thing missing. I lifted my hand, placing the inside of my wrist against his lips. He moaned deep in his throat and I could feel the vibration of it against my lips. "Kristair...," I gasped as his teeth sank into my flesh. My eyes stung with imminent tears. Not from the pain, for that was fleeting, but from the wealth of emotions that were flowing out of him. Even as I wallowed in the tenderness that he held for me, he fed off of my own emotions. He drew the lust, love, and need from me and enclosed them around him like a cloak. It was the same tenderness that had undone me since the first night.

My hips snapped hard and relentlessly into him. He trembled so sweetly against me that it was all I could do to keep some measure of control. My thrusts became frantic and I reached around to wrap my hand around his cock, stroking with my erratic movements. I drew in my breath in quick, harsh pants that came out again as mewling, sharp cries muffled against the side of his throat.

Kristair's cock throbbed in the circle of my fist. I felt his rippling contractions around my own cock as I emptied myself into him. Never enough, I didn't think that I would ever get enough of him, or the explosive passion that erupted between us.

"Don't forget, Jacob. Don't you ever forget. I'll always be with you."

I WOKE up gasping, my body shuddering through the last stages of my orgasm. Oh god, I could still taste him on my lips; my wrist still ached.

I squeezed my eyes shut against the slow, painful thuds of my heart and I turned into the twisted sheets, shaking. I was afraid to open my eyes. What if I saw broken skin? What if I saw an empty bed?

Inside, my soul howled, the sound full of despair and fury, desolate and alone. I gritted my teeth and forced my eyes open.

My wrist was whole.

There wasn't even a lingering impression of teeth and Kristair's scent, his taste fled. It had been just a dream. It hadn't happened like that. Kristair had left to confront the Syndicate; he hadn't stayed with me, though I doubt that would've stopped the Syndicate. The rhythm of my heart started to slow.

"But it's how you wanted it to happen, mo chroí.*"*

"Kristair?"

Chapter 6

MY BODY felt like I really had been up all night long making love with Kristair. My eyes were gritty, a headache throbbed between my temples, and my muscles ached. I should've gone back to my dorm between classes and taken a nap, but I sure as hell didn't want to go to sleep again. The dream had left me feeling cheated, like I was caught in a goddamn monkey-in-the-middle game where everything I wanted was tossed around just out of reach, taunting me.

And the day was hardly over with yet. Somehow I had to get through practice, work my shift at the cafeteria, and then go to the meeting at Pooh Corner. At least the meeting was something to look forward to. I had to believe that Tony was on the level and Ussier would see it.

"Corvin."

My head jerked up at the sound of my coach's voice. I realized I'd been so caught up in my thoughts that I hadn't even started getting ready for practice. "Sorry, Coach," I muttered, tugging off my T-shirt. The last thing I needed right now was him giving me shit again for my attitude. Out of the corner of my eye I saw his mouth tighten at the sight of my tattoos. Well, he was just going to have to deal. For fuck's sake, he'd known about them for eight months now. It wasn't like they were going anywhere.

I turned to face the locker, slipped off my nipple rings, and put them in the little box I kept in there, hoping he didn't see the motion. They were yet another bone of contention between him and me. "Hurry up and finished getting dressed and get your ass out there. And, Corvin, you're benched for Saturday's game."

I froze in the act of slipping Kristair's torc off from around my throat, and then I forced myself to lay it down before I spun to face Coach Latimer. "I haven't broken any rules." How I kept my voice even I didn't know. In the past I would've already been shouting. I was building up to it though, anger grumbling in the background as I seethed.

"Your attitude is unacceptable and your performance is suspect. I don't like the changes I see in you," Coach Latimer said, his voice flat and unwavering. Not the first time I'd heard that particular tone.

"Let me get this straight. This year my grades have improved to the point where you don't have to get on my ass anymore about keeping them up." I put on my pads and jerked my jersey over them, glowering at him the entire time. "I've submitted to every request you've given me for a physical and drug test without argument. I haven't been involved in one damn brawl on or off the field this year. And you're benching me? Are you fucking kidding me? There are scouts out there, Coach. This is my last year. If I'm going to be invited to the combine again, I need to be playing. I haven't done shit to deserve this."

"Yeah, you've learned how to keep a hold of your temper, but you've grown cold, Corvin. I don't like it, nor do I like some of the feats you've pulled on the field. People are starting to talk and it gives me and my department a bad rep I don't want."

Kristair believed that telling a bit of truth sometimes made your case stronger, so I opted to try that strategy now, though only out of sheer desperation. Dammit, I needed to play. I needed to get out there and forget for a while, to have something that was normal. As normal as I could get with having to make sure I kept any supernatural bursts of speed or strength locked deep inside.

"Look, Coach, cut me some slack, okay?" I paused, my throat tightening, my eyes stinging just thinking about my admission, and I forced myself to meet his eyes. God, it was so hard. Admitting it out loud made it real and I'd gotten really good about not saying anything.

"Last year I met someone who changed my life and then he was killed. Right now the only thing I give a shit about is football, so please, let me play. I'll do whatever you want. I'll go take another physical. I'll piss in a fucking jar whenever you ask. I swear to god, I'm not on drugs, okay? I'm not doing anything illegal, or anything that's gonna let the team down. Come on, please."

My legs were trembling by the time I'd finished and I sat down hard on the bench. He was silent as I continued to get dressed, waiting for his answer. I had to act like he was going to give me permission. Then I was ready. I rose with my helmet tucked under my arm and my heart beating an uneven tattoo in my chest as I studied his face. Jesus, I didn't need this now. Everything was crumbling out from underneath me. I wanted to start screaming and never stop.

Coach Latimer's eyes hadn't changed and my heart sank. I'd learned the hard way during my sophomore year that winning didn't matter so much to the man as did the personal integrity of the team and every man on it. I'd been convinced that as long as I kept playing the way I had been I was golden. So I'd let my grades slip and the next thing I knew, I'd been sitting on the sidelines watching the team play without me. I'd had to do extra credit on top of the make-up work just to satisfy Coach.

"I'm sorry, Jake. I really am." It was the unfamiliar and unexpected gentle note in his voice that made my throat close up more so than the rejection I knew was coming.

Coach handed me a slip of paper and I took it before sinking down onto the bench again. It had the name and address of a doctor on it. "This isn't some damned head quack, is it?" I glared up at him, some of my anger coming back to chase away the despair. "I ain't crazy."

"I'm not crazy, not ain't. You are at a university now." Kristair gently teased and my heart twisted.

"No, it's not, Corvin, though that might not be a bad idea either. You've got a lot of rage bottled up inside you. It makes you dangerous; to yourself and to your teammates and to the men we play against. I can't take the risk."

I stared blindly down at my hands. I wanted to rail, shout, punch the lockers until the pain in my hand drowned everything else out. But I couldn't. It just wouldn't come out, and the fucked thing was I got where Coach was coming from. My jaw worked and I nodded, looking up to meet his eyes. "I understand."

He studied my face for a long time as if trying to weigh the sincerity of my words. "I expect you do. Maybe you're finally growing up, Corvin."

I shrugged, my lips twisting into a smile. Shit, if getting wisdom was always this painful, I'd much rather be a cocky brat instead.

"So, if this isn't a shrink then who is it?" I gestured with the slip of paper in my hand. A sudden suspicion hit me with a wrenching in my gut and as soon as I had the thought I knew it was true. The profound disappointment in Coach's eyes confirmed it. Oh god, how had he found out? I had been so careful.

"I know you forged the results of your physical, Corvin. I don't know why and I suspect you're not going to be telling me either. The only thing I do know is that you're not using, which is damned smart of you because I'd have no qualms about kicking you off the team, talent or no talent. Why you did something as asinine as fake a doctor's clearance, I don't know. If you have a medical condition and you're worried it might keep you from playing, you have a responsibility to yourself to take care of it. Football is one thing, your health is another."

A medical condition. That was a fucking laugh. I couldn't be more disgustingly healthy. I hadn't had so much as a cold since the night I got those tattoos, not even when everyone else around me had caught the stomach flu the month before. No, I'd fudged my results because I was terrified of going to the doctor.

Over the past year I'd been changing. I wasn't used to the idea of holding back in practice and especially not during a game. But I was faster than I had been, more agile, stronger. You name it. What if they found something in my blood that indicated these abilities weren't just a product of my imagination? What if I received proof that I wasn't quite human anymore?

Yeah, the thought scared the shit out of me. I wanted some semblance of normalcy left in my life. I could've taken it if I'd still had Kristair, but I didn't. He was gone and there was no one else around to help me. I didn't trust Ussier that much and I wanted to keep Steve and Kayla out of this craziness as much as possible.

"I'm not sick, Coach, and I'm not risking my health." I glanced down at the paper then turned to tuck it into my bag. "I'll make an appointment tomorrow."

It hurt. It hurt so fucking bad for him to think I'd betrayed him and not be able to defend myself. But what the hell was I supposed to say? I was afraid to go because I had a second heart and I never knew when it was going to decide to start beating inside me. That would be just what I needed to nail the proverbial coffin of my life, to become some kind of medical freak everyone wanted to prod at.

"You do that, Corvin, and when the results come in, if they're acceptable, you can play again."

I met his eyes with a bitter smile. "What about my attitude?" That sure as hell wasn't going to change anytime soon.

"I understand about losing someone. You know my door is always open. You should use it sometime."

I glanced away, the lump in my throat swelling even larger, and nodded. It was a nice gesture and damned if I didn't appreciate it, but nothing was going to make the gape inside my soul go away. I was being bombarded with reminders every second and it was getting worse. Kristair talked to me more often, more personally, and God help me, the dream the night before had been so vivid and real. I may have tried to let him go, but my past was clinging with a vengeance.

"Yeah, I'll keep it in mind."

"Warm-up is getting ready to start and you need to be out there the same time as the others." He turned to walk away.

"Coach Latimer." He stopped, though he didn't turn around again.

I just couldn't let him believe whatever it was he was thinking about me and my reasons for faking the physical. I may have felt like I'd lost everything that meant something to me, but I still had my pride, and as hollow as it seemed, I clung to it. As much as Coach Latimer and I butted heads, I couldn't let him think I was using. I knew he said he didn't, but the suspicion had to be lurking in the back of his mind. After all, there were a hundred different ways to fake a drug test.

"I swear to you I'm not juicing, Coach. I know my game's improved and I've heard some of the talk behind my back. Truth is I've been working out somewhat obsessively, anything to get my mind off... well, whatever." My chest tightened to the point I had to drag breath in. God, when would it stop hurting so fucking much?

To mask my emotions I bent over to retie my cleats. "I didn't go to the physical because I was embarrassed and I knew I was healthy enough to play." Out of the corner of my eye I saw him turn to look at me so I busied myself with my laces, hoping he would take it for shame instead of lying through my teeth. I didn't care if he thought I was worried about eczema on my ass or an STD, just as long as he didn't think it was drugs.

I steadied myself and met his eyes again. "It was wrong and I'm sorry."

Coach Latimer didn't answer; he merely nodded and walked away. The enormity of what had just happened crushed down on me and I sagged back against the lockers. I wasn't going to be allowed to play. Football was the only thing I looked forward to anymore. When I was out on the field I could stop thinking, just lose myself in the moment and pushing my body to its limit. Or at least, to the limit I'd allowed myself.

Now I was going to be stuck watching while the scouts wondered what I'd done. The rumors could hurt my chances. Frustration surged and I banged my head back against the lockers several times. Fuck. Fuck. Fuck.

The locker room emptied, the sounds of my fellow teammates fading as they went out to the field one by one. Had any of them listened in? How much had they heard? I supposed I could've made more friends on the team if I'd wanted to, but when I'd started I'd been too cocky and hot tempered. Now I had zero interest in letting anybody else in.

I brushed my fingers over Kristair's torc, hoping to gain some balance, then headed out to the field. As I fell into my first lap around its circumference, I started making lists, anything to block my mind and my emotions. First get through practice, then go to work and concentrate on the paycheck coming in instead of the people I was serving. I'd make an appointment with the doctor the first thing in the morning if they'd let me. They had to let me. I couldn't wait weeks before the doctor had an opening in his schedule.

Fuck, what was I going to do? I knew jack shit about human anatomy. Even if Kristair's heart behaved itself and remained quiet, I didn't know if there would be some kind of echo effect since it was still taking up space in my chest. And what if they wanted to do blood work? Ugh, I was gonna go mad with all the what-ifs and uncertainties.

I passed by the rest of the guys and settled into an easy lope at the head of the line, though I held myself back from really running the way my bones and muscles longed for. Staying just ahead of the guy behind me, no matter how much he tried to catch up, eased some of my seething frustration.

I hated limiting myself. That wasn't how I did things. I pushed myself, constantly. Only now I had to give some real consideration to what Kristair told me when he'd done his little hoodoo ritual, which had permanently implanted his heart in my chest. I'd thought the effects would've worn off with his death, but it was only one of many things I had been wrong about.

Hell, I didn't even know if trying to limit myself was even going to work. I might continue to get stronger. Who knew where it would end or what other abilities of Kristair's I'd develop? It kept escaping me, like I was under too much pressure. It came in little spurts, a great rush if I took off the restraints. One day I was just gonna explode.

Come to think of it, I had no damned idea how a vampire created another. Kristair had never discussed it beyond refusing to turn me. I shook my head and realized I had pulled ahead a little too much and once again forced myself to hold back. I didn't want another bitching out on top of the one I'd already had. I needed to put a stop to these thoughts. I had enough damned trouble without worrying if I was turning into a vampire on top of it. In paranoia, I ran my tongue over my teeth, but they didn't seem any sharper than they were before.

Tony was a vampire and it had happened in the space of a single night, not this gradual change over months. I finished my laps and paused to grab my water bottle. Tony'd be able to answer my questions, some of them anyway. There had been a point not too long ago when he would've done anything to help me. My gut churned. It seemed like an awfully personal thing to ask, especially all things considered.

I swallowed hard and blinked back the almost overwhelming burning in my eyes. Yeah, well, I'd royally fucked that one up. Tony wouldn't help me. Kristair couldn't help me. I was on my own.

Still running at the easy lope, I started the second lap. It didn't help, though. My inner demons continued to chase after me. No matter what I did, I couldn't escape the memories, the regrets. How things had ended with my friend was as much of an open wound as losing Kristair, and there was no chance of a resolution there either, even if his conversation went well with Ussier.

Chapter 7

THE crowd at Pooh Corner hadn't changed much at all from the night before except that Deke wasn't at the bar. The lady in his place wore a tight leather vest and the first genuine smile I think I'd seen in the place. I studied her as I walked up the long aisle. The problem with vampires was there was no real way to tell who was a vamp and who was human. I'd recognized Kristair instantly, but now I knew it was because of the bond developing between us, not because he had a huge neon sign over his head that announced he liked to snack on humans.

Deke's replacement was human though. I'd stake my life on it. No pun intended. There was an openness about her that was missing in most vamps. They, of course, had to live in secrecy. Still, did she know about her boss? How could you work that close to something like him and not suspect?

"You Jake?" She asked as I neared the bar.

I grinned. "The one and only."

"Deke and Mr. Ussier are in the back room. They said to go on in."

"Anybody else with them?" If Tony didn't show, I swear I was gonna kick his ass just 'cause.

"Not yet. They're still expecting Ms. Dupree and another gentleman."

"Thanks." Frowning, I went around to the back room. It was twenty 'til so Tony still had time to arrive. I just worried though. What if he chickened out? And I couldn't really blame him either. This was a big thing and he had no reason to trust me.

The body guards Ussier assigned to me didn't follow me into the back. I actually hadn't seen them once since I'd gotten back to my dorm last night. Not until I arrived at Deke's place. The only thing that told me they were still hanging around was the prickle of awareness at the back of my neck.

Deke and Ussier were at the small table. It looked like they were modifying the range of semiautomatic weapons arrayed before them. "Is that what you spend all your spare time doing? Making weapons?"

"I'm always looking for a better way to kill my enemy."

The casual way Ussier said it about made my hair stand up on end. "You guys scare me." That was no damn joke. I joined them at the table, curious despite myself.

Ussier gave me that wolfish grin of his, complete with dimples. "I believe in survival and I'm not stupid enough to think I'm safe just because I'm at the top of the motherfucking food chain."

Deke grunted. "Makes you a bigger target if you ask me."

"You talk to that friend of yours, Mr. Corvin?" Ussier shook my hand.

"Yeah." I still wasn't sure Tony would show, but I could hope. "I think he's suspicious it's a setup."

"Good."

"Good?" Ussier's logic baffled me. "Won't it be harder to strike a deal then?"

The vampire leader lifted his head from the gun he was putting back together and shot me a glance of disgust. "Now I know that's not your old man talking. He'd have known better. Deals are for dipshits." He shook his head. "I said 'good' because it means he's picked up some brains in the last six months. If you walk into a situation like this without thinking twice about it, you deserve to have your brains bashed in."

"What are you if you think twice and still come?"

"You've got balls." Deke laughed. "And you just might make it."

"Glad you think so."

I started at the sound of Tony's voice coming from the door. How long had he been there? I twisted around, studying him now that we weren't in some murky alleyway. He was definitely paler, but I'd expected that. There was a dark fringe of hair dusting his upper lip, as if his hair had continued to grow for a bit after he was turned and he never bothered to shave it off. The thought made me cringe inside because it made me think of Tony locked in that coffin for who knew how long before he was released.

I pushed those thoughts away and watched him as he came to the table. I think the thing that changed the most about Tony was the way he moved. Catlike and soundless, with an easy grace, his eyes more green than gray now, gathering the light from the naked bulb hanging overhead.

"Good to see you, youngling. I would've been pissed if I had to call a hunt on you." Ussier gestured to the empty chair. "Go ahead; sit."

"I aim to please," Tony murmured and sank down into the chair, studying us each in turn.

"Are we waiting for the wench to show?" Deke asked, starting to pick up all the paraphernalia on the table.

"No, my youngling waylaid her. I suspect they'll be occupied a while."

"I hope Taylor knows what she's doing," Deke said under his breath and rose to stow the box of gun parts on top of the crates along the wall. "Anyone want a beer?"

"We'll all have one," Ussier said and then grinned at me. "Though I'm sure Mr. Corvin would appreciate the tame version."

I frowned as Deke opened a fridge. I didn't think vampires could drink beer. I remember many a time Kristair sitting with me as I ate and drank and he never had anything. Then the answer came to me, filtered through one of Kristair's memories of vampires taking blood from intoxicated humans and saving it. I shuddered. That was fucking foul.

Warily, I eyed the bottles Deke set down on the table and my skin crawled as Ussier handed one to Tony then opened up his own. I had to look away as he drank. God help me, I'd loved Kristair, but this was not a world I wanted to be a part of. Deke returned from the bar with a brimming mug of beer. I muttered a "thanks" as he set it down in front of me. It may be genuine, but my stomach roiled at the thought of touching it.

Ussier sat back in his chair in a pose that somehow seemed indolent and superior all at once. "So youngling, Mr. Corvin tells me the Syndicate's decided to ignore my promise and has returned anyway. You can start by telling me how many of your people are in my city and where they're staying."

"They're not my people," Tony retorted.

"Semantics. Are you going to argue with me, or are you going to answer my questions?"

Tony took a deep breath and shoved his hair out of his face. "For right now there's only about a half a dozen. They've rented a house in Oakmont and are planning on bringing more in during the next few weeks. Bit by bit to keep anybody from getting suspicious."

Ussier and Deke exchanged sharp glances and Ussier's eyes narrowed. "Now that's real interesting. Oakmont, you say?" Tony nodded. "Well now, that's real, real interesting."

I had to admit, I didn't get it. What was so interesting about Oakmont other than the Syndicate could argue that they weren't exactly in Pittsburgh? Before I could ask the question, Ussier leaned back in his chair and gestured for Tony to continue. "And you say they're here to grab Mr. Corvin."

"Actually, he's not the main target." Tony kept his eyes on Ussier, neither looking at me nor Deke. I didn't blame him. Ussier could probably leap across the table and have Tony by the throat before he said goddamn.

"They plan on using him as a distraction and if they manage to nab him as well they'll look on it as an added bonus." His gaze flickered to me for a second, coldly amused. "They have plans for him if they do."

I swear my insides twisted at the nonchalance of his comment. I don't think I could be expecting another rescue from him if I managed to get myself into another bind. "So last night was a setup. They weren't really planning on grabbing me and torturing me for what I know." I didn't know whether to be pissed or relieved.

"I think last night was a mistake, or somebody acting outside of orders. The Council is in chaos ever since Roland Montrose was killed. There's a lot of infighting between the remaining members. If anyone manages to seize control it would be Gabriel Castillo. He's the most ruthless one there now, only he's been closeted with his pet prophet for years now, from what I understand. They may have gone after Jake because they wanted Ussier to hear about their presence and distract him. I don't think they really believed he'd go out of his way to protect you, especially now that the Ancient One is gone. And they honestly don't think you know a damned thing."

Tony studied me, his brows drawn in thought. "But if Ussier's chasing shadows then that leaves them free to get what they really came for. Or, for that matter, it could've just been a pact between those guys hoping they'd score extra points for bringing you in. In that case, they're lucky they're already dead because the Council would be furious they've alerted Ussier. Nobody seems to know what anybody else is doing. The only thing I can say for certain is what the cell in Oakmont is planning."

"Enough with the background bullshit," Deke growled. "Why are they here?"

"They've come for Artemise Dupree."

Ussier went still, the kind of terrible stillness that comes just before striking. Deke began cursing under his breath. Tony shrunk back in his chair as he stared back at the vampire lord. "The Council knows that he isn't due to go through the changes for at least another century, but they reason that if they get him now, they can watch the process from the beginning. They think they waited too long last time before trying to bring in the Ancient One."

"Whoa, whoa, whoa, wait a fucking minute," I broke in. "Pittsburgh cannot be the only city with Ancients. Wouldn't it be easier to go somewhere else and get an unsuspecting one? One who doesn't have friends already gunning for ya?"

Tony shrugged. "They carry a grudge. Quite a big one."

Ussier leaned over to Deke. "Get Artemise here, and for god's sake don't breathe one word of this to Alette. The last thing we need is her going ape shit on us." Then he pinned Tony with his gaze, all trace of dimples gone. "Tell me, youngling, how is it you know so damn much about what the Council is up to? You're too young to be wandering about alone. Isn't someone missing you back home?"

"That place isn't my home," Tony hissed. "Pittsburgh is. In case you forgot, my sire died that night and the people in the Syndicate weren't too keen on taking me in at all, despite their bullshit philosophy about helping out the younglings and banding together."

Deke returned to the table. "He's on his way. Hugh and Lisabeth are with him."

They returned to grilling Tony while I stared at my hands and tried to figure out what I was gonna do from here on. I wasn't the target, which was cool, but I wasn't exactly safe either and that was decidedly uncool. I had experienced the Syndicate's unique brand of torture once before and wasn't eager to go through it again. I guess the one thing I had going for me was I did have everything they wanted locked inside my head. I just didn't know if I could stomach using it.

Then there was my doctor appointment tomorrow afternoon and my meeting with Kayla and Steve whenever it was I got out of here. The anxiety weighed down my chest so badly it made it hard to breathe. One thing at a time. That's all I could handle, one thing at a time, and right now that one thing was Tony and what was going to happen with him. At this moment, I couldn't focus on anything else.

Ussier and Deke conferred in low voices. Tony's eyes were strained and his mouth was tight, but when he saw me looking at him he scowled. Then to add to the tension, Lisabeth, Hugh, and Artemise stepped into the back room. As Deke rose to gather more chairs, I began to think I never should've come. I didn't belong here. Artemise I had no problem with. He seemed almost friendly, his blue eyes merry as he came forward, leaning on his ever-present cane. He greeted both Tony and I with a handshake and a smile. He was the one who had urged reason over wanton destruction that night. And that had always stuck with me, made me a little ashamed of myself.

Hugh could've been a linebacker. I'd never seen him smile, not once. Granted, I hadn't spent that much time in his company and I didn't really want to change that either. Now his scowl was so deeply etched into his dark face it emphasized the harsh planes. It was Lisabeth, however, who really gave me the creeps as she took the chair between Ussier and me.

I realized I was leaning away from her as Ussier filled them in on the details, but if she made me nervous, she downright freaked the fuck out of Tony as she studied him unblinking. He tried to meet her stare, but ended up glowering down at the table after only a few moments. His fingers twitched as if he wanted to drum them and only managed not to through a supreme effort of will.

Lisabeth couldn't have been more than eleven or twelve when she was turned. It was weird to see those old, old eyes on that tiny, midnight-dark face. What kind of person turned a child into a vampire anyway?

Artemise frowned thoughtfully as Ussier finished his recap and turned to Tony. "I'm curious to hear how this all started. Go on; tell us what happened after you first arrived in Rome."

Tony stared at the scarred tabletop and then downed half his beer. "They were divided on what to do with me. Some just wanted to destroy me on the spot. But eventually this other group within the Syndicate took me in. They oppose the Council. They believe that the Council's methods are going to lead to all of them getting killed."

"Well, at least the entire group isn't butt-assed stupid," Deke said.

"Claudia was a member of that particular group."

"Who?" Ussier asked.

Oh Jesus, he had to be joking. "Claudia? You mean the same bitch who attacked Kristair the night he met with the Syndicate? The same bitch who tried to kill him?"

"She wasn't trying to kill him—" Tony started, and I jumped to my feet.

"Ya could've fucking fooled me. I was there that night and I saw her attack him." She had been insane, I'd swear it. I don't think I'd ever forget how her eyes had burned, her fanaticism glowing from within them.

"Hold up, Mr. Corvin," Ussier said in a soft voice. "I want to hear what he has to say."

Fuming, I shut up, glaring at Tony as I struggled to get my temper under control. He turned away from me and focused his attention on Ussier as if I wasn't even there. "The Council was fairly certain the Ancient One wasn't going to agree. They wanted to put him off guard with the meeting, make them seem harmless, reasonable. Claudia made sure he knew they were a genuine threat. She went in there, knowing she was going to die."

"God damned extremists," Deke said. "I hate 'em, crazy fucking mooks."

"There has to be more to it than that," Ussier disagreed with a frown. "The old man told me something similar and my Razor Children confirmed it. She attacked him to make sure there was no chance of a compromise between Kristair and the Syndicate, ever. The question is why."

I frowned, remembering my conversation with Kristair when he'd come to my apartment after the fight. "Okay, so maybe she wasn't trying to kill him," I grudgingly admitted. But she was still a nutso freak. "Kristair told me that her faction believed the Council was gaining too much power."

"That's partially it," Tony said. "It's how the Council is going about getting the power that disturbs us." I shivered. Us, Tony grouped himself in with the vampires like Claudia.

"The Syndicate's original purpose was to provide a haven for younger vampires to give us a chance to survive by banding together, but the Council has perverted that purpose. All the Council cares about is getting more power and knowledge, by whatever means necessary, and they can't see that those very methods are going to destroy them."

"That's the damn truth," Ussier said. "If they keep trying to abduct Ancients, they're going to have every older vampire in the world emerging to tear out their throats."

"Claudia took it a little further, though. She believed that getting this knowledge the hard way, by learning over the centuries, led to a higher purpose. There are some others who believe it as well and they're all as fanatical as her. The rest of us just want to get by and not draw attention to ourselves."

"Kristair believed something similar," I said. "He was mostly offended by the Syndicate before things got bloody because he thought the knowledge had to be earned, not freely given." It was like with his books in his precious library. He shared them, but on his own terms and no more.

"I can agree with that," Ussier said. "The things we learn to do, they're hard won. It gives us our edge. I'm not going to share that with very many people. And who even says it can be taught? It's like a talent. Either it emerges or it doesn't."

That tickled something in the back of my brain, but I remained silent for now. If Tony and the other members of the Syndicate believed I knew nada, I was kinda inclined to keep the truth to myself. Besides, I wasn't sure I wanted to explore the niggling thought despite my promise to Ussier to tap into Kristair's knowledge. God only knew what it would do to me.

"Now that Montrose is gone, Castillo is trying to consolidate his position, promising the rest of the Council immortality if they back him. Or at least that's the rumor."

"Immortality? Aren't vampires immortal already?" I asked. "That's kinda overkill, don't you think?"

"There are many definitions of immortality," said Lisabeth. "A vampire can still be destroyed, no matter how powerful they are. Perhaps they seek a way around that."

"I don't know what their goal is." Tony shrugged. "As to your earlier question, I know about the Council's inner workings because some of my faction are old enough to sit in on the Council meetings. They included me when they decided to interfere again because of my past history here. They figured if you were going to talk to anyone from the Syndicate, it would probably be me."

I couldn't fault them for that logic. "So what now?" Tony had given his warning, though it wasn't one I'd expected. Did that mean I was off the hook now if the Syndicate wasn't really after me? Maybe it was stupid to want to believe that last night's attack had been a fluke, but I didn't like the idea of being followed around all the time by Ussier's minions, especially if it might be unnecessary.

"Now, your friend here gives us the address in Oakmont," Ussier said. Tony's face tightened. Probably more because Ussier referred to him as my friend than out of any worry over betraying his… what? Family? What did they call themselves? "Then we'll pay them a visit and see if he's on the level."

"And in the meantime?" I tried not to show my frustration, but I wanted an answer now. What was going to happen to Tony, dammit?

"You're still on my watch list, Mr. Corvin, despite what the youngling says. You may not be the target, but you're still a mark and that's unacceptable. Tony will be your new bodyguard. If he's knows these people as well as he seems to, then you can use that to keep one step ahead."

"I'm not a babysitter," Tony snapped. "I gave you your warning. At least let me help you get rid of the Syndicate cell instead of following this tool around."

"Fuck you!" I snarled right back. "I didn't ask for yer damn help, not last night and not any other night. You can go to hell."

We glared across the table at each other, fists clenched, and I swear, guilt or no guilt, I wanted to punch that sneer right off his face. "Thanks, but I've already been there cuz of you."

"Enough, gentlemen," Hugh said in his deceptively soft voice. "We get it. You hate each other's guts, but Ussier gave you an order, youngling. In his city. There is no argument."

Tony pressed his lips together then nodded shortly. "Fine. I'll watch over him."

"Now just wait one damned minute. Don't I have a say in this?"

"No." Both Ussier and Hugh spoke as one and with enough implacable authority in their tones that my intended arguments died in my throat. "Remember what we talked about last night," Ussier reminded me, his eyes grim.

"I don't like the youngling being the only one watching him," Hugh said. "Especially since we're not sure which side he's on. We should add someone else."

"Mr. Corvin can take care of himself," Ussier replied, and Tony snorted. I shot him a dirty look to hide my attack of nerves. Ussier really did intend for me to use what I could of Kristair's abilities. Fuck. Not that I liked his goons creeping behind me all the time, but still.

"Besides," Lisabeth cut in with a cold smile. "The youngling's own survival depends on the Ancient One's lover. If one dies so shall the other." She hopped down from the chair and crossed over to Tony. An expression of fear flickered over his face, but he stood his ground as she caught his head between her tiny hands. I had to give him credit for having balls.

"Jacob Corvin, come here." I found myself by her side without a chance for thought or refusal. Alarm bells went off; if she didn't already freak me out, this would've cemented it. "Give me your hand."

Hesitant, I held out my hand and jumped as she sliced my palm with her fingernail, drawing blood. "Hey, what the—" The fierce glance she shot me shut me up. Tony tried to draw back, but the vampire girl grabbed his ear and held him still as she smeared my blood on his forehead. As she muttered softly in another language, the blood became an incandescent blue before sinking into Tony's forehead.

I took a step back, my skin crawling, my palm throbbing. Vampires were bad enough, but vampires with magic were a whole new set of scary. I'd seen too much to disbelieve anything was possible. I rubbed my thumb over my palm, smearing the blood, and the pain eased. My stomach twisted as the skin knit together before my eyes and was whole once more.

"There now." Lisabeth released Tony with a satisfied smile. "Now the youngling has no choice but to guard Mr. Corvin's life as dearly as his own."

Shit. I wouldn't blame Tony if he killed me himself, just out of pure spite.

Chapter 8

THE night was bitter cold, the wind whipping between the buildings to lash at us as we left Pooh Corner. Tony didn't say one word to me until we had walked the entire way back to campus. Not that I could blame him. My thoughts were pretty troubled too, and every time he fingered his forehead I was struck with another little stab of guilt. He shouldn't have that extra burden. If he was out to betray me and did, then they could hunt him down clean. It just didn't sit right that they used hoodoo shit on him.

"You didn't say anything," he finally said.

Frowning, I turned toward Tony. "What?"

"You didn't speak up for me *again*. You didn't try to stop her." Once more Tony touched his forehead and for a split second his expression became haunted before it returned to the now familiar cold indifference. "Guess all your talk about being sorry was bullshit."

The accusation dug the thorn in my conscience that much deeper. Truth was I hadn't even thought about protesting at the time. It had happened so fast and I wasn't expecting it. I should've said something. It wouldn't have stopped Lisabeth for a second—I knew that, at least— but I still could've tried even if she had scared the shit outta me.

Last time, not only had I not tried to stop them, I'd encouraged them with my own disavowal of Tony, my own cruel words and bitter, angry indifference to what was happening to him. What goes around comes around, and it was biting me in the ass. "I had no idea they could even do anything like that. That it was even possible." I paused and shook my head. "But you're right. I should've said something. I'm sorry."

"Bite me." Another time, a comment like that from Tony would have me on the ground laughing.

"What do you want me to do? Do you want me to call Ussier and demand he have it removed? It won't do a damn bit of good. They don't trust you. According to them you're an outsider."

"What about you?" Tony shot back.

"Huh? What are you talking about?" Ignoring the wind and my desire to just get inside so I could give Steve the news and take one more step to moving on, I stopped to face Tony. Obviously, there was something he was working toward.

"Do you trust me?" Tony demanded.

I hesitated a second too long and his expression hardened and he began walking again. "Fuck it, Jake. Never mind."

"It's not that I don't trust you." Fuck, he could read me too well. I wasn't very good at hiding things and the quirk of his brow told me he read my hesitance loud and clear.

"Really? Enlighten me then."

"I don't think you're out to see me dead, but I don't think you'd grieve for very long if I was killed. And I couldn't blame you." It was a fine line, but it still was a distinction, an important one in my mind.

"Damn right, I wouldn't cry over you." The slash cut quick with the bitter edge of Tony's voice. "But then I'll be dead myself and I'm not ready to lie down and give up yet." That was a sentiment I could appreciate. "You don't really think she used magic, do you? I mean it's just—"

"Crazy?"

He nodded. "Yeah, maybe."

"I don't think she's the kind of person to fake at anything. If she threatens you, it's real." I eyed him uneasily, wishing the damn mark was gone. "Besides, I've seen too much shit to disbelieve anything."

Tony shut up again and it wasn't until we turned toward Kayla's dorm that he spoke up. "Where are we going?"

"I promised Kayla and Steve an update. They're waiting for me in her room."

"Motherfucker." I glanced back to where Tony had halted and stood glaring at me. "You said you wouldn't say anything."

"That was last night and I didn't tell them anything." Kayla finding out was not my fault at all. The chick was too smart for my own good. "Tonight's different. You said you wanted to see where things stood. Now you know."

"Jake, I don't want them finding out I'm here."

"Why the hell not?" I continued on, figuring if Tony was serious about his assignment, he'd follow. "Steve doesn't deserve this bullshit. He's been going nuts over you, jackass. Unless this is another way of punishing me. Well, it's not going to work. I'm done with keeping secrets." Silently, I cursed my conscience for panging right then. The knowledge planted in my head from Kristair was a whole other issue, unconnected with this situation, and telling would cause more problems than keeping my mouth shut would.

"It's not your story to tell. Jake, I'm fucking warning you," Tony growled, grabbing my arm in a hard grip.

"Or what?" I turned around and snarled, my eyes going to the invisible mark on his forehead. "What? Ya gonna kick my ass? Go ahead and bring it." My fists balled up and it was an effort to keep them in my coat pocket. "Give me one good reason why I shouldn't tell them, for chrissake."

We glared at each other for a long minute while Tony seemed to struggle with it. Then he scowled and stalked past me. "Fine. We'll do it your way, as usual."

I gritted my teeth until pain stabbed through my jaw and then counted to twenty. Not trusting myself to speak I just began walking again before we ended up brawling in the middle of the quad. The remainder of the walk did nothing to blunt the edge of my anger and I was still fuming when I knocked on Kayla's door.

"Are you coming? Don't be such a friggin' coward," I snapped at Tony, who was hanging back. His face tightened.

Kayla must've been listening at the door or else I was louder than I'd meant to be because the door popped open then. "Jake," she said, with enough reproof that she didn't need to say anything else. Her eyes flew to Tony and she gave him a smile that lit up her face before glancing over her shoulder back into her room.

"I assume Steve's here. Let's get it over with." I gestured for Tony, though I was no longer impatient. We both were going to have to deal with the fallout in one way or another.

As I stepped into the room, a grin broke out over Steve's face. "Good to see you, man. So fess up. What happened?"

Stomach jittering I stepped to the side, allowing Tony room to come in behind me. A quizzical look crossed Steve's face and then his eyes widened. "Tony? Tony! Holy shit!" Laughing, Steve jumped up and caught Tony in a bear hug. "Damn, it's so fucking good to see you!"

Their exchange hurt to watch, especially when Tony hugged Steve back, but I made myself do it anyway. The strained relationship I had with them was entirely my own doing, not theirs. Kayla caught my eye and gave me a small smile of sympathy. She always seemed to know just what I was thinking, sometimes before I did myself. I shrugged and she rolled her eyes as Tony and Steve continued their reunion.

Damn, it was good to see Steve all excited like that though, and for a moment Tony almost looked like his old self. If it wasn't for this aching hole inside of me or feeling like I was an outsider peering in, I could almost believe this was a year ago. "When did…?" Steve started, then turned to me, his eyes narrowing. "You knew, last night…. This was what you wanted to meet with Ussier about. This is what you said you couldn't talk about."

Oh god, here it came. Steve's expression had already darkened even before I started to speak. "Yeah, but—"

"But what?" All the coiled tension I'd been holding inside for the past twenty-four hours stretched taut to the breaking point as Steve stepped up into my space, forcing me to tilt my head up to look at him.

"Jesus, Jake, why didn't you tell me? You looked at me right in my eye, knew Tony was back home, and you didn't say a word."

The sick expression on Steve's face, like he was staring at someone he didn't even know, made me shrink inside and the tension broke, ripping through me in a haze of rage and bitterness. What I was going to say died in my throat. Fuck him. I didn't owe him an explanation. I didn't owe any of them anything. Not any fucking more.

Shaking inside, I took a step back, not trusting myself to speak. I just needed to get the fuck out of there before I did something I regretted. "Jake. Don't," Kayla said softly.

Her, I could acknowledge. She wasn't one of the ones constantly poking and prodding me, seeking a reaction or new ways to cut at me. I shook my head and she nodded, giving me my space. She was the only one who understood.

"Wait, we're not done yet."

Even as Steve reached out to grab my shoulder, something inside me snapped. "Back the fuck off," I snarled, shoving him hard enough to send him hurtling back to land on his ass on Kayla's bed. "I don't owe you a damn thing."

My glare took in Tony as well, who was staring wide-eyed with surprise at the both of us. "Neither of you." Something flickered over his face, maybe regret, but I didn't care, not anymore.

Out of the corner of my eye Steve leapt up and his punch landed on my face before I was even aware of what he was about to do. "You'd lay hands on me, boy? Come on, Jake, let's go."

I touched my tongue to my lip, tasting blood, something feral and ugly clawing inside me as I started toward Steve. He wanted a fight, fine. I'd be fucking happy to give him one.

"Don't you dare," Kayla spat, leaping between us and glaring at us in turn. "Don't you two start on each other." She put her hands on our chests and nudged the both of us apart. "Both of you get a grip."

Tony stepped forward and grabbed Steve's bicep, leaning in to whisper something to him. I didn't even bother to wait around and find out what it was. Next thing I knew I was out the door, running. Who needed friends anyway? They either sat around and judged or became targets. Either way, I wanted nothing to do with it, nothing to do with them.

Behind me I heard them shout my name. I ran faster, the walls flying by me in a blur of color and texture. I ran the entire way back to my dorm, my chest burning, and locked myself inside. I didn't need anybody.

Chapter 9

MY FRUSTRATION overwhelmed me. I could feel Jacob. He was so damned close and he was hurting. His pain lashed out at me, tearing into my psyche. The epiphany I had in the warehouse was a mockery now. I couldn't do anything. The Ascended blocked my efforts with damning ease.

If only I could reach him. Then what? What would I do? Follow him around like a ghost? Reassure him that I was okay? Say goodbye? None of those options were palatable. I wanted to be with him. Simply that.

Our time had been so short and neither of us had been given any peace during it either. If it wasn't the Syndicate hounding us, it had been my degeneration, though I suppose I really should say evolution. Though at the moment it didn't matter how powerful I was, not when I wasn't in control of myself.

I couldn't see Jacob and the whispering unintelligible voices of the Ascended drowned out his thoughts until all I was left with was his pain, ripping at me. I was trapped by those who I was a part of now, but who also avoided me, as if I carried a taint. The double isolation was keen.

Then my prison walls changed. Instead of nothingness, I now stood amidst the vastness of the universe, a multitude of stars around me, below and above, some bright and strong, others flickering out of existence. The Ascended were gone, their voices mute. The new silence was deafening and far lonelier than my mere isolation had been.

I concentrated my psyche on taking form, nebulous as it was, of how I used to look. Did this mean I was free? Were they finally letting me go? Hope dawned as I stretched out my awareness, searching for Jacob. My connection with him had become tenuous as well, barely a wisp of emotion.

Again, I was blocked, and the anger that whipped through me frightened me with its immensity. I wanted to shriek out all my fury, storm and rage until everything around me lay in ruins. Again and again I hurled my thought and will against the invisible adamant tethers, searching for a weakness, some flaw I could exploit so I would have voice and means to retaliate.

"You have no concept of the power you have at your fingertips. You can do anything and, like an ignorant babe, you will destroy without thought of the consequences. Your blunders could have erased your very existence from the fabric of time."

Next to me, my old Mistress appeared, as hazy and wan as I was. I remembered her now. I remembered everything from the moment the Ascended seized me. She was the one who kept beckoning me back in when I was almost free. Once again, she was the instrument of a change I did not want.

"What would have happened to your precious Jacob if he had never met you?" she asked, looking around at the vista spread out before her, though I sensed every bit of her attention was on me.

"He'd probably be much happier." The thought was crushing, though true. I wouldn't be plagued with his torment had I never interrupted his life with my own problems.

"What about Kayla?" my Mistress persisted. "Would she have submitted to the perversions of her father if she hadn't known of you?"

"Don't pretend as if you care about them. You don't!" I snarled, turning to face her and meeting her calm gaze.

"No, but you do."

Her matter-of-fact tone cut through my fury and I laughed sardonically. "Jacob used to accuse me of manipulation, but I learned it from my Mistress."

"We're trying to teach you responsibility, Kristair. Your old life is over with. Jacob and Kayla's existence is only a wink of an eye. In the grand scheme of the universe, they don't matter."

Fine. If she wanted to discuss philosophy, then we could argue it as long as it got me what I wanted in the end. I could play scholar to her teacher. I'd had enough practice at it. "What is our purpose then if nothing matters?" I asked, my voice as emotionless as hers. "Everything has to have meaning or else nothing does. Isn't that what you once taught me?"

"Knowledge, Kristair. You've always enjoyed learning, though you were as stubborn about it in Rome as you are being now. There's a whole wealth of knowledge that you have barely tasted waiting for you: other dimensions, whole civilizations come and gone. We could spend our eternity studying and still not touch the surface." For the first time, something almost passionate colored the threads of her words.

"That doesn't answer the question, Mistress. If we can do anything, then why don't we? We have the power of gods and you want to merely sit back and watch as things unfold?"

"Why must you always question me? And cease calling me Mistress. You make a mockery of it, and such titles have no meaning here."

I paused, mulling over her words. In the beginning she had insisted I call her Mistress. I had always done so, but with an undertone of derision, even after we had reached somewhat of an accord. And when she had asked me to use her given name I refused. I suppose it was my own petty way of revenge. However, now that the tables were turned once again and I was forced into a position of subservience to her for the second time, I could not refer to her as Nerissa.

"I don't like being pushed into a corner, you know that. Yet it's the tactic you like to use on me. You also were the one who taught me the value of questioning, of not taking things at face value, and looking for the deeper meaning." I grinned. "I'm only following your teachings."

"We suppose we must acknowledge your point, though you would've argued anyway just for the sheer joy of vexing me."

I shrugged and the distinctly human gesture of it reminded me of those I'd left behind. "And your answer?" I prodded.

"Balance must be maintained, child. Everything we do must shelter that balance. That is why we exist. That is our purpose. Balance is the key to nature, whether it's destructive or constructive."

I laughed, the sound rich with contempt. "Our very existence is an imbalance, Mistress. From the moment we're created as vampires we're an aberration of nature, living beyond the span allotted us, preying off of other life. Now that we've evolved we're even more unnatural. We threaten the balance if what you say is true. Therefore shouldn't nature call for our destruction?"

"Nature probably would if we didn't keep ourselves in check. I have no doubt we would be destroyed. That is why when we were vampires we were careful about whom we fed from and how much. We were careful to remain quiet."

"Not all of us." Some enjoyed the thought of the lifestyle too much, wallowed in it, destroying without care. Ones like that were quickly destroyed, either by other vampires whose territories they encroached upon, or by the bands of humans who hunted them down. "But, I concede your point."

"You should've realized that not all who join our ranks were once vampires. There are psychics, sorcerers, beings from places long since turned to dust. Anyone who has trained their mind and will enough to have earned the right to become one of the Ascended. You would know this if the boy had not blinded you. That is why you must give up your connection to your lover. He ties you down to emotions you no longer need. They will cloud your vision and judgment. Jacob is holding you back."

She stepped forward and laid a hand on my arm. "It's not that we're without sympathy, Kristair. You're in a situation none of us have ever dealt with before. When we evolved, our earthly cares fell away with the destruction of our bodies. Your body isn't completely destroyed. It lives on in Jacob, and that has to end."

I knew she was only speaking the truth. I sensed the difference between myself and the other Ascended and sensed their distaste for the havoc my presence brought them.

It should be easy to sever the link between myself and Jacob. In his mind I was already dead. He was young. In time he would heal and move on. And Kayla was strong; I had no doubt she would thrive. As for myself, well, once the last tie was gone I would be free in a sense. No more worries or cares pressing upon me. In my new state, thoughts of Jacob and my former life would merely be another curiosity to observe. I'd had an inkling of what it would be like before Jacob's pull had separated me from the Ascended. In its own way it had been glorious. A life I would've quickly embraced at another time, before Jacob.

I don't know why I couldn't let go. That life was over with even if the ending had come too fast upon me. When I had been created as a vampire, I had found it hard to let go then too. Not this much, though. To turn away from Jacob and what we had seemed a travesty to me. To remember him, but not be able to recall the feeling of loving him, the wealth of emotion between us…. To turn my back on it and give it up would be like turning my back on him. Even if he would never know I had, that was something I couldn't bring myself to do.

All of that aching pain came rushing back in: the longing to be with him, the need to tell him I still loved him. My Mistress stepped back, removing her hand from my arm, an expression of baffled distaste crossing her hazy features. I wrapped the pain around me, savored it and let it remind me who I still was, despite what I had changed into.

"Mistress, I understand the reasons why you say I have to give him up. I do understand." That was the screwed-up part of it all. Here I was stuck in limbo and more likely to do myself and the Ascended harm. And it wasn't as if I had a real choice in the matter. I had already changed. One of the few absolute truths I'd learned was one could never go back. Right now I just couldn't accept it.

"Yet, you're going to continue to fight us, every step, as you did when I turned you and you had to give up your human life."

"You always did know me well." It was a relief to have her understand even though it wouldn't stop us from battling each other. "If I had had my epiphany a couple of months earlier than I did, things would be different."

I paused, studying her with almost pity. "You don't remember what it's like. You can't as you are now, without emotion. I will admit, what you offer is very tempting: unlimited knowledge, the chance to study and observe for the rest of my existence." The possibilities made me hungry for it, answers to all the questions I'd had, to be a part of a whole that was similar to me instead of seclusion. I would still be on the outside looking in, but not alone. Never alone again.

"Only the cost is too high. Maybe if I had succumbed to the same ennui that happened to so many of us toward the end of our lives. I never really understood that. I always thought it was laziness on their part, content to merely exist instead of looking for something new. There is always something new to explore, but I suppose it made the change easier to bear."

"That is why you belong with us, Kristair. You are a seeker, a questioner like the rest of us. You are finally home," my Mistress persisted.

"Knowledge isn't the only thing I've sought."

"We know. We've watched you, both when you were under my care, and after I'd changed. Then you were afraid of being alone, yet you isolated yourself too. The logic escapes us now as it did then. Just as your refusal to merge with us now makes no sense. You've experienced the joining with the whole. You know you'll never be alone again." If she had been my Mistress of old, her frustration would be almost palpable.

I smiled. "That's because logic had nothing to do with it."

I thought of Jacob and everything he had given me in our time together, his complete trust, his loyalty, and how he had the unique ability to draw me out from behind my walls. It was rather difficult to hold myself back when he fiercely fought every barrier and knew when I was trying to put one up. I ached with the memories. Being with him had been a true joining and, for me, the Ascended could not begin to compare, despite what wonders they offered.

"You cannot understand, Mistress. You, with all your wisdom, your knowledge, this is something you can't ever hope to comprehend, no matter how much you study. You may have evolved into something higher, but you lost a piece of yourself in the process."

"Every birth is painful. And you don't have a choice whether or not you're going to be born; it is thrust upon us all. You know that. The same thing happened when we became vampires and you enjoyed your existence as one. You reveled in it."

"Eventually, I did." In truth, I hated more where I was taken, so far from home, so different. I hated that more than I did becoming a creature of the night. Becoming a vampire had opened me up to my true potential and, perversely, I could see how I was holding myself back from something more once again. But matters were different this time.

"Without change we become stagnant and wither," my Mistress continued. "Some never survive the first stage and at each rebirth there are fewer of us who go on. That is the way of things, the way of nature."

"Darwin would've loved this conversation," I murmured. "So is this the end then? Or is there another life awaiting us?" I couldn't imagine there being anything else, but then, before I'd become this new entity, I hadn't been able to imagine this life either.

"You know we're not permitted to tell you that."

I hid a smile at her prim tone. It meant she didn't know, and not knowing, wondering, rankled my Mistress. "I know, but I had to try."

"Come, Kristair. Now that you are truly awake, let us show you what this life can give you."

The easy camaraderie I was beginning to have in my Mistress's presence fell away as my suspicion returned full force. "I am not going back into that prison you've all been holding me in."

I grabbed a hold of Jacob's fury and pain and hurled it at her mind, all of it with full force. In her moment of surprise, the bonds around my mind weakened and I tore free from her grip, forming a picture of Jacob in my head. The world blinked and I found myself staring at him, no more than a foot away from his face.

If I had breath it would've frozen. He was here, really here right in front of me. I wanted to weep. If I still had the capacity for tears they would be falling, endless rivers of sorrow coursing down my cheeks. Only I had no eyes from which to cry, no outlet for my grief. Nothing.

Still, I reached for Jacob with phantom fingers. Or at least tried to, and was met with the same barrier that had prevented me the last time I'd attempted to make contact with him. I couldn't remember when it was—time had no meaning where I was—but it couldn't have been long ago.

Jacob stared at me, or to be more accurate, right through me. Shadows darkened his once summer-bright eyes, circles marred the finely etched skin below and spoke of tormented nights where sleep proved to be elusive. *Jacob,* mo chroí. As I had no eyes to shed tears, or hands with which to touch him, I also had no lips to speak, so my lover didn't hear me.

Instead, he turned from the mirror and headed out of the bathroom. Panicked, I followed, terrified of losing sight of him and having him slip away yet again. I reappeared in the reflection in his window. There was a familiar reassurance to watching Jacob from this vantage point. I used to perch for hours on the other side of a pane of glass similar to this one as he slept, or ignored me, or tempted me, depending on his mood or how exhausting his day had been.

Jacob paced his room, muttering under his breath and clenching his fists. I couldn't read his mind; either he or the Ascended kept me from that final link. Nor could I read his emotions, not like how I used to, but his frustration and upset reached across to me, even without the link.

He sat down on his bed and grabbed one of the books littering its surface, pulling it toward him with a notebook and pencil. His brows furrowed as he bent over his work. Within moments the pencil found its way between his lips, and he gnawed absently on it as he read. The familiar gesture filled me with longing.

Just to be able to sit beside him as he studied, to respond to his occasional comments or gripes, would have been a blessing. To distract myself, I looked around the room I found myself in. It wasn't Jacob's old apartment. There was no iron fire escape behind me, merely a long fall to the ground. It looked to be one room with no connecting bath, smaller and more cramped than his old place.

Late into the night, I lingered as he worked with dogged determination on whatever assignment it was he was doing. Several times his phone rang, but he ignored it, only the clenching of his jaw to show he'd heard it at all. It was so much quieter than the past when either Tony or Steve would barge in at one point or another. Jacob's door was shut, instead of open as he used to have it so he could talk to whoever was in the living room or kitchen at the time.

It almost seemed as if Jacob had locked himself in a self-imposed cage.

Tony. I had forgotten about him. *Oh, how his memory must haunt you, Jacob.* I wondered what had happened to the boy. Everything had been so chaotic when the Ascended claimed me. I didn't know what happened to him or Steve. One had betrayed him and the other had been threatened with harm. Which brought to mind, I didn't know what had happened to Kayla either; whether or not she'd been hurt that night and if she was doing well now.

It hurt to think Jacob and Kayla might be all alone now. Well, not entirely. I knew my daughter well enough to know that she would attach herself to Jacob, whatever he had to say on the matter or not.

Jacob sighed, his shoulders slumping. Damn the entire lot of them for keeping me away from him. I watched with impotent fury and helplessness, wanting to run my fingers through Jacob's unkempt hair and pull him close, as he shoved his books and papers onto the floor and shut off the light.

In the darkness I could see him lying back, staring up at the ceiling and brooding. I hated it. Jacob didn't brood. He sulked, he got angry, he threw fits and then got over it. He had changed. There was suppressed anger in every line of his tense body. I could sense it despite our severed link.

Wait, that couldn't be right. It couldn't be entirely broken or else he wouldn't have been able to reach out to me with his pain. Unless Jacob had learned some new tricks. Oh, but if I was right, if a thread still remained…. Hardly daring to hope, I reached out with my thoughts, chaotic emotion playing a madcap dance in my mind, and encountered yet another wall.

Seething, I walked out of the window, disappearing and reappearing in a frame on his desk. Jacob was so close, had I form, I could reach out and brush my fingers across his cheek. I snarled. I was so damned close. The barrier was thin, some spots weaker than others. I struggled to pierce through, throwing myself at it again and again, sensing victory when he stirred and his face turned toward me.

Then my world turned topsy-turvy as I fell end-over-end only to reappear in the window again. Stunned, I watched Jacob lean over the side of the bed. Then he straightened and replaced the picture on his desk. He glanced around the room, his brows furrowing before slowly laying back down, his tension stronger.

Perhaps I wasn't as powerless as I seemed. Maybe if we both reached out to each other…. I raised imaginary fists, prepared to pound them against the window. Jacob had seen enough odd occurrences; he might just take it as a sign instead of becoming scared. Instead, at the gentle rattle I managed to produce, he merely wrapped a blanket around his shoulders and curled up on his side.

I had watched him fall asleep many times and it never failed to amaze me how quickly he could drop off. It didn't matter how upsetting his day had been or how much there was on his mind. Jacob could fall asleep anytime, anywhere.

I waited until I sensed his dream consciousness and then pushed myself out to merge with him as his defenses lowered. Jacob's dream wrapped around me and enfolded me within its colors and nuances of emotion. I lost myself in the wash of abstract and disjointed thought. Even here during his sleep, he was still tormented.

It was a struggle to not allow my own frustration to take over and influence Jacob's fragile balance. He was walking a razor-thin edge between crushing depression and self-destructive rage. The wall he had erected against the seething morass on either side was a thin veneer at best, but somehow he clung to his façade of calm with dogged stubbornness and kept the insanity at bay.

"Jacob, mo chroí, *I'm here. Please, talk to me."*

The images in his mind froze and my lover's heart picked up speed, thundering in his chest. He stirred, sheets whispering against his skin as he rolled over onto his other side and curled up even tighter. His shields battered at me, trying to force me out of his mind. If he had conscious control over such skills, he would've been able to do so with ease. It seemed that what he had learned in the months since my passing hadn't been limited to pushing his body to its limits. His mind had grown as well. It seemed that all the barriers between us were not only those created by the Ascended.

It was hard to wait until he had settled down again. I didn't want to scare him out of his wits, or make him think he was going insane, as unsettled as his emotions were. I considered waiting until he was awake to try to contact him again, but then immediately rejected the idea. Too crazy. No, it was better to introduce the idea now.

I caught the thread of his dream and began weaving my way into it. Bit by bit, I unraveled the tangled skein of his emotions, becoming the warp and weft until I became a part of the whole. This time when I intruded on his thoughts, he didn't try to shove me out. What he had been dreaming about scattered away as I built a different illusion, one of us naked in his bed, the sheets tangled around our waists. We lay there, our heads on the pillows, arms casually draped across each other, and just looked. I found that now that I was here and he was accepting me I couldn't speak.

My eyes caressed Jacob's face, the lines of weariness around his mouth, the way shadows lingered in his eyes, clouding their usual crystal-blue clarity. I moved my hand, cupping his face, and then slid it into his hair.

Jacob's eyes closed and his mouth tightened. Sorrow etched the lines deeper in his face and I moved closer, gathering him into my arms and pressing his head down onto my shoulder. He was stiff, holding himself apart, his mind terrified that he was about to break down and lose all sense of control that he still had. My hand caressed his back, silently urging him toward the release he needed. Bit by bit, the tension started to ease from him.

"Jacob, love, it is all right. You can let go. I'll be right here to catch you."

Chapter 10

MY WORDS had the opposite effect I intended, and Jacob jerked out of my arms. My mind reeled as his dream ended abruptly and I found my focus shifting from lying in his bed in the dreamworld, to occupying his mind once again.

Jacob's breath came in harsh gasps as he ripped the sheets from around him and lurched out of the bed. He gripped his hair in his hands, cursing in an intelligible stream. His mind was in chaos, his emotions tearing at him, ripping new holes into his already damaged psyche. I tried to reach out to soothe him only to find myself shoved back and blocked again.

If he'd just let me reach him or if the Ascended would just give me my natural abilities back, I could help him. I knew I could and the frustration of not being able to ate into me.

Jacob stumbled out of his room and across the hall into the bathroom. I recognized the dorms now and couldn't fathom how he'd ended up back here. He'd been so proud of the fact that he was on his own, worked at a job he hated so he could do it. What would have possessed him to give that up?

My lover trembled all over as he turned on the water in the shower and stepped inside. At first, the cold sting of it against his skin made us both gasp. Then the water soon became scalding, stinging rain and Jacob slumped against the wall, making no effort to step away or turn the faucet to a more comfortable temperature. It was almost as if he was doing it on purpose, inflicting some kind of self-imposed punishment upon himself.

I couldn't make sense of his thoughts. Either he was suppressing them out of a conscious effort or he was so far gone tonight he couldn't think straight. His emotions dragged him down. Flashes of rage were directed at himself, then at a shadowy figure lurking in the background, and then much to my surprise, toward myself.

I didn't know what to make of that. Then, as his shoulders began to shake, it all fell into place. I'd deserted him. And not only had I left him, but I'd also initiated our relationship thinking at the time that I was dying. I'd let us get so far into it, become so close, there was no hope of us remaining detached, not when our minds and souls were as one. No, I'd given him all that. Opened up a new world for him and then abruptly snatched it away with my disappearance.

"Ah can feel ya, but I can't hear ya. And then other times fuck, ya talk, but it ain't you, just yer memory talkin'."

Oh, Jacob. My conscience bled at the sound of his despair. I'd been incredibly selfish and shortsighted. The depth of his agony renewed my determination to get through to him. I couldn't, wouldn't, stand by and let him continue torturing himself in this manner. I needed to find some way of returning to him. How could he move on into another relationship after what we'd shared? I knew that, were our positions reversed, I never would be able to. Who else would be such a part of me as Jacob was?

A harsh sob startled me out of my caustic reflections, so it took a moment for me to register that Jacob was crying. It seemed so out of character for him, but after the first one escaped his throat, another sob quickly followed, opening a torrent of raw emotion that battered the both of us. Jacob punched the tiles several times then sank down to the floor of the shower, his body shaking harder, wracked with anguish.

I was torn. My conscience said I should leave him in peace instead of intruding on a deeply personal moment. Jacob wouldn't be comfortable with the idea of me watching him break down. I wasn't invited, even if I was the catalyst for his tears. At the same time, I wanted to pull him into my arms until the storm had passed.

I cursed the Ascended for putting us in this predicament and even more so for not giving me the tools with which to aid him. I couldn't hold him, I couldn't kiss him, and if I spoke I might be giving him false hope, only to have it destroyed when the Ascended took me back if I didn't find a way around my new fate.

Jacob muffled the sounds in the crook of his arm and, as his crying jag continued, the urgency to interfere gradually eased. The storm was violent, with dark emotions pummeling the both of us until we were raw and bleeding. Only, I sensed that it was a much-needed release and, though the wounds were open again, maybe this time they'd be able to heal cleanly.

I wasn't sure how much time passed, but the water had grown cold. Jacob shivered both from the chill and the release of tension he'd stored in his body. My lover had sunk so deep into his mind and sorrow that I doubted he would notice anything amiss if I took steps toward contact.

It took all of my concentration to find a small hole in the limits the Ascended had set on me, but it was enough to grasp the shower faucet with my mind and shut it off. Jacob didn't even stir and there was no indication that his upset had woken up anybody else in the dorm. I don't think his pride would be able to handle knowing someone had seen him like this. Not when his psyche was so brittle.

I settled down to wait him out. I wanted to implant the suggestion to find warm, dry clothes, but he'd become so mentally adept I knew he'd notice that interference. I wanted to speak, only I was sure it would only spur him to kick me out again. He wasn't ready to believe that my voice might be real. I suppose I couldn't blame him. In his reality, I'd died months ago.

All too soon the tension started to return to him as he recovered from the shock of what had just occurred. In dismay, I listened to his dark thoughts start to reemerge, and with each one, the rage grew. Gory images of intended personal revenge toward the Syndicate shocked me with their brutality and cold-bloodedness. They shouldn't. I'd been a warrior my entire life and had seen worse, but somehow, coming from Jacob, it seemed dreadfully wrong.

Then the images switched from fury to guilt as Jacob lashed at himself with them. Pictures of Tony being dragged into the coffin meant for me while Jacob stood by and let it happen. And then came a whole cascade of fevered imaginings of Tony being tortured and of his parents crying at a funeral, Steve turning away from him. On and on it went.

"Oh, mo chroí, *don't do this to yourself."* I had to say something. His ongoing cycle of self-flagellation had to stop. I sifted through his memories of the past couple months and caught onto the truth he kept ignoring. *"Tony isn't dead and you did try to help him in the end. Torturing yourself won't change the past."*

Jacob jerked back his shoulders, slamming them hard against the tiles. I used his shock to grasp his mind before he could evict me again. This was too damned important. Before I could speak again and lend him further reassurance, my lover dropped his head into his trembling hands.

"I'm going fucking crazy."

"No, no you're not. I swear to you, you're not. I'm not completely gone." One day I would find a way to return to him permanently.

This night had to have the most surreal quality for him and I decided that we should try again another time, when he'd be able to process it more. Jacob was dazed and lost; arguing with him right now wouldn't help. *"Get up, Jacob. Dry yourself off and go to bed. Things will seem different in the morning."*

He whimpered, childlike, and fisted his hands in his hair. *"You're not real. You're not real."*

"Go on. You can argue whether I'm fact or fiction in the morning," I urged even softer. After a moment, he rose stiffly and stripped out of his clothes, leaving them in a sodden heap on the bathroom floor.

"Get back to your room and get some clothes on. You don't want to get sick."

Jacob was still shivering from a combination of chill and shock. He slung the towel around his hips, muttering something about not ever getting sick again, and grabbed up his sopping clothes.

Once he was back in his room, he dried himself off with mechanical motions, rubbing hard against his skin. I sensed his hope that the friction would prove to him that this was a dream or not. I was able to talk him into tugging on a pair of sweatpants. Then he sprawled back on his bed, covering his eyes with the crook of his arm. It took even more prodding to get him under the covers.

Then I switched my awareness out of his mind to hover beside his bed so I wasn't watching from out of his eyes anymore. The sight of him huddled, so lost and young, ached with painful clarity.

Before I realized it, I had reached out with phantom fingers and brushed back a lock of hair that had tumbled across his forehead. Jacob's eyes closed tightly. "I thought you were gone again," he whispered.

I don't know how I had broken free of the injunction set upon me by the Ascended that had kept me from touching him, but I wasn't about to pass up the opportunity it afforded me. I laid my presence down behind Jacob and wrapped my arms around him, pressing against his back. *"Sleep; it'll all be clearer in the morning, when you've had an opportunity to rest."*

"I don't want to wake up. Not if it means this was only a dream."

"That is not a worry for right now, mo chroí. *You've given yourself no surcease. Please, Jacob, do you trust me?"* I shifted up and kissed his temple then laid my head against his shoulder, soothing my palm up and down his arm.

"Always." His response was immediate and fervent.

"Then put yourself in my hands and rest. Let me hold you. Whether you feel me or not, I am with you."

Jacob sighed as his body relaxed by slow degrees, his shivers tapering off. I held him close, listening to his breathing as it evened out to the steady, low throb of his heartbeat. I waited until he had completely drifted off, savoring every second of my contact with him even though it was on a limited scale. We had shared, in a way that had not been possible in such a long time. I steeled myself, knowing he might not remember it in the morning, and if he did, he would probably dismiss it as a dream. It was a start and more than we'd had before tonight.

This time, when I sank into his subconscious, there was no anger, no guilt. The deep scars he'd carved into himself were being soothed by a deep contentment. I allowed it to lull me into a state of similar ease. We drifted together, linking more intimately than we ever had in the past, neither thought nor emotion clouding who we really were. It was almost as if our souls had now truly become one.

When Jacob's dream started, it drew me in as well. This time there was no sense that I was intruding, no attempt by him to kick me out. We wrapped ourselves around each other, closed our eyes, and indulged in what we'd both been wishing for: the chance to hold each other and to be together once more.

This was well worth whatever fight I had to put up in order to keep it.

Chapter 11

"KRISTAIR, when are you going to put that boy out of his misery?"

I hissed as Jacob and his room fell away to find myself once again back in my prison. It took all of my self-control not to lash out at the Ascended surrounding me. I must be getting stronger, or more aware, because now I could make out distinct psyches among the mass.

Bit by bit, I regained my self-mastery, building up my wall with the sheer force of my convictions. They couldn't keep me from seeing Jacob; they couldn't keep me from contacting him. It was all a matter of time, wasn't it? And for once, time was something I had in abundance.

"If you would return me to where I belong then he will be tormented no longer!" The words came out in a near roar as my frustration threatened to overpower the fragile control I had gained. "I don't belong here! You know this. It's why you choose to isolate me. Let me go." A great weariness settled over me. The same words were said over and over again, on both sides with no progress being made either way.

"It is you who needs to let go."

There it was: their eternally echoing ultimatum. Had they gone so far into this dimension of existence that they no longer cared what went on elsewhere? I could have almost laughed if I wasn't already about to splinter into a thousand shards. No headway, on either side.

The urge to give up pressed in on me from all sides. It would be so easy, for the both of us. It would be so easy. I would forget my feelings for Jacob and then he would be able to move on, without fear of changes he didn't understand, to move on and find someone new.

I stiffened in fury. "LEAVE ME ALONE," I snarled, shoving back the oppressive minds that threatened to suppress my will. They fell back with frightening ease. My rage continued to grow and power surged through me. It was their entire fault. If they'd only left me alone, then none of this would've happened.

"That's true, Kristair." Her voice came again and gave me pause. "If we had left you alone, you wouldn't be going through this self-torture, nor would your lover." Before I could rejoice and press my point, my Mistress continued. "Nor would you have met him, but the changes that happened to you would have still occurred. They didn't come about because of our interference, but because of the way you trained your mind and your will. We merely sought to guide you and ease your passage. You still would have evolved and Jacob would still have been left behind, with no knowledge or memory of you. Only your daughter would've mourned, yet there would have been no preparation for her. One night, she would've gone to look for you and never found you."

I paused, my fury stilling as the cold truth sank in. They were not at fault, as much as it made it easier to blame someone, to have something to fight against. If I were to think rationally, which I had done little of since I'd heard Jacob's call, I'd cease fighting. Our relationship would've been difficult enough as it was with me being a vampire and him being a human, but now it was all but impossible.

My thoughts were carved of ice as I considered the matter from all angles, forcing down the emotions that threatened to cloud my judgment. I'd let defeat and weariness color my mind and sensed them closing in, the circle growing tighter. "Unless the connection is reversed, I will continue to feel what Jacob feels and it will affect my reactions," I warned, and the presence drew back.

"Then you must sever it, for the good of you both." My Mistress's voice was as devoid of emotion as my own had been. "You are the only one who can do it since you set it in motion and magic has its own laws. Since the rest of your race is dead, only you have the innate ability necessary for such a task. Each individual's thought is unique, so one of us cannot erase something that has already been initiated. We can only try to mitigate the damage and make what repairs we choose."

I nodded. So there were some limits in what they could and couldn't do. Good. No matter how much will was put behind their desires, they couldn't go back and make it so I had never met Jacob or never done the ritual. Though whether it was because they really couldn't or more a matter that they dared not screw with time didn't matter, just as long as they didn't. That was good to know. If I continued to refuse, they were helpless, but I didn't want to push them so far that they'd opt to take care of the problem in another way. But how far would they go in order to keep me as one of their number?

"I'll need to be present with him and reopen the connection before I can reverse it." It was difficult to keep my emotions on an even keel and, as I sensed them pick through my psyche, I knew the decision to do so had been a good one. They would be suspicious of any strong displays. "The magic of my people requires a close bond and harmony of thought. Jacob will have to be aware of me and what I intend for it to work. It will take a bit of time to reestablish that bond after so many months and upheaval."

They were mistrustful. Darkness battered at my mind as they continued to probe, looking for a loophole or trick I might be trying to play. "How long?" They asked.

I considered the months I had hunted Jacob, working tirelessly to create the bond, to connect with his thoughts and emotions before I had deemed it satisfactory enough to work. It wouldn't take nearly as long this time, not with it already being somewhat in place and certainly not with the way Jacob felt. What would take longer was getting my lover's cooperation. He would not agree, not at all, not if he thought there was some chance we could be together on some level, no matter how small. On that, we both agreed. It would be a hard-fought battle.

"What does time matter to you? Several weeks, months. It matters not how long it takes."

My Mistress laughed. "We are not simple, Kristair. We know what game you are playing with us. You still seek to circumvent your fate."

"What if I do? It doesn't change the truth. You want me to be free of him and I say to do so I need this time. You know I am not lying. He has to agree to the ritual. It won't work if he holds on."

The silence stretched out as the Ascended considered it, weighing my words and intentions against each other as I suppressed all hope to keep them from sensing the feeling. Even if I could be allowed to interact with Jacob for a short time, it would be something. Somehow together we'd find a way around my recent change or attain some kind of closure. Either would be better than the terrible limbo we were stuck in now.

"You have two weeks."

I froze, stunned beyond belief that they had relented even that much. Two weeks wasn't long, but it was far more than I had before. My mind raced as I tried to tie up the loose ends and questions before they released me. "Once I reverse the spell, the remainder of my corporeal body will be destroyed?"

"That is correct, and your soul will rejoin with your mind instead of unnaturally existing in two places. You'll be whole again."

That, however, was entirely a matter of opinion. How undamaged could a person's soul be if they felt nothing? I recalled some of my recent conversations with my Mistress. No, the Ascended weren't entirely devoid of emotions; they were just in complete control of them, their minds ruling all. Once my heart was destroyed there would be no going back, no more fighting. The idea made me very uneasy.

"What restrictions are you going to put on me?" I was no fool, there were always limits, and since they considered me enough of a danger as it was, just as long as they didn't follow me every second, and they afforded me some privacy, I could work around their rules.

"Your consciousness will be locked within Jacob's form since that's the vessel you chose. You will not be able to move between time and space. Where he goes, there you will be as well. You can choose to project yourself so he can see you or so he can feel you. Not both at once. What you choose to tell him is your own affair, but bear in mind there are some concepts he isn't capable of understanding." There was a pause. "And this is only between you and Jacob, and only for the purpose we set you to. Do not use this reprieve as an attempt to connect with Kayla again or to set other mortal affairs to right. Only he will be able to connect with you."

I pondered over their strictures. They were both more than I hoped for and still not enough. I was greedy. I wanted to hold Jacob, not just occupy a corner of his thoughts. He could see me or feel me but not at the same time. At least he'd always be able to hear me. Two weeks. Such a short time in which to share everything I wanted to share, to convince Jacob to let go if I didn't come up with an alternate way for us to be together.

"I understand." Excitement spiked before it became muted by sorrow and fear. So soon and we would be linked again. The very weight of it, the anticipation, overwhelmed all thought. What was I going to do? What was I going to say? As much as I wanted them to release me this very moment, I knew the two weeks were going to pass quicker than either of us would be ready for. It hurt that I wouldn't be allowed to contact Kayla though, and seemed unnecessarily unfair. If anyone would understand the limits and oddity of it all, it was her.

"If you are ready, we will send you back now."

"No."

They seemed a little startled at my vehemence and when my Mistress spoke there was an undercurrent of amusement in her tone. "We thought you were anxious to see your Jacob again. Why do you delay now? Do you seek yet another way to thwart your destiny?"

"For me to reverse it, I need Jacob's cooperation, and that might take some fast talk and hard arguments on my part." I smiled inwardly. "*Mo chroí* is more stubborn than most."

"In another time and place you would've been well suited to him."

"We still are, despite the circumstances." I considered the problem, again trying to quell my excitement. "Leave me be. Let me think on it." I drew my thoughts and emotions in on myself, blocking off my connection with Jacob so I could think clearly and isolating myself from the Ascended. They pulled back, leaving me to my privacy and, for the first time since Jacob's pull had separated me from my companions, their presence seemed less of a prison and more the community it should have been.

Two weeks. *Mo chroí*, why does it seem like we never have the time we both desire?

Chapter 12

I WOKE up, my eyes gritty and muscles sore from having slept too hard and too heavy, yet tempered by a deep sense of peace. Kristair was no longer with me. I wasn't sure if he'd ever really been there or if I'd finally cracked, and frankly, I didn't give a shit if I had. Last night had been so strange, so unreal, and remembering it now, it was very cloudy and mixed up. It didn't matter how much I thought on it; it still seemed more fantasy than reality.

I wanted to linger in bed, roll over and see if I could capture my dreams again, but a new sense of purpose drove me from the bed. I found my clothes in a damp heap on the floor so I knew at least that part of it hadn't been a delusion. The nagging headache also told me I'd lost it and bawled like a freaking baby.

Scooping the clothes up, I tossed them into a hamper and quickly got dressed. I wasn't ready to deal with Steve quite yet and the sun was streaming through the window, so I'd have to wait before I could talk to Tony. But, I knew right where to find Kayla. Probably best I started with her anyway.

The walk to the cathedral didn't take long. Even if she was in class, this was where she always came in between them. In Kristair's office. Her office now, I should say. Bet the university hated that, having Kristair's library in the hands of an undergraduate student. Picturing their expressions of arrogant dismay had me grinning. The expression seemed almost strange.

Kayla's eyes widened in surprise when I walked in. I hadn't been back up here since I'd retrieved Kristair's torc from his burned-out rooms. It had been completely renovated; Kayla had made it her own. Old maps hung on the wall, matted and framed, some of countries long since gone. The desk was less utilitarian than Kristair's had been, made of gleaming hardwood, and a fancy computer took up most of the top.

"Before you say anything I want to apologize."

Kayla tilted her head. "Are you okay?"

"I don't know honestly. I'm better, I think, or I just might be going crazy. Either way, I'm tired of that damn rollercoaster I've been on. I can't take it anymore, for myself or for you either." Kayla was dealing with her own shit and she didn't need me bringing her down anymore with mine.

"You've certainly seemed hell bent on losing it lately... but you seem different today." She rose and came around the desk. "Come on; we can talk in the library. No one will disturb us there."

I experienced a warm rush of pleasure as I stepped into Kristair's old haven, and not entirely my own either. That little section of my brain where Kristair's presence lingered almost hummed. For myself, I couldn't believe it had taken me so long to come back to this place.

Kristair's spirit lingered in the rows upon rows of bookcases, some locked and some containing artifacts other than books. The sense of his presence struck me, more here than any other place. I wasn't sure if it was because this had been his legacy or because of what had happened last night. A quick glance at Kayla's expression told me I wasn't the only one who felt it, though.

"Do you think he's gone? I mean really gone?" I asked.

She closed her eyes, a quick rush of sorrow crossing her face, but when she opened her eyes again, her gaze held acceptance, almost peace. "I didn't used to think so. I held on thinking one day I was going to come here and he was going to be sitting right at that table or puttering through the shelves. He could spend hours here and did so many times," she said, her voice lost in the warmth and comfort of memories.

"When did it change? For you I mean? When did you start thinking he might be really gone?" I walked over and slung my arm around her shoulders.

"The other night, when I got his letter." Kayla moved away from me and ran her fingertips down the leather spine of a book. "We had made emergency provisions for this library when I started school here and I put them into effect when you came back last spring and told me he was gone. But now I have the paperwork guaranteeing everything in here is mine. I suppose I should get a lawyer. I'll find one in a couple days when I'm a bit steadier."

"I'm sorry. I'll never be able to say that enough. I know I've put you through the frickin' wringer with my attitude all these months."

She cast a glance over her shoulder, warm and loving. "Attitude doesn't even begin to describe it, hotshot." She hesitated then gestured to the table. "Sit down. We need to talk."

I pulled a chair out for her at the table then braced myself for whatever was coming. There was something else in that paperwork Kristair had left for her, something that had to do with me. I reached over and took her hand. "Out with it. I can take it."

Again she cocked her head and studied me, then kind of nodded as if she had come to a decision. "He left some things for you too. A house in town and half his savings."

I stared at her, appalled. "No way, Kayla. That's yours." I couldn't take it, even if I wanted it, which I didn't. I couldn't in good conscience accept such a thing.

She shook her head and let her gaze drift over the shelves again. "I have everything I want here in this room. As for the money, he'd set up a trust fund for me years ago. That will be more than enough to keep me secure without the additional half. So it's not like you're stealing anything. It was Kristair's money to begin with."

"But the house—isn't it the same place Kristair raised you in? Don't you want your own damn home?"

"God, no." I blinked at her insistence. She was serious. "Bless Kris for trying and he was a good father to me, but that place was too lonely. I was by myself all day and I only had so much time with him in the evenings. I mean, he stayed with me all night and he tried his best, but it never really felt like a home. For either of us."

"But school's going to be over in the spring. You're not going to have the dorm. What do you plan on doing then?" I argued, not ready to back down. That was her place. I had no business taking it, even if she just sold the thing.

"I have some property of my own, some land Nerissa owned. Kristair had a townhouse built there and put the deed in my name years ago. I could always go there if I wanted to, or maybe go to grad school, or travel. I don't know. I haven't decided yet."

It didn't sit well with me. It didn't sit well at all. Hell, to be honest, I hated it, and my lover had known I would've too. I wanted to earn what I got, not have it handed to me. As for Kristair, well, he had to take care of what was his and I couldn't argue with him about it, and the bastard knew that. From the look on Kayla's face, I knew I wouldn't be able to argue with her either. Her mind was made up and she was far more stubborn than her father was.

"I don't like it."

"I know you don't, Jake, but look at it this way: it was his last wish."

"Damn, girl, you're as good with the arguments as he was." It still hurt. The idea of a will made the reality of him being gone so much realer. Was that even a word? For once Kristair's voice didn't correct my choice of words. I sighed. Maybe all I'd have of him was his voice lingering in my head and dreams of us together as I slept, but at least I wasn't entirely alone.

"Does that mean you're not going to give me any grief?"

"I think I've done enough of that already." Besides, it didn't mean I had to use the money. I could save it for her kids or something or maybe a house for my mom instead of that dinky little trailer of hers. I'd think of something.

"What changed, Jake? Something happened last night. You're different."

I shrugged. "Maybe I decided to listen to you after all."

"As much as I'd love to believe you now recognize my natural wisdom, I don't. Something happened. Steve tried to call, you know, to apologize. I don't know what happened with Tony. He disappeared right after you, and Steve was rather upset about everything. He was sorry even before I sat him down and had a talk with him."

For some reason that image put a smile to my face. I could only imagine Steve's reaction to a lecture from a white girl who only came up to his shoulder. Kayla's features may be delicate and those dimples would always throw me off, but she was almost more forceful than my Ma. I almost wished I'd witnessed her telling Steve off.

"Don't worry about it. It was just as much my fault as his. We were just blowing off some steam. Guys do that."

"Bullshit. You know what Steve's biggest problem is? He feels guilty too. And just like a man, he's taking it out on someone else instead of dealing with it. And you are letting him get away with it instead of just talking to him!"

I glanced at the exit. Somehow I got the impression Kayla was just warming up to her lecture, only it didn't seem half so funny now that I was on the receiving end. "What's he got to feel guilty about? He ain't done nothing." Her observation surprised me. I knew my friend took things too seriously, but not so much that he'd beat himself up over something I'd done.

"Jake, when are you going to drop the ain't?"

"When it stops annoying you." When Kristair's voice in my head stopped correcting me.

Kayla rolled her eyes and muttered something under her breath. "The point is Steve wishes he could've done more and not just for Tony, but for you as well. I guess he thinks of himself as an older brother to you two idiots and he blames himself for what happened."

"That's stupid. He shouldn't be taking that shit on himself, big brother or not."

"He also hates it that you don't confide in him anymore."

"Really?" That gave me pause. Kayla nodded. "Well, he doesn't make it easy. I mean, he blames Kristair for everything and I don't have the energy to defend him all the time, you know." It was damned frustrating.

"Actually, I do know."

"You would." I gave her a small smile. "Okay, I'll talk with Steve later. I promise. I owe him an apology anyway." Not for keeping that last secret, but I shouldn't have lost my temper the way I did. It never should've almost come to blows between us.

"Thank you." She patted my hand and smiled back with that impish twist to her lips.

"Before I go, there's something I need to tell you. I don't know if it'd help explain things or not. Before Kristair... before he left, he finished that ritual of his people's. You know the one we talked about. The one where he left his soul behind in me." At least that was how I understood it.

"I kinda figured that. You're different. Not quite the way you used to be, yet not quite all Kristair, but like a combination of the both." She paused and when she spoke again her voice was troubled. "Though there were times when I swore it was my father's voice coming out of your mouth."

"Must've been hard on you."

She shrugged. "I've learned to live with it. I just don't want to lose you, Jake. As annoying as you can be, I kinda like you."

"Thanks, I think." I laughed then sobered.

"You don't understand what it's like to carry that." I shook my head, feeling the weight of it once again. Only this time I was determined not to let it drag me down. "I can hear his voice, commenting on things I'm doing, pointing out things he'd learned, trying to guide me. Some of his memories have become my memories to the point sometimes where I can't remember which ones belong to who without stopping to think about it. Sometimes I forget who I am. And when I hear his voice, but he's not talking to me, you know... it cuts all over again. And I'm changing, in all kinds of little ways. I can't hold onto anything anymore. I have no control and it's scaring the shit outta me." I forced myself to stop. Damn, I hadn't meant for it to come out all in a rush like that. I'd said more than I'd meant to.

"Oh my god, I had no idea." Kayla linked her fingers with mine. "Is there anything I can do to help? I can look at Kristair's old journals. Maybe there's some way of breaking the spell, or at least lessen its effects."

"Actually, I don't want to, at least not yet. Maybe later, but for now I'm not ready to let go of that last link with him. Funny thing is, if you'd suggested it yesterday, I would've jumped at it."

"What happened last night?"

"I don't know how to explain. It was different from hearing his voice. It was like he was really there, Kayla. Like we were linked, the way we used to be. He was hurting for me, missing me too...." I trailed off and shook my head, remembering my breakdown in the shower. "He helped me to let go of some of the stuff I've been carrying around. Hell, he practically forced me to do it." Then he'd held me afterward. I couldn't be mistaken about the way his arms felt around me. If it had only been an illusion, if I was just losing my mind, it wouldn't have felt that good, right?

"I... I don't know what to say."

"That's a first," I teased.

"You really must be feeling better." Kayla threw her arms around me and gave me a hard hug. "I don't know whether you're the luckiest or unluckiest bastard ever."

"That makes two of us." I glanced at my watch. "I've got to go, babe. I've skeeved off my classes, but I have a doctor's appointment I can't miss. I'll call ya later."

Kayla rose with me and brushed a kiss over my lips. "Thanks for coming by."

"You're welcome, trouble," I said, tugging on a lock of her hair.

"Oh, you're impossible. Get out of here."

Chapter 13

I CALLED Steve on my way to the doctor's office. He picked up on the first ring and I clamped down on the immediate prick of guilt. I spoke as soon as I heard the click, before he got a chance to say hello. If I was going to spend my day apologizing, I wanted to get it out of the way quick. "Look, Steve, I wanted—"

"Forget it, man. We were both asses."

"So we're cool?" Another knot of tension unraveled.

"Yeah, we're cool, bro. You've been honest with me ever since your boy landed me in the hospital. Sometimes, I forget that. And Tony told me he asked you to keep your mouth shut."

"Actually, I was coming over last night to tell you anyway. I promised Tony I wouldn't say anything until after he met with Ussier, no longer." I couldn't help but wonder if Tony would've let Steve know at all if I hadn't forced his hand. Now that was one thing I didn't feel guilty about.

"Where are you now? Want to meet on campus for lunch?"

"Can't. I have to get another physical for Coach. He thinks I'm either on drugs or hiding an illness, so he's benched me until I meet with his own physician."

"That sucks. I can kind of figure where he's coming from. Not that I think you're using, but he's a sharp man. He knows something's up with you. Think the physical will get him off your back?"

"I hope so. It's worth a shot at least." A warning sensation trickled up my spine, raising the hair on my neck, but when I glanced around, I saw nothing. It was a gray day, clouds scudding low and dark. Even with the lack of sunshine, there was no way vamps were out today. Still, some instinct warned caution. "I have to go, but I need to tell you something real quick. I doubt Tony had the time last night." I ran through the conversation with Ussier and of the blood spell Lisabeth laid on us to keep Tony in line.

Steve let out a string of violent curses, so I waited until he'd vented some of his frustration. "Is there anything you can do to reverse it?"

I started to say no then paused. Was there? Maybe Kristair would know. He had some of the hoodoo knowledge. There were so many of his memories filed away in my head. I didn't even try peeking into most of them. I had too much to deal with as it was, without opening that Pandora's box. "I don't know. I'm not quite sure how magic works, but maybe. It's an idea to think about."

"You do that and maybe we can all get together tonight and put our heads together. My place, though, 'cause Kayla's is too small. Makes me feel like an idiot."

"And too pink and lacy," I added. "I'm afraid to move in there. One of these days I'm gonna break something. Then she'll kill me."

"There's that. You think Tony will come?"

"I can guarantee it." I glanced at my watch. Damn, I was going to be late if I didn't get moving. "You get Kayla there and I'll get Tony. What about your roommates?"

"They're not going to be there. Some frat thing going on, so we'll have the place to ourselves."

"Awesome. Grab some beers too." Despite the situation, I was kind of in the mood to celebrate a bit. This would be the first time we were together, really together, since the night Tony came home from his short disappearance. If only he'd confided in us about what had happened to him then that whole night in the warehouse could've been avoided. He didn't know though, I reminded myself. He didn't know Kristair wasn't hurting me. And none of us could've guessed what it would lead to. "Steve, I'm going to tell him about what Kristair left in my head. He doesn't know anything about it, thinks I'm completely normal."

"You sure about that, man?"

"Yeah, I'm sure. He needs to know." The funny thing about trust was sometimes you had to take that leap first before someone could trust you in return, and I was going to make that leap. Ussier would probably cuss me out, but I didn't care.

I hung up the phone and darted across the street just before the light changed. Since that was taken care of, the nerves regarding my doctor's appointment hit again. This had to go well.

"Okay, Kristair. I don't know if you can hear me or not, but let's make a deal here. No crazy shit, for the next hour. Just let me get through my appointment and then you can make your heart do flips if you want to. I'm just asking for this one hour," I said under my breath and hoped no one on the street thought I was talking to myself.

There was no answer, but his heart remained silent in my chest as well so I took it as a confirmation. Otherwise, I'd drive myself crazy worrying and probably drive my blood pressure up so bad the doctor would commit me to the hospital.

Once again, that prickle of awareness hit me. I was being followed or watched, I just knew it. Only this time there was no way I was gonna lead them down an alley to take care of it. I fingered the gun in my pocket, hating its presence there. Whoever it was could wait to bug me later on, hopefully when I had backup.

I glanced around the street once again, seeing nothing out of the ordinary, just a whole shitload of people going by on their own business. And any one of them could be crazy. Didn't matter, though; they could stare at this building all afternoon. I reached my hand out to enter the building holding the medical offices and another mind grabbed a hold of my own, shoving my presence into a corner, and took over my body.

Just like what Kristair had done to me, only this wasn't my lover. My heart kicked into high gear.

Stunned, I watched myself turn away, heading toward a sedan with tinted windows that pulled up in front of the building. I could sense eyes boring through me from the other side of that dark glass. Snarling, I fought, tearing at the bonds in my head, trying to dig my heels in so hard that I stumbled as if drunk. People averted their eyes and quickened their pace as they walked by me.

"Fucking A! Motherfucker no! Get outta my fuckin' head or I'll blow your fuckin' brains out!"

I struggled to pull the gun out of my pocket and Kristair spoke up. *"Trying to shoot in this state is not wise."*

"THEN TELL ME WHAT TO DO!"

"You know what to do. It's all in your head," Kristair whispered. *"The eyes, Jacob. The eyes are the window to the soul."*

The doors to the car flew open and two men got out, taking me by the arms and leading me to the back door. I fought harder, snarling in rage in my head, and panting as if I were running a goddamned marathon.

"Hurry! He's too strong," a young girl's voice cried out on the edge of some extreme emotion.

They shoved me inside next to the girl, whose face was pale, lines of stress around her eyes, her mouth pinched in pain, and sweat dotting her brow. Her gaze punched right through me, a living creature. *HER!* I lurched toward the girl, felt a part of my psyche pierce through her eyes into her, and then a presence in my mind ripping. A presence that didn't belong there. She screamed, a high piercing shriek that made the bones in my ears rattle. Then something sharp pierced my leg, a needle, and a gray fog rolled in.

"MO CHROÍ, you have to burn the medicine out of your system. Hurry. You have to wake up. It'll be dark in a few hours."

"Wha.... Kristair? What's happening?" I couldn't hear him clearly, though I knew it was him. I concentrated on pushing back the fog that seemed to have me snared within its tendrils. As it began to clear, my other senses woke up. I was sitting on a hard chair with my hands cuffed behind my back.

Both hearts began to pound in my chest. Fuck! What was I gonna do now? I kept my head down, my eyes closed, somehow managing to keep my breathing even. *"Kristair?"* I held my breath and prayed, straining for an answer. I couldn't have imagined his voice, but, once again, I was met with only silence.

I was on my own.

I could do this. I didn't need anyone. Suddenly my world lurched and tilted, spinning me over onto my side. My eyes flew open with a gasp and I lifted my head. What the fuck? I was still in my chair and the room was empty. I was losing my mind; that was the only answer. I had gone over the fucking edge. My own heart was still beating a rapid cadence in my chest, but Kristair's had calmed down, settling into an even, almost sleeping, pattern.

Taking several deep breaths, I willed my own to do the same and studied the room. The floor was unfinished concrete and the windows were high and small. It must be some kind of basement. There was a chill in the air and the light outside was rapidly fading. The room was lit with a naked bulb and it reminded me of a b-movie setting. One I was not anxious to star in. There didn't seem to be any cameras set up to watch me, but I wasn't taking any damn chances. I needed to get out of there before they realized I was awake.

I tugged on the cuffs, but they were threaded through the chair back. I might be able to break the slats, but that would mean I'd have to use Kristair's abilities.

Fuck. If I didn't know any better, I'd say it was a goddamned conspiracy to make me use them. Well, if I did, I did. Now wasn't the time to get squeamish.

I tugged on the cuffs then pulled until they cut into my wrist. Where the hell was that stupid strength and speed Kristair had given me now that I really needed it? Using it on instinct was one thing; trying to work myself up to it deliberately was something else entirely. What if I was wrong? What if I couldn't really use it? I could hurt myself trying and end up alerting the bastards who took me to the fact that I was awake. Even worse, if I used it on purpose, could I shut it off again? Or would that door remain open forever?

Voices approached the door, so I immediately dropped my head, pretending to be asleep. There had to be at least four of them, but I seemed to remember the girl screaming like she was hurting or something before I had blacked out. When the door opened, I had to force myself not to tense up.

Those fuckers made me miss my damned appointment. The urge to lash out at them and make them pay was strong.

"Is he still asleep?"

"He's out cold."

"Are you sure?"

"Yes, I'm fucking sure. He hasn't moved since you tranked him. Maybe you gave him too much."

"Didn't you see what he did to Angie? I'm not taking any chances." The voices came closer and, through slitted eyes, I saw a pair of sneakers stop in front of me. My fingers ached to tense into claws, but I held them still. I'd probably have one chance to break out of here and I wasn't about to blow it. If they drugged me again, I wouldn't wake up until after dark, and then my chances would go from fucked up to I might as well bend myself over and beg for the dry corn-holing I was gonna get.

I started to think of all the reasons why I was pissed. Maybe I couldn't try on purpose to break the handcuffs, but if I worked myself up to a really good mad, I could use that. Kinda like the Hulk. After all, these were the same assholes who took over my mind and that really made my blood simmer. And they were the fuckers who'd made me miss my doctor's appointment, and there was no way my coach was gonna believe this story. My gun was gone, and if something happened to me, Tony was going to pay the price. Then I realized that my throat felt oddly light.

Those trifling motherfuckers had stolen my torc! Choking rage boiled up inside. I swear to god, if I didn't find it, I'd kill every last one of them.

"Get the syringe. I'm going to give him another half-dose just in case."

"But Ted said he had an idea to keep him in line if he woke up." My blood turned to ice even as the other figure came all the way into the room, though he seemed reluctant. Smart guy, because when I got my hands on him I was gonna hurt them both. "What if it sends him into shock or something?"

"It won't. He's a jock. They're used to being juiced up on something. The man will be here at dusk to get him. I'm not taking any chances until then. Will you hurry up?"

When the man in front of me half-turned to face the other, I exploded out of my chair. There was a momentary pain at my wrists as the links between the cuffs broke, but that disappeared as both men shouted. Fuck, please don't let there be more than the four in the car. Two here, maybe one taking care of that psychic freak, but all I could do was concentrate on the two here and hope to take them out before reinforcements arrived.

I leapt over the chair as the guy in front of me took a swing, and charged the guy with the syringe. He lifted it as if he was going to stab me and I caught his wrist, twisting it around, and injected him with his own shit. "Take that, asshole," I snarled.

He staggered as I let him go, but I was already turning to meet the other guy who was rushing at me. "Russell, get your ass in here," he shouted.

Fuck. More of them, but at least it was only the one. I ducked under his blow then rushed him, jamming my shoulder into his chest and stomach until we collided against the wall. "Fucking bitch!" I snarled, backing off, and began pummeling him with my fists. He got in a few good blows himself, but I barely felt their sting as fury took over.

I wanted to kill them, could almost taste their blood on my tongue. I needed to hurt them, to see them suffer. I pulled myself back from those dark thoughts before I could give in to them. I was human, not some monster.

Some instinct had me ducking and rolling out of the way, and the guy I'd hit with the syringe cold-cocked his friend with the chair I'd been sitting in. As his unintended victim crumpled to the floor, I met his dazed look and grinned. "Thanks."

He took a stumbling step back, but before I could deck him to finish the job, he slid to the floor as well. "Well, that was no fun," I muttered, nudging him over with my toe.

"Why don't you try me?" a voice rumbled.

I glanced over at the door and groaned. The guy was huge, at least twice my size if not more. Hell, I would've recruited him for our team if he wasn't so butt ugly. "Well, aren't you a big Samoan-looking motherfucker. The buffet is around the corner; sorry."

"Bring it, pipsqueak."

"Why don't you come get me?" This couldn't have been one of the guys who nabbed me. I would've remembered somebody this big. Probably couldn't fit in the car so they'd left him behind. "Or can't ya fit through the door?"

I angled my body and half-crouched as his face darkened and he came through the door at me in a rush. Fuck he was quick, much quicker than I would've given him credit for. He was halfway across the damn room before I had a chance to process it. I dealt with guys just like this every day on the field. I could handle him too.

Cursing, I tried to dodge out of the way, but he caught my arm and whipped me into the wall. The breath left my lungs at the impact, leaving me gasping for air. He caught me before I recovered, wrestling me toward where they kept the drugs.

Get home. I had to get home. The stray thought flitted through my brain.

Screw this bullshit. I wasn't playing their games anymore. If they wanted me they were gonna get all of me. Pushing the possible consequences out of my mind, I tapped into my inner reserve and shoved. It was even easier now to unlock those abilities inside me. The guy flew across the room and I pounced on him again as he landed. The blood in my veins was a furious fire. Snarling, I picked him up and he screamed. Everything in me cried out for his blood. Kill him. Bite him. Tear him to shreds.

Shuddering, I pulled back. "What are you? Jesus, what the fuck are you?" the guy stammered, his eyes huge.

I landed a good one on his jaw and his eyes rolled to the back of his head. I let him slump to the floor as the second guy who'd gotten knocked out by his friend started to stir. I went over and put him back to sleep too. That animal instinct inside of me told me to finish them off—they knew too much—but I yanked myself back from the edge.

I wasn't that far gone. At least not yet.

GET home. Get home. Get home. I don't know where the urgency came from. It was there in every beat rushing through my veins, propelling me onward. It was so strong I found my steps turning toward campus before I realized my direction or where I was in relation to home.

Dusk was falling swiftly, bringing with it a bitter chill and the hint of coming snow. As the first flakes began falling, I couldn't help but be charmed, despite my situation. Snow was nonexistent in Louisiana, and even though it seemed to snow all the time in Pittsburgh and was balls cold, it never got old.

Before I left, I had tied the three idiots together and somehow managed to wrench the cuffs off of my wrists. Now I tossed the remnants into a garbage container in the alley. There had been no sign of Angie, or the other guy who'd driven the car. At least I'd managed to find my torc, which now lay safe again around my throat. Russell had been packing so I took his gun and managed to recover mine as well. I almost tossed it with the cuffs, but something told me it might come in handy later on.

Now I had this sudden overwhelming desire to be back at the dorm.

Glancing at the sky, I began to walk faster. I might have waited too long. It was getting darker every second, and who knew how long it would take for the vamps to get active? Gloaming. That's what Kristair would call this time of evening when the senses began to stir and the day stood at a crossroads. It worried me that I hadn't heard one little peep from him since I'd woken up handcuffed to that chair. Not one comment or piece of advice, not one sigh or mutter.

Not wanting to ponder the implications of his silence, I pushed my thoughts back to the scene I'd left. If Kristair were awake in my head he would've had things to say about me leaving them, especially the big dude, knowing what they knew. Ussier would probably kick my sorry ass. I didn't plan on telling him.

The Syndicate would soon know something had gone wrong. I just hoped they didn't realize I wasn't exactly human anymore. I don't know how I could hide it anymore, not after what I'd thought I'd done to Angie. There was nothing I could do to change that and I didn't intend on adding cold-blooded killings to my conscience. It was heavy enough.

Still, there were other ways to delay them and maybe add a final "fuck you" to the whole screwed-up situation. Not to mention if I could get some corroboration for what happened this afternoon, Coach might be inclined to believe why I'd missed my doctor's appointment. I pulled out my cell phone and called a number I'd gotten way too familiar with in the past year.

"Detective Aderson," the cop's smooth voice answered. I handled him better than his partner, who always seemed to be disgusted to deal with me.

"Detective, it's Jake Corvin."

"Mr. Corvin, what brings you to call me? I would've thought you'd be sick of talking to us by now."

I was, but these guys somehow knew all about this whole other world I was a part of no matter how hard I tried to stay free of it. They had some kind of truce with Ussier. As long as bodies didn't pile up or too many people didn't go missing, they didn't try to make war on the vamps and the vamps left them alone with the things they knew. For all I knew they probably helped each other out.

"Yeah, maybe, but I thought you might want to take a ride to check something out." I rattled off the address where I'd been held. "I was out running errands and they yanked me into their car, drugged me up with something. I managed to wake up before they expected and knocked them out. I left three of them tied up back there."

"You do manage to get into no end of trouble. How is it you're always in the thick of things?"

"Tell me about it. It's a skill."

"Tito and I will check it out. Come down to the precinct later and give a statement."

I grinned in relief. His partner would've made me come now and lost the bastards in the process. Not to mention that the urgency to get home was so strong it was a fever under my skin. I wanted something familiar around me, something sane and safe.

"Yeah, I can come down sometime tonight."

"You have any idea why they wanted you?"

Oh, I'm sure there were reasons, a whole damn list of them. But I wasn't positive they were working for the Syndicate. And since I was pretty sure I hadn't pissed anyone off lately, I didn't know who else it could be.

"Haven't a clue. I left there not five minutes ago, but they said something about waiting for nightfall. So that only leaves one thought in my mind." Uneasiness stirred in my gut. What if these cops didn't have a deal with Ussier? Was I stirring the pot, getting them worked up over things better left unsaid?

"Where's your protector? Isn't he going to want to take care of this situation?"

I clenched my jaw. "He's gone. Besides, I don't want them hurt. You understand?"

The cop's voice softened. "I understand. Will I be able to reach you at this number?"

"Yeah, it's my cell." I hung up and debated for a quick moment what I had just put into motion, and then decided it was the right thing. Whoever kidnapped me had been human and I'd rather have other humans deal with them, even if they'd been working for the vamps. At least then it wouldn't be an immediate death sentence.

I followed up with a quick voice mail to Tony so he'd have it when he woke up, which should be soon. Then I gave in to the urgency churning within me and ran, faster and faster until the world blurred by on a rush of fierce exhilaration.

Chapter 14

AS I unlocked the door to my dorm, such a profound sense of relief swept through me that I almost sank to my knees. Home. I was home. I pushed inside and my heart stopped. It literally stopped dead in my chest then gave a single painful lurch.

Kristair lay in the center of my bed naked, his long legs drawn up and tucked in close to his body. His forehead touched his knees and his arms clasped around them. He was still, both his body and mind at peace, almost as if waiting to be reborn.

I couldn't move, dared not blink. I just stood there, staring like a fucking idiot. Waiting for him to disappear, waiting for the illusion my fucked-up crazy head had conjured to fade and leave me alone. But it remained, Kristair continuing to lay there looking so damn real, so solid, it broke my stuttering heart all over again.

"Kristair."

I breathed his name and approached the bed, sinking down onto it beside him. Hesitantly, I reached out a hand, pausing just before touching him, my heart pounding in my ears. It was so real, he was so real, yet it couldn't be possible.

My lover stirred, his head turned toward me, his long, dark lashes fluttering open. He smiled. A slight tugging of his lips as his eyes warmed. "*Mo chroí.*"

"Oh mah god, Kristair." I leaned over him to throw my arms around him and let out a little yelp when my hands went right through him. I almost fell flat on my face. My heart, which had started beating again, stopped once more. "What the fuck?"

Kristair sat up, sorrow flickering in his gaze. Oh god, I felt him. I felt him inside like I used to. Felt his emotions wash over me, his need to touch, sensed the same fear in him that I carried. This wasn't a dream. Somehow he really was here in some screwed-up way.

I scrambled from the bed, trembling all over. This was way too much, too close to what I'd had, too much of a mockery of our past. I was going crazy. "What are ya? Some kind of ghost?"

"No, Jacob, no ghost. It's me." He rose as well. Unsure of what was happening, I backed up when he took a step toward me. "Close your eyes."

"What?"

"Trust me, mo chroí. *Close your eyes."*

They stung, but I did as he asked and sensed him approach. Oh god. Then his hands framed my face. *"Keep them closed,"* he whispered in my mind before his lips closed over my own.

Hesitantly, I wrapped my arms around him, felt the strength in his body as we came together. This time my mind wasn't clouded with a dream and I wasn't in the middle of a major rock-bottom meltdown. He was here and I could taste him, I could smell him. My senses reeled it was so real.

I opened my eyes, overcome with the need to see him as well. As soon as I did, the sense of his body against mine, the sensation of his kiss against my lips immediately disappeared and my arms fell through him. "Jesus fucking Christ. What the fuck, man?"

I was losing it. I was seriously fucking losing it.

But Kristair stood there, looking as solid as I was, such sadness in his eyes that it eased my frustration. "I'm so sorry, Jacob. But they placed restrictions on my return. You can see me, but not touch me, or you can touch me, but not see me. Never both at once."

"What?" I couldn't wrap my brain around it, not him being here, or in such a screwed-up manner. I had walked into a nightmare.

"You've got to be joking, Kristair. Who the fuck makes up rules like that?"

"Sit down," Kristair urged, gesturing toward the bed. "We have much to talk about."

Stunned, I did as he said, once again sensing our connection flow between us. It was so achingly sweet, so painfully beautiful, that I almost couldn't bear it. Kristair started to ease back and I shook my head, grabbing a hold of the connection and holding on as hard as I could. *"Don't."*

"You've gotten stronger." Kristair's eyes roamed over me, locked on my face as if seeing me could somehow feed him. *"I have a great deal of explaining to do, so much to go into and very little time to get it all together."*

"You're leaving again!" I shouted, jumping up from the bed. "No! No, ya can't." I didn't know if I could live like this, with him only half here. My brain chose that moment to give my emotions a good swift kick as if to say, "Think, idiot." It couldn't be very different from him being a vampire who ran around at night and whose world I could only be a reluctant part of. I paused. If I thought of it that way, yes, I'd damn well try.

"Not if I can help it." Kristair's voice bore the same grim determination as his dark eyes.

I sank back down, unable to tear my gaze away from him. "You're really here? I'm not just imagining this?"

"I'm really here. I swear to you. I am and you're not going crazy," he said, echoing his words from the night before.

A hot, hard lump settled in my throat, making it impossible to talk. *"And it was really you last night too? I didn't dream that?"*

"Yes, it was real, though in a much more limited fashion."

I closed my eyes, stretching out my hand to him and swallowing hard when he grasped it and tugged me into his arms. I squeezed them shut tighter, then buried my face in the crook of his neck. I realized then that Kristair's heart was still beating within me and had been steadily since I'd woken up from the tranquilizers. He must've been here the entire time, asleep and waiting for me.

"I knew you were in trouble, so I came back earlier than I intended," Kristair said in response to my mental thought.

"What do you mean earlier than you intended?" I glared at him, unable to help myself. "You mean you could've been here months ago? Why'd ya wait? Kristair, for fuck's sake, you know what I've—"

He shook his head and lifted his hand, pressing phantom fingers I didn't feel against my lips until I closed my eyes. Fuck, I couldn't take this. I opened them again, my eyes burning. "What's going on?"

"Lay down with me, Jacob, like we used to, and I'll explain it all."

Like we used to. Nothing was like it used to be. I was caught in a tailspin, spiraling out of control and heading for a fiery crash. There was something I could cling to if I let myself take that chance.

Sighing, I stretched out on the bed and turned toward him as he lay down beside me. It was crazy how solid he seemed, how real, as if nothing had changed, right down to the scar on his shoulder. There was nothing about him that screamed ghost unless I tried to touch him.

I closed my eyes and traced my finger over the scar. We may not have been lovers for very long, but I knew Kristair's body better than my own. He wrapped an arm around my waist and tugged me closer. I regretted not getting undressed first so I could feel every inch of him against me with no barrier.

His skin was warm under my palms. I kept wanting to open my eyes to make sure I wasn't imagining it all, but I kept them closed and held on tight.

Kristair leaned his forehead against mine. *"Open your mind. I can't explain what happened to me. It's too much. But I can show you, give you an understanding of what it's been like."*

I relaxed, sensing him take control as our minds merged together like they had during his meeting with the Syndicate. For a brief, glorious moment we were one, existing together. One mind. One soul. Our bodies pressed together, heartbeats in sync. If it had to end, couldn't it just end right here, just like this?

Then my sense of the world blurred and faded away as Kristair unveiled what had happened since his disappearance in the warehouse.

He must've held back the full weight of it, but still my mind spun, my psyche buffeted with the overwhelming enormity of what he'd become, what he'd experienced in the many months he'd been gone. I could only taste the edges of it, yet it was still too much.

Then he showed me his arguments with Nerissa, his desire and desperation to get back to me, and the decision to have him sent back to break the link.

"NO!"

Abruptly, I was flung back into my body. The break was so violent that my heart stuttered in my chest. I sat up, my head spinning as I struggled to catch my breath.

"Jacob, are you all right?" Kristair asked with concern in his voice.

"Yeah, just give me a minute." I turned my head toward him and laid it on my knees. Kristair watched me, a slight furrow between his brows. I couldn't begin to understand it all, even with Kristair's memories in my head of those last moments of his argument with those creatures who had once whispered in his head. If I thought things had been unequal between us before, now… now it just seemed damn near impossible that we could make any kind of a relationship work.

And perversely, that made me want to try even harder.

"What are you?"

Kristair winced. "They call it being one of the Ascended. I think some of the more arrogant ones would liken it to being a god, but I don't hold to that belief. I am what I am, who I've always been, only more."

"Kristair, next time, don't answer." I thumped my forehead against my knees a couple of times before realizing that I just wasn't going to be able to process what Kristair had become. Dating a vampire had been enough of an adjustment. Being in love with what he was now was something else entirely. So I ignored it and focused on what I could understand.

"They want you to end it and you came back to do it, didn't you? You were going to let me go," I accused.

"I was trying to work around that. It's why I wasn't planning on coming back right away. I wanted to come up with a solution so I wouldn't have to go back." Kristair brought his hand up to my hair but this time was unable to ruffle it to make the cowlicks stick up the way he liked so much. "But then you went and got yourself snatched off the street and as soon as you woke I had them send me back so I could help. I didn't expect them to make me sleep until you returned."

There was a whole number of uncomplimentary words Kristair aimed toward those whom he called the Ascended on that matter.

"What are you going to do?" I demanded.

What could he do? Even if he wanted to fight them, he wouldn't be able to hold them off. They were the ones who had caused his change last spring, with all their pushing and prodding, driving him crazy by making him lose control. I seethed. Just let me get my hands on them. I'd give them hell for….

Kristair began laughing, the wonderful sound startling me out of my thoughts. "Oh, I'd missed you so. If anyone could tell the Ascended off and make them listen, it would be you." He clasped his hands around his ankles, holding back his desire to touch me. His expression told me how much he didn't like not being able to any more than I did. "They can't make me. For all their power, they cannot force change upon another of their number."

"But they can make you miserable and keep us apart anyway."

Kristair nodded. "As usual, you see right to the heart of the matter. They can do all that and more. They've kept me from you all these months. At first they even kept me from sensing you, though that actually might have had more to do with me being overwhelmed at first. It was so huge, all I could do was drift and try to soak it all in."

"So what are we going to do?"

The rush of tenderness that went through Kristair just about made me hum with happiness inside. I'd missed this, just this, so very much. Maybe we could make it work even if I could only touch him when I couldn't see him, because it did nothing to dampen our connection. I sensed him just as strongly now as I ever had.

"We will think of something. I won't give up."

I scowled at him. "See that you don't." I couldn't deny the need to touch him anymore, to taste him. I closed my eyes and reached for him, groaning as he came into my arms.

"You're wearing too many clothes," Kristair complained and dragged my coat off of me, then my T-shirt.

Blind, except for my sense of touch, my lips found his throat and I kissed my way up to lips, kissing him hungrily. I couldn't get enough. Time wasn't on our side, but fuck, I swear if I wasn't inside him in the next few minutes, or him inside of me, I was going to explode. It was like a bonfire had lit up inside of me.

I kicked out of my shoes while Kristair tugged off my jeans with impatient jerks until I was as naked as he. We knelt on the bed, our bodies pressed together. It was like coming off a withdrawal and being consumed with need as we indulged in each other. No matter how much I touched, how much I kissed and tasted and breathed him in, it wasn't enough. I craved more. I had to have it like it was a basic essential to survive.

"You still wear it," Kristair breathed against my mouth, brushing his fingers over the torc around my throat.

"Only take it off for showers and football."

My lover chuckled inside his mind. *"Only the important things then."* He cupped my ass in his hands, urging me to straddle him as he sat back on his heels. I was going crazy, his skin scorching as it brushed against mine, his cock hot and hard pressing into my stomach.

"Bite me, Kristair. Can ya still do that?" I wanted to feel that pain again. I had to have it; it would make it so real. Like pinching myself, only better.

He hesitated, his mouth lifting from mine. "I don't need to feed anymore, not like I used to. The instinct is no longer there." Before I could protest, his lips slid down to my throat and he licked my pulse point. "But I've missed your taste."

My lover struck so quickly, I had no time to register he was going to do it before his fangs pierced me. I cried out, clutching his shoulders, hissing in pain, almost crying from the pleasure. This was nothing like my dream experience. This felt like it used to, complete with the sense of satiation from Kristair. He might not need the exchange to survive, but he still desired it as much as I did.

I clung to him, shudders wracking my body until he lifted his mouth from me. "Oh god, oh god. Jeezus, screw the foreplay, Kristair. I need you now." I wrapped my hand around his cock and gave it a squeeze, before releasing him and turning around on my hands and knees. "Fuck me. Fuck me now."

"Just as demanding as ever," Kristair murmured. I gasped as I felt the slick head of his cock rub against my entrance. I dug my hands into the blankets and pushed back, my body raging. "Where's your lube?"

Blindly, I gestured toward the desk. "I can't believe you're talking about lube at a time like this. You won't kill me." With the way I was healing, I knew he couldn't hurt me that much either.

Kristair groaned and then his weight was gone from the bed. A few moments later he was back and my breath caught as his slick cock pushed into me, the burning sting so very welcoming. I clenched my teeth and drove back. "Oh fuck." He was inside me, filling me up, and it was so damn perfect I thought I might die. "More," I gasped and drove myself back again as he guided my hips.

My lover didn't say a word. Then again, he didn't need to. His hands were gentle on my hips, his thumbs brushing my skin in tender sweeps even as he met me with hard thrusts of his own. His emotions rolled me over, swept me under, and I closed my eyes and lost myself in the undertow.

Our minds came together, merged, and I sensed how it felt for him to be inside me so hot and tight, saw the way he imagined how my body looked to him as we fucked. I would have killed to be able to see the expression on his face. I could picture it, though. I'd seen it often enough, his lips parted, desire hazing his dark brown eyes.

"Fuck," I panted, almost sobbing. "Not enough." Maybe it would never be enough, not after our forced separation. "More. Jeezus, don't stop." Dimly, somewhere, I think I heard my cell ring, loud and insistent until it finally fell silent.

Laughter echoed in my mind. *"Good thing you have me as a lover; you'd probably kill a human man."*

"Ain't I just good for yer ego."

Kristair stretched out over my back. I savored the heat of his skin against my own as he nuzzled my neck. All of those sweet, tender gestures amidst our heated fucking drove me wild. *"You're good for much more than my ego,* mo chroí. *I need you. I think I forgot how much you make me whole."*

If Kristair kept talking like that he was going to turn me into a wreck. He'd managed it last night somehow, but I'd be damned if I would allow it two nights in a row. I snaked my hand around to the nape of his neck and turned my head to kiss him. Ours tongues tangled wildly and then Kristair pulled back with a rough curse.

"Don't you dare open your eyes."

I cried out as his cock left my body. The sudden aching emptiness was too much like what I'd been through all those months. My eyes flew open and I looked over my shoulder at Kristair, breathing a sigh of relief when I saw him kneeling behind me. "What the hell are you doing?" My body ached, demanding to be filled again, to be used until I couldn't take any more. "Don't stop now."

"You don't listen worth a damn, do you?"

I laughed and rolled onto my back, sensing that's where he wanted me. It was so odd to hear him curse. "Language, my love, and you're always saying something about me." I closed my eyes, a come-hither smile crossing my lips as I crooked my finger. "Now get your sexy ass over here, before I get violent."

"Who do you think I learned it from?"

Then Kristair was over me again. I groaned, wrapping my legs around his lean waist and arching up against him. He slid one hand under my back, lifting me higher, and then he was inside me again, driving into me over and over, until it seemed all I could do was hang on for the ride.

As he buried his face in the crook of my neck, I slid my hands down to his ass, feeling the play of hard muscle beneath my fingertips as I urged him on, harder and faster. My cock throbbed between our slick stomachs, the friction making me crazy for more.

"Jeezus fucking a...."

Kristair kissed me, silencing my demands. I kissed him back, plundering the slick heat of his mouth. *"If you say 'more' one more time...."*

If I could have, I would've laughed because I knew his threat was idle. I knew Kristair loved how demanding I could be. It didn't matter if I was topping or not. But I couldn't because the tension had built to such a fevered pitch inside of me I thought I was going to explode.

I dug my fingers into his skin, clenching hard around him. I don't know who climaxed first. Fuck, it didn't matter, because one sparked the other, dragging out the pleasure in long rippling waves.

Chapter 15

I'M NOT sure how long we lay there, wrapped up in each other. It couldn't have been that long because my body still held that heavy drained sensation it always did after intense sex. Then when some stupid fucker began pounding on my door, my eyes flew open and as soon as I did the sense of Kristair in my arms faded.

Cursing viciously, I sat up and dragged a hand through my hair. "Go the fuck away," I snarled.

"Open the damn door, Jake, or I'm kicking it in. You've got thirty seconds," Tony snapped right back.

Oh fuck. I glanced at the clock and heaved a sigh of relief. It wasn't that late; bad enough Tony was freaking on me without adding Steve and Kayla to it as well. "Can't it wait? I'm busy."

I ground my teeth together as I heard the bastard start counting through the door. I'd had Kristair back with me for less than an hour and already we were being interrupted. "All right. Hold on a damn minute and I'll be right there." Muttering more curses under my breath, I fisted a hand through my hair and rose. Kristair lounged back on his elbows, watching me as I dragged on a pair of sweats. *"Aren't you going to imagine some clothes on or something?"*

"Even testy is sexy on you." His grin was wicked as he stretched out his long, lean legs. *"Nobody can see me but you."*

"Oh for crying out loud, doesn't matter if he can't see you," I hissed in his mind. *"I can, and it's damned distracting."*

Kristair's low laughter almost had me smiling, until he disappeared. My heart lurched. Then his presence manifested itself again in my mind, occupying a corner of it just as I had with him in the past. I caressed him with my thoughts and sensed the reassurance of his answering touch. Drawing a breath to calm myself down, I opened the door.

"You're a dickhead and your timing sucks," I said with a heartfelt glare.

Tony scowled right back and pushed his way into my room. He'd certainly gotten more self-assured and forceful since he left Pittsburgh. That would've been a good sign on any other night than this one. "Come on in. Why don't you go ahead and make yourself comfortable."

He ignored my sarcasm and glanced around the room, his eyes narrowing in suspicion. "You here alone?"

"Nope." I hooked my chair with my foot and sat down. "Now you're here too."

"Smart-ass. Then what was so damned important you couldn't open the door?"

"I was jacking off." Disgust flickered over Tony's face. His reaction was almost worth the interruption. "Actually, I suppose it's a good thing you came. Your timing's still awful, but I'd needed to talk with you anyway."

"No, I need to talk with you," Tony broke in. "You had no damn business running off like that last night. It's not just your life you're risking by going around all half-cocked like you do. It's mine too, asshole."

"I wasn't in any danger last night." Tony's savage glare had me dropping that argument, so I moved on to the next one. "You could've followed me, you know. Or couldn't you keep up?"

"You could've answered your phone and let me know you were okay."

I had been pretty fucking far from okay, but I decided to keep my mouth shut on that point too. Kristair flooded my mind with a rush of tender warmth, but thankfully remained silent. I didn't want to think about last night.

"I wasn't in the mood to talk to anyone last night, but you already knew that. And you knew I was home too. This is the first place you would've checked. So don't give me any bullshit about wondering if I'd been taken or not. You would've been able to smell if I was home through the door just like you did tonight."

Maybe it meant he'd been worried about my state of mind, maybe not, and right now I didn't care to explore it any further. Our constant bitching back and forth wore me down.

"That doesn't change the fact that you risked both our lives by running off," Tony replied, his voice more subdued than before. Then he dragged over another chair and sat down. "Look, I'm sorry. I knew you were pretty close to cracking and kept feeding into it, but I swear you piss me off every time I see you. You get under my skin then dig in even deeper."

Maybe things between us weren't as irreparable as I thought. One could always hope, and it seemed I was doing nothing but that lately. Maybe it was finally beginning to pay off.

"I'm sorry if it seems that way. I'm not trying to set you off. Well, mostly I'm not. Last night was a very bad night and, before you say it, I know it sucked for you too."

"I had a taste of your state of mind last night, Jacob. If anyone had tried screwing with you, you would've ripped them apart."

"Like I said, it would've been a bad idea to run into anyone." I didn't want to rip anybody apart, even vamps. Well, for the most part, I didn't. If they kept fucking with me, I'm sure my feelings would change.

"Let me tell you what the Syndicate has planned for you and maybe then you'll take it more seriously."

"I do take it seriously."

"Shut the fuck up and listen. There are some on the Council who want to turn you." My blood turned to ice and Kristair went deadly still in my mind. "They want to make you a vampire so they can torture you for the next thousand years. Take a moment and imagine how that would be. As pissed off as you make me, I still don't want to see that, okay? So please, no more luring vampires into alleyways and no more running off by yourself. Think before you do something moronic. Okay?"

As I soothed Kristair's fury, my mind raced. It was weird. I wasn't scared; not really. Wasn't even that angry. Probably because I'd spent all those months before now pissed and upset. Besides, becoming a vampire was never going to happen. I would never let it happen. I wasn't sure I even could be turned with the way Kristair was influencing my physiology.

"Kristair, you really have been in my head too much if I'm thinking words like that."

"It's good to know I can influence you as much as you do me." Kristair paused. *"You may have a point. They may not be able to turn you, but that's not a theory I want to test. But you do heal quickly. They can use that to prolong your torture and it wouldn't be the first time."*

I shook my head, trying to block out the images of what I'd gone through at Montrose's hands, and turned my attention to Tony. "Okay, I've heard you out. Now it's your turn to shut up and listen. I've got some things you would like to hear, things that might set your mind at ease some."

"Don't tell him I'm back. You're the only one who is to know," Kristair said. That brought me up short. He seriously couldn't mean for me to not say anything to Kayla.

"Yes, I do certainly mean Kayla. We can talk about it later."

I frowned and pushed it aside for another time as Tony spoke up again. "Are you going to get around to it or sit and stare off into space?"

Trying to run two conversations was going to end up giving me a headache. I turned my attention to Tony and promised myself I'd find out what Kristair was talking about later on.

"I'm telling you this because I trust you and you'll realize just how much in a minute. I'm also telling you because keeping secrets is what fucked us up in the first place. I should've told you what Kristair was and what he meant to me. Maybe if I hadn't been so hell bent on protecting you, and been honest with you from the start, you wouldn't have thought I needed saving and we wouldn't be in this situation."

I think that was the first time it really hit me. Maybe because I'd never said it out loud before. Tony had thought I was in danger and he'd risked his hide to help me and gotten turned into a vampire. I'd never even asked him what happened that night with the woman who'd picked him up. But, I don't think he'd tell me even if I did ask.

"Forget it. It's in the past. We both did shit that we've come to regret and, honestly, being a vampire is pretty fucking cool. Well, most of the time."

I used to be able to tell when he was lying, or at least I'd thought I could. Now, I had no damn clue. "You know how the Syndicate was so concerned with Kristair's secrets?"

"Yeah, but I think it's a bunch of bull, since it didn't help him too much in the end." Tony's brows furrowed. "Though I'm not sure what exactly happened to him. So much shit happened so fast."

"Do not go into what happened to me."

"Don't worry, Kristair. I won't." There were some secrets I'd never give away and that was one of them. Kristair started to speak again, but I hushed him or else I'd never get through this conversation.

"Tony, listen to me. I swear everything I'm going to say is the absolute truth. I have in my head everything Kristair knew and I mean everything. Those damn secrets the Syndicate wanted so bad I know. On top of that, Kristair did something to me, changed me somehow. Most of what he could do, I can do, or at least I think I can. If I ever bothered to put the effort into it, that is."

Now that Kristair was back and we were connected, I bet it would come even easier. *"You've given this some thought,"* he said.

"From time to time, and reluctantly, I might add. More lately though, since vamps have started to come out of nowhere and harass me again."

Tony didn't say one word. I wasn't sure if it was because he didn't believe me or because he just couldn't believe the fucking crazy situation. There were times when I still had trouble believing it myself.

"Today while you and Ussier and every other vamp in the city were sleeping, some humans with crazy mental mojo nabbed me off the streets. I haven't really delved into these abilities he left me. I didn't want them." "*I'm sorry, love, but it's true,*" I said to Kristair before continuing on with Tony. "But I had to, to get free of them." I studied my hands. "It was the first time I'd used it on purpose and, you know, it felt good. Not like in the alley when I just let myself go. I hate to say it, but it's true, it was damn good. And now that I've unlocked them I don't think I can put them away again."

Wasn't sure I wanted to, which was kinda scary, because I'd been against the idea from the beginning. Even if the abilities disappeared, I'd changed. Guess it was just a fact of life I'd have to accept.

"About time."

I stuck out a mental tongue at Kristair. Mouthy bastard. Damn, it was good to have him back.

"Okay, let me get this straight. You were kidnapped today? What the fuck?" Tony jumped up. "I thought somebody was watching you during the day."

"Really? I have a babysitter then too?" I didn't know that. "Well, I didn't see anyone else and it happened so quick. Even if someone had been there they probably wouldn't have had time to react." I hadn't been paying as much attention as I should have. I thought I'd be safe while the sun was up.

"What do you mean mojo? What did they do?"

"Some kind of psychic bullshit. It was like my brain had been seized or something. I fought it, and I'm pretty sure I was close to winning by the time they dragged me into the car and then unloaded some drugs into me."

"You just can't stay out of trouble, can you? You're like a freaking magnet for bad shit." Tony touched the spot on his forehead and glanced up at the ceiling. "I'm so fucked. Jesus, I never should've come back. I must've been crazy."

"Calm down. I have a couple ideas."

"I just bet you do. Thanks, but no thanks."

"Stop being such an ass and shut up and listen, okay?"

Tony plopped back down in the chair and glared. "What? Is there something in that thick head of yours that he left behind that could actually reverse the spell so I don't get destroyed when your idiocy finally gets the best of you?"

"Well, I asked Kayla to look into it because Kristair did know some magic."

"What do you think, Kristair? Is it possible?" Fuck, I hoped so. I hated knowing Tony had what amounted to an invisible bull's-eye between his brows.

"What happened? I need to know that first. I could sense your emotions after I left, but very rarely have I gotten to see you since then to know what you've been going through."

I ran down our meeting with Ussier and what Lisabeth did to Tony to keep him in line. Even before I'd finished, I already knew Kristair's answer. Regret weighed down his thoughts. *"You can't do anything, can you?"*

"Her magic isn't mine. I wouldn't even know where to begin."

My disappointment must've shown on my face, because Tony grabbed my arm. "What is it? Why do you keep zoning out?"

"Doesn't mean Lisabeth and Ussier can't be reasoned with," Kristair went on. *"If you can prove to them your friend is trustworthy, they may take you're assurances. All you have to do is delve into his mind. He won't be able to hide his true intentions from you. He's not strong enough."*

"I'm not doing that!" The very thought of mind-raping Tony in that manner made me sick to my stomach. "Okay, so Kristair's magic can't reverse it like I'd hoped." Tony stared at me like I'd lost my mind. "What?"

He shook his head. "I dunno. Sometimes you don't look like yourself and you act different from the Jake I remember. It makes me jumpy. Just like right now it was like your mind wasn't here."

"Try having two thousand years of memories and shit stuffed into your head and you'd act differently too." I immediately repented my bitter tone as I felt the shaft of remorse run through my lover. *"I'm not saying I wish you didn't do it; just sometimes it's hard to deal with."*

"I can just imagine." Tony stood up. "Talking's not going to solve anything. I thought the trouble with the Syndicate was over with when I came by. I'd tried calling you last night to let you know Ussier destroyed that cell in Oakmont. Figured it was a done deal then, but I guess not if they tried taking you today. We need to let him know."

"Truth is they're going to keep coming and coming until either I'm dead or Ussier manages to put enough fear into them. You know this as well as I. Anyway, Steve wanted to meet with us tonight to discuss some things."

"Dammit, I don't want him to get involved."

"Neither do I, but I didn't want any of you getting involved last time either. And look what happened. Keeping you out of the loop proved to be a huge mistake. Steve and Kayla both are less likely to do something crazy if we tell them what the fuck is going on."

"What can they do other than get themselves killed?"

"It's not a question of what they can do; it's how much they'll kick our asses if they find out that we've kept them in the dark. Not to mention all the trouble they'll get into on their own. Neither one of them will accept us trying to keep them out of it." They wanted to support us. They'd made that more than clear on several occasions. The dawning resignation on Tony's face told me he realized it was pointless too.

I sighed. As much as I wanted to stay inside and wallow in Kristair's presence, I couldn't. Damn, that pissed me off.

"We have some time. This is important too and I'll be right here with you the entire time," Kristair murmured in my thoughts.

"You'd damn well better be." I rose and grabbed a T-shirt, tugging it on. "Come on; let's go talk to them. I've got an idea simmering in the back of my head."

"Fine. Doesn't seem like I have much of a choice."

I paused and addressed my lover, holding up a hand for Tony to wait. *"Is there any way I can share with him some of your abilities?"*

"He hasn't earned them."

"Don't give me that bullshit. He's trying to keep me alive and I'm trying to keep him safe too. There has to be something we can do to augment him. And when you get right down to it, I haven't earned them either." Jeezus, I'd used "augment." I wasn't even sure what it meant, only that it sounded right. *"Will that mind thingy work on him?"*

"Even if you could share it with him, it still takes time, discipline, and will to master the abilities. It's not like, poof, and suddenly you're powerful. It's different with you, because you're permanently linked to me. Even then, notice how you're stronger now than you were at the start."

I couldn't help but smile at the testiness of his voice. Kristair hoarded his knowledge like a damn miser sitting on a mother lode. "Tony, I have an idea. I don't know how well it'll work, but it's worth a shot."

He cocked his head. "What is it?"

"You know how I said I've got Kristair's stuff in my head and how I can do some of it, all of it probably, if I put my mind to it?" Except for the trick of walking through walls; that was just a little too creepy for me. "I want to try to see if I can share a part of it with you."

Tony studied me, his face thoughtful, before he finally responded. "Maybe you are on the level and maybe you're telling me the truth, but I'm just not ready to open my mind to you."

I bit back the rush of disappointment and nodded. "It's a standing offer, so if you change your mind...."

"I'll let you know."

Chapter 16

I WAS very grateful Kayla hadn't arrived yet when we'd arrived at Steve's. Kristair was too stirred up at the prospect of seeing her again. We'd even had a quick, heated argument about her on the way over. He insisted she wasn't to know he had returned. In a way, I understood, if it didn't work out, and fuck I didn't want to contemplate the possibility. Then her grieving would start all over again. That didn't seem to be the only reason, though, and I didn't have the time to dig any further. Besides, it didn't matter in the long run. We'd find a way to make it work this time.

Tony and I filled Steve in about what had happened to me. As he listened he unloaded the dishwasher, banging the dishes together and downing a second beer in the process. Then we sat down and went over plans and possibilities, losing track of the time.

For the moment, it was good to be with Tony and Steve again. To have some hope that after this whole mess was over, the three of us might be able to salvage our friendship. And to make the day near perfect was having Kristair with me again. Being connected with him again made me believe in just about anything. The only thing that would make it better would be to have him next to me in the flesh.

My cell phone rang and my stomach tightened when I glanced down and didn't recognize the number. After the day I'd been through, I was starting to listen to all these little stabs of intuition. "Yeah, who's this?"

"It's Detective Kuykedal returning your call. You never came in to see us." The sound of his nasal voice had me curling my lip. The man grated on my nerves, even when he was trying to help. The only thing that made me feel better about the whole situation was knowing I irked him just as much.

Damn, I'd forgotten all about my call to them. My pulse picked up. *"Who is it?"* At Kristair's silent question, I quickly relayed my conversation with Aderson. *"You shouldn't have gotten them involved. The situation is murky enough."*

"It'll be worth it if they lock those idiots up for a bit. Hell, even if it's only overnight."

"Sorry about that. I got a little sidetracked," I replied to Kuykedal.

"Another imaginary kidnapping, punk? We checked the place you called about and it was clean. Nobody tied up, no drugs, nothing."

At first I was so stunned, I couldn't even find the words to reply. Steve shot a questioning glance my way and smacked Tony on the arm, nodding toward me. I waved them to silence. "Then you got there too late." I couldn't imagine how if they'd gone over right after I'd talked to his partner.

"Next time you come down here and make a proper statement or I'll haul your ass in for making a false report."

I opened my mouth to curse him out when Kristair interrupted. *"Let it go, Jacob. It's not much of a surprise that they cleared out. It was close to nightfall. Besides, he seems eager to get his hands on you. Don't give him reason. We can always deal with him later."* There was an awful ring of finality in his words.

"Thanks. I'll keep that in mind." I didn't even try to stop the sarcasm in my voice.

"See that you do."

I swore as I hung up. "Guess all the goons who grabbed me managed to get away clean."

I sensed Kristair's disquiet over it and gave him a mental nudge. *"I couldn't just kill them."*

"I know, and to be honest, I don't expect you to, but it certainly would've made things tidier."

"I don't like the sound of that," Steve grumbled as Tony stared out the window, his frown thoughtful.

"I more than don't like it," Tony said. "They must've sent more than one cell to the city. I should've thought of that. You should let Ussier know, if he doesn't already."

"Why don't you?" I suggested. "You're a part of this team too, and if you decide to stick around you'll have to put up with him more than I will."

As Tony made the call I went over to the window and looked out at the empty street. Something was off and it made me restless. "When did you say Kayla was gonna get here? She's coming, right?"

Steve glanced at his watch and scowled. "She was supposed to be here an hour ago."

"She's never late. She would've called if she fell behind." Kristair's alarm had my stomach jumping as Steve echoed his thoughts aloud.

"I'm sure she's just primping or something," I said, though I didn't believe it any more than they did. I pulled out my cell again and tried her number. As it rang, the tightening in my gut became stronger until it hurt. The tension in the room thickened.

I tried telling myself I was just being paranoid about the whole situation, but my instincts screamed when someone picked up on Kayla's end. A voice I didn't know; a man.

"Hello, Corvin. I hope that's you."

"Just who the fuck are you? Where's Kayla?" Kristair went still inside me, his predator instinct leaping to life as Steve's expression went flat.

"I see I've gotten your attention. Good. The pretty girl has something she wants to tell you."

I waited, tense, but nothing happened. I strained to hear as a muffled curse came across the line, then a woman's outcry of pain. Kayla. My insides turned to ice. Then the sensation was lost under

Kristair's white-hot wave of killing fury. "You leave her the hell alone," I snarled, trying to fight off Kristair as he struggled to take me over. *"Calm down. I hafta hear what he has to say. Please, Kris."*

"What do you want?" I asked, striving for calm as Steve began demanding answers until I shot him a glare. Tony grabbed his arm and shook his head and Steve shut up, his jaw clenching.

"You take that blood traitor youngling who's hanging with you and head to the access tunnels underneath the campus. You know the ones?"

I closed my eyes. "Yeah, I know them." Too well, in fact. The three of us had stumbled across them drunk once and had gotten lost in there for hours before we'd come to our damned senses. I mouthed the info to the two of them and Steve swore under his breath.

"We'll find you down there. And if Ussier even twitches from his hidey-hole tonight, we'll know about it. She'll become one of us long before you can rescue her."

I laughed grimly. "That would be a bad idea. She'd end up yanking out your guts and feeding them to you." Hanging up the phone, I tried contending with Kristair, who was deep in a bloodlust frenzy.

Tony and Steve began demanding details as Kristair began raging for blood. My skull pounded. "Hold it! Jus' hold it for a damn minute." I was deeply shaken by the rabid man inside my head and could only deal with one thing at a time. Kristair must've shielded the worst of his instincts from me when we were together, but now either he couldn't, or he'd forgotten to do so. I shot Tony a stricken glance. Was this what all vampires dealt with? It was far worse than the rage that had come over me when I'd fought my kidnappers.

The intense craving for the hunt filled my mouth. I was hungry for the sharp tang of blood, to chase my prey as they ran from me, to hear their scream as I tore them open.

"Kristair, you've got to calm down. I can't take this."

"They've got my daughter," he raged. *"I'm going to rip them apart."* The list of rather inventive tortures he had in mind flashed across my brain, making me ill. Not that I could blame him, but I didn't want to be the one to do all those things.

"I know," I tried to soothe. *"And we'll get her back safe. I swear it. Come on, love. I need your brains, your instincts to get through this. They aren't going to be suspecting what we're capable of what we have coming their way, okay?"*

Kristair muted the edge of his rage and I realized my hands were shaking. Damn, that had been intense.

When I turned to address my friends, Steve's expression was grim, Tony's wary. I drew in a breath and tried not to think of Kayla stuck in those damn tunnels for god knew how long. Abruptly, I remembered what the goon who'd kidnapped me had said, that one of them, Ted, was working on something to ensure my good behavior. He must've meant Kayla.

The hot taste of blood and fury filled my mouth. Ted was one dead motherfucker.

"Okay, here's the deal. They've got Kayla and they want Tony and me to meet them in the access tunnels under the quad." I turned to face Tony. He really had no stake in all of this. He didn't know her at all. "Will you go with me?"

Surprise crossed his face and then he nodded. "Yeah, I'm with you."

"You're not cutting me out of this," Steve said, his eyes narrowing. "I'm coming too."

"He'd just be somebody else we'd have to keep an eye on. He'd be a liability," Kristair said.

"Out of the three of us, he knows the tunnels the best, unless you spent some time down there."

"I have not. I'd forgotten they were even down there, to be honest."

"He's a good man, Kristair. He's the most level-headed of the three of us. He can get Kayla out while we deal with the rest. Besides, he'd follow anyway. He and Kayla have a thing going right now and he won't just sit here while she's in danger."

"A thing? What's a thing?"

I thought it best, seeing as I was talking about his daughter's personal relationship, if I just ignored the question, so I gestured to Steve and looked at Tony. "I think we should take him with us, Tony. What do you think? They said we couldn't bring Ussier into this, but they shouldn't consider him a threat." I glanced at Steve. "But, if it does jeopardize her to bring a third person, I'm sorry, but I'd have to ask you to stay back."

"No, he's human and probably known to be a friend of ours," Tony replied. "They won't think him a threat at all. More bang for their buck. He'd be a bonus, as food or extra leverage."

"Well then, they're a bunch of idiots." I checked the gun in my pocket. "Let's go."

"Wait. Don't we need a plan?" Steve asked as he grabbed a flashlight.

"The plan is to get Kayla free and for you to get her the fuck out of there," I said, exchanging a grim look with Tony, who nodded.

"What about you two?"

"We'll be the cleanup crew," Tony replied. "Before we go, Jake, that thing you said you can share with me. Do you really think it's possible?"

I nodded. "Yeah, but I've been told time and again that I can share the theory with you, but you need to work on the practical application. It might not all catch on at once."

"Lord, you sound like you've downloaded an encyclopedia into your head since I've been gone. Can it or can it not be done?"

"Kristair?"

He was very reluctant, I could sense that much, but his concern for Kayla outweighed his hesitance. *"Some of the changes would probably be immediate. For example, the physical changes that you went through because it's a part of every vampire and he would've started on them already whether he's realized it yet or not. Others will take time. It's just the way of things. Still though, the Syndicate members would be expecting him to have the abilities of a youngling, so they'll underestimate you both. Whatever extra he gets will have a much heavier psychological impact because it will surprise them."*

I pondered that a moment. Well, it couldn't hurt in the long run. "It'll help. You won't be able to walk through walls tonight, but it'll give you an edge they won't be expecting."

"I'll take anything at this point. You know we're walking into a trap, right? Are you sure you don't want to call Ussier?"

"Fuck no! Not until I know she's safe. Don't argue with me on this, please, Tony."

"Will somebody care to fill me in on what the hell's going on?"

I realized that I'd never explained to Steve about the legacy Kristair had left me. "I'll explain along the way. We're wasting time." I gestured to the chair. "Let's sit down, Tony. I don't think this'll take long. After this, trust me, these guys won't stand a damn chance against us."

"There needs to be a connection between you two, an empathic one. You were friends for a long time. That might suffice," Kristair spoke up.

"We'll never know until we try. What do I do?"

"We're doing this in a hurry, so touch your fingers to his temple and close your eyes. I need to take a hold of you for a moment. Do you mind?"

I smiled at his politeness and teased. *"You asked. You're learning. Go ahead. Let's get this over with. I don't want Kayla down there one second longer than she has to be."*

I figured that she was the only reason why he was agreeing to this and right now I didn't care for the reasons, just that it was getting done. I brushed my fingers against Tony's temple. *"Now reach out to your friend,* mo chroí, *to the heart of him. If he is the man you think him to be, if you know him as well as you claim, it should be rather easy. If he's not, you'll never be able to reach him without tearing through his defenses."*

I hoped I was right. Now was not the time to find out Tony was trying to screw us all. I doubted it, though. He never would've agreed to this intrusion if he was lying. Long, tense moments passed and I blocked out Steve's grumblings. Then I sensed the whisper of Tony's thoughts, his nervousness, and grinned.

"Like that, babe? Is that what I need?"

"Yes, very good. Follow that connection, make it stronger. Once you've got it established I'll take over."

I concentrated and soon heard Tony's startled voice in my thoughts. *"Jake?"*

"Hey there, buddy. Yeah, it's me."

"Who else is with you? There's an echo."

"Trust you to get too deep. A lighter touch would've sufficed without alerting him to my presence," Kristair said in a tight aside to me. He hesitated and for a moment, I thought he was going to break the link and refuse.

I sent him a silent appeal and he gave in, deftly taking control and shunting me off to the side, though this time I wasn't overcome with the same feeling of helplessness I'd had before. There was a confused welter of emotions, images, the babble of voices that went on for I didn't know how long. Then the connection was broken and I fell back gasping.

"What happened?"

"You held on too tight, made the connection too complete." Kristair sounded shaken.

"Was he hurt?" I rose up on shaky feet and looked down at Tony, who had fallen out of the chair and lay on his side, cursing.

Steve bent over to help him up. "What did you do to him?" he demanded.

"I'm okay. It's just a lot to process." After several long moments, Tony raised his head. "I see what you meant. It's going to take a bit, but…." He hesitated then a slight smile tugged the corner of his mouth. "Thanks, man."

I grinned back at him, greatly reassured by the connection we'd shared. I'd wanted to trust him before and now I knew I could. "No problem. Now let's go kick some vamp ass. No insult intended."

"None taken."

Chapter 17

WE FILLED Steve in as we walked to my dorm to grab the extra gun I stole from my kidnappers, before heading over to the tunnels. I don't know whether he was shocked or pleased or how to read his thoughts at all on the whole damn situation. Steve was almost as good hiding what he was thinking as Kristair. By the time we arrived at the quad, my heart was pounding and Kristair was a tightly coiled presence in my mind, tense and ready to spring.

The tall buildings thrust up high into the night, obscuring the sky, their height turning the quad into nothing more than a dark, narrow alley between the buildings. As we went inside the main building, I was sure we'd attract attention. Between the way we looked and our determined swagger, our presence had to scream "dudes up to no good." Yet, no one commented as we passed the bank of elevators and loaded ourselves into the freight elevator.

The basement was empty as we made our way over to the access door. "Still know how to pick locks?" Tony asked me. "I could rip the hinges off, but that might draw too much attention to us."

"Yeah, though last time I did it I ended up locked inside a room at the top of the cathedral." I crouched down in front of the door and studied the lock as my lover filled me with a rush of warmth.

"*It was a nice surprise to wake up to,*" Kristair said, and I grinned.

"*I bet.*"

"You'll have to tell me that story sometime," Steve murmured and switched on the flashlight as soon as I'd popped the lock. "Are you sure you won't need a flashlight coming out? We should've stopped and gotten another one at least."

"Positive," Tony replied. "I don't need the light to see. Neither should Jake."

"I'll be cool. Think of me as Super Jake without the burning need to be a vigilante. Most of the time anyway." I gestured to the door as the thrill of the hunt rose in Kristair then filled me in turn. "Shall we?"

The flashlight did nothing to banish the oppressive dark behind the door. Though the corridor was wide and the ceiling high, the sense of walls still pressed down. Pipes of all sizes covered the walls, some sticking out or hanging free. The air was tainted with mildew and damp dust, and as we stepped in and shut the door, the dark swallowed everything but the little ray Steve had aimed at the floor. There was a wall to our immediate right and the tunnel stretched out on our left, disappearing into the gloom.

"Nobody waiting for us," Steve commented, flashing the light down the corridor as far as it would go. "What now?"

"See if you can catch her scent," Kristair said, his predator aura making my blood stir in response. I was beginning to share his excitement of the chase despite my resolve to keep that separate from me. *"You should be able to follow it straight to her."*

"How do I do that?" I took a cautious sniff of the air, but the only thing my nose caught was damp and rust.

"I don't know how you've managed to block yourself so well," Kristair grumbled and rummaged around in my head. It was a very weird sensation. *"You've got so many walls up I'm surprised I ever managed to get through to you."*

That gave me something to think about. I had been so intent on trying to go back to normal, maybe I could have had Kristair back sooner if I hadn't spurned what he'd left me. Suddenly, my nose flooded with scent, so much at once that at first I couldn't figure out what belonged to any one thing or person. I sneezed.

"Jake?" Tony asked.

"Give me a sec." There that cold, almost disturbing scent had to be Tony and the other one rich with warm blood was Steve. *"Ugh, Kristair, I don't want to think in vampire terms."*

"Sorry; that's the only way I know how." There was a tense pause. *"She didn't come in this way."*

"Yeah, I agree." There were other indications of people having been through here, but all days old, and nobody carrying the old chill like Tony, either. "Okay, I'm not keen on waiting around for the goon squad. If they want us, they'll find us. In the meantime, we'll look for them."

"How? These tunnels cover blocks," Steve said in frustration.

"I can track her if we come across her scent."

"I probably can too. I'm not as familiar with her as you two, but we have met." Tony hitched his shoulders and started walking. "One of us should scout ahead."

I didn't like the idea of us separating, and from Steve's expression, he wasn't fond of the idea either. *"Don't trust him. I know you want to, but the odds are bad anyway and not just for Kayla but for you too, Jacob. Please, stick together,"* Kristair said.

"How about you? Can you go ahead for us and let us know what you see?"

"It's worth a try." Kristair materialized next to me, looking as solid as if he were really there and still stark naked. To my relief, neither of my friends gave any indication they saw him.

"Hold up, Tony. I might have another idea," I said as Kristair took a few steps away down the hall. *"For chrissake's, put on some clothes. You're killing me."*

"Don't have any to put on. Most likely my Mistress's idea of a joke." He moved faster down the hall until he'd reached about fifty yards or so, then stopped. I sensed Kristair's regret before he spoke. *"This is as far as I can go. It won't give us much warning."*

"If Tony's out to get me, keeping him close won't make much of a difference, but if he isn't we can use the extra edge," I argued then nodded at Tony.

"Be careful and for god's sake don't get caught." It was wrong of me, but I swear I smiled when Kristair growled in my head. *"Trust me."*

"It's not you I don't trust. I will admit I do admire your loyalty, as stubborn and misguided as it is sometimes."

"Jake, I don't think…." Steve's voice trailed off as the shadows seemed to wrap around Tony before he melted into them and disappeared.

"Wow, that's a neat trick." He'd done something similar that night in the alleyway, though I'd been too worked up to really notice it. "How'd you learn that one?"

Tony chuckled softly. "Those first few months in Rome I didn't want to be seen, so somehow I made it so I couldn't be. I won't go too far—no more than a few corners at the most. I'll let you know if I see anything."

"You sure he'll be okay?" Steve murmured, searching the shadows, but there was no trace of Tony. I couldn't be sure if he was still there or if he'd already gone on ahead to scout.

"As sure as I am about any of us. I've seen him in action. He can take care of himself."

"It's just ass backward, you know," he sighed. "Guess I'm not used to being the low man on the totem pole. He's all vamped up and you've got super powers. Not that I'm looking for them, but it's just weird."

I knew what he meant. Steve always took care of us. And Tony, damn, he had been like the baby brother and now he was taking point. Then it hit me: the real difference was that before Tony had had an innate trust in people. It used to drive Steve and me crazy. Now, that kind of innocence was gone. It was a little bit ridiculous, but I missed it.

I drew my gun as we started down the corridor, grateful for the way the pipes deadened any echo effect from our low voices. "You may not be able to kick my ass anymore, but I'm still glad you've got my back."

"Trust me, Jake, I'd find a way to kick your ass if I believed it necessary."

"Kristair, if you can't scout, do you mind disappearing again?"

Kristair laughed and then he was in my mind again. *"Better?"* he teased.

"It depends on your point of view, love." Yes, not seeing him naked was less distracting, but the intimacy of him in my mind reminded me that we'd just been reunited and weren't in a position to enjoy it.

"Soon," Kristair promised.

As we made our way deeper through the tunnels and we didn't see or hear any sign of the people we were seeking, I began to worry that this was some kind of sick hoax, a way to distract us. That they laughed at us as we skulked around underneath Pittsburgh as they pulled some shit above. Frustration eroded my patience with my worry for Kayla growing as each minute trickled away.

"No, they're down here. Somewhere," Kristair said.

"How do you know?"

"I can just sense it." He paused. *"Have Tony check your back trail; they may be setting you up for an ambush."*

"Thought you didn't trust him."

"Don't have much of a choice at the moment."

I caught Steve's arm. "Let's wait 'til Tony checks in again. We're getting nowhere."

"That's the damned truth."

I turned and scanned the darkness behind me, but with Steve's flashlight, any advantage from Kristair's night vision was lost to me and I was reluctant to leave him alone while I went back to see if anybody was following us. I strained to hear and picked up nothing more than dripping water and the scurrying of tiny feet.

"How long has it been since Tony last checked in?" I asked.

"About half an hour or so."

Late, but not too late. Still, with everything else, it made me uneasy. For once, Kristair was silent, and I blessed him for it. Somehow I sensed Tony, so I knew he was still alive at least, but nothing more than that.

"How come I can do that? I couldn't before."

"I told you, you held onto him too hard." Kristair still sounded a little disgruntled about that.

"I'm not going to start hearing his thoughts all the time, am I?" One man in my head was enough. I didn't want to share this connection with anyone else.

"Not if you don't let him."

"Trust me, I don't want that." Something eased in Kristair and I realized he'd been the tiniest bit jealous. I'd have to tease him about that later on.

"How much ground do you think we've covered?" I asked Steve.

"No more than a quarter of the tunnels, I'd think. It's hard to tell," Steve replied. "And we can't be sure we haven't missed a smaller side tunnel."

I gnawed my thumb, weighing our options. I hated this shit. "Let's backtrack for about five minutes or so," I said in an undertone. "Make sure no one's following us."

"Wouldn't they just back off when they see our flashlight?"

"Yeah, maybe, but I'd be able to smell them if we cross their trail. Then at least we'd know if they are hounding us."

"But what if Tony comes back and we're not where we're supposed to be? Won't he...." Steve stopped and gave me a rueful smile. "Never mind. He'd be able to track us too."

"You've got it."

"You know, Jake, I'm beginning to believe you were right. I shouldn't have come. You guys don't need me along screwing this up."

I stared at Steve in surprise. "Are you feeling okay?" Steve shrugged. "Don't go there, man. Besides, there's no one I'd trust more than you to bring Kayla safely out, and that's the damn truth."

We hadn't gone back more than a hundred yards when I caught their scent. Two of them, and, from their cold abnormality, they had to be vamps. Kristair went very still in my mind then let out a slow hiss. *"You'll have to take them out. Leave one aware enough to talk."*

His merciless tone bothered me, but not enough that I couldn't see the sense in it. Besides, they'd taken Kayla, and even if Kristair wasn't in my head spurring me on, I'd still want them to pay for dragging her into this.

"What is it?" Steve whispered.

"There's at least two of them back there." Why they had kept back from ambushing us didn't make any sense. If they'd wanted to attack us they should have done it long ago before we realized we might be on to them. *"Kristair?"*

"They may be herding you." Ice trickled through my stomach. That didn't sound pleasant.

"Let's go get them. One of them will talk." Steve's voice was grim and implacable.

"Go for their heads. It'll slow them down, at least."

We started forward, moving cautiously. "Jake, thanks for not trying to tell me to stay behind."

"I know better." A recess between the pipes opened up, hiding an old door. I gestured to it and Steve and I stepped inside. "Douse the light," I said on a breath. As long as they saw it coming they were going to keep backtracking, and I wasn't gonna chase them all the way back to the start.

It didn't take long. I could hear them start to run as soon as the light disappeared. Couple of fucking idiots, but better for us. I squeezed Steve's hand and brought my mouth to his ear. "I'll knock them down," I whispered. "You shine the light in their eyes and shoot." I trusted his shooting far more than my own. Where the hell was Tony? I tried reaching out to touch his mind, but the approaching bad guys had me so distracted I got nothing.

The blur of their outlines came closer in the pitch dark. "Wait!" one shouted just as they pounded past us and stopped turning toward the door. I launched myself at their feet and the three of us went down snarling in a tangle of limbs.

"Too late, motherfucker," I growled, and kicked free of him. I let Kristair's instincts take over and jumped to my feet as shots rang out.

"There's no silencer on the gun. What were you thinking? The sound will draw others," Kristair snapped.

"For crying out loud, you knew I had one. Why didn't you say something earlier?"

"I've never touched a gun. It didn't occur to me at the time."

"Well, that makes two of us! At least until recently." The other vamp grabbed me and spun me around. I punched him in the nose, drew my gun, grabbed him close, and unloaded it into his chest. It muffled the sound, but not by much, and the vamp fell back with a scream of pain. Damn, that would be heard just as much as the gunshots.

Steve still grappled with his vamp and I rushed over to help, grabbing the knife from my belt that Tony insisted we each take. Fuck, where was he? I was gonna kick his ass when he showed. His absence was beginning to worry me. The vamp who was fighting with Steve half-turned to meet my charge and I buried the blade in his chest. Much to my surprise, he fell to the ground and didn't move.

"Huh?"

Kristair's sigh would've been comic if the other vampire hadn't decided to take off, lurching down the hallway. *"Did you make any use at all of my memories? As long as something is lodged in their heart, they are defenseless."*

Several things clicked into place. Kristair had done something similar to Dominic, only I'd been too worked up at the time to notice. *"That's not a part of the legends."*

"It's not something we try to advertise. It's bad enough that the heart is a known vulnerability without revealing the entire truth."

Steve cursed and took a shot at the retreating vampire, but he'd already gone past the circle of light from his fallen flashlight. Then a short scream cut off with a squishy thump. Steve and I exchanged glances and bolted toward the sound.

We found Tony wiping his blade clean on the shirt of the headless vamp. Seeing us, the tension around his mouth faded. "Watch where you're shooting that damn thing, will you? You two sure make enough noise. Three more are heading right toward us. I got caught up trying to avoid them."

Kristair made a sound of suspicious dismissal in my head, but otherwise didn't say a word. "We'll have to take them out too," Steve said, nudging the loose head out of the way with a grimace.

"One's staked back there." I jerked a thumb over my shoulder. "We can ask him questions once we're done with your goons."

"Excellent," Tony said with a Monty Burns-esque smirk and undertone. Then his eyes narrowed before he spun around. "They're coming."

"What? I don't hear anything." Steve peered down the dark corridor and fingered his gun as my ears caught the sound of pounding footsteps.

"He's right. Get ready."

Tony melted into the shadows as Steve and I retreated several yards. The vamps appeared, closing the space between us with a speed that left Steve cursing. Without warning, the shadows came alive behind them as Tony attacked. It didn't take the three of us long to take them out.

"*Younglings,*" Kristair sniffed in disdain.

"*I, for one, am glad they were and not the souped-up version. We're not the bad-ass vampire lord you are.*"

"*Your sarcasm hasn't dulled one bit.*" Kristair gave me a tender nuzzle as Tony checked the bodies to make sure the vamps were destroyed.

"We're cool?" Steve asked.

"Yep." Tony rose from his crouch. "Let's see what we can get out of the one you left behind."

The vampire still lay where we left him. Though he didn't move as we approached him, there seemed to be something desperate and terrified in his eyes. A youngling. He was older than I was, in his late thirties, I'd guess, with a receding hairline. *"How long are newbies considered younglings?"* I couldn't miss the disgusted undertone older vampires like Ussier and his gang used when they discussed them.

"Depends on the vampire and when they start learning and cease acting like spoiled brats. I must admit, your friend has potential. That's if he survives his first few years."

"What if he doesn't talk?" Tony asked, crouching down next to him and touching the knife hilt.

"Oh, he'll talk," Steve promised. "One way or another."

Kristair made a quick suggestion, one that filled me with a kind of sick, fascinated horror. "Or we can just go the quick route." We didn't really have time to waste with a prolonged torture. "And rip the answers from his mind."

Tony cast me a shadowed, worried glance. "Can you really do that?"

"Think about it." Kristair had shared his abilities with him, after all. "Both of us should be able to do it."

"I don't care what the fuck you two do. Just do something, dammit. She's been stuck here for hours," Steve snapped.

That more than decided it for me, and the surge of fury from Kristair melted away any lingering misgivings. Tony shrank back as I reached forward and touched my fingers to the vamp's temple. I drew in a breath, closed my eyes, and let Kristair guide me. *"It won't be pretty,* mo chroí. *He'll try to resist."*

"Oh well. It's on him then." I clenched my jaw.

I sensed another mind, one cursing and shouting, but the vampire's attempts to hold both Kristair and me off were laughable. We pulled down his defenses and laid his mind bare, searching through his thoughts until I lit upon Kayla. Wow, it was kinda like having a GPS device locked in my brain now. I could pinpoint where they were holding her without any effort.

"She's not too far," I said, opening my eyes and locking my gaze with the vamp whose brain I'd invaded. "Hell, we would've stumbled over them in the next ten minutes. There's a service room nearby where they're keeping her."

"How many people are with her? Have they touched her?" Steve demanded with a sharp edge to his voice.

Kristair went tense in my mind and I attempted to soothe him as I glanced up at Steve. This vamp didn't know anything past where they were holding her and I didn't want to think about her being hurt in any way. We'd find out when we got there.

"They'd better pray to whatever god they hold dear that they haven't."

Kristair had my wholehearted agreement there. As it was, none of them were going to walk away after kidnapping her, which didn't bother me in the least. It should have, but it didn't. I guess I'd have to deal with the repercussions later on.

"With these goons out of the picture, there are only three more," I replied to Steve.

"If they're anything like those creampuffs, it won't be hard, but we'll have to be quick. Get in and get out with her. They might have additional backup. This entire place could be riddled with them and we'd never know," Steve said.

That was a very good thought, one I hadn't considered, and Tony nodded as if he agreed it was a possibility. *"I wouldn't put it past them,"* Kristair said. *"These tunnels would be an ideal hiding place from Ussier. Many exits, many bolt holes."*

"One thing at a time. As soon as we get free from here, Ussier's getting a call. I've got faith he'll take care of the problem."

"He'd consider their presence here a personal affront," Kristair agreed.

"Let's go then," Tony said, rising and taking out his short sword. "Move out of the way, Jake."

"Wait." I delved into the vamp's mind again, trying to get a sense of how powerful the remaining goons were and how many were left in the city. The minutes ticked by as I probed and sifted before finally withdrawing with a sigh. The vamp glared at me, his eyes dark with hate.

"You have a far gentler touch than I do." Kristair laid a mental kiss on the side of my neck. *"I often forget that brute force isn't always required."*

"All yours." I gestured to Tony and stepped out of the way.

"Whoa, wait a sec," Steve started as Tony stepped forward and I grabbed Steve's arm, stopping him from interfering. A moment later it was done. Steve scowled down at the mess. "He couldn't move. Was that really necessary?"

"Did you want one of his friends to free him and have him sneak up behind us again?" I asked. "He wouldn't hesitate to do it to us and if we'd let him go he'd try his damnedest to take one of us with him."

"Besides, you already beat him in a fair fight," Tony added. "They'd have killed him anyway for giving us information, even if he couldn't have stopped us. It implies weakness. And he's one of the ones who took your friend."

"Okay, fine, point taken. Let's go."

Tony wouldn't quite meet my eyes as we headed out again. I wracked my brain, trying to figure out what I'd done this time to set him off, then decided it didn't matter. He'd always been moody.

"It's because you plundered that youngling's mind. He realizes you can do that to him as well, and it bothers him."

"So what? I won't."

"Think about it, Jacob. He's hiding something and seeing something like that would dig under his skin because he knows he's vulnerable to it."

"Or he's worried because he's not sure if I'd already done it or not. You didn't go rummaging around when you were sharing with him, did you?"

"You wouldn't have been happy with me if I had, so I managed to resist my instincts."

"Thank you." I eyed Tony as we wound deeper through the pipelined labyrinth. Kristair's instincts were sound. I'd known Tony long enough to recognize when he was sitting on a secret. True, he'd gotten defter about hiding it, but there was still no disguising that I made him skittish. When this was all over and done and Kayla was safe, we'd have a long talk.

I paused halfway down the next corridor and held up my hand. A faint light glowed on the wall from the intersection and at my signal Steve shut off the flashlight. "According to the vamp, she should be in a maintenance room right around the corner."

"So what's the plan?" Steve asked, fingering the gun at his waist.

"Jake and I can be on them before they're even aware we're here. We'll make them chase us around the next corner. It'll give you a chance to get her and get out. Kinda like Han Solo and Chewie in the Death Star."

"You do remember they ran into more trouble, right?" Steve asked dryly.

"Sounds good to me, but I'm Han," I replied. *"Does rushing them work for you, love?"*

"Do I have much of a choice?" I sensed Kristair's feral grin in my thoughts. *"Let's get on with it."*

I masked a chuckle and exchanged a glance with Tony. Then we rushed toward the three vamps who were crouched down playing with a deck of cards. One of them stared at us, stupefied, as we bore down on them. We'd almost crossed the final yards between us before he had a chance to shout and ready himself.

Tony went for the two on the ground and I tackled the other one, shouting as I bore him down to the ground. Then I was scrambling up again and bolting down the hall. I peered over my shoulder at the vamp's snarl and saw to my relief that Tony was right behind me. All three were chasing us. Idiots. *Time for a touchdown, baby.*

We exchanged grins and darted around a junction. Tony split off one way and I ran in the other direction. There were some confused shouts and a curse from Tony. When I risked glancing over my shoulder again, all three were on my ass with Tony tailing behind them.

"Looks like they want you more," Kristair commented.

"Tell me somethin' I don't know."

With any luck Steve was getting Kayla out of there and I didn't want to get too far away from him in case he ran into trouble. So I pulled my gun and turned around to shoot. Only Tony was too fucking close. Cursing, I braced for the impact as they fell upon me and I felt a hot slash of pain rake across my ribs.

"Watch out for their claws, Jacob, and don't let yourself get bitten. Once they latch on it's hard to get them to let go."

My skin crawled with disgust at the mental picture. *"Claws and fangs? Dammit, that's not fair. Why don't I get claws and fangs too?"*

"Because you're not actually a vampire."

I sensed Kristair merge more deeply with me and we began to move as one, fluid and deadly, ripping through our opponents as if they didn't exist. The wound on my side started to close and the pain eased.

When the last one went down, Tony shook his head, disbelief on his face. "I see what you meant about taking care of yourself. I've never seen anyone move like you do." He bent to wipe his sword off on one of the vamp's shirts.

"Kristair did warn me about what would happen, back at the beginning of our relationship. But as usual, I jumped into things without thinking about it. Not that I'd go back and change it."

"I hope not at this point." The little surge of warmth from my lover had me smiling.

"Let's go check on Steve and Kayla. I'll feel better when I see her with my own eyes. Then we can let Ussier know what's going on."

"Actually, there's no need to."

I paused in mid-turn and cast Tony a questioning glance. "What do you mean?" Kristair went still inside of me and a ripple of unease went down my spine at his reaction.

"I already told him." Tony shrugged and didn't meet my eyes. "When I was away from you, I searched for a spot where I could get a cell signal and I called him. He should be here soon."

I swore and shoved him against the wall. Asshole! I ran around the corner, terrified I'd find Kayla hurt or dead. Steve would've shouted if that was the case, unless there had been more waiting in the room and he'd been hurt too. I was so furious I could've pounded Tony's face in with my fists. "What the fuck were you thinking? They said not to!"

"I was thinking that we were walking into a goddamn trap. And that once again you didn't seem to give a crap about your own safety or how that would affect me either."

The maintenance door stood wide open, but the room was empty except for the ragged remains of a rope around some pipe. Kristair hissed in my mind. *"I smell her; she wasn't hurt. There's no blood in this room."*

It eased my anger a little, but not by much. I glared at Tony as I shoved by him. "We could've taken them. Hell, we did." I began following Kayla and Steve's trail back the way we'd come. "Maybe what everybody's been trying to tell me is true. I can't trust you."

Chapter 18

STEVE and Kayla were just around the corner and the angry tension inside me flowed away when I saw them. They were both alive. Then Kayla turned around and the answering jolt from Kristair had me staggering to a halt. Whatever Tony was trying to say was lost in a meaningless buzz.

"Little one."

I closed the distance between myself and her as the smile on her face faded into an expression of concern.

"Are you okay?" I demanded, or maybe it was Kristair or some strange combination of us both. I didn't feel entirely in control as I grabbed her hands and examined the ligature markings in the faint light. My blood raged. I was gonna kill them all. Every last one.

"Jake?" Kayla pushed against my chest as I pulled her into my arms and gave her a fierce hug. "I'm okay, I swear. See? I still have all my finger and toes."

I don't think I'd ever appreciated how much Kristair loved Kayla. Hell, I wouldn't know how much he cared for me if it wasn't for our mental link. My lover kept his emotions locked inside too much, rarely revealing what he felt. His relationship with his daughter was one of those areas where he'd always kept up a wall. And she was as much an integral part of his life as me.

"Jake, come on. We shouldn't hang around here," Steve lightly punched my shoulder and cast an anxious glance around. "You can have your reunion later."

I nodded past the lump in my throat and tried to make myself let go, but Kristair held on. *"Love, we've got to get out of here. She's okay. She'll tell us all about it later."*

I drew in a deep, shuddering breath and released her, not trusting myself to speak because I couldn't be sure what would come out of my mouth. Not with the emo kick Kristair was on. She grabbed my face between her hands and scrutinized me, her eyes widening. "Kris?" she whispered. "Is that…?"

I tugged her hands down and gave them a gentle squeeze. "Yeah, I'll explain when we get out of here."

"Jacob! She wasn't to know."

"You made that agreement, not me. And she already recognized you, and for that you only have yourself to blame. 'Sides, deep down you want her to know and, for crying out loud, you only follow the rules when it suits you. Why toe the line now?"

"And you make it a point to never follow the rules," Kristair retorted.

I couldn't tell if he was disgruntled or pleased. *"You've got me there."* Behind us somewhere in the corridors we'd just left there came a shout of anger and surprise.

"There's our cue." Steve gave Tony a shove to start him running. "We'd better get our asses in gear."

"Fuck!" I grabbed Kayla's hand and took off as fast as she could keep up. I could've sworn I'd only seen three in that bloodsucker's head.

"That he knew of, or he could've hidden the remaining from you. We didn't linger over him long enough to discover what else he knew."

That wouldn't be a mistake I'd make again. Steve and Kayla couldn't see very well, and it slowed us down as we bolted without care through the labyrinth. The way the walls deadened the sounds in some places or echoed eerily in others made it hard to tell how many vampires were chasing us. More than what we'd already dealt with so far, that was for sure.

We skidded around a corner and Tony cursed as his sneakers slipped in the pool of water, almost taking him down. "How far?" Steve gasped, steadying Tony before taking off again.

"Fuck if I know. You know this place better than me." In fact I was beginning to wonder if we were headed in the right direction or if we'd taken a wrong turn somewhere. This didn't look all that familiar, but one section of pipe was the same as any other so it was hard to tell. *"Kristair?"*

"I'm not sure. You don't have the best sense of direction. At least not underground."

"Tony, I take back what I said earlier. I hope your gamble pays off."

"That makes two of us." Tony stopped and turned around.

"What the fuck do you think you're doing?!" Steve shouted. "Come on."

"Keep going. I'm going to try to head them off and buy you time."

My stomach lurched and I pushed Kayla to Steve. "Get her out."

"NO!" The shouts, both mental from Kristair and verbal from my friends, left me reeling.

"I'll be fine," Tony insisted. "Hurry up and get out of here. I'll lead them in another direction then hide in the shadows and sneak back around. I'm not looking to start a fight. Now go, damn you!" With that he disappeared into the shadows and I sensed him run off.

I gave into the inevitable and Kristair's mental prodding, gesturing for Steve and Kayla to run ahead of me. "I'll stay with ya. Quit yer bitching."

There was nothing I could do at the moment to help Tony, and I promised myself that once I got Steve and Kayla out of there I'd go back for him. The sounds of pursuit began to fade and it immediately raised my suspicions. It was too easy. "Faster."

"We're trying," Kayla gasped.

A couple of turns later, I caught our scent again and knew we were on the right track. It couldn't be too much farther. *"No, it's not. Keep going straight and you'll spill right out into the basement."*

Behind us a sudden shocking scream of pain lashed through the hallways. All three of us stumbled to a stop and stared back the way we'd come. "Tony. Oh shit," Steve said.

"Oh my god," Kayla whispered. Another scream full of rage and pain came, and she took a small step forward. "We've got to do something."

"You go; get her out of here," I said to Steve. "I'll go back for Tony." For once, Kristair didn't disagree with me.

"No, we'll all go together," Kayla insisted, and I saw the decision flick across Steve's face as he took her hand again.

"The next door you see should be the one out of here," I told him.

He nodded and Kayla's eyes widened as she tried to yank her hand out of Steve's grip. "No. I'm not some fragile little flower. You can't go alone, Jake."

"I'll be okay. After all, I've got Kristair's kung fu." And so much more. Before Kayla could protest further or Steve could change his mind, I ran back the way we'd just come. "Go!" I shouted to them.

Partway down the corridor, I turned and shot, puncturing the pipes twice with bullets. There was an angry hiss as scalding steam filled the corridor. That would keep them from trying to follow me, and with any luck, it would keep any bloodsuckers from continuing after them. I was sure they weren't any more interested in being parboiled than I was.

The sound of Tony's screams grew shriller. The sense of his pain and fear drew me on as the shrieks became more terror-stricken and weak. I came around a bend and stumbled to a halt at the sight of a whole damned flock of vamps huddled around a twitching form on the ground. "Get your filthy fucking fangs offa him!" I roared and charged them.

Kristair snarled in my mind and his bloodlust mingled with my own as they closed in around me. I remembered with sickening clarity how it felt to be fed on by so many. The memory of the horror and pain turned my stomach and fueled my rage.

They dragged me down to the floor, but I fought free of them, using every bit of strength and speed I had inside of me. Blood covered my hands; injuries to my body quickly mended. And though I brought several down, it seemed more and more took their place. Weariness stole through me as inch by inch I was pushed back away from Tony.

"Any more tricks you've got that you ain't told me, love?"

"Has anyone ever told you that your grammar becomes more atrocious the more stressed you become? Don't worry, mo chroí. *We're not anywhere near done yet."*

The image of a fireball formed in my mind and as soon as it did I realized I could do it. Pulsing heat formed a sphere in my palm. It wasn't very big, about the size of a baseball, but it was enough that the fuckers surrounding me suddenly fell back. "Dodge this, bitches."

I drew back and hurled it straight toward the thickest bunch of them. Shrieks pounded the walls as a big fucker erupted into flames, setting those closest to him on fire as well.

"Sweet fucking Christ, that's awesome!" I held up my hand again and another ball formed. *"I didn't know you could do this."*

"Neither did I, but now seemed like a very good time for experimentation."

The remaining vampires who weren't busy dodging the ones on fire fell back even more when I lifted my hand again and more fire blossomed. I stepped forward, reached down with my other hand, caught Tony's foot, and dragged him toward me. Just as I was prepared to hurl the other fireball, another hand caught my arm. "I like your wicked curveball, but you've done enough. Take the youngling and get out of here."

Ussier gave me a grim smile and released my hand. He was flanked by Hugh and Deke, who grinned and clapped my shoulder. "That was a good one, kiddo."

The fire in my palm died and I scooped up Tony, tossing him over my shoulder. Now was not the time to argue. If they wanted to take out the rest, I sure as hell was not going to bitch. Not when Tony wasn't moving.

"They can't kill him by draining all his blood, can they?" A terrible worry gnawed my conscience. I'd just gotten him back and once again, just after I'd yelled at him and said I couldn't trust him, he'd gone and gotten himself hurt. Really hurt. I was such an ass sometimes.

"No. Only the one who created him has that power. Since she's no longer around, it's not a worry, but he will need blood to recover. His wounds are numerous." There was a pause. *"I'm sorry. You were right to trust him, it seems."*

"I'll tell ya I told you so later."

I could only hope people thought Tony was drunk off his ass as I carted him back to Kayla's dorm. He wouldn't be the first undergrad dragged unceremoniously home in such a way. I was betting on Steve taking Kayla there because it was closer than his place. That fight in the tunnel had drained much of my energy and Tony just seemed to get heavier as I carried him into the building.

"You need to rest and eat. You've lost blood. That's why you're so weary."

"I didn't lose that much. I kept healing every time one of those bastards got me."

"It takes blood and energy to heal. Not to mention using your abilities," Kristair said with exasperation. That made sense, I supposed.

As I stepped on the elevator, another student spoke up from behind me. "Hold it." Oh crap. I jammed the shut button as he came running up, but he managed to wedge a foot in and get on anyway. "I said to hold it."

"Sorry, man. Was just trying to get him back upstairs before he puked all over the place again."

The guy in the elevator eyed Tony. "He looks fucked up. Did he get caught in the middle of a riot?" He chuckled a bit nervously.

Tony's clothing was torn and bloodied, and I cursed myself for not thinking about that. "He tripped in a mosh pit. Bad idea. I wouldn't recommend it. The people in there have no mercy."

"You know you could always enthrall him, plant a suggestion so he'll forget meeting you and Tony."

"I can't do that."

"Why not? Some moral code of yours that I don't know about?"

"No, people irritate me too damned much. I'd be brain zapping left and right if you showed me how to do that." It would be too much of a temptation.

The elevator doors opened on Kristair's mental sigh and I gave the guy a cheery wave. *"You do already know how to do it."*

"Stop tempting me or I'll start calling you Darth Kristair." My lover's confusion had me grinning.

Someone must have been looking over me because I managed to make it to Kayla's door without encountering anyone else. I'd barely knocked when the door opened and Steve peered out, the lines of anxiety on his face easing some. "About damn time," he said and grabbed my arm, hauling me inside. "Is Tony okay?"

"Lay him down here," Kayla said, getting up from her bed.

"I need to get him to heal himself and then he needs to feed. I don't know how bad off he is. There was a whole damn herd of them on him." I slung Tony down on the bed. Shit, he was heavy.

Kayla glared at me as she straightened his legs and smoothed back his hair. "He's not a book bag, Jake."

"You try carrying him all the way back, unconscious." Worn out, I sat down on the edge of the bed beside him and tried to gauge how many bite marks there were on him. I was damn nervous at the thought of him feeding. How the hell were we going to control him? The memory of Kristair's feeding after he'd been burned so badly came back to me. With all of his willpower, if he'd lost control, what chance did Tony have?

"So what do we do?" Steve asked, worrying his lip.

"I'm still trying to figure that out. He's gonna go ape shit when he tastes blood." Ugh. The thought of anyone else biting me other than Kristair was gross, even if it was my friend.

"Here," Kayla said, pulling out a bunch of silk scarves from her dresser. "We'll tie him down and sit on his legs."

My brows shot up as I picked up a bright blue one with a flower pattern. "That's my kinky girl."

"Perve. It's called knowing how to accessorize." Kayla picked up one and tied Tony's foot to the metal frame of her bed as Steve slapped the back of my head.

"Don't give me that. You thought it too," I muttered, and tied Tony's other foot. I still wasn't sure it'd be enough to keep Tony in line.

"Get your thoughts off of my daughter's bedroom habits and concentrate on the task at hand." Kristair's prim tone had me snickering until he gave me a mental buffet same as Steve had. *"You can set a leash on his mind. Between the two of us we should be able to control him until the worst of his hunger has abated."*

"I'll go first," Kayla said as I scooted up on the bed and laid my fingers against Tony's temples.

"No, I will," Steve replied, rolling up his sleeves. He cut Kayla off as she began to argue. "I need to do this for him. Are you sure he's okay, Jake? Fuck, he looks dead to me."

"He's an unconscious vampire. He's supposed to look dead. Trust me, you'll see him react the moment he tastes your blood. But give me a sec." I probed Tony's consciousness until I caught the rush of his emotions, raw terror and savage hunger. I shuddered and gave Steve an abrupt nod. "Go ahead and nick your wrist."

The moment he laid his wrist against Tony's mouth, Tony tensed under my fingers. His eyes flew open, his gaze feral and inhuman as he snarled and jerked against his bonds. Kayla plopped down on his legs and Steve cursed as Tony latched onto his wrist.

"Tony, it's us. Steve and Jake and Kayla. We'll make sure you're okay. Calm down. Focus on my voice. Fight through the frenzy. You've

got to heal yourself. Slow down. You don't want to hurt Steve. We'll make sure you get everything you need. Come on, buddy. Trust me."

I repeated it over and over again, hoping to break through the animal haze in his head. I sensed Kristair's ruthless control over him, forcing Tony to pull back from Steve after several long moments. Tony hissed and snarled, jerking and half-rising up off the bed.

Then Kayla was sitting down next to him and tersely muttered to Steve, "Don't frickin' argue or try to get all overprotective. It's a bad habit you've developed." Kristair's hold on Tony tightened until my friend's mind cried out in distress, pain lancing through him. *"It'll be okay. Kayla's stronger than the rest of us,"* I soothed. *"Ease up, Kristair."*

She made no sound as Tony sank his fangs into her wrist and I couldn't help but wonder if Kristair had ever bitten her. Mentally, he shook his head. *"That wasn't something I wanted to open up between us, especially with the way she felt. It would have only complicated matters."*

Tony didn't fight as much this time when Kristair and I forced him to let go of Kayla. His gaze was almost lucid as he watched me with hard eyes. *"Let go of me, Jake,"* he hissed in my thoughts.

"Promise to behave."

He snarled in response. It was so damned surreal to see my friend with fangs, blood around his mouth, and a predator's light in his eyes. Knowing he was a vamp was one thing; seeing proof fucking positive was another.

"He should be fine. His injuries weren't as extensive as mine were and his wounds aren't deep."

"Who's that?" Tony demanded.

"It's my alter ego. Now shaddup. Here's the deal. I'm gonna let you bite me and then you're gonna heal yourself. Got it?"

"Fine!"

It was over with quickly. Even as Tony fed, the bite marks closed up and his gaze lost some of its rabid hunger. He ceased straining against Kayla's scarves and relaxed back against the bed. He didn't make one sound of protest as I pulled back, grateful for the loss of contact. I couldn't stand anyone other than Kristair biting me.

The room was silent at first as he licked his lips. "How are you feeling, Tony?" Kayla asked, nudging me aside.

"I'll be fucking dandy once you untie me," he snapped.

Without hesitation she picked at the knot and undid it. Steve stirred uneasily and I gave him a reassuring smile as I started on one of Tony's ankles. The scarves would have barely slowed Tony down for a moment now that Kristair wasn't holding him still with his mind. They'd only been an extra deterrent if I hadn't been able to control him as much as I had. If he was showing enough restraint to keep from ripping them off, then I trusted him not to go crazy once he was released.

When the last scarf fell away, Tony uncoiled himself from the bed in a fluid, dangerous move. "Don't wait up for me. I'll call you tomorrow night."

"Hey, Tony." He paused and looked back at Kayla, who gave him one of her winsome smiles. "Thanks for everything."

He grinned back at her, an odd mix of Tony's old boyishness and lupine grace. He winked at her. "You can tie me to your bed anytime, sweetness."

Steve let out an explosive breath as Tony left. "I don't think I'm ever going to get used to this." I didn't even have to ask to know exactly what he meant and I shared his feelings one hundred and fifteen damn percent.

"Oh, he'll be back to himself once he's hunted," Kayla said, plopping down on her bed with almost obscene casualness.

I winced. I'd hate to be the poor sucker who ran into Tony tonight. *It won't be so bad, Jacob. He's not hungry enough to hurt anybody, and if he does it right, they won't even remember.*

"The thought of being somebody's midnight snack is unnerving."

"You never minded being my midnight snack," Kristair reminded me. *"No one animal is at the top of the food chain, no matter how much they'd like to delude themselves. There's always something or a*

pack of somethings ready to take you down. Gives life a certain zest, don't you think?"

"I think you're trying to ignore the fact that Kayla's sitting a foot away from you, and you're doing a rather bad job of it too."

I glanced over at her only to find her studying me calmly. I swear nothing ever seemed to rattle her. *"You just don't know the signs. She's rattled all right, and not liking it one bit."*

I gave into Kristair's want and sat down next to her, skimming my fingers over her jaw. "How are you holding up, troublemaker?"

"Just fine, and glad to be home." Even that little of a hint of relief told me Kristair was right and she was on edge. I slung my arm around her and after a moment she leaned in and laid her head on my shoulder. As much as I wanted to go back to my own place and be alone with Kristair, I couldn't ignore what had happened to her today.

Steve took the chair and sat down across from Kayla and took her hands, kissing her knuckles. I had to smile. I don't think I'd ever seen Steve quite this way with a girl. I wondered if he realized yet that he was in love with her.

"What are you talking about?" My lips twitched at Kristair's outraged tone.

"Just hush. They're good for each other."

"Are you okay?" Steve asked, studying her face. There was tenderness in the question that had me eyeing the door before his voice turned fierce. "They didn't touch you, did they?"

"They didn't dare. I think they were a little scared of the situation they'd gotten themselves into. They were worried enough about what Jake would do and not so certain you wouldn't bring Uncle Ghedi into it. I'm surprised you didn't actually."

"I didn't, but Tony did." Steve's eyes jerked toward me and I shrugged. The gamble had paid off. Tony had risked himself in the end, so I wasn't going to bitch about it anymore.

"Well then, since you're okay and I see that Steve isn't going to let you out of his sight, I'm heading back to my dorm. It's been such a freaking crazy day I don't know which side is up anymore."

"Wait." Kayla grabbed my hand and studied my face. Kristair fell silent and drew back into that small corner of my mind, walling himself up. I knew what she was searching for and hesitated. Despite what I'd said to Kristair earlier, I don't know if this was the best time to reveal that he was kinda, sorta back. "I guess I was just imagining things," Kayla murmured, releasing me with a tired sigh.

She turned away, her tawny hair falling across her face so I couldn't see her expression. I let her be. She wouldn't appreciate me making a big deal out of her mourning and it had been a rough day for all of us. Maybe telling her that her father was back, but unable to communicate with her, was a bad idea. At least for tonight.

Steve tugged Kayla into his arms and I slipped out the door. *"Thank you,* mo chroí," Kristair murmured, emerging fully once more into my thoughts. *"I don't want to get her hopes up if this doesn't work."*

"It'll work," I replied with grim determination. I'd make damn sure of it.

Chapter 19

I LAY on Jacob's bed on my stomach, watching him prowl the room like the predator he so ardently claimed not to be while he spoke on the phone with Ussier. As much as I enjoyed the intimacy of being one with him when I occupied a corner of his mind, I missed watching him like this.

My lover was so expressive, and not just in his face either. He showed what he was feeling in how he moved and in the shade of his voice when he spoke. I didn't need our connection to know his emotions, and right now Jacob was trying to work through something in his mind before speaking of it. I could dip into his thoughts easily enough and nudge him to talk, but I preferred for him to tell me, in his own time, and his own words.

I savored our bond after having only a shadow of it for so long. It still didn't seem real. I was back home in one fashion and reunited with Jacob, though my Mistress had arranged it in such a way that we'd be left frustrated and unsatisfied with our reunion. Or at least I believe that was her intention.

Jacob wanted to look at me and touch me at the same time. And I wanted to be free to walk beside him, to aid him in his battle against the Syndicate instead of dispensing advice from inside his head.

Still, I think she had underestimated the impact my return had had on the both of us. And the restrictions only had made us both more determined.

We had slipped so easily into our connection, almost as if we'd never parted. Merging with him had been as natural as feeding once had, and far more fulfilling. This was where I belonged. Yet time weighed on my mind. Fourteen days. We had so little with which to destroy the Syndicate beyond any hope of recovery and to ensure Jacob's safety.

Jacob's shoulders tightened further and he scowled at me as he shut off his phone, tossing it without a care on the desk. "The Syndicate isn't our main problem, Kristair. In fact, it's not even our problem at all anymore. Ussier's gonna take care of them."

I propped my chin on my fist and studied him. At last, we were getting to what troubled him. I could count on it not taking long with my lover. He was not one to sit around and brood for days on end. He was driven to action, even when action wasn't called for. Jacob was in a dangerous mood, emotions swirling in a volatile mix, yet I couldn't deny the thrill of excitement it gave me. "Just because Ussier's leading the charge doesn't mean they'll leave you in peace."

"I know that," Jacob snapped. "But I have more damned important things on my mind than worryin' about those bastards. Ever think about that? Fuck, you say I'm stubborn, but you, once you get yer mind on a goal, you don't drop it for nothing."

Jacob's accent had thickened, always a sure sign that something was really eating at him, versus a rush of temper that always disappeared as quick as it came. I took time sitting up and drawing my bare knees to my chest to give myself a chance to think out what I wanted to say. "They aren't the kind of people we can just ignore. They won't stop until they get what they want or they are destroyed."

"That's not why ya came back!" I blinked at Jacob's shout, but before I could respond, he was moving on. "God fucking dammit, Kristair! You came back so we could figure out a way to be together again, not to get involved in the middle of another bloodsucker war."

"I just need to be sure you'll be safe if—"

"No, don't you fucking say it," Jacob raged. "Don't say if; don't even think it. I swear I can't handle you giving up once more. It's happening all over again."

I tried to probe his mind, but couldn't make sense out of the welter and confusion of emotion and his seething thoughts. I wanted to reach out to him, but knew he wouldn't welcome it until he got everything on his mind out in the open. "In what way? What's happening again?" I asked. I didn't think he meant the Syndicate's attacks, at least not for the most part.

"First, you show up all unexpected again, not that I'm complaining. Then the Syndicate starts making asses out of themselves again. And at the same time we've got this short amount of time where we need to figure out how to save you, but you'd rather fight the Syndicate instead of using that overstuffed brain of yours to figure out a way to get us out of this mess. I'm not watching you give up again. Not this time."

Shocked, I stared at him until my mind could pull together my thoughts. "How can you say such a thing? I wouldn't give up on you. Not ever." And the thought of Jacob ever giving up on his own was unfathomable.

"That's the point. Can't you see? You may not give up on me, but you sure as hell are quick to give up on yourself." He leaned against the wall with a cynical smile. "You stopped fighting last time, distracted yourself with the Syndicate and stopped looking for answers. Don't try to deny it, because I know it's true. I have all your memories, remember? That last night in the hotel, you had made the decision to stop looking for an answer."

"Jacob." My heart lurched at the sudden wave of anguish within my lover. "I'm sorry, *mo chroí*. There was nothing I could do anymore. Nowhere else to look. It was inevitable and I hadn't wanted to waste what time I had left with you. I wanted to savor it."

"You didn't know that for certain. You can't look me in the eye and tell me that you knew it then, and just because you've discovered it since then doesn't count. Even if you did know, I can't do it again. Losing you is one thing. Maybe we won't win this fight either, but I need to know you're going to give it everything you've got this time. Everything, until the bitter fucking end."

Unable to stay away anymore, I began to rise so I could go to him. He shook his head and the surge of denial I sensed in him had me sinking back down, trying to ignore the little stab of hurt. Jacob ran a hand through his hair, standing it up in little spikes and tumbled waves.

"And then you admitted to almost not coming back at all, of letting me go, which I get, sorta. But just tell me now, are you here to ease your own worries about me or are you really back so we can find a way to keep you here?"

What could I say? Of all the ways I'd known I'd hurt him, this had never even occurred to me. This time when I stood up, Jacob only looked at me as if I somehow could give him all the answers he sought. I reached out to take him by the shoulders then remembered I couldn't touch him and let my hands fall. I had not realized how difficult that rule would be to bear, hadn't recognized my own need to touch and look.

"Just answer the question, Kris. It's not a hard one."

Didn't he know already? Couldn't he sense my commitment to him? To us? "I am here to stay." I paused, sensing it wasn't enough, and searched his face, felt his doubt echo my own fears. "I swear to fight 'til the end, if need be."

Jacob didn't say anything for a long moment. Then he nodded. "Okay then. So why don't you tell me what's been nagging at you. I know it has to do with the deal you made to get here, but I haven't been able to figure it out."

"Let's lay down." I gestured to the bed and was reassured by Jacob's fleeting smile.

"I don't know if lying down while you're naked is a good idea," he said, but followed me as I stretched out. "Can you imagine up some clothes?"

"Are you the same Jacob I left? You keep trying to clothe me. Besides, if I did get dressed you'd be furious with me." I couldn't take my eyes off Jacob as he tucked his hands under his head and rested his cheek against them. "I've missed this, you know. Just watching you. Though, I will admit, your bed is far more comfortable than your windowsill."

Jacob snickered. "I can just imagine, my beautiful stalker."

"I wish you wouldn't call me that."

170 | Marguerite Labbe

"You only have yourself to blame, love. Now spill, and don't you even dare think of the Syndicate once."

Pushing that menace out of mind was easy for the moment, though I knew it would come back. I couldn't just pretend the threat didn't exist. It was harder, though, to put words to my worry. Jacob closed his eyes and I followed suit. His hand touched my shoulder then slid up to curl around the nape of my neck. I let him pull me closer and sighed as he slung his leg over my own. "They want you to reverse the ritual, the bond you set up with me," he said.

I nodded. "Yes."

"And that frightens you. Why? Not that I want to lose it either, but that's what's bugging you."

"I know how I can return home for good. In theory. And it's a good theory. I'm certain it'll work if I'm given the chance. And before you ask, I can't tell you. If I don't think about it and keep it locked inside, I'll get the chance to pull it off. If I tell you, or ponder it too long, they'll find out, and I have no doubt they can block me indefinitely."

"If they know so much, don't they know you're trying to pull a scam on them?"

"I'm sure they do, but necessity dictates their actions. They had to let me come back because they have to have the link broken. It's like a chess game. Whoever has the best strategy and luck wins."

I closed my eyes as well and pressed my forehead against Jacob's, wrapping my arm around his waist. A little spark of excitement came to life inside him. "You *are* sure." I knew he was smiling without looking and I returned it. "What's the catch then? What's got you so worked up?" he asked.

"It's hard to explain. The Ascended…. I wouldn't say they're emotionless because that's not true, but their emotions are buried deep and they refuse to allow them to influence their decisions. I don't think they would've forced me to come back if our connection wasn't creating havoc with them. We're all linked together. What one feels, the whole feels. You don't have to stay a part of the whole—you can go out and explore on your own, though I doubt they'll consider me ready for that anytime soon. But even if you're apart, you're still connected."

Even now, I could sense them. It was distant, a thin thread, but still there.

Jacob gave me a mental poke. *"You're straying. Get to the point."*

I gathered my thoughts back together and tried to suppress my growing fear. Jacob's fingers stroked the nape of my neck. The simple contact soothed me. "Because I was connected with you, I didn't experience the same divorce of emotion the rest of the Ascended have. Everything you were going through pulled at me. I was made to feel it just as keenly as you. They tried blocking it, but you broke through every time."

"And since you felt it, they all did."

"Exactly. It was akin to setting off a tornado in a monastery. It upset our balance more and more the longer it continued."

Jacob burrowed closer and I accept his wordless comfort, sinking into it. *"Tell me, love, what about losing our connection frightens you so much?"*

My lover had the uncanny ability to draw from me what I usually buried deep, and the words poured forth from my mind into his. *"What if I become just like them when we break the link? What if you become just a memory and what we had becomes just another curiosity to study? Then where will the drive be to make that change, that sacrifice for you? That is what scares me."*

I struggled to pull myself back from that brink and get my emotions under control, and Jacob's grip tightened. *"No, don't push it away. Just let yourself feel, Kristair. You bury too much even as you fear having it buried forever."* That was easier said than done, but this was Jacob and he let all of his feelings run rampant. *"Now come on, you really think you can forget me that easy?"*

A laugh broke free because I knew he was only half-joking. "I'm not worried about forgetting you." Though I had done just that in those initial months when I'd been reborn and inundated with all the new knowledge and experiences, I didn't anticipate that happening again now that I'd become somewhat accustomed to the experience of being open to the universe.

"I worry that my memories will cease to matter. You don't understand how seductive that world is, how easy it would be to be pulled in. I could spend forever in there and just touch the surface. If I don't have the connection with you anymore to keep me grounded, if I become just another part of the whole… I don't know, Jacob. If I had to make the choice now, while I am entirely myself, I'd choose you. But if I'm incapable of feeling the way I feel when I'm with you then I'm afraid of what my choice would be." I couldn't even say it because then it might make it real. It was shaming to admit, because in my mind it lessened what we had and it shouldn't be allowed to.

Jacob was quiet for a long time and I opened my eyes again so I could look at him. There was disbelief and sorrow, but underneath it all, there was his strength of conviction blazing in his eyes as he stared back at me. "You won't forget," he insisted. "I'm not dismissing your fears, but I know you won't."

My lover had far more faith in me than I warranted at the moment. He didn't understand what it was like. Jacob propped himself up on his elbow and shook his head. "I do understand," he said. "Or at least in part. When you shared what happened with you earlier today, I got a taste of it. And knowing you the way I do, I get how attractive that life would be for you. You've always claimed to be more unfeeling than you really are and you do a very good job of hiding it on the surface, but from the first moment your mind touched my own, I knew it was just another mask you put on."

"I'm not like you, Jacob. I can't take it on faith. I need a plan, something to fall back on."

"Then we'll come up with something. Between your brains and my sheer awesomeness, we'll think of a way in the next two weeks." Jacob traced a finger in the air over the tattoo on my shoulder. "If nothing else, Kristair, you've proved to me that anything is possible."

Anything was possible. That was true and it was also what had gotten me into this mess in the first place. I'd trained my mind and will to the point where I could do just about anything I wanted. If only I had access to that power right now. Normally, I didn't mind gambles, but this time, too much was at stake.

Not to mention that the Syndicate was still out there as well. Jacob's blue eyes narrowed. "You're damn lucky I can't touch you or else I'd thwap you on that bald head of yours."

"I'm sorry, but ignoring them isn't going to make them go away, and they're a problem I can do something about."

"You know what your problem is?"

I cast Jacob a curious glance. At least most of his frustration and anger was gone and now he seemed more exasperated than anything. "What?"

"I think you've got this complex about protecting people, and that somehow keeping them in the dark makes things better. Hell, I don't even think you do it deliberately, not really. So it's not like you're lying. You're just used to keeping things close inside. And if it's something you don't think you can handle, then you bury it, ignore it, and concentrate on something else. That's what's going on here."

"Maybe I do." At Jacob's pointed look, I held up my hand. "Okay, you're right. So, what are you trying to get at?"

I tried to probe his mind, but couldn't make out where he was going. He wasn't upset, more calm than anything else, almost reflective. Either this was something he'd pondered for a long time or else he was holding it in remarkably well.

"You used me." Jacob said it in such a matter-of-fact way that it took a moment for his words to register and my conscious to twinge in remorse. "You went into this relationship knowing from the moment you spotted me that there was a very good chance you'd disappear sooner rather than later."

I couldn't deny it. I had been selfish from the start. Even before I'd found Jacob and knew he was what I wanted, I'd known that my chances for a long-term relationship were slim. Maybe given my experiences in the past, the idea of a fling had been more palatable. But Jacob had changed my mind, just by being who he was. And, by then, it was too late to back out, even if I'd been inclined to do so, which I wasn't. From the moment I'd first seen him, I'd wanted him with everything in me. He was mine, my true other half. The mate I had been searching my whole life to find.

"What you say is true," I admitted. "Before I got to really know you I was just thinking of myself and not the consequences to you. Maybe I should've stopped when I stopped thinking of you as more than a potential vessel. Please, don't ask me to regret doing it, *mo chroí*, because I can't. All I regret is hurting you. But, I can't be sorry for making you a part of me."

"I'm not looking for apologies."

I cocked my head and studied him, uneasy with his calm. This wasn't Jacob, but something stirred beneath his demeanor and I hoped we were getting close to the heart of what was on his mind. "Then what do you want?"

"I'm not sure. Acknowledgment maybe, which you just gave me. I was so pissed after you were gone. Partially because of that, mostly because you'd given up. I kept thinking that if you'd given enough of a shit, you'd've fought harder."

My mind spun, and my heart, which was the only physical part of me left, lurched in Jacob's chest. How could he even think that? At the same time, given the circumstances, I could understand where his anger came from. It wasn't undeserved, but it still hurt.

"Jacob, I—"

"No, don't." Jacob lifted his hand as if to touch me again and then gave me a rueful smile. "I said don't apologize. Come on, love, I know you better than that. It was easy to be pissed and to blame you when I was hurting, but now that we're together again…." His gaze caressed my face. "It's hard to stay upset when I know what's going on in your head, when I can feel what you feel toward me."

He cocked his head. "I think I understand better now why you're so worried. It's funny. Back when you were here and we'd be separated all day long while you slept, I would get so confused and muddled. Until sometimes I had to ask myself what the hell I was doing. Then you'd wake up and it would all become clear."

"You've summed it up perfectly." We were so different, in temperament, in outlook and philosophy on life. But when we were together, we clicked, even when we fought. There was an intensity between us because of the bond, because there were no walls. What would happen when the link was destroyed?

"We'll figure it out. No sense in stressing over it," Jacob soothed, giving me a mental embrace.

Exasperation snapped through me, and if I could, I would've shaken him. "Might I remind you that you're the one who brought this all up and said I wasn't worrying enough about the problem?"

A lazy smile crossed Jacob's sensual lips. "That was earlier. You're falling behind. This is now. We've talked about it and you promised you'll behave." His grin widened as my mouth fell open in indignation. "It's been a long, crazy, fucked-up, wonderful day. We're both on edge."

He closed his eyes and shot me a very erotic image of us twined together. "Why don't we do something about it instead of arguing?"

Chapter 20

I SURRENDERED; I never could keep up with the twists and turns of Jacob's whims even if I tried. I suppose it made us even. I closed my eyes and pressed a kiss to the center of his chest. "What am I going to do with you?" I murmured.

"Oh, I can think of plenty."

"I'm sure you can." I shifted closer to him and waited until he opened his eyes and looked at me again. "I love you." I sensed the aching lurch of Jacob's emotions and then a wry smile touched his lips.

"We haven't said that yet, have we? I guess it's been crazy." He lifted his hand and stopped just before his knuckles would've brushed my cheek. "We knew it, felt it, so maybe the words weren't necessary."

"But you like hearing them."

"Hell yeah I do, and I love you too. Now close your eyes and kiss me."

I smiled and leaned closer, my eyes on his face as he let out a low hiss of frustration. "I have an even better idea. Do you have anything we can use for a blindfold?"

"Silk scarves, bondage, and now blindfolds? What a kinky night this is turning out to be," Jacob said, but rose from the bed to go rummage in the top drawer of his messy dresser. "I should have something. I've indulged from time to time."

"I'm sure you have." I rolled onto my stomach and watched as he pulled out two long black cloths, arching a brow. "Me too?"

"Oh yes." Jacob tossed the blindfolds down on the bed then stripped out of his clothes, his eyes on me, hot and loving. "Are you going to put yourself in my hands?"

"Don't I always? Just let me get my fill of looking at you first. I was too busy earlier to appreciate." I knelt up on the bed and let my gaze wander over him. Jacob was as beautiful as he'd always been. Muscles taut from working out and playing football, the little golden rings at his nipples and my silver torc the only items gracing his body, and he didn't need anything else. Broad shoulders tapered to his trim waist then flared out to strong thighs. The tattoos stood out against his golden ruddy skin and my hands ached to touch him.

Jacob wasn't embarrassed at all, not that I expected him to be. If anything, I'd say he preened from the attention. He huffed and snatched up one of the blindfolds. "I don't preen!"

"Yes, you do. You love the attention." I closed my eyes as he approached then felt his fingers fumble against my face as he tied on the strip of cloth.

"That's different," he said, tying it on before pressing the other blindfold against my palm. The bed dipped as he knelt in front of me and slipped his arms around my waist. "I know how good I look."

I covered his eyes with the second cloth as his fingertips caressed sensual circles at the small of my back. His lips feathered over my own and I slid my hands from the knot in his hair then down the length of his body. "I want to take my time," he said, kissing along my jaw. "I was too impatient earlier. Not this time."

Jacob's breath teased my skin as he laid me back on his bed. My lips found his pulse at the base of his throat and tasted. I could still smell his blood, though the craving to feed no longer existed. That particular hunger didn't drive me anymore. The instinct had died when I'd become one of the Ascended. But my longing for the intimacy we shared when I bit him was as strong as it ever had been.

Jacob caught my lips in a dizzying kiss. *"I'm calling the shots tonight."*

"Do I have a choice in the matter?" The ache spread throughout my body as he touched me, his hands possessive and reverent.

"You don't want a choice, love," he whispered in my mind and deepened the kiss in a way that made me weak. *"You're the kind of man who likes to surrender. You just bury it deep. Let that side out tonight, Kristair."* Jacob didn't wait for my agreement. He pulled my hands above my head and pinned them there as his mouth broke away to torment my throat.

Jacob's access to my memories, to my soul, provided him with entirely too much insight. He chuckled and gave my wrists a light squeeze before caressing down my body. It didn't matter if he knew how to manipulate my desire now when he didn't know it before. My lover had the innate ability from the start to just look at me and make me want.

His lips traced trails of fire across my chest. His tongue circled around my nipple then drew the aching peak into his mouth, nibbling, tormenting. I couldn't keep my hands still any longer and drew them down so I could touch Jacob in return.

Searching by touch, my fingers found the ring piercing one of Jacob's nipples and gave it a light tug. "You should get your own piercing," he groaned, and I knew that mischievous smile of his graced his lips. He rocked his hips against my thigh, his bare cock pressing into me, making me very aware of my own cock rising hard between us.

"Keep dreaming."

Jacob laughed and slid lower, his tongue dipping into my navel as my hands caressed the strong contours of his back. It was strange not to be watching him, seeing the flickers of pleasure cross his face. It seemed I'd always been watching him in one way or another. Instead, now I allowed myself to be guided by my other senses.

The soft cotton ends of Jacob's blindfold brushed against my lower stomach and my muscles tightened in response. He eased my thighs apart and moved to settle between them and I grabbed his shoulders.

"No. Wait. I want to taste you too."

I sensed Jacob's mental nod and then he shifted again as I rolled onto my side. I slid my hand down his hip; the scent of his arousal so close stirred my senses and my hunger. Jacob's heartbeat quickened and my own echoed its call in his chest. I kissed the tender skin on the inside of his thigh and felt his breath shiver along my cock before the wet heat of his mouth slid over it.

"Jacob," I whispered, inexplicably feeling like I'd come home, with his scent and warmth surrounding me, his hands stroking my body. And as I touched him in return, only one thing was missing.

I turned my head, sliding my tongue along his thigh, tasting the thrum of excitement in his mind as my own mouth found his shaft. I guided it to my lips, teasing my tongue over the velvet head before slowly sinking down. His groan vibrated against my own cock and I sighed in response.

This was so sweet, unlike our heated fucking earlier when we needed to prove to ourselves that being together wasn't an illusion. The heat still simmered underneath the surface the way it always did, waiting to explode, but for the moment we savored our reunion.

Jacob tasted of spice and musk, a flavor that was just as addicting as his blood. His mouth moved along my cock in a hard suction. His fingers toyed with my balls before sliding back to tease along the cleft of my ass.

Desire surged stronger and I caressed my hand over his thigh, then up along his side and around to knead his ass. He had a perfect one, high and tight, and it looked amazing in his football uniform with the fabric clinging to every curve. Each time I saw him in it I wanted to touch him.

I stroked my tongue along the shaft of his cock and began a slow bob, sinking lower each time to take in more of him. Jacob's fingers pressed against my entrance and the same liquid sense of surrender that I felt whenever he penetrated me stole right through my body. The sense that I was wholly his in a way I'd never let myself be with anyone else.

He pushed his fingers deeper and I rocked my hips, wanting more, even as he began to stroke. Jacob groaned as I penetrated him as well, searching out that spot that would drive him crazy and moaning helplessly as he found mine.

We found a rhythm, slow and sensual. The taste of my young lover grew stronger on my tongue as our passion deepened. It was incredibly erotic and one of the most sweetly intimate experiences in my life. We whispered endearments, encouragements in our thoughts, spurring each other on as the tension spiraled higher.

I sensed the first ripple of Jacob's orgasm in his mind and it sparked my own even as the taste of him spurted in my mouth. His breath panted against my skin, working his hips and gripping my fingers in velvet heat even as he tormented me with his own fingers and sucked harder on my shaft.

I slid my mouth off of his cock and stroked my fingers along his hip as his trembling eased. Turning my head, I nuzzled his thigh and drank in his scent. I shifted as Jacob's mouth continued its torment on my cock, his fingers nudging deep inside me, pressing against my now over-sensitized prostate. Little jolts of electricity sizzled through my body.

"Jacob," I groaned and again tried to shift away to give myself a chance to recover. I sensed his intent just before he moved and turned to scramble away, but he was so quick. I found myself on my stomach with Jacob on top of me pinning me to the bed.

When had he gotten to be so fast and strong?

Instinct had me struggling. If I had been my old self, I could've easily gotten out of his hold, but it seemed the Ascended had made us equal in many respects. Jacob chuckled against my ear; his wicked sense of triumph was exhilarating. He nudged my thighs wide apart with his knees and pinned my hands at the small of my back.

"Where do you think you're going?" Jacob's lips nuzzled my neck before he gave my earlobe a sharp nip. "You're not trying very hard. You can do better than this."

Pride had me redoubling my efforts, but my lover countered each one with ease, his laughter breathless. "Let go of me," I insisted.

"Now where's the fun in that," Jacob teased. I groaned helplessly as his fingers brushed my entrance again. "We did it the nice and sweet way. Now, I want to hear you begging."

He pushed deep inside me and, for a moment, I went limp as desire returned with a dizzying sweep. Then he found my spot again and massaged it with ruthless intent. The taste of his goal was sharp and insistent. He really did want me to beg.

The sensations were overwhelming. Jacob's cock surged against my thigh as I began to writhe, trying to find some surcease from those wicked fingers.

"Retribution will be a bitch," I swore and then cursed in my head again as it came out more breathless than the promise I'd meant.

Jacob snickered and then began to thrust, hard, deep strokes that gave me an indication of the fucking that was to come. "Liar. You're enjoying this as much as I am. You like being held down and helpless. You just haven't had much of a chance to explore it. Now you do."

When our relationship started, Jacob had this driving need to dominate me and, I must admit, that side of him had evoked a forbidden thrill in me that I had buried a long time ago. Now that need had been tempered. It wasn't so much that Jacob was driven to prove himself as it was because he wanted to be in control. Which made him all the more dangerous and me all the more tempted to give in to him.

"What do you want, Kristair?" Jacob asked, nudging my thighs wider apart. I sensed a momentary pang of regret in his mind that he couldn't see me pinned down and helpless, my thighs splayed and entrance exposed. The picture he had in his head was explicitly detailed and made me groan. He had me on fire and unable to think past the inferno.

"For you to kiss my ass."

Jacob laughed and dropped a kiss on one cheek. Then he nipped me there too, and then on my hip. Little stinging bites that licked heat along my skin. "Where did you learn such language, love? Maybe I'll need to punish you as well."

I went still as pure glee whipped through the brat. "You wouldn't dare." I turned my head, the blindfold slipping enough for me to see a sliver of light, but nothing more.

"You should know better than to dare me."

A sound suspiciously like a whimper fell from my lips as Jacob knelt between my thighs and slid his fingers free from me. The emptiness ached and I wondered when it went from being too much to wanting more. His hand caressed my ass while I tried to pull my wrists free from his grip.

"Jacob," I warned.

"You just keep digging yourself in deeper." His hand cupped my ass and gave it a squeeze as I brushed my thoughts across his, trying to judge whether or not he'd actually have the audacity to do it.

He laughed. His hand came down just hard enough to sting, and if I hadn't been so indignant and excited, I would've admired Jacob's flair for the drama of the moment. I jolted, my nipples rubbing against the sheets as I gasped. The heat generated by that one smack surprised me by its scope.

"You've had your fun, brat. Now let me go." My voice lacked conviction, even too myself.

"Love, I haven't even gotten started." He was fearless, I'd give him that, as he peppered my skin with several quick slaps. I was torn between cursing and laughing at his audacity. Jacob paused, his hand now caressing. "What do you want?"

"I want you to let me go before I turn this around on you," I retorted.

"Liar." Jacob kissed the small of my back, licking a small circle there, making a wet trail with his tongue down to the cheek of my ass. He smiled against my skin and when he pulled back, I took advantage of his distraction to try to break away again.

He cursed, and heat flooded through my body as he wrestled me down again, his hand making another sharp imprint on my ass. I bit back a groan as Jacob laughed in my mind. *"You can't hide that you're liking this."* He dragged out each blow, touching me everywhere in between until my skin was hot and my cock raging.

"What do you want?" Jacob asked again next to my ear.

Another quick retort came to my lips, but I held it back. I could egg him on with further curses and struggles and we would enjoy ourselves with the power play, yet I sensed Jacob was searching for more truth underneath our little game.

What did I want? I think my lover understood my own needs better than myself.

"Come on, Kristair. Tell me," Jacob urged with another quick slap.

"Why don't you show me instead?"

There was a breathless pause and then Jacob released my hands. A bitter pang of disappointment surprised me, but soon enough he was lying over me, the head of his cock rubbing against my entrance. "That's a good idea," he agreed.

Jacob's lips brushed against my jaw and I turned my head to meet them. He linked our hands together, deepening the kiss. The power of it shook me to my core. He was more sure of himself than he had ever been before, more sure of us, and what we both wanted.

I moaned, feeling myself giving in to his silent demand and, for a moment, I fought it, afraid of the fall. But Jacob didn't relent. His tongue continued its erotic claiming of my mouth, tangling with my own tongue, his hands keeping a tight hold on me when I would've pulled away. When his cock began to push inside of me, I couldn't fight it any longer.

Fierce triumph whipped through Jacob as my mouth softened and I kissed him back, but instead of surging into me with one hard thrust like I'd expected, he held himself in check. It still stung without lube to ease the passage, but I couldn't deny how excited I was and if he'd stopped to grab some, I don't know if I'd have let him get so close to this untapped part of me again.

Jacob burrowed into me, both in body and in mind. I swore his fingers touched my soul, laying me bare as he began to thrust, hard, deep, and relentless. I couldn't fight him. I couldn't hide. No one had ever made me need so much, not like he did.

I clung back to his hands, clinging to him as he fucked me and laid his claim. One I would never forget. *"Please, Jacob."*

"You're mine," he replied with more love than possession, but that was there too.

I shuddered, rocking my hips back to meet each thrust, surrendering to the eddying passion. *"I'm yours."*

Chapter 21

I WOKE up in a daze, alone in my bed. Frantic, I searched my room for Kristair's presence, which I sensed was still near. I found him standing naked by the window, wreathed in moonlight and shadows, staring down at the campus grounds below. It struck an odd chord within me. How often, in his many centuries of existence, had he stood, in just the same manner, watching the world go by?

"You need your sleep," Kristair said without turning around. "I'm sorry if I disturbed you."

I sat up, cocking my head at the tone of his voice. It seemed almost detached, almost clinical. "What is it? You're worried about something."

He shrugged and I rose, going to join him at the window. It was late and the quad below was still, most of the windows in the other dormitory towers dark. Kristair's thoughts were moving so fast that I couldn't keep up with them. There had been times in the past when I'd found it hard to follow his mind, but not like this. He was analyzing, computing, filing data away in that over-big brain of his with freakish speed.

Fear jolted through me as I remembered how Kristair had been before, when the Ascended tormented him. How he seemed to be not quite there, in this reality with me.

"Hey."

Kristair half-turned his head, looking at me out of the corner of his eye. When I tried to touch him in concern, my hand passed right through him. Biting back a curse, I calmed myself and said, *"Come back to me."* His heart wasn't beating in my chest and deep inside his mind I heard the all-too-familiar whispers. *"Who is that?"*

A shudder rippled through his mind and, with a lurch, his heart started again. His emotions swept up, erasing his detachment and breaking the whispering link. "They wanted to remind me of what I left behind," Kristair answered, turning to me with a rueful smile. "I thought they would leave me alone these two weeks, but I supposed wrong."

"They can't have you," I said fiercely. Damn bunch of freaking cowards, hiding behind Kristair so I couldn't give them hell for bothering us this way.

"On that we agree." He hesitated, debating, and I gave him a mental prod.

"What are you hiding?"

Kristair smiled, but it didn't look quite right on his face. "I've been back home for less than twenty-four hours and I'm already in trouble." As light as his tone was, I knew it rankled him to be answerable to somebody, how much it grated after all those centuries of being on his own.

Alarms triggered in my brain, but I silenced them, or at least hit the snooze button. Kristair was still with me, so it couldn't have been too bad. "What did they say?"

"They're not thrilled about the fireball down in the tunnels. You could say they're morally outraged, if they were capable of such emotion."

I frowned, thoroughly confused. "You're losing me. What does that have to do with them?"

"They think it's not an ability you would've been able to do if I hadn't returned. They're concerned about you gaining too much, too quickly."

"Seems to me they need to mind their own damn business. Tell them to go stick a star up their collective ass." I shook my head, pissed by how they kept dragging Kristair into this bullshit. "Just tell them I won't do it again. Will that make them happy so they'll leave you alone?"

"They've already taken steps. I'm sorry, Jacob."

Again alarms went off, this time all of them blaring at once. "What do you mean?"

"They've limited the tricks you can do." Kristair's lips tightened in anger and kept myself from cursing. He was worked up enough without me adding to it.

"No more fireballs?" I said as plaintively as I could to make light of the situation and as I hoped a tiny smile touched his mouth.

"No more fireballs. I'm sorry—"

I brushed a mental finger over his lips and he quieted. "No, don't be sorry. You didn't do it. Besides, to be honest, it's a good thing. I'm an immature idiot." Kristair's eyes flashed, but I continued before he could interrupt. "Me and fireballs is a bad idea. I'm glad to be rid of them."

And, if things went the way I wanted them to, I'd never have to use them again anyway. His dark gaze searched my face before he gestured to the bed. "Lay down. You haven't let yourself rest in a long time. You need your sleep."

"You're not sleeping either."

Kristair laughed, low and rich. "I have no need to sleep, not anymore, but I'll lie with you. I like watching you sleep. That hasn't changed."

I frowned, but followed Kristair back to the bed. How could I sleep now when I was so restless? The Ascended were still out there, waiting to take him away from me. "I'm not tired," I said, plopping down on the bed next to him.

I couldn't help thinking about what he'd said earlier tonight of his fear of their detachment and its effect on him. I think I understood it better now. I turned on my side and studied him in the dark. "We'll figure out a way to get around them."

It was strange how sometimes I still couldn't read him. Though we were such a part of each other, Kristair had turned holding himself aloof into an art form. The shadows heavy in the room only made his eyes more enigmatic and he buried the truest part of himself behind that damned mantle of self-possession.

"What is it?" I demanded.

"I'm trying to figure out how you did it. How you've come to matter so much. How you make me need you." Kristair's voice sounded troubled, fear touching his mind before he shoved it away.

I smiled and he frowned. "And what do you find so funny about that? I thought my comment would've gotten your temper up."

"Maybe it would've at another time, but I just take it as a sign that I'm winning, and you know how much I love to win." I traced my eyes over his face, memorizing every line, every hard angle. "You've never let someone come so close before, have you? And I don't think you intended it with me, but now it's happened and you're scared."

"Don't be ridiculous. We've been through too much for me to be afraid of what we have."

"It's not that you're afraid of what we have; it's your fear of losing it. We happened so quickly, Kristair, and we got too distracted to do much more than go along for the ride. This time, we've had a taste of what it's like to lose each other. And there's more riding on us this time, on us and our bond. It's got you all worked up."

"The Syndicate is still making trouble and I still have a time bomb hovering over my head. As you pointed out, it is very similar to before."

"There are some big differences," I insisted. Sometimes I thought Kristair liked to argue just for the sake of arguing.

"Name some."

"For starters, we're already in a relationship so we're not dealing with all the craziness and confusion of getting to know each other and figuring out how we feel. The first time was so intense and so immediate, and you tend to over-think things. Second, the Syndicate isn't as much of a distraction as before because I'm not letting them.

And third, you may have a time bomb hanging over your head, but at least this time you have a plan you think will work."

Only there was one big worry that still nagged at Kristair. How he was going to keep his feelings for me after he truly became one of the Ascended. That worry now bugged me too, big time. If I hadn't already made a lasting impression on him, how could I up the ante? We were a part of each other. Didn't that count for something? "You know, I was just thinking, and it made me wonder."

"Mmmm, were you? Sounds dangerous." Kristair smiled and I knew he was attempting to relieve the tension that had sprung up.

I gave him a mental poke. "Stop that. I'm serious. What happens when you break the link? Do I lose the tats? What about your memories?" The mental link had been broken between us before and that had been painful enough, but to lose everything this time? I didn't know if I could handle that.

"I'm sorry. I know the tattoos irk you, but they are permanent."

I shrugged. "To be honest, I've gotten used to them. I think I'd actually miss them if they disappeared. What about when your heart's gone? What's going to happen to the rest of me? Am I going to go back to the way I was before I met you?"

"It's impossible to go back to an original state." His voice automatically settled into a mode I recognized from every professor I'd ever had. "That's not how nature works. You'll still have my memories; that can't be erased. There will still be an echo of me inside you, but that's all it will be: an echo. As for your physical abilities, your mental ones… I don't know. I would think you'd retain a part of them but you might have to re-teach yourself."

I'd lived with an echo of him for months. At least this time I had a better idea of what I was getting into. It was better than nothing and it sparked an idea, though I couldn't quite fully form it yet. So, I pushed it to the back of my head and figured I'd let it brew for a day or two. If I worried about it, I'd lose it altogether.

Kristair laughed softly, and if he could've, I know he would've touched me then. "You and I are so different, *mo chroí*. How is it we fit so well together?"

"Some things just are."

"You should get some sleep."

"So you keep saying. I'm wide awake though." Well, at least my mind was. My body would love another few hours, but there was too much to think about. In less than a day my entire life had turned around again. At least this was for the better. I didn't want to sleep and lose more precious hours.

"I'm going to try to reschedule my doctor's appointment tomorrow. At least now I can make sure he doesn't hear a double heartbeat." I scowled at his flicker of amusement. "It's not funny."

"You're right. I'm sorry. I promise to behave. Now will you sleep?"

There was no way I could sleep now. Too much was running through my mind. "Do you think anything odd will show up in blood tests during my physical? Some kind of vampire gene mutation or something?"

"I'm a librarian, not a scientist. How would I know? I think you're safe. Your changes are more mind over matter than physical. They don't have tests for psychic abilities, not yet at least."

"You're awfully sexy for a librarian. We should sneak into your hidey-hole and do obscene things to each other there."

"Are you ever serious, Jacob?"

"I am being serious. The scent of old books and sex." I wanted it, even more so because Kristair was so adorably scandalized by the idea. "You know, you're the only one who ever calls me Jacob. Not even my Ma does."

"Does it bother you?"

"No. Somehow I can't see you calling me Jake. It fits you…." I trailed off when I heard footsteps approaching my door. It was late enough that the sound of someone wearing shoes and not stumbling around drunk was odd enough to capture my attention. I gave the air a cautious, instinctive sniff. "It's Tony."

Kristair nodded and disappeared. Then I felt him settle into his corner of my mind. I tugged on a pair of track pants as Tony knocked. When I opened the door, he raised an eyebrow. "You're up late."

From what I could see, he seemed to have recovered from his ordeal earlier. In fact, there was an air of restless excitement about him. "What's up, Tony? Or did you come by to stare at me half-naked again?"

Tony gave me a light, playful shove as I stood aside to let him in. "Your ego hasn't changed a damn bit. You still think everyone wants you."

"You mean they don't? I'm crushed."

He laughed, then cast me a considering glance. "You've changed, since just last night. What's going on?"

"I've got a lot of things off my mind, dealt with some others, and been too busy to mope anymore. I think that's plenty, don't you?"

"Yeah, guess so. There's another thing you can stop worrying about while you're at it."

"I'll take anything I can get." I gestured to a chair and sat down on the edge of my bed. "And since it's after three in the morning, go ahead and spit it out. I have this nagging voice in the back of my head that keeps telling me I should be sleeping."

"I haven't said a word yet."

"But you were thinking it—loudly."

Tony shook his head and remained standing. "I met with Ussier. They're still hunting down rogue vampires and having a damn good time of it. He sent me to check up on you."

I had no doubt Ussier was as happy as an arsonist on Bonfire Night with all the cops busy in another town. The man had some serious bents, but at least he seemed stable. "How sweet. But that's not why you're knocking on my door."

"True. I figured I'd call, but I wanted to say this to your face." I shifted and leaned against the headboard to stretch out as he moved about the room. I'd learned not to prod with Tony or else he'd change his mind and not say another word.

He picked up the new country CD I'd bought a couple weeks ago, shook his head, and set it back down. "Don't know how you can listen to that stuff."

"Try growing up in Louisiana and see what you listen to."

Tony grinned and it was infectious. I hadn't seen him look like this in too long. "Lisabeth took off her spell."

"Really?" I didn't think she'd do it. I'd hoped, but figured it was a long shot at best. "That's good news."

"Ussier said you'd vouched for me and told him what happened in the tunnels."

"I thought it was worth a shot. He wouldn't listen earlier without something to back it up. After everything you did to help us, I had to try. Does this mean you're welcome in the city, free and clear?"

"Yeah, it does." Tony shoved his hands into his pockets. "If I want, I can stay here."

"Sounds like you're not sure anymore." I frowned; I liked the idea of Tony sticking around. Maybe one day, things would go back to normal.

"Guess it's like you said. You can never go back. Huh, Kristair?"

"No, you can't. Only it doesn't mean you can't find a new path together."

"Now who's the philosopher?" I teased.

"No, I do want to stay here. The last place I want to go back to is Rome, but this war isn't finished and I think—no, I know—I need to see it through."

"Tony, there's no damn rule that says you have to take on the Syndicate just because they took you in at one point. It's not like you had much of a damn choice. You don't owe anybody anything."

"So you keep saying, but if I see this through, then maybe I won't have to look over my shoulder anymore, wondering when they're going to retaliate. Then I can be free here in Pittsburgh."

"Tell me you at least have a plan, 'cause seriously, I'm not letting you leave without one."

"You won't let me leave?" A little smile hovered over Tony's lips. "And just how would you plan on stopping me, toolbox?"

"I'd tell Steve," I snickered. "Let him handle you."

"Bastard."

I laughed even harder at the genuine chagrin on his face. "Yeah, I know. It's a part of my charm. Seriously, do you have a plan?"

"Not yet, but I promise, I won't do anything until I do."

"Ask him how many serve on the Syndicate's Council."

Tony frowned at the question and then shrugged. "Seven. Well, actually six. They haven't replaced Roland Montrose yet. There's some in-fighting over his seat. Everybody wants it."

"The hydra," Kristair said.

"What? It's too damn late at night for you to go all cryptic on my ass. Speak in full sentences."

"The hydra was a mythological creature with multiple heads. If you destroyed one head it still lived, spawning another two in its place."

I scratched my temple, trying to keep up with him. *"Um, thanks for the mythology lesson. What does that have to do with anything?"*

"If Tony can get Ussier's help, they can destroy the entire Council at once."

"Wouldn't others just rush in to replace them? And be pissed off too."

I sensed Kristair's sudden mental smile, a malicious glee in his tone. *"Isn't your friend here aligned with another faction who opposes the Council's tactics?"*

I grinned. My lover was damned clever at times. "Okay, I've got something that just might work, but it'll depend on your friends in Rome. Do you think they'd help?"

"Depends on the plan. Shoot."

Quickly, I gave him an outline. He listened, his eyes narrowed, his lips pursed in thought. "If Ussier can find some people to help then

I think I could convince them. I doubt they'd be willing to take on the risk alone, even though some of us have been pushing for a coup. But if we had some older vampires as allies, damn, I can almost guarantee it."

I began to get excited. This could really work. *"Do you think Ussier would be interested in helping Tony?"*

"He'd consider it a good time. Trust me, leaving the country and blowing the Council to bits will seem like a vacation to him."

"Okay, here's the deal, Tony. Why don't you go talk to Ussier and lay it out for him? It should come from you rather than me anyway. The sooner we can take the Syndicate out the better." I paused and winced, bracing myself for the coming firestorm. "And tell him I'm going with you."

"WHAT?" Kristair and Tony shouted at the same time.

"Jake, it's not your fight. Come on; be serious. You can't walk into a vampire den, no matter what kind of badass abilities Kristair gave you. That would be insane," Tony said as Kristair seethed.

"I'm not talking about us going at it alone. Let me remind you that I'm a part of this too. I'm one of their targets and I'm going to see it to the end with you." Kristair's anger settled into a cold fury.

"What happened to not wanting to be a part of the war?"

"You don't have to do this," Tony argued. "You know, in order to fix things between us or some dumb-assed thing like that. We're cool. Hell, you came back for me earlier and got Ussier to remove the spell. Dude, we're cool. Stay in Pittsburgh."

"Like you said, if we do this, we won't have to look over our shoulders anymore. You got into this mess 'cause of me, so we'll get out of it together. Then neither of us will have to look back anymore."

I thought he'd argue more, but after a moment Tony grinned. "It'd be good to have you at my back. And to show my appreciation, you get to be the one to tell Steve what we're doing."

"Thanks." I grimaced. "Can we let him in on it after we get back from Rome?"

"You're out of your mind." Tony shook his head and glanced out the window. "Sun's gonna rise pretty soon. If I want to catch Ussier before then, I'd better get going. I'll call you tonight and fill you in on what's going on."

"Cool." I ignored Kristair's continued mutterings, rose, and held out my hand. After a moment, Tony clasped it with a roll of his eyes.

"I'd give you a hug, but you'd probably consider it a come-on or something, freak."

I laughed and pulled him in for a hug anyway. It was so good to have my friend back. "You know, ever since you went all creature-of-the-night on me, I must admit you are sexier."

"Jackass."

"Dweeb."

I prepared myself for Kristair's explosion as Tony left, but my lover remained quiet. That couldn't be a good sign. He also didn't reappear in the room after the door had closed as I'd expected. Instead, he remained in that corner of my brain. *"Look, I know you're pissed but I have to do this."*

"Didn't you get angry with me, this very evening, because I thought taking out the Syndicate was a priority?"

"Yeah, but that was different."

"How was it different?" Kristair's voice was icily precise in direct contrast to the hot fury I sensed lashing from him.

"Because I'm not going to let myself get distracted from the goal. Besides, this time, thanks to you, we have a plan instead of just sitting back and waiting for them to come to us. I don't want a long-drawn out mess. In and out, then it'll be over with."

"I don't want you going," Kristair insisted.

"That's just too bad, isn't it?"

There was a very quiet pause and my lover's temper sparked hotter. *"It'll be too dangerous."*

"Earlier you argued that it was too dangerous to sit here and do nothing while they're hunting me. Make up your mind."

"I didn't mean for you to go chasing after them in their territory!"

"You would. Why can't I?" I crossed my arms over my chest and glared at Kristair in my thoughts since he wasn't letting me do it in person.

Kristair growled. He actually *growled* at me. *"You don't owe this to Tony, like he told you. Don't go. You don't belong in Rome. You shouldn't be getting mixed up in the affairs of vampires."*

I laughed and stripped out of my clothes again. "I can't believe you're seriously saying this. Damn, you haven't been back a day and we're already fighting." At least no one was around to witness me talking to an empty room.

"We're making up for lost time."

"It's not because I owe him. It's because he's my friend and he needs my help. Kristair, he'd never ask for it. Not now." That shut him up, and my lover was quiet as I lay back down. As soon as I was settled under the covers, I sensed him rummaging around in my head, nudging. A yawn overtook me when he somehow triggered my brain to sleep. *"What ya think yer doin'?"*

"You need to sleep."

Exhaustion rolled over me, driving me under. That sneaky motherfucker....

Chapter 22

"I CAN'T believe you pulled that shit on me again. Didn't you swear you wouldn't do that?" I complained as we walked down the hill on Lothrop Street.

"I swore not to take away your will. Moving your brain into a sleep pattern is different. You'd had a long day, and what you're planning is not going to make it any easier, especially if you keep this fool notion of going to Rome."

I couldn't be irritated as much as I wanted. It had been the first good night of sleep I'd had in a very long time, plus my meeting with the doctor had gone well. I'd had to skip my statistics class to go, and hearing Kristair bitch about it had put me in a better mood. The test results from my physical would take a week, enough time to get me to Rome and back, if everything went well. Then I could play football again and put this all behind me.

"You have a one-track mind, Jacob."

Kristair seemed more talkative today than normal. And his emotions kept swinging between skittish and awed. Every few minutes, he'd make my eyes jerk up to the sky where the sun was peeking out of the clouds. He was going to make me permanently cross-eyed if he kept it up.

"Relax, love. It's not like you're a vampire anymore. You're one of the big, bad Ascended, remember. You can go anywhere."

"I can't erase two thousand years of instincts overnight."

"Thought you said it was all mind over matter." I gave him a teasing poke. *"Couldn't you just will yourself to walk outside?"*

"You have to believe it. If there's any doubt, it would be fatal. Not something I'd have been eager to risk. Besides, we know what happened when I realized the power I'd had. I think either way, we'd never hear from the vampire who tried that trick again."

"I get your point. Either you end up as a crispy critter or you're snatched by the Ascended the moment you realize you're a badass." I paused then grinned again. *"I bet you'd risk it under certain circumstances. Say, if Kayla was in trouble."*

"True."

"You'd do it for me too."

"That's debatable."

I laughed, warmed by Kristair's surge of exasperated affection. *"Yeah, I love you too, old man."*

"The last time I saw the sun rise was the morning our raiding party left to destroy the Roman fort. It wasn't much of a sunrise. The mists were heavy, blocking out everything behind a gray wall. It had burned off by noon, but I wasn't paying much attention. I was too busy." Kristair's voice became quieter in reflection. *"I didn't know it would be the last time I'd see it."*

Abruptly, I was drawn into a memory so real I could feel the mist cooling on my skin as I ran through that ancient dawn. The air stirred and eddied around me, around the men I was running with, dark-eyed men covered in blue tattoos, many more extensive than my own.

"Jacob!"

"Sorry," I muttered out loud and pulled myself out of the memory. It had been incredibly detailed, as if I'd actually been there.

"It's a part of the exchange I did with you. It's how it works, how we share our memories so our history is not forgotten." Kristair sounded shaken after his brush with his past.

Why hadn't I taken the chance to explore this before? I had all those months with this part of Kristair locked inside of me. All the questions about him I'd had harbored, who he'd loved before, how he'd ended up a vampire. And I'd ignored this gift.

Once again, I found myself in the past. It was pitch black, one of those moonless nights, and patches of clouds obscured the stars. A beautiful monster swept down out of the sky and the screaming started. Hair-raising horrified screams as the night came alive and ripped open flesh. I was overcome with terror and rage as everything I knew fell down around me.

"Please don't, Jacob. Please."

I jerked myself out of the memory, ashamed by how lost Kristair had sounded. *"I'm sorry, love. I had no right."*

"The memories are now yours too. I just don't wish to relive them again."

We both fell silent as I turned back toward campus. I supposed I should hit the rest of my classes, but I wasn't in the mood to sit in on a boring lecture. What I'd like to do was lock myself away someplace private with Kristair for the next two weeks and ignore the entire world. But that wasn't gonna happen anytime soon.

"If you hurry, you'll be back in time for your statistics class."

"You sound way too excited about it, Kristair, and that's a little scary. I think I'll grab something to eat instead. Maybe go by my favorite hangout."

"Would you mind if we took a detour first?"

"As long as you don't suggest schoolwork." I was going to have a very hard time concentrating on classes until all this was settled. My grades were up to some slacking. I should be able to dig myself back out of any hole I put myself in with a little effort.

"I wanted to check out the place where you were being held yesterday. See if there's any new information we can pick up."

"Why not? Beats going to my last class." I laughed aloud at Kristair's surge of consternation. *"Relax, love. I've been a good boy all semester. Coach hasn't had to ride my ass about my grades either, so I can afford to miss one day."* Or a week or so.

"You'll miss more than a day if you go to Rome, and that is sure to piss off your coach. You may be benched for the time being, but I'm sure he still expects you to go to practice."

"Anyone ever tell you that you nag, Kristair?" I said acidly. He went still with indignation. *"I'll call Coach from the air, tell him it's a family emergency or something."*

He didn't respond and I sighed. Nothing like having a sulking two-thousand-year-old vampire haunting your head. Guilt struck immediately after that snide thought. He was worried about me and we had such little time. Why were we arguing again?

"I'm not sulking, impudent brat." Then Kristair sighed and gave me a mental kiss. *"Can't you understand I don't like it because I'm worried about you?"*

"I can handle myself."

"It's not about you handling yourself. I know you can." That comment surprised me, the warmth of it chasing away my irritation. I really needed to stop trying to prove myself to everyone. Only I wasn't sure how to after all this time. *"And you won't be taking them on alone, either. I'll be there as well as Ussier and whoever he brings along."*

"Then why are you so upset?"

Kristair was silent again, but this time it seemed more like he was trying to gather his thoughts, so I let him as I walked through the cold afternoon. *"You don't want this life. You're not a warrior, though you're capable of defending yourself or those you choose to defend. In reality, you'd rather be left in peace. You don't go out seeking fights. Maybe on occasion when you have your temper up, but for the most part you're not a violent man. You didn't want to change, remember? But you have. When I left, you'd never killed before, and now you have. After the first time, it gets easier."*

I remembered Montrose with an uneasy stirring in my gut and that god-awful momentary shock I had after I looked down at his destroyed body. That horror had been missing yesterday in the fight down in the tunnels. Uneasiness stirred before I pushed it away. There was nothing I could do about that. I needed to see this through.

"Okay, I get your point. You understand, though, why I changed my mind about going?" I asked.

"Your loyalty has always been one of your strongest traits."

I snorted. *"You wouldn't say that if you'd seen what happened after you disappeared."*

There was a long pause, and when Kristair spoke again his voice was so gentle, a burning ache rose in my chest. *"I did see, when you were torturing yourself the other night, mo chroí. You stood with Tony when he came back, even though it would be easier to continue to be his enemy. I'm not saying to forget about what happened the night he vanished, but remember how you defended him too."*

"So what were you hoping to see at the house?" I asked, grateful when Kristair let me change the subject without comment. The whole situation with Tony was still a sore subject, though it was getting better.

"I'm not sure, but I want to take a look at it anyway. I want to get more information on this girl, the one who grabbed a hold of you psychically. She concerns me."

"I don't think she was at the house. She was hurt making me get into the car."

"Good. I'm not sorry you hurt her. She attacked you." Kristair's voice was grim. *"You didn't kill the men you fought with and the police didn't find them, so we should be able to track them back to where they ran to and make sure they aren't a threat to you or Kayla in the future."*

"Wouldn't the Syndicate have gotten back at them for failing?"

"You watch too many movies. It's possible, but it's hard to find people who are willing to be a vampire's eyes and ears during the day, ones who can be trusted. Especially ones with her little gift. Chances are they're still alive."

I thought they'd be dead for sure. *"You're not planning on us, well, you know...."* Killing vamps in the heat of battle was one thing; killing humans in cold blood, even if they were asses, was another.

"What is it with you and vampires? I'm one, remember, or has that little fact slipped your mind unless you want me to bite you?"

"Correction: You were a vampire, and I've never claimed to be consistent."

It didn't take long to walk to the house. When I got there it was quiet. Still Kristair made me scope the place out before he let me enter through the same back door I'd escaped from the day before. The house was deserted, but someone had done a thorough job of cleaning up. I glanced in the basement room where they'd held me, but it was empty except for the busted-up chair sitting all alone in the middle of the room with one of the rungs bent out of shape. But there were no syringes and drugs, just like the cop had said. I started wandering around, seeing if I could pick up a scent to trail that would lead us in the right direction.

"I don't think we're going to find much here," I muttered, after searching outside before coming back in for one last sweep of the place. "I followed the trail like you showed me, but you saw it ended on the street. They had to have had a car. Wait, they did have a car. I'm an idiot. The one they took me in."

"What do you remember about it?"

I shook my head. "Not much. I was distracted when I was fighting. It was dark; some sort of four-door sedan. Beyond that, my brain seems to have shut down."

"You were fighting off a psychic attack and drugged. Don't beat yourself up over it. Did you get any details after they shoved you into the car?"

"No, the drugs hit quick. Last thing I remember was the girl screaming."

"Talking to yourself and trespassing? Not a good record you've got there, punk," a nasal voice said from behind me.

A shout lodged in my throat as I spun around. Kristair hissed in my mind. Just my freaking luck. The two cops who knew me better than the sheriff in my hometown stood framed in the doorway. "Hey, guys. What are you doing here?"

"Could ask you the same." Detective Kuykedal's eyes were hard on me as he came into the room, looking just as thuggish as ever in his sweats and ratty T-shirt. If he hadn't been with his partner, it would look like he was breaking and entering too.

"Just thought I'd look around, since you guys weren't too keen on doing anything."

"Scram, kid," Detective Aderson said. "Unless you have something new to tell us. Anything else happen after we talked yesterday?"

"Only running a rampage through the tunnels," Kristair said in such a bland tone I almost snickered. *"Who are these guys?"*

"Just some cops I ran into when Tony and Steve were in the hospital. They've taken a liking to me."

"I can see that."

"Nothing with them." I walked over to the chair where I'd been bound and gestured to it. "You might want to check this. One of the dudes clocked his friend with it when I ducked. After clearing out the rest of their things, I don't think they came back."

"Stop playing Frank Hardy and get out of here, before I haul you in," Detective Kuykedal said, stepping to the side so I could leave. "Don't let me catch you snooping around here again."

"You read the Hardy Boys?" Detective Aderson murmured.

"Yeah, and Tom Swift and Nancy fucking Drew. Got a problem with that?"

"That's so white bred of you."

"You can only read *Roots* so many times, you racist motherfucker. Now can we get back to the case?"

The two of them reminded me so much of Steve and me that I had to bite back a laugh. "Sweet little moment there, guys. Really. I think I'll be going now and leave you two alone."

"Aren't you a mouthy one." Kuykedal glared. "We'll give you a call if we have any questions." He shook his head and muttered under his breath, "Stupid punk is going to get himself killed."

"He isn't dead yet," Aderson replied as I edged past them, heading for the door.

"Well that was a waste of time. What now?" I asked Kristair as my stomach growled.

"Now you eat before you get cranky, and we'll figure it out."

Kristair could be as bad as my Ma sometimes with his fussing. I couldn't bring myself to mind it, though. I listened to him think as I made my way to find food. I could just picture the serious expression on his face, the faint furrow in his brow as he ran through options. As much as I loved having him one with me, I missed being able to see him.

I almost groaned in pleasure as Originals Hot Dog, better known as "The O," appeared down the street. It was near packed all twenty-three hours they were open. It was the best place in Pittsburgh to grab a quick, cheap bite to eat, and the food rocked.

"When was the last time we just talked about bullshit, instead of all this life-and-death stuff?" I sighed with pleasure at my first bite of pizza. Damn, I'd been hungrier than I'd thought.

"It's been too long." Kristair's interest was piqued by the pizza. *"You really like that stuff?"*

"One day I'll introduce you to it. Tonight I'm making it a rule, when we're back home and in bed we're not gonna talk about the Syndicate or curses or hunting people down. Got it?"

"Sounds like a good idea to me, but until then, I've been thinking. How did you follow me to my tower the night after we initiated our bond?"

I considered it as I finished my first slice. *"I dunno. It was kind of like following breadcrumbs in my head. I just knew where you'd been."*

"When the girl attacked your mind, she would've left a psychic trace. You might be able to do something similar with her."

"You mean lock in on her, kind of like one of the GPS devices?" That might be handy for the moment. Not something I'd want all the time, though. *"How many people am I going to get stuck in my head? You, I don't mind, but I don't want a whole platoon of characters running around up there. I've got enough to deal with."*

"It won't be like that. Afterward, we can see about keeping her permanently out."

Still, I hesitated and ran a hand through my hair. *"Okay, just tell me first. What do you plan on doing with this chick if we do find her?"*

"I promise you, I won't ask you to kill her or to hurt her. I only want answers to a few questions."

I didn't like it, mostly because I knew Kristair wouldn't be so kind if he'd had a choice. He didn't like loose ends, especially ones that had been proven dangerous in the past. If I wasn't standing between them and Kristair, he would be ruthless. At least in this case he'd given me his word and I knew he wouldn't break it. I finished my soda and set it down. *"Okay, sexy. What now?"*

"That's up to you, Jacob. You're the one with the ability, not me. You came up with that one all on your own. It might help if you close your eyes and concentrate."

"Lord, not here. I'd look like a freak." I tossed my trash. *"I'll do better if I'm walking around anyway."*

I wandered down the street, letting my thoughts drift until I picked up on the taste of someone in my mind, a taste that was feminine. It wasn't like what I had with Kristair. Even when I hadn't understood it, it had been strong. This was different, more like the lingering scent of a burning wick long after the candle had been blown out.

"I think I've got it."

"Good, good." Kristair's mental fingers brushed over the link. *"She was very strong, wasn't she? Let's see where she leads us."*

Twenty minutes later, I stood outside an old apartment complex, one that was even rattier than the one I'd lived in with Tony and Steve. The front door sat atilt in the frame and a flickering bulb lit the dirty entryway. I glanced at the mailboxes. There were no nametags and one was busted open. I headed up the stairs until the trace stopped me at the fifth floor.

She was in the first apartment just off the stairs. I knew it in my bones. At least it meant she was still alive.

"There's no reason to feel guilty if she wasn't, Jacob."

"I know that." I still would have, and Kristair knew me well. I took a deep breath and knocked on the door. When Russell opened the door, I almost groaned. It would have to be the big motherfucker.

He scowled, huge fists bunching. "What do you want?"

"I'm just here to talk. I don't want any trouble."

His face darkened further. I cussed under my breath as he grabbed my coat and yanked me into his shithole of an apartment, shoving me up against the door. "You've got trouble, asshole." Russell was working himself up to a real good mad. His nostrils flared and his face was scrunched up and furrowed. I'd never seen anyone simmer with fury like that, building it slowly to a full boil. If it wasn't directed at me, it would've been amusing. "Do you have any idea what you've done to her?"

Kristair snarled, the sound rumbling in my head. He was ready to break loose and take over if I'd let him. *"Relax. He's not ready to beat my face in yet."*

"Why give him the opportunity? Strike first."

"Look, you guys jumped my ass, not the other way around, so back the fuck off, because if you think I was freaky badass yesterday, you haven't seen me today." Uncertainty appeared on Russell's face, but his grip didn't lighten. "Where is she? I might be able to help."

"What can you do?" he growled.

"I'm the one who hurt her, aren't I?" Rage leapt in his eyes. "If you knew anything about psychic mumbo-jumbo you'd have helped her already. Since she's still hurt, I'm guessing not." It was a gamble—one I wasn't sure I could back up—but it was worth a shot.

Russell let go of me with a snort of disgust. "What's your price?"

"Information."

His jaw tightened, but he nodded. "Fine. She's back here, but if you hurt her again I'll break your scrawny neck."

I didn't dignify that with an answer.

Angie sat up on the unmade bed, wrapped up in a blanket with her arms around her knees. She stared straight ahead at nothing, but when I stepped through the door she flinched, then began rocking, tugging at her dark hair in agitation. She was barely more than a girl, fourteen or fifteen maybe.

"Holy hell, Kristair."

I sat down on the bed and she continued to stare ahead. There was so much tension in her body, I was afraid she'd shatter. Russell shifted on his feet. "If you hurt her, I swear...."

"So you keep threatening." I turned my head and glared up at him. "I won't. I promise, okay? I didn't want this either."

"What do I do, Kristair? Where do I start?" I had done this to her, but I didn't know how to fix the damaged I'd caused. *"If the Ascended has limited my mojo, is that going to stop me from healing her?"* My big mouth might just have promised more than I could deliver. Wouldn't be the first time.

"She's not completely catatonic; that's a good sign. She's at least aware that you're here, so the damage should be reversible. And the Ascended didn't touch this ability of yours. You've always been very strong minded and you caused the damage before I came back. It doesn't follow under their rule of anything new. You should be able to help." Kristair paused, concern creeping into his voice. *"Are you sure you want to do this?"*

"Yes," I insisted.

"Then reach out like you did with Tony. Physical contact would make it easier, but I don't know if your twitchy friend would like that. You'll be vulnerable enough as it is."

"Got it." Her hair half-covered her face and I hunched over until I could see her features better. Her eyes cleared and focused on me as I caught her gaze. She made a small desperate sound of fear, her skin turning paper-white. Russell shifted closer and I held up a warning hand. "It's okay, Angie. I won't hurt you. I want to help."

She didn't move as I inched closer and touched my fingers to her temple. Pain struck with stunning force as I delved into her lacerated mind. It felt as if a grenade had gone off inside her brain, leaving behind shrapnel and still-bleeding wounds. I didn't even know where to begin. I had done all this?

"She caused damage herself. It wasn't just you. She could've let go when you started fighting back and saved herself, but she didn't. It was her choice to fight you. Beating yourself up isn't going to solve anything."

I took a deep breath to ease my frustration and worry. Following Kristair's instructions, I let the sound of his voice guide me as I eased the unnatural pressure in her mind and began knitting Angie's psyche back together. Energy seemed to drain from me quicker the longer I worked and I lost all sense of where I was, which only added to Kristair's uneasiness.

"You need to stop. You've done enough for her. She can do the rest on her own if she wishes a full recovery," Kristair urged and gently nudged my will aside, taking control of my actions as my hand fell from Angie's temple.

"What?" Even my mental voice sounded slow and slurred.

"You pour too much of your heart into things, Jacob. You don't know how to hold back," Kristair chided in exasperation and concern, lending me his strength so I didn't fall on my face and embarrass myself.

It took a monumental effort for me to open my eyes, but when I finally did, I found Angie staring at me, her eyes stunned. They were a light brown with golden highlights and a slight almond cast. Color had returned to her smooth cheeks and the pinched look in her features had lessened as her pain faded. Russell sat down next to her on the bed. It struck me how similar they looked. Brother and sister, maybe, not that it mattered.

"Angie? Angie baby, talk to me."

The girl looked up at Russell then hurled herself into his arms, clinging. He let out a sigh of relief and glanced my way with grudging respect and awe. "You really did it. Holy fuck."

I shrugged. "She's not in the clear yet, but she will be. I think she needs to sleep, and give her brain a rest. You might want to knock her out." Goddamn, that sounded good. I could use a long nap myself, like maybe into next week. *"Okay, Kristair, what questions did you want me to ask them? I want to go home before I fall over."*

"Why had they used Angie? There were other ways they could have subdued you other than trying to grab you psychically. It makes me wonder if they wanted something in particular and planned on using her to dig it out of your head."

Russell shook his head as I relayed the question, his big hand stroking through the girl's hair. "I'm not sure. They talked more with Angie than me. They were looking for something they thought you knew; some bullshit key to immortality, I think." Russell barked a laugh. "Which made no damn sense. They're vampires. I'm not sure what they'd need with more immortality than what they already had. Angie was supposed to probe for the secret. They were talking about flying us to some council meeting, but they didn't say where." He paused, bitterness flashing across his face. "They didn't warn us that you were psychic too."

"They didn't know. It wasn't something I was born with. I kinda inherited it." I frowned and absently gnawed on my thumb until Kristair made me stop. This whole brain-rape thing just to learn what I had stashed in my head didn't make any sense. It was too much effort to discover the extent of Kristair's abilities, especially when they'd earn it on their own only if they just waited. No, there had to be something else.

"Do you mind if I take over, Jacob?"

"Why the hell not? You're halfway there already." I relaxed and Kristair slipped deftly into control. It was getting easier each time, this fluid give-and-take, as if we were really two separate and whole personas sharing one willing body. Like we belonged this way, two people in one, joined forever.

"Why does the Syndicate believe there's another path to immortality?" Kristair was troubled by this and I tried to soothe him, but he shrugged me off.

"You think they suspect something about the Ascended?" I asked.

"Perhaps."

"How would I know? All I heard was something about some prophet of theirs had predicted it, I think. They talked about a really old vampire called Chris something, but when he disappeared, I guess they shifted their plan and named you instead. But Angie didn't find anything about immortality in your head." Russell drew her closer, his brows furrowing. "They questioned her for hours, but she kept screaming there was nothing there. They wanted us to check someone else out, but their damned interrogation made Angie even worse. She almost died. Once they'd decided they weren't going to get anything more, they left, and I haven't seen them since. For all I care they can go fuck themselves."

I spotted one of Angie's eyes peering at me through her hair, the sight of it chilling me to the bone. "But you know it now," she said softly. "You've unlocked the Ancient's secret, and they're going to come for you."

Chapter 23

"ROME! You're going to Rome? Are you crazy?" Kayla's eyes blazed with outrage as she moved in close enough to take a swipe at me. "You're not some damn cowboy, Jake. You're a football player. What the hell do you think you're going to be able to do against the entire Syndicate Council?"

"Ouch, that hurts," I tried teasing her then took a step back when her mouth tightened. "Okay, sorry, no more joking. I'm not going to be going alone. I'll be safe. You trust your Uncle Ghedi's abilities, right?"

"I trust that Ghedi Ussier has his own damn agenda and you might be smart to consider that."

"She's right, you know."

"Please don't start, Kristair. One of you is bad enough and neither of you are going to change my mind." My lover muttered some snide comment about being stubborn and then fell silent.

"Thanks for the advice. I promise you, I'll trust my instincts. I won't be gone long. You won't even have a chance to get over being mad at me before I'm back to harass you."

"You are fucking nuts. You are." Kayla grabbed my jeans out of my carryall and began putting them back in the dresser, much more neatly than how they were in there before. I don't think I'd ever seen her so rattled. "You think it'll be over with just like that." She snapped her fingers. "That you'll be able to waltz in and take over their Council as easily as you rescued me. It's just like another football game to you, isn't it? It's not a fucking game. People are going to die. You could die."

She stopped and sat down on my bed, her hands trembling. "Don't go, please."

I crouched down in front of her and took her hands in my own. They were chilly and, damn, she looked miserable. I felt a twinge of regret for putting her through this. "I have to go. As someone pointed out to me, those jackasses are not going to stop just because I want them to. And I can't let Tony go by himself."

"No, I guess you wouldn't." Kayla scrubbed a hand over her face, wiping away a tear I hadn't seen fall, and then her jaw tightened. "I could go with you. I have a townhouse in Rome I've never seen before." She began to talk faster, trying to convince me, as I shook my head while Kristair made it known to me how much he disliked that suggestion. "You don't have to take me to the fight, but I could just be there, in the same city at least."

"Do you have any damn idea of what Kristair would do to me if I agreed? Maybe I am crazy, but I'm not that crazy."

"You act like he's going to find out. He's gone, Jake. He'll never know. Besides, he wouldn't want you going either."

"Kristair would find a way to get to me and kick my ass. You're right; he wouldn't want me going either. But if he was here, he'd be the first one to head over and take the Syndicate out himself."

"Why the hell am I even arguing with you?" Kayla glared, her mouth settled into an adorable pout, though I didn't dare point that out. "You've got your mind made up. I suppose I should be grateful you even took the time to tell me about your damned jaunt."

"I'm not trying to hide things from you. I wouldn't." I sat down next to her on my bed and slid my arm around her shoulders. At first, she resisted, but then she laid her head on my shoulder and burrowed in.

"I don't want to lose you too. You're the only family I've got left."

"You're not going to lose me, I promise."

"You can't promise something like that. You don't know what's going to happen."

Damn she was stubborn, just like someone else I knew. "Fine then. I'll give it my best damn shot. Is that better?"

"Ass." Kayla gave me a hard hug. "I guess that'll have to do. I don't know why I keep surrounding myself with so many hardheaded men."

"Like you can talk," I retorted. Kristair was hurting, having her so close and upset, so I gave in to his wish and settled back, gathering her into my arms.

"God, you're so much like him sometimes it's scary," she said, her voice muffled against my shoulder. She lifted her head and gave me a smile, her eyes hard and damp. "I swear to god, if you get so much as a scratch, I'll hurt you bad, Jacob Allen Corvin."

"Yes, ma'am." I touched her face. "You take care of yourself too, trouble. No more kidnappings while my back's turned."

"Yes, Daddy." Kayla gave me a hard kiss on my mouth. "Come back quick, Jake. I'm serious."

AS THE private jet taxied down the runway, I tried to figure out how I had managed to get myself into this predicament. I was the only human on a plane full of vampires. There really had to be a better way to travel. Of course, with them I could use a doctored passport and didn't have to worry about the authorities when we landed. On the other hand, I'd almost rather have handled those inconveniences over wondering how long it was going to be before one of my traveling companions got hungry.

"You'll be just fine, Jacob. Older vampires have more control when it comes to feeding. Seems to me the only one you should worry about is Tony." There was an undercurrent of amusement to my lover's voice.

"Aren't you a barrel of laughs." I couldn't help but smile, though. It was going to be a long trip and having Kristair with me to

occupy my attention would keep my mind from wandering places I didn't want to go. I especially didn't want to think about the Syndicate, or what was going to happen the next night. *"Why don't you pop out of my head and lounge naked across from me? Maybe do a little dance."*

"You'd really love that, wouldn't you?"

"Oh yes, I would." I grinned and sent Kristair a mental image of him with pasties and a pole in the middle of the plane.

"Sorry. I'm not into cheap thrills, but if you want a distraction I could do this."

That was all the warning I got before pleasure rippled through me. I stifled a gasp and gripped the armrests as the sensation of Kristair's mouth closed around my nipple and tugged on the piercing. That evil bastard. How the hell was he doing that?

"You okay there?" Ussier asked as he sat down next to me. "You look a little shell-shocked."

"I'm cool," I managed without my voice squeaking like I'd just started puberty. *"Stop that right now, Kristair. I swear when I get my hands on you...."*

Kristair's chuckle filled my mind, but he took mercy on me and stopped his torments. My body throbbed, on edge. I had to admit I was very distracted. It was hard to think when my balls ached.

Ussier had chosen to bring only a few others with him besides myself and Tony. There was Alette, whose plane we were using and who thankfully sat with Hugh at the front of the plane. Tony was sitting with Artemise, looking both awed and a little frightened as he talked with him. I almost laughed. He still fidgeted when he was nervous.

Four older vampires against a whole infestation of younger ones. It didn't seem like good odds to me.

"It's better than you think," Kristair said with a nuzzle to the back of my neck. The sudden sensation of his tongue tracing just under my earlobe made the blood rush out of my head. I shifted in the chair and prayed Ussier wouldn't notice my hard-on.

"Cut it out!"

"So who's manning Pittsburgh?" I asked, trying to make conversation despite the surreal situation I was in. Other than traveling with vampires and having Kristair whispering naughty suggestions in my head, the fact that I was in a private jet threw me. I'd always dreamed of being in one someday, but the dream had been very far away, almost out of reach. The seats were covered in butter-soft leather and spaced so there was more than enough room for me to stretch my legs. It was decadent and sinful. I loved it. I'd like it even better if everyone else was gone so I could stretch out Kristair against all that leather and give him the fucking he had coming.

"Lisabeth," Ussier answered. "There's no one better to keep an eye on things for me. I almost brought her, but then I would've had to leave Alette in charge and I'd rather keep her close. She's capable of bombing the entire city and believing she's saving it in the process."

I cast a glance at her and was glad she was on the other side of the plane. She was more beautiful than any starlet out of a movie, but whenever she turned her eyes on me, a chill ran through every nerve ending in my body, urging me to run away as fast as I could.

"She's, ummm… a little unstable? Why would you want to bring someone like that?" I whispered, hoping her ears weren't as good as Kristair's had been.

Ussier laughed. "Because even a rabid dog has his uses, and Alette is very, very good. She's steadier when she has Hugh and Artemise around. I'd stay away from her if I were you, though. You're just her type: young and good-looking."

I shifted in my seat and wet my lips. *"Why the hell did you bring me into this mess?"* I complained to Kristair.

"You're the one who chose to come to Rome." Then Kristair took pity on me. *"Don't worry. Ussier's messing with your head. Alette does prefer men like you, but she likes musicians the best. So unless you can play the trombone, you're safe."* He paused. *"I'd still keep my distance from her."*

"So what's the plan for tomorrow?" I asked Ussier.

"Tomorrow night you stay put in that house of Kristair's while me and my Razor Children check out the place where the Syndicate is headquartered. Tony can meet with his contacts and then we'll meet with you at the townhouse and make our plans from there."

Two days in Rome versus one. I sighed. One week had almost passed, or at least that's the way it seemed, and I only had two weeks with Kristair. What was I thinking? We still needed to figure out a way to counteract the remoteness he felt when he was a part of the Ascended. They'd visited him again last night after I'd fallen asleep and I was sure they'd come visit again as soon as I drifted off tonight. If I could get away with it, I wouldn't sleep for the next week.

"What are Razor Children?" It was safer to ask Kristair, but I was not at all reassured by his response.

"You don't want to know." Kristair's lips drifted down to the pulse in my throat and I almost jumped when he nipped it hard. It became a struggle to concentrate on what Ussier was saying.

"If everything goes right, then we'll set up a new Council for the Syndicate and then be on our way back home."

"What if everything doesn't go right?" I asked, a trifle breathless, and hoped it didn't show. At least Ussier's expression never altered.

"Then we move on to Plan B."

I shouldn't ask. I knew I shouldn't, but I did anyway. "And what's Plan B?"

"We blow everything to hell and let the devil sort it out."

"Oh." I knew I should've kept my mouth shut. "No offense, Ussier, but you scare me a little."

He laughed again, a low, rich sound. "I'm the reason why God has a thousand eyes."

That sounded vaguely familiar. "LL Cool J?"

"No. Redman."

Kristair's lips were everywhere. Places they shouldn't possibly be, considering I was still clothed. I was very conscious of Ussier sitting next to me and he wasn't the type of man to miss anything that was going on around him. I'm sure he could hear my heartbeat thundering.

"Kristair, for the love of god, behave yourself."

"Words I never thought I'd hear you say. You wanted a distraction." There was such wickedness to his tone I knew I was screwed.

"Excuse me," I muttered to Ussier and bolted for the bathroom, ignoring the curious eyes on the back of my neck. As soon as I locked the door, Kristair appeared before me, his dark eyes hungry.

"You'd better be getting down on your knees, troublemaker," I growled, undoing my jeans.

Kristair sank down without a murmur. I don't think I'd ever seen anything so beautiful as this proud man on his knees, sensuous lips parted, a dangerous glint in his dark eyes. I leaned back against the wall, cursing the fact that I wouldn't get to watch him going down on me as I closed my eyes. But then his wicked lips were around me, my cock sinking into the wet heat of his mouth, and I couldn't think anymore.

I bit my lip against a strangled curse, but couldn't stop the moan. Kristair's tongue lashed and his fingers toyed with my balls as his voice in my head urged me on. *"Fuck my mouth, Jacob. I'm so hungry for you."*

I slid my fingers over his scalp and thrust my hips. It was like I was in a mad, delirious dream, and it was over with far too quick. Kristair knew every trick I liked, knew just how to suck and tease and torment. And as my orgasm erupted, he sucked harder, lapping up every drop.

Panting, I opened my eyes as Kristair sat back on his heels. He was licking his lips, his eyes gleaming in satisfaction. "You bit your lip too hard," he teased in a low voice. "Now it looks all swollen."

I glanced in the mirror. He was right, and my cheeks were flushed on top of it. I was gonna have to walk back out there smelling of sex and looking like I'd just gone a round. "Just you wait," I promised, tucking myself back into my jeans. "When this is all over with and I've got you to myself…. Just you wait, Kristair."

KRISTAIR'S tension increased the closer we got to Rome and by the time we landed it was almost unbearable. He resisted my efforts to draw him into conversation and grumbled as we took Alette's private car to his townhouse. I tried to ignore Kristair's unease and tried to watch the city go by, but couldn't see much at all through the tinted windows.

I was exhausted and lost track of what time it was. We'd taken off just after sunset in Pittsburgh and I'd not been able to sleep on the plane at all. From what I could tell, it was early evening in Rome the next day. Or something like that. I wish I knew if the Ascended took into account different time zones or not. Did we lose a day or not?

All I wanted to do was crawl into bed and wrap my arms around Kristair. For once I envied the vampires. The sun was down and they were wide awake, didn't matter at all how long they'd been up. For all I knew Ussier and his creepy Razor Children were on their way now to check out the Syndicate's headquarters and Tony was meeting with his people.

My thoughts were scattered and my muscles felt like leaden weights. I'd wanted to go with them, but Ussier had railroaded me into the car and sent me off like a damn kid. As much as I hated to admit it, I was glad nothing was going down tonight. I'd be useless. At least there was one good thing I could say about being in Rome: it was at least twenty degrees warmer than back in Pittsburgh.

"*I'd take the cold,*" Kristair said.

"*So you've finally decided to talk to me?*"

"*Conversing would've been a bad idea, considering both of our moods. I did not wish to argue with you again.*"

I almost sniped back at that, only I sensed how true that statement was for Kristair. Even during the madness last year, when he didn't know if he was going crazy or not, when he didn't have control over whether he was coming or going, even then, I hadn't sensed this deep unquiet with him. Arguing would relieve my tension, but it would only add to his.

The car pulled to a stop and the driver asked me to wait a moment as his friend checked out the place. I suspected that they were guards of some kind for me. Just as long as they didn't try to hang around inside with us, I was fine with them. *"What do you think, Kristair? Is the house clean?"*

"I would be very surprised if the Syndicate knows I own this place. I have not made it a point to visit and the upkeep has always been done through an intermediary."

"Why keep it if it bothers you so damn much?"

All I got back was another mental shrug, and I bit down my rising frustration. It was amazing how little I could get from him when he was like this. How I could share someone's thoughts and emotions and still not understand all his layers was a problem I'd never get straight.

Once the all-clear was given by the guard, I stalked inside the house and shut the door in the man's face. If they wanted to keep an eye on me, they could do it from outside. I shook my head when Kristair retreated deeper into my mind as I locked the door. "Nope, we're having this out before you drive me outta my mind."

Kristair's confusion followed me as I started up the stairs. *"What is there to have out?"*

"Please, just get out of my head so I can look at you."

There was a momentary pause and I sensed Kristair's vast reluctance before he did as I asked. As he appeared ahead of me on the stairs and walked on, he didn't look back. There was something about his quiet dignity that seemed very vulnerable to me. His nakedness only added to the impression.

I followed him into a small bedroom and frowned in confusion as he went to the double doors that opened out onto a balcony. He stepped outside and laid his hands on the railing, staring out, his mind a chaotic mix of sorrow, anger, and loss.

I reminded myself that no one else could see him naked, and joined him. It occurred to me then that I had never seen such an open expression on his face. Everything he was feeling showed in the downturn of his lips and his lined brow.

I couldn't begin to imagine Kristair letting anyone else see him like this, so off balance and upset. Only me. Somehow it helped to put things into perspective. With anyone else, he would've gathered his composure around him like a mantle, shrouding himself behind his poise.

My heart twisted, ached, and filled. If it was possible to fall in love all over again, I think I just had, and all because Kristair was lost in thought and miserable and letting me see him in this state. How many times had I argued with him about the walls he had up? Now there wasn't any kind of barrier.

I wanted to touch him so damn bad and gather him close. I settled for wrapping a mental arm around his shoulder as he stared out at a city sparkling with lights and heavy with sounds that cities all over the world seemed to make. "I didn't think it would've changed so much."

"It's been a long time, Kristair." I glanced down, trying to see it as Kristair had known it, but even with his memories, I couldn't grasp it. It was too different from what I knew, seemed more like looking at a memory of a movie than reality. "What made you leave?"

"My Mistress was gone and the city was falling apart from the inside out. The Empire was failing and Rome had already been sacked once, destroying everything we had, when I decided to go. There was going to be another invasion; it was only a matter of time."

"If you hated it so much why didn't you leave earlier?"

"At first I wasn't allowed to. I was a prisoner until my Mistress thought I'd learned enough to not embarrass her. Then I had nowhere else to go. Or at least that's what I believed."

I glanced at Kristair's face and noticed he wasn't really looking at the city, but at a long-gone memory. So this wasn't the house where Nerissa had taken him after she'd made him a vampire. I wasn't sure why, but it made me feel better.

"No, it's not," Kristair said, glancing back at the townhouse. "There are some belongings of hers that I'd saved and returned here and the land is hers, but I had this built later, after Kayla came to me. I thought the property should belong to her and that she should have something to go to, some remnant of her ancestry, if she wished."

"You're a good dad, Kristair." It kind of made me wonder what it would be like if things were different. If he were human and we weren't caught up in such a supernatural mess. What would it be like to raise a family with him? I'd never had those kinds of thoughts before, and damn, I must have been more tired than I'd thought if I was having them now.

He laughed, but there was no real humor in it. "Your opinions are prejudiced." He turned away from the balcony, some of his upset sloughing off under renewed determination. Now that was the Kristair I knew. "The city still stinks though," he said with a snide twist to his lips.

"So says the man who lived in Pittsburgh during the steel era. Now whose opinion is prejudiced?"

"There's a different heartbeat to Pittsburgh. It's built on toil and common folk. The steel mills may have left their mark, but at least it was honest work. Rome is imperial self-indulgence, corrupt and rotting from the inside out."

All the bits and pieces were beginning to come together. Kristair had already been set against what this place had stood for, given his people's war with the empire. Being brought here against his will would've been enough to give him a grudge, but it went even deeper than that. Kristair valued self-possession, moderation. For all of his own wealth, he lived in an unassuming manner. Given the way Rome was when he was here, he would've been disgusted and horrified by its excesses.

"Do you intend to go out and explore?"

Another time I would've jumped at the chance. Pittsburgh had been the farthest away from home I'd ever been before and now I was on a whole other continent. But right now, the thought was unappetizing. As much as I was sure Kristair would dislike the thought of needing comfort, he did.

"No, I'd rather stay in. I'm beat."

A smile flickered over Kristair's face. "Your motives are transparent."

"Who cares? I might only have ten more days with you. Rome can wait for another day. Why don't you show me where the bed is?"

The quick whiplash of longing that went through Kristair made me want to pull him into my arms. The fact that I couldn't do that *and* watch the surrender I knew would be on his face was maddening.

I followed him as he turned back inside, locking the balcony doors as he drew the curtains shut, plunging the room into dark shadows. I pulled off my shirt, fumbling toward him in the dark. The tension in his body eased as I put my hands on him and pulled him close. He threw himself into my kiss with wholehearted abandon, surrendering to the moment without one hint of reservation.

I loved him so damn much I didn't know how I could contain it, I ached so.

Chapter 24

"Now, tell me again why I'm doing this," I muttered as Hugh tossed the rope and hook up over the crumbling stone wall.

"*Because you don't listen to reason,*" Kristair grumbled in my mind.

"Why not?" Hugh grabbed the rope and tested its grip and security before clambering up, hand over hand, moving his bulk with incredible ease.

"*I think I prefer your explanation,*" I said to Kristair as I hauled myself up behind him.

As I crested the top, I saw the crumbling ruin of an abandoned school filling the courtyard. I crouched low on the top of the wall, peering through the shadows to figure out where the hell Hugh had gone.

"*Get down. You're too exposed up here,*" Kristair snapped.

I leapt down with a sigh. "*I'm not as used to all this covert stuff like you are.*" The dark, broken windows stared down at me like dead eyes. It was more than a little creepy. One of the shadows near the wall moved, making my heart jump until I realized it was Hugh. At least Ussier had taken Alette with him. I didn't think I could take her freaky intensity at that moment.

Tony dropped down behind me, followed quickly by Artemise. He unstrapped the cane off his back with a nostalgic smile on his lips.

224 | Marguerite Labbe

"Ah, raiding a Catholic girls' school. Now this brings back memories. Have you ever done that before, youngling?"

"Only in my dreams, though Jake and I did raid the girls' dorm with water guns during our freshman year."

Those were the days. I shared a grin with Tony at the memory. *"You mean Steve didn't tag along for that one?"* Kristair asked.

"Nope. He was actually working the security desk in the lobby. He's the one who let us in. He ended up losing his job over it and bitched about it for weeks."

"Where are Ussier and Madame Dupree?" Tony asked in a whisper as we moved deeper into the shadows.

"Doing things," Hugh grunted. I glanced at Tony and shrugged. That was all the info I'd been able to get out of Ussier before he'd taken off a couple hours earlier. "Jake and I are going to go ahead and get into position near the Council chamber and wait for Ussier," the big man said as he pulled out a modified blueprint of the old school. He pointed toward the old dormitories. "You're meeting your friends there, youngling. You sure they're in with us?"

"They were pretty excited about the idea even before I promised Artemise would speak to them." He gave Artemise a tight grin. "The thought of an Ancient being on their side has got them riled up, and they're sick of what the Council's doing. They're sure it's going to lead to their destruction. They'll go along with it."

"Okay. Get going then and good luck," Hugh said.

I caught Tony in a quick hug. "Be careful."

"You too," he whispered back.

I clasped Artemise's hand and then they were gone. Hugh gestured to the blueprint again, capturing my attention. "We'll go through the kitchens, kid. The Council chamber is on the second floor overlooking the inner courtyard." A scowl deepened the crags in his face. "The youngling has a trick of drawing shadows around himself and I can move without being seen. Ghedi says you know some things. Got any tricks like that?"

"I never worked on sneaking around," Kristair said. *"I think your best bet is to move quickly and silently. The sooner you're in place, the lesser the likelihood that you'll be spotted. Unless you feel like melding through the walls."*

"I'd rather be shot in the face." I shuddered. *"Sorry, Kristair. That's just freaky. Besides, the Ascended blocked anything new."*

I shook my head at Hugh. "Sorry, man."

"That's okay. This place has lots of hidey-holes and old servant passages. We'll take our chances."

"What happens if we get seen?"

"We'll have to take steps to make sure that doesn't happen, but if it does…." Hugh let the thought trail off ominously then pointed out the trail he wanted us to take.

"He means to kill them, doesn't he?" I asked Kristair.

"You can't be leaving possible enemies behind. This coup d'état of yours is going to be difficult to pull off if the Council gets advanced warning."

"But what if it's somebody who'd be on our side?" I argued.

"My suggestion is the same as Hugh's. Don't be seen. Then you won't have to worry about these little moral dilemmas."

Grumbling, I followed the vampire, amazed at how quietly he moved for such a big man. Bits of broken glass and stone rubble littered the ground and he didn't make a whisper of sound. The door to the kitchens was solid. I'd kind of expected it to be half hanging off the hinges and in as much disrepair as the rest of the place, but I guess the Syndicate wasn't entirely lax in security.

Their efforts didn't matter because it only took Hugh moments to break through the lock. The creak seemed too loud to my ears and I cringed. Hugh paused a moment then gestured for me to follow.

The lower-level windows were boarded up and the inside of the kitchens was pitch black. I had the impression of a cavernous space as my breathing seemed to echo in the room. After a few moments, my eyes adjusted to the gloom and I was able to make my way across a floor covered with trash and debris. From the scent of things, no one had been down here for a long time.

It was eerily quiet as we made our way toward the Council chamber. There were only a few people wandering the hallways and those were avoided with an ease that made me suspicious. *"I don't like this. I mean, I know we got rid of a whole bunch of their dudes, but I thought this place would be crawling with vamps. The Syndicate is a big organization, right?"*

"They don't all stay in one location. There are cells all over the world. The Syndicate is more of a network than a place for them all to congregate. The Council itself is here. That's all that matters."

"And what if the Council isn't here?"

"Tony's contacts indicated they've been meeting often as of late. Do you trust his information or not?"

It's not that I didn't trust him. Nerves were making me second-guess everything. *"I guess that makes sense. Their shenanigans back in Pittsburgh must be keeping their attention occupied. I just wish I knew what they really wanted, and I don't like the idea of them causing all this mayhem on the say-so of a psychic."*

"It'll all be over soon."

Hugh gestured toward a well-lit corridor. According to the blueprint, the entrance to the Council chambers should be around the corner. I sensed Kristair leave my mind and started visibly when he appeared in front of me, sauntering naked to the corner.

"Kristair! What the fuck do ya think yer doin'!"

"They can't see me. I just want a peek to see what we're up to. Don't worry. I can't go far from you."

"Kristair! Get yer pretty ass back here. Dammit, Kristair, I mean it!"

My lover gave me a cheeky smile then disappeared around the corner. Hugh was watching me with a skeptical expression on his face. "You okay, kid?"

"Just peachy fucking keen." I scowled in the direction Kristair had gone. "What now?"

"Now we wait for the signal. Ghedi and Alette are taking care of what they need to do and your friend and Artemise should be arriving soon." Hugh pressed his ear to a door then opened it before motioning me in ahead of him.

"There are two guards outside the doors. Tony's friends were right. The Council is in session. I couldn't get close enough to peek inside, but the guards are talking between themselves."

"*Fine,*" I snapped. *"Can ya come back now?"*

"If it'll get you to stop swearing at me. I'm perfectly safe."

Relaxing some, I glanced around the room Hugh had stuck us in. It was an office and one of the few rooms I'd been in inside this heap that was actually in use. A computer hummed on a battered desk and books were scattered across every surface. It reminded me of Kristair's old office, only less neat.

Curious, I started picking through the books, which seemed to be journals for the most part. Kristair would be interested in that. I glanced up to see him walk through the door as Hugh finished his quick examination of the room and locked the door before turning toward me. "I should be back in time for the signal. I want to check a couple things out."

"Wait a minute," I hissed in exasperation. Hugh's body went filmy and indistinct before he turned into mist and slipped out under the door. I turned my glare on Kristair instead. "This is really beginning to piss me off."

"You could follow him, I suppose, but it would take time and concentration for you to turn into the mist. You don't concentrate very well when you're irritated. Oh wait, no, you can't." He grinned. "And even if you could, it freaks you out."

"I thought I was supposed to be the smartass in the relationship." I ran my hand through my hair and fisted it, barely feeling the sting. It had been too easy; made me think of a trap. "Something's off. I don't like this."

"You're not becoming psychic on me, are you?" Kristair's voice was light, but his dark eyes were penetrating as he studied me. Disquiet stirred in his mind as well.

"That's not even remotely funny." I cocked my head at the sound of a woman's shout of outrage, muffled as it was through the doors and passages. There was something about that voice....

"Kayla!" Kristair gasped and bolted through the door. *"Stay inside."*

"The fuck I will." My heart pounding, I fought the lock, threw open the door, and chased after him, honing in on the sound of Kayla's continued shouts. What the hell was that woman doing here? I swear, if she followed me....

The two guards in front of the doors jumped when I burst around the corner. I felt Kristair pop into my head again and we were on them before they had a chance to shout for backup.

"Jacob, I don't think barging in there is such a good idea!" Kristair shouted in my head. But, by then, it was too late. I'd already knocked the guards aside and flung open the door.

Several men and a single woman sat around a long oval conference table. Tied up, lying in the middle of that table, was a struggling Kayla, furiously cursing. What I wouldn't give for fireballs now. I'd torch every motherfucker in the room.

I bounded up onto the table while they were still half-turning, their mouths falling open with expressions ranging from shock to dismay to pleasure. There was a shout behind me from the guards as I began to yank at the bonds around Kayla's wrists. She fought me off, shoving at me, trying to tug her hands free of the rope as her struggles redoubled.

"Stop fighting me!" I roared.

Kayla yanked the gun out of my waistband and half-sat up, leaning to the side, and unloaded the clip. I cursed as a wet spray hit the back of my neck and scrambled back off the table, dragging Kayla with me and shoving her behind my back. "There's a knife in my pocket," I said in an undertone. "Cut yourself free."

"Stop!" one of the councilmen ordered in a ringing voice as the second guard closed in on me. The conference table stood between us and the door, not to mention the entire Syndicate Council. Fuck. How the hell where we supposed to get out of this one? "Leave them both with us." He gestured to the other guard on the table, who was scrabbling, trying to right himself in the bloody mess Kayla had made of him. "Take that with you."

I lifted my newly loaded gun and pointed it toward the guard, feeling Kayla struggle behind me. "How's it going back there?"

"It's coming. At least, you managed to loosen them somewhat."

"Back off," I warned the guard. He did, pausing to bow before the Council members. He tossed the other guard over his shoulder and left.

Great. Just great. Now what was I gonna do? Another one of the Council members shut the door, locking it behind the guard. There were only six of them. *"We can take them. Can't we, Kristair?"*

"These are not younglings, Jacob. You won't find them to be so easy. And there's Kayla to consider. She could get hurt in a struggle. Let's not be so hasty. They seem inclined to talk. Let them. It's not as if you're truly alone here, so stall for time."

"Please sit," one of the councilmen said, gesturing to the blood-smeared table. "We've heard quite a bit about you. Nothing that would've led us to believe you'd charge in here so rashly, but intriguing nonetheless. Maybe we were wrong about you."

"Yeah, you were. I thought it was me you wanted. You royally fucked up by bringing Kayla into this."

"The Ancient One left his secrets behind to someone. When the little girl in Pittsburgh told us it wasn't you, that left this Kayla Mercer. It had to be someone close to him. It made more sense anyway. She'd been with him for years before you."

I breathed a sigh of relief as Kayla slipped my knife back into my pocket. She was free. I reached back and handed her the gun, then drew out the knife for myself. I could do a lot of damage with Kristair's abilities and that blade. "She doesn't have what you want and, like you said, I don't either, so we're leaving."

"I don't think so. Neither one of you is going anywhere." He pressed an intercom on the table. "Bring in Chaziel and some extra bindings."

I glared at each vampire in turn. None of them made a move toward me and Kayla, but they didn't seem all that concerned about our weapons either. I got the impression they could take them from us at any time with considerable ease. With any luck, Hugh was already back in the room where he'd left me and cursing my absence. Please god, let him be looking for me.

Another one of the councilmen approached, moving cautiously, but stopping out of reach. "So you're the one who killed Roland Montrose."

"That's right, and if you get any closer you're next."

Kayla pressed against my back. Though she was tense, the gun she had pointed in their direction was rock steady. "You'd better have a damn good plan, Jake."

"Trust me."

"This is not a damn adventure," she grumbled, then raised her voice to address the Council members. "Who's Chaziel and what's he got to do with us?"

The lone councilwoman gave us a thin smile then sat down on one of the chairs seeming at ease, though I suspected it was a show. The set of her shoulders and the tiny line between her brows betrayed her nerves. "Chaziel is the one who's going to get into your heads and tell us what we need to know." She tilted her head to the side and I felt the brief touch of another mind try to probe my own, which I shoved away with a stinging slap. Behind me Kayla shuddered.

"Keep your filthy mental fingers away from us," I snarled.

"You have good shields, both of you, but we can wear you down. If nothing else, listening to each other scream should weaken your will," she said with a chilling smile. She reminded me of an evil, scrawny bird with her sharp features and inhuman eyes.

Kristair's mind stiffened in fury. His outrage must've shown on my face because the one closest to me took a hasty step back. "You have no idea what you're fucking with," I snarled. "But it really doesn't matter because you're all fucked to begin with."

The councilman who had spoken first laughed. Before I could ask him what the fuck was so funny they all leaped toward me as one.

Kayla's gun went off as I began to move, letting Kristair meld with my actions until, once again, we moved as one.

I tried staying close to Kayla, but each feint and attack drew me further away from her. The sound of the gun stopped and I turned to toss her another clip as one of the vamps clocked her in the back of the head. She crumpled into a heap onto the floor, the gun falling out of her hand.

I rushed toward her with a roar of outrage and shouted again as the rest drove me down. There was a hard blow against my temple and I struggled against the darkness, until another blow dragged me down.

Chapter 25

"JACOB, wake up. Please, mo chroí. *"*

I wasn't sure if it was Kristair's voice that brought me around or the excruciating pain in my shoulders. The moment it slammed into me, I wished for oblivion again. I sensed Kristair try to take some of the pain on himself and it eased a bit, though not enough to stop my groan. My head was fuzzy and my stomach roiled with nausea.

"He's already coming around," someone whispered. "Perhaps he is the one."

"Then she's expendable?"

"No, not yet. What do you think, Chaziel?" The voices echoed and the air smelled of cold, rusty dampness, as a steady dripping sounded from somewhere in the room.

"Let's not be hasty, sir. We've waited too long to get them. Now that we have them, let's be sure."

"Send some others up to the Council chambers. He may have brought friends," the woman said.

I tried to move, but it brought a new wave of white-hot pain that shot through me, banishing the fog. I bit back a scream, tasting blood on my lips, and opened my eyes. I had the quick impression of old tiles, mirrors spider-webbed with cracks, and broken stall doors. I was slumped against the wall, though nobody was holding me up.

What the hell? I shook my head in disorientation and turned it to see a silver stake driven through my shoulder, pinning me to the wall. An equal pain in the other shoulder told me there was one there too. Clammy sweat broke out on my brow and I retched, tasting bile in the back of my throat. *"Oh fuck, Kristair, oh fuck. What the fuck!"*

"It'll be okay, mo chroí. Once you're free you'll be able to heal the damage," he tried to soothe, though he was even more upset than I was over the situation. *"They took you to the showers in the lower level. There are guards all over the place."*

"Where's Kayla?" I shouted, terrified by her silence. *"Fuck, Kristair, what if they've done the same to her? What if—"*

"She's okay, for the time being. Unconscious and tied up, but that is it. They consider you to be more dangerous."

"Lucky fucking me." Oh fuck, it hurt, even more than when I'd been shot. It was hard to think around the agony that consumed me.

"You're lady friend is quite okay." The first councilman came into my line of sight. "And she'll remain that way if you cooperate." He made a gesture and another man approached his side, a young Indian-looking dude, with a high-peaked forehead and dusky skin. "You will let Chaziel into your mind and every time you resist the girl will be hurt. Wake her up," he ordered.

I clenched my teeth and took a deep breath, straining against the spikes in my shoulders. The pain increased a hundredfold and I slumped against the tiles, fighting to keep from hurling. My head spun with the agony and fury. Where the fuck was Ussier? Where the fuck was anyone?

"Kristair, we can't let this happen!"

"I'm aware of that."

"Then come up with something! You're supposed to be the brains!" I finally spotted Kayla as the vampires who were standing in front of her moved aside. She had been dumped onto a chair with her hands tied behind her back. She was slumped over, still unconscious. The vamp grabbed her by her hair and slapped her across the face several times until her lashes fluttered. "Wha…?"

Kristair snarled inside my mind, growling curses. Damn, if only he could take form now, because those guys wouldn't stand a chance in hell.

"Welcome back, Ms. Mercer." The vamp stepped back and Kayla cried out as her eyes lit on me. She struggled against her bonds, trying to stand up.

"Jake! What did those bastards—"

There was a sharp crack as one of them slapped her again, the imprint of his hand standing out sharp and red against her cheek. "Shut up," he said flatly then nodded to a young boy standing in the background next to a huge brute. "Let's show the human how serious we are."

The duo came forward and the big guy grabbed Kayla as the kid ripped open her shirt. Kayla shouted and kicked the boy in the chest, sending him stumbling back as the brute dragged her toward the open showers. "GET YOUR FUCKING FILTHY HANDS OFF HER!" I roared, venting all of Kristair's and my fury.

Kayla shrieked as the big guy turned on the water, holding her under the spray, and my eyes widened in horror as the boy approached her with a cattle prod. No, they wouldn't, not when that guy was still holding her. "No, wait! Don't!" I tried to move forward and gasped as a lurching wave of pain washed over me.

"Do something! She's your daughter. You can't let this happen."

"I CAN'T!" Kristair shouted in frustration and rage, making my temples pound even more. It wasn't fair. Kristair was as helpless as I was, if not more so. What was happening to both of us sickened him.

The kid's expression was vicious as he approached Kayla. I could only watch in rising horror as he touched the prod to her chest. Her screams pierced the air, but the goon holding her only laughed when his arm smoked, as if he got his rocks off on the pain, both Kayla's and his own.

Then it was over and Kayla sagged, whimpering as the water ran over her. The vamp looked at me, a sick smile on his face, and I imagined my hands tightening into claws. If I'd had the strength, I'd rip myself from the wall and tear him to shreds.

"Wait, Kristair. You can take me over, right? You can do it, pull me free."

"Jacob, the damage—"

"Ah don't care about no fucking damage! Ah'll heal. Just fuckin' do it!" I steeled myself against the pain that would come, but Kristair was already mentally shaking his head.

"You still have a mortal body. You'd pass out and when you woke up again you'd be in the same spot and weaker. We can't do it."

The chairman stopped in front of me, his gray eyes alight in anticipation. When I got a hold of him, he was gonna wish he'd been the one in the shower. "I'm not sure how much she can take. Ari can hold her for however long I want and if he needs to feed to heal, she'll be rather handy. So I suggest you think about that long and hard." The vamp gestured to Chaziel. "You may start."

"Jacob, I need you to relax as fully as you can," Kristair urged. *"You need to concentrate past the pain."*

"What fucking good is that going to do?"

"Remember how Hugh changed into the mist? You can do that, but you have to let go of the pain and the fear you have of changing. You have to trust me. The Ascended couldn't have foreseen this. It's at least worth a try."

I fought harder as Chaziel approached. I couldn't even make my fingers twitch, but I kicked. And every jolt sent more agony through my shoulders until I sagged, gasping for air, my chest aching and frozen as the pain stabbed repeatedly throughout my entire body.

"Please, mo chroí, you're only hurting yourself further."

I jerked my head to the side as Chaziel's hands came up to touch my temples. "Get away from me! And don't you dare touch her again!" I shouted, so infuriated I could barely hear Kristair's pleas in my mind.

Chaziel's fingers dug in and I cried out at the mental stab, the touch of his mind oily and obscene. I felt contaminated by it. Kristair retaliated, whipping out a thought, slashing at Chaziel's psyche, and the vampire staggered back from me, clutching his head with a shout. Once again, Kayla's screams echoed throughout the bathroom along with the sizzling jolt of electricity.

"There's someone else in his mind," Chaziel rasped, shaking his head and staring at me with glittering eyes. "I'm sure of it now. He is the key."

The head vamp lurched toward me with such hunger in his expression that a slither of fear penetrated through my rage. "Tell me what I want to know. Give me the secret to immortality."

"Fuck you," I snarled.

The vamp's face went dark with fury. He grabbed the spikes in my shoulders, wrenching and twisting them until metal ground against bone and flesh. I screamed, unable to hold it in. Vaguely I heard through the mind-numbing torment, "Get the girl again. Longer this time."

I fought the darkness trying to take me under and I fought Kristair, not hearing what he was saying. However, his will was stronger than my own. Gently, he stole over me, taking possession of my body and forcing my mind to retreat back. *"What are ya doing?"*

"The only thing I can do under the circumstances." Kristair's frustration lashed out, until he got it under control again. *"I know, I promised you I wouldn't do this, but I can't watch them torture you anymore. At least I can help you somewhat."* With that, he cut off all sensation to my body. The blessed relief was so overwhelming it took me a moment to realize he hadn't done the same for himself. He was still experiencing the same agony I had been.

"Leave her alone," Kristair snapped coldly through my mouth, the timbre of my voice changing to match his. "She is not a part of this."

The vamp stepped back in startled surprise, his eyes widening. Chaziel gasped. "It's him. It's the Ancient One."

Kristair tensed as the doors burst open. I cried out in relief inside his mind when Tony strode in with a number of others right behind him, including Artemise. Oh thank god, thank fucking god.

"What is the meaning of this?" the vampire holding Kayla snapped. "Explain yourself, youngling."

The councilman in charge turned away from me and gestured to some of his goons. "Just kill him. Kill them all."

"No, wait. I know the secret," Tony said, stepping forward. "I know what you're looking for and I'll share it with you, but you have to let them go first."

"Kill them," the leader snarled. The vampires behind Tony pulled out weapons as the rest of the Council and their guards started forward. Imminent violence hung in the air as both sides eyed each other.

"Wait," Chaziel said, throwing out his hand and staring hard at Tony. "He's telling the truth."

Kristair went terribly still as horror stole over him. His will wavered, letting me have control over my own body again. I bit my lip, tasting blood as the agony slammed into me again. I almost passed out as he cursed in my mind. *"Get your idiot friend to shut up,"* he said with terrible intensity.

"Tony! Don't!" I didn't understand what had Kristair so upset, but his urgency infected me. *"I don't understand. How can he know, Kristair?"*

"You went too deep with him. The connection was too strong," Kristair hissed in frustration. *"It had to have been then."*

Tony's gaze flickered toward me, then to Kayla, and his mouth tightened. "Well, Castillo, what will it be?"

"Give me the secret and I'll let them go."

Artemise stepped forward, his cane tapping on the tiles in the sudden silence that followed Castillo's counteroffer. Tony closed his mouth on the retort I know he was dying to give. "Don't be ridiculous, child. We'll have no leverage once you have the secret. Release them." He looked us over critically. "It's not as if either Kayla or Jake is in any condition to run."

The tension stretched out, but then Castillo made a little half-bow toward Artemise. "As you say, Ancient One. Let them go."

The big man sneered, but shut off the water and set Kayla down half-senseless on the chair. He glanced at Castillo and at the man's nod, cut her bonds. She clutched the ragged ends of her shirt together and crossed her arms, lifting anxious eyes to me.

"Now Jake," Tony said, with a grim glance at the spikes in my shoulders.

Castillo made an impatient sound and moved out of the way, gesturing to the hulk. "Go ahead."

I braced myself as the vampire approached me, but all the mental psyching in the world couldn't prepare me for what I felt when he ripped those goddamn spikes out of my body. I fell forward with a sharp scream, my legs giving out on me. I writhed on the ground sobbing, until the pain receded enough for some sense to return. I felt Kristair applying mental pressure, easing the bleeding, and then warmth spread through my shoulders as he began to knit the muscle back together over the gaping, mutilated holes.

I glanced over and found Kayla out of her chair, fallen onto the tiles. She clenched her jaw together, her eyes fierce, as she dragged her way over to me. Everyone stared, but no one tried to stop her. "Are you okay?" she asked, kneeling next to me, touching my shoulder as she bit her lip.

"Nice boobs," I said, the corners of my mouth lifting in a devilish smile. Kayla gave a laugh that sounded suspiciously like a sob.

"Ass." She blinked back tears and brushed a wet trickle of blood off my chin. "I love you."

"Ditto."

"Your friends are free," Castillo said, spreading his hands. "However, you'll understand if I don't hand them over to you right away. Otherwise, I'll lose my leverage." His eyes narrowed on Tony. "The secret now, youngling, or she dies."

Tony glanced at me. I struggled to push myself up and wrapped my arms around Kayla, trying to shield her as best as I could. They couldn't strike at her without hitting me first.

"Do you really want me to share it with everyone in this room?" Tony asked in contempt.

I'd give Tony marks for becoming cleverer in the past year, or at least warier. "You will share it with us all," the councilwoman said with a snarl. The tension in the room tightened when Castillo hesitated.

"Of course," he nodded in her direction, his voice smooth. "With us all."

Kristair sped up the healing process he'd been doing in my shoulders, forcing a gasp from me as the flesh knit together, pulling, itching, and sending a wave of dizziness through my head. Drawing away the lingering pain, he bolstered my strength and gave me a mental nudge. *"Stop him,"* he hissed. *"Stop Tony, before it's too late."*

"He won't tell them. He's stalling. Ussier's somewhere around. He won't give up when help is so close."

"He's running out of time. Castillo is not going to wait!"

"Fine; have it your way," Tony started. There was a flash of steel behind him as one of Tony's companions raised his sword. Everything seemed to freeze.

"NO!" I shouted in horror as it slashed down and Tony's head went flying. Kayla screamed and Artemise roared in fury, turning on Tony's murderer, raising his cane. The Council and their goons rushed toward the other faction, but Castillo turned on me as I jumped to my feet and ran toward my friend. A blazing golden light surrounded him and the body disappeared.

"What the fuck!"

"Jacob, you and Kayla get out of here now! The Ascended took Tony."

"But that means...."

"GET OUT!"

Castillo grabbed a hold of me, fingers stabbing the still-healing wounds. He snarled when he found whole flesh. Though, it was still tender enough to make me flinch. Out of the corner of my eye, I saw Kayla dart over and grab the discarded cattle prod as I tore myself free. "How do you think you'll like it?" Kayla asked with a malicious smile as she shoved it down his pants and danced back out of the way. The vampire went down with a roar of pain.

There was a crash of glass as Ussier came through one of the windows, followed by Alette. I grabbed Kayla's hand. "Time to go."

I snatched up Castillo's fallen gun as the vampire tried to get the prod out of his pants and shot him several times in the chest. He fell back, body twitching as electricity continued to course through him. When he opened his mouth to scream, blue bolts sizzled between his teeth and smoke began to pour from his mouth, nose, and ears, and the reek of burning flesh assaulted my nose.

Hugh came through the main door, his scowl darker than normal. "Come on, kid." I fought another wave of dizziness as I shoved Kayla toward him and dodged my way through the fighting crowd.

"What's wrong with me?"

"You lost a lot of blood. I used even more to heal you and that takes an enormous amount of energy. You need to eat."

"You mean feed?" I asked, sickened by the thought as we reached Hugh. He fell in behind us, guarding our backs as we left the battle behind.

"No, Jacob. You're still human. Food and sleep will suffice."

"Faster," Hugh ordered, scooping up Kayla before taking off down the hallway in a blur of speed. "This place is going to blow in two minutes."

"That sounds like Ussier. He was probably laying charges earlier. He likes to be thorough, especially when he's out of town. Better get moving."

I bit back a curse and bolted after Hugh like I had the football and my team needed one more touchdown to win the game with fifteen seconds left on the clock.

Chapter 26

JET lag was the world's biggest bitch. I could hear Kristair calling me urgently. I stirred, felt his rough hands cradling my face. *"Jacob, mo chroí?"*

My bones ached as memory came rushing back. Memories of night air against my skin, exhaustion dragging me down, the fierce heat and brilliance of an explosion and then welcoming darkness. I opened my eyes with a groan and smiled up into my lover's anxious eyes. "Hey there, gorgeous. I'm awake. Stop fussing."

Kristair's relief flooded through me, a smile tugging on his lips. *"Welcome back. You were starting to scare me."*

"Talking to yourself?" Kayla stepped up to my side with a tray in her hands and sat down on the edge of my bed. Wait. My bed? I sat up and stared around my room in the dorm in surprise.

"Whoa." Had it all been just a freaky dream? "When the hell did we get back?"

"Crack of dawn this morning. You just missed Steve. He dropped this off for you." She set the tray on my lap as I sat up. It was then that I noticed the dark circles under her eyes and lines of weariness around her mouth. I was still wearing my clothes from our raid, bloodied, tattered, and singed. It was surreal to have Kristair lounging next to me and Kayla sitting on the other side. Then my gaze fell on the food in front of me and I couldn't think anymore.

Kayla remained silent as I devoured the omelets, toast, and orange juice. There was enough on the tray for the both of us with food left over, but I ate every damn bite and I think I could've eaten more.

"I'm sorry," I started, and she shook her head.

"Uncle Ghedi said you'd need it after all the healing you did. You were hurt in the explosion too. Hugh had thought you were closer to us than you actually were."

The memory wasn't clear. It was full of weaving walls and echoing screams. *"You'd used too much of your will, not just in healing yourself, but with expending your strength running and fighting. The toll finally caught up with you."* A sensation of lingering fear and anxiety still clouded Kristair's thoughts. *"I couldn't reach you. I could see that your body was whole, but I couldn't reach you inside your mind."*

I could only imagine how terrifying it had been for the both of them. "Guess I needed to sleep, and eat. Thanks," I said to them, then set the tray aside and combed my fingers through my hair. It was damned embarrassing, knowing I'd passed out like that, regardless of the circumstances. "How are you? Oh, wait. Steve." She'd said I'd missed him. I needed to call him, tell him about Tony. Only I wasn't ready to face that yet. I still couldn't wrap my brain around what had happened. It was too unreal. Had it really happened? I couldn't have lost him again.

"No, don't worry about it. I already talked with him about everything."

"And he still let you hang out here looking like you're about to fall over?"

"He's not my daddy. It's time he remembered that." Kayla crossed her arms. That argument had to have been a doozy. "I think it's time for some answers, Jake."

Kristair stirred and I sent out a soothing thought. *"She deserves answers, love, especially after what she just went through. Besides, she's your daughter, and as somebody else who loves you, I know I wouldn't be happy about not being told."*

"You wield pressure very well." Kristair grumbled, but his heart wasn't in it. To be so close to Kayla and not have her know he was okay bothered him a great deal. *"Do what you think is right. You will anyway."*

I almost gave him a snippy comeback, when the truth hit me. No, I wouldn't, not if he asked me to. Anybody else and I'd go with my gut reaction, whether it was wrong or right, but Kristair I actually listened to. Sometimes.

"At least that's something."

"You haven't slept a bit, have you?" I asked Kayla. She was still wearing her jeans from the previous night, though someone had given her a T-shirt to wear in place of her torn blouse. I should've been awake and taking care of her. It irked me that someone else had.

"You're not going to get me off your back that easily. Spill it, Corvin."

"Give me a minute to figure out how to say it. It's complicated even with all the madness we've been living through." After a moment, I took her hand in mine. "Remember when I came to see you in your office?"

"Yeah. Feels like ages ago. I can't believe we're still in the same week."

"Me neither." I'd had enough action-packed adventure to last me two lifetimes. "Remember how I said I thought I sensed Kristair the night before and we talked about knowing whether he was really gone or not?"

Kayla tensed, her eyes searching my face before she drew herself up straight. "He's not, is he?"

I let out an explosive breath. At least she hadn't gone nutso on me. "No. The day we were first kidnapped, I came home to find him here." I ran through everything that had happened, including Kristair's promise to the Ascended, and she listened without interrupting, an expression on her face I couldn't read.

She rose, went to the window, and stared out of it for a long time. Kristair turned to watch her and I wished I could touch him. It occurred to me that I could do what my lover always did for me, so I mentally wrapped my arms around him and was rewarded with his warm rush of gratitude.

"So you're saying he's in this room. He's here right now," Kayla said.

"Yes."

"And I'm not allowed to talk to him or see him?" The catch in her voice gave me a pang of regret. I rose to go to her, but then she spun around to face me, her eyes wet and furious. "What kind of fucked-up shit is that?"

"I think those were my exact words." She believed me. I'd been sure she would think I was crazy. "But we're working on it. We still have time before…." I paused, my words trailing off as Kayla froze and Kristair hissed. "Kayla?" I waved my hand in front of her face, but got no response.

"She can't hear you, or see you for that matter," another woman's strangely choral voice said behind me. "We are between time, in a manner of speaking, and she is still in the ordinary world."

"What are you doing here?" Kristair demanded as I turned around looking for the speaker. I don't think I'd ever heard his voice be so cold as it was now.

The woman appeared to be older than Kristair and me. There was something familiar about her, though I swear I'd never seen her before. Her honey-brown hair was caught up in a fancy knot on the back of her head with ringlets cascading down. She was dressed in a toga with scarlet edging around the hem and another piece of scarlet cloth draped over one shoulder. Rings adorned her fingers and multiple bracelets clasped her wrists.

"Just who the hell are you?"

"Don't be foolish, boy. You know who we are."

I looked around in confusion, trying to figure out who she meant by all this "we" business. The strange multi-person timbre to her voice was unsettling.

"You have no business being here," Kristair snapped as he rose to his feet and went to stand in front of me.

"Hush, Kristair. You've caused enough damage, and we're curious to see what your fascination with the boy is." A wave of choking fury went through my lover, but he didn't say a word, neither aloud or in his head. I stepped up beside him and glanced at his face, on edge at his silence. He glared at her, his eyes black with rage. Somehow, she'd gagged him with a thought and all the pieces fell into place. This was Kristair's Mistress.

"Leave him alone!" I shouted, my hands clenching into helpless fists.

"We don't think so. He's an interfering lout and we're growing rather tired of his pitiful attempts to prolong a life he should've left behind by now." She pointed to the bed. "Sit."

There was no shove and my feet didn't move, but I found myself sitting on the bed, next to my lover. I started to pull myself to my feet again. "What if I don't—" Then I found myself to be just as voiceless and paralyzed as Kristair.

Fuming, I crossed my arms and glared at her. To my further irritation, she only smiled and walked over to Kayla. I could see the resemblance now. They possessed the same delicate features, though Nerissa's eyes were a rich brown and carried none of Kayla's easy affection, and there was a more worldly and arrogant expression on her face.

"You've done well with her. She's grown up strong," Nerissa said in approval, touching Kayla's cheek. "We should've known you'd keep your promise."

She glanced at Kristair and laughed as a surge of snarling possessiveness went through him. It bothered me that she could sense his emotions as well as I could. "You think she's yours?" She laughed again. "We could take her back anytime we wanted to, old friend, but that's not why we're here."

"Then please enlighten me," Kristair ground out. I opened my mouth to add my own opinion only to find myself still mute.

"Your time here is up." Her expression hardened when Kristair began to protest. "That debacle in Rome never should have happened. That youngling was on the verge of giving secrets he never should've had in the first place. Secrets you let out because you shared them with this boy!" She waved a hand in my direction. "Do you know what his inclusion into our ranks has done? He wasn't prepared for this."

"He had the strength of will to use it or else you never would've taken him in the first place. You would've let him perish."

"That's not the point!"

I didn't know if Tony was better being off dead or not. After everything Kristair said, being with the Ascended didn't seem like a heavenly paradise to me. "The point is the Syndicate didn't get what they wanted. They don't even exist anymore and I don't believe Tony had any intention of giving them the information. You know that as well as I, so why don't you tell me why you're really here?"

"As we said, your time is up. We know you didn't really need the two weeks, yet we gave it to you anyway. As of now, the offer is rescinded."

I jumped to my feet before I'd even realized I'd shoved off the compulsion to stay put and remain silent. "You can't do that!"

Nerissa's eyes widened in surprise and then she gave me an appreciative smile. "Well now, aren't you a surprise. You would've made quite a formidable vampire."

"No thanks. You promised him two weeks. I still have one more week with him."

"Not anymore. You have until dawn."

Kristair drew himself up straight. "You cannot make me."

Nerissa laughed, the sound containing just a touch of fondness, and reached up to touch Kristair's cheek. "My dear friend, how naive you still are. There are many ways to coerce, and some methods you've even used yourself in the past. Break the link, Kristair, or he's dead at dawn. That will also give us the results we want."

Kristair took a step forward, his face livid. "You will not harm him," he growled low in his throat.

"Not unless you force our hand."

I sensed Kristair's decision to back down before he said a word. "No! No, you're not going to take this bullshit!"

"I know them, Jacob. They're not lying and I'll not risk you." He shot me an apologetic glance then turned back to Nerissa. "May I ask one favor?"

"Of course. If we're able it's yours."

Kristair locked eyes with me, sorrow evident in his gaze, and I found I couldn't be angry anymore about his lack of putting up a fight. "If it's our last night, remove this ridiculous rule where I can't see him and touch him at the same time."

My stomach clenched, hope colliding violently with my sense of helplessness and despair. It wasn't fucking fair. What the hell had we ever done to the Syndicate or the Ascended to deserve them interfering in our lives? Though, if it wasn't for them, I never would've met Kristair at all. Still, I hated every last one of them.

"Very well. At nightfall," Nerissa agreed then pointed at Kayla. "And she cannot be here. This is just for the both of you. If anyone else sees Kristair, you'll revert back to the way you were."

"And privacy," Kristair said, his tone fierce and unbending. "Just him and I. You are to keep yourselves out of it."

"Ah, Kristair, only you would ask such a thing. No wonder you were always our favorite." She gave me an arch look, an appreciative glint in her eye. Anyone else and I might've grinned back or given her a wink, but this time I glared. She laughed again. "Agreed. You'll have your privacy. Until dawn then."

"Mistress," Kristair said by way of a goodbye, inclining his head ever so slightly. Then she was gone.

"What are we going to do?" I demanded, turning on Kristair.

"Jake? What are you talking about?" Kayla's voice sounded so faint that she had me spinning back around in alarm. Her face had lost all of its color and she was trembling.

"Christ!" I jumped forward and wrapped my arm around her waist, steadying her. *"What's going on?"*

"I'm not sure. Could be delayed reaction. She's gone through a lot lately and she didn't rest at all last night. Or it could be a reaction

to what my Mistress just did, or, for all I know, the Ascended could be causing it just to make sure she doesn't interfere."

"Is she going to be okay?"

"She'd better be."

"Stop fussing," Kayla said. "I'm fine."

"Bullshit. I'm getting you back to your room and calling Steve. We can argue about it tomorrow." Tomorrow, after Kristair was gone. Fuck, I couldn't take all this shit at once.

It didn't take me long to change and bundle her up. She barely argued, which worried me even more, but at least Steve was waiting for me when I got to her dorm. She didn't mention Kristair once, which meant either she was really out of it, or else somehow the Ascended erased our conversation from her mind.

"I'm not a baby," Kayla complained, trying to shake off my arm and glare at Steve. "I don't need you two hovering over me."

"Payback, *chica.* You did the same to me not even an hour ago." I gave her a light push and she sat down hard on her bed. "See, you're a pushover. Now take a nap or I'm going to start being mean."

"You already are mean. You called him." She pointed at Steve.

"Thanks, man," Steve said.

"No problem."

"I hate men." Kayla grabbed the knit blanket at the end of her bed and pulled it over herself. "Fine. I'll take a nap if you two will please leave."

"Lay down first and then we'll leave," Steve said.

Kayla rolled her eyes and stretched out. As soon as she did, a huge yawn struck her. Kristair sighed in relief. *"She'll be fine. I'm sure of it. They may have tampered with her, but she needs the sleep anyway."* There was a wistful note in his voice and, as impatient as I was to leave so we could make a game plan, I waited. This might be the last time he ever saw her.

No. It wouldn't. I refused to believe that. I was not going to lie down and give up. Not now. Not ever.

Kayla's eyes were already drifting closed when Steve caught my arm as I turned to go. "Is it true? What she said happened? Is Tony?"

"Yeah, he's gone." Even if he was one of the Ascended, he was out of our reach. It hadn't hit me yet, that he was gone. I wasn't sure it ever would. Maybe I was just numb after everything that had gone down. Or maybe I just couldn't believe it had all happened. Being in Rome seemed more like being in a dream than reality.

That seemed to be happening often lately.

"You'd have been proud of him though." An image rose in my mind of Tony standing there, staring down an older vampire. He'd been so smooth and certain… confident.

"You'll have to tell me about it."

"Yeah." I smiled as his gaze drifted to Kayla. "Not today, though. I'm going to go do what she's doing, probably until tomorrow." That should keep them both off my back.

"Get out of here, man. You're damn lucky neither of you were hurt, but I'll kick your ass for going out of the country and not taking me with you later."

Oh damn, she hadn't told him everything. But I let it lie and left after getting Steve's promise that he wouldn't leave Kayla. Maybe her omission was for the better anyway. Steve didn't need the images of her being tortured in his head any more than I did.

Kristair was just as quiet as I was as I wandered around the campus and then ventured out. For some reason I wasn't ready to go back to my room yet. The clock over the Mellon Bank said it was just before eleven. We had plenty of time before nightfall.

My cell phone rang and I winced when I saw Coach Latimer's number. I was gonna end up missing practice again. Fuck. I'd deal with the fallout tomorrow. At least it would give me something to concentrate on.

"It's kind of silly in the light of everything else, but I'm going to miss watching you play the game next weekend. I'd been looking forward to it," Kristair said.

"You'll see me play again."

I sensed Kristair's smile and he nuzzled close. *"I swear I'll be sitting with you at your table when you're drafted."*

"I know you will." I sat down on a bench, watching people go by. The wind had died down, but the cold was just as biting as ever.

Kristair's biggest worry was that somehow he'd forget about what we had, what I meant to him, or that it would cease to matter. Maybe that's why I couldn't wrap my head around the problem. It just didn't seem possible he could lose what we had. Even with his memories of what it was like with the Ascended, I couldn't understand.

Memories.

I jumped up as an idea hit me, practically dancing in excitement. It was so elegant and brilliant in its simplicity. I wondered why it hadn't come to us before. *"What? What is it?"* Kristair asked. *"Your thoughts are moving too fast."*

"Welcome to my world, love," I shot back, unable to contain my glee. *"What if you transferred all of my memories, a piece of my soul to you as well? You said I wouldn't lose that part of you, even if you broke the link, so that means you wouldn't lose that part of me either. No matter what the Ascended did."*

There was a breathless pause. Then Kristair laid such a mental kiss on my lips that I had to sit back down. *"That's perfect. The emotional link would be gone so it wouldn't set them off anymore and I wouldn't lose you, not really. I think it'll work!"*

"What do we need to do? What kind of paint did you use on me? Where can I find it?"

Kristair laughed. *"That will be easy to find. The harder part will be getting a tattoo gun and needles. We don't have time for an argument or a hard sell and I'm sure none of those guys in the local shops will be interested in letting you borrow their tools. You'll have to use your abilities to sway them."*

"Wait a minute. What happened to the paint? I liked the paint. You're really going to tattoo me?"

"Of course. Then you'll paint the design on me. Just be grateful there are tattoo guns now and you don't have to get them done the way I did. This is much quicker." Kristair nudged me up and I was walking

down the sidewalk before I realized I was moving. *"You'll have to say the words of the ritual as well."*

"But I don't speak that language. I don't even know where to start. And I'm not a very good artist either. What if I fuck it up? And do you even know how to use a tattoo gun?"

"My memories will guide your hand and your mouth. You just have to relax and slip into them." There was a pause then Kristair's voice turned teasing. *"You're not afraid of needles are you? I think it would be a little anticlimactic after getting your nipples pierced."*

"Don't be an ass. Of course not. Just wanted to make sure I'm still beautiful after you get your hands on me. How many tattoos will I need?"

"A few. We have a couple hours to prepare. In the meantime, I want you to think about significant events in your life, things you believe shaped who you are."

"Gotcha." I followed Kristair's directions toward a tattoo parlor he knew. With any luck, they'd be open. If not, I was more than ready to practice my breaking and entering skills again. The sun seemed to slide faster across the sky now. We had to hurry. Dawn wasn't too many hours away.

Chapter 27

I COULD barely keep still and knew my agitation was driving Kristair batty. I could hear him behind me at my cleaned-off desk, puttering around with whatever it was he needed to do so he wouldn't give in to his threat to tie me up and gag me. How he thought he was going to pull that one off eluded me.

Instead, I stared hard at the sun, watching it sink its way ever more slowly below the horizon. Later on I'd curse again about how quickly time was slipping by, but not now. Now I wanted Kristair's hands on me and to be able to look into his eyes as he touched me.

The sky darkened in little increments. Kristair lit the candles he'd had me purchase earlier, complaining under his breath about them not being homemade. I watched him walk up behind me in the glass, a sense of déjà vu hitting me as we looked at each other through our reflection. Then he slipped his arms around me, pressing close, and the wonderful shock of the contact rippled through me. I reached my hand around the nape of his neck and leaned back into his embrace.

Minutes slipped by as we held each other and watched. I could stay like this forever, but if we didn't get moving, we might not have forever. I turned my head, twisting to look up at him, my heart beating faster as I brushed my lips over his. "Ready?"

Kristair nodded then leaned down to kiss the puckered scar on the back of my shoulder. It would be a continual reminder of what had happened in Rome. Four new scars. I'd have a hell of a time explaining their sudden arrival at practice, but at least it was something I had been able to heal. If I had to rely on doing it the natural way, I might never have recovered enough to play at all.

It brought back another rush of memory I didn't want: Kristair realizing he had this limitless power and using it to heal me and save my life after Montrose shattered my spine with that bullet. Knowing he doomed himself at the same time.

Kristair would have that power again. This was going to work and he'd come back to me.

I stretched out on my back and watched Kristair intently as he brought his tools over to me. He cleaned the skin on my shoulder near the scar and laid down the transfer paper. When he peeled it back, the image he'd drawn was left on my skin. "Seems like you've done this before."

"I have." Kristair picked up the tattoo gun, adjusting the rubber bands before setting out the little pot of ink. "I've always followed the art. It wasn't something I wanted to lose. Before I made the deal with the university for my library, I was a tattoo artist." A smile flitted across his lips. "The hours were better."

As hard as I tried, I couldn't picture Kristair working in a tattoo parlor. Despite his own tattoos, he seemed too serious to me, too proper. "I'm not as dried up and old-fashioned as you make me out to be," he said with asperity.

"I'm not so sure about that," I teased. The gun whirred as Kristair turned it on and I watched curiously as he began outlining. It didn't hurt, not really. Felt more like a scratchy burn. But after having had spikes in my shoulders, and being shot, any sort of pain was relative. "So am I supposed to meditate or something?"

"Nope, just lie back and take it."

"Sounds kinky."

A little frown formed between Kristair's brows as he bent over me. He was so intent. It was a little sexy. "You know, we never broke out those body paints," Kristair said, with a quick glance up.

"The night's still young."

Kristair smiled, but I sensed in him the same anxiety I had, compounded by helplessness. The night may be young, but there was so much left to do. The worry faded as he concentrated again on his work and I distracted myself by watching the tattoo take shape on my skin.

It was an odd design, kind of tribal, and I wondered if it meant anything in particular or if it was just a pretty design. It reminded me of three interlocking stylized petals woven around a circle. "What is it?"

A faint smile appeared on Kristair's lips and he didn't look up but concentrated on what he was doing. There was such an odd sense of sudden shyness, so out of character for him that my curiosity roared to life. "Come on, Kristair, tell me."

"Our minds have been linked and our bodies, many times." He sat back and took up a wet wipe, cleaning the area he'd just gone over with the needle. He lifted his gaze to mine. "Now our souls will be linked. They may be able to take the first two from us, but not the third."

There was something more to it than that. As much as I liked the symbolism of that idea, it didn't account for the strange shyness which was still strong in his mind. "What else?"

"You know me far too well, *mo chroí*."

"I don't think that's possible. Now give it up."

Kristair traced a finger over the circle trisecting the symbol and I savored the simple touch. "It implies a commitment as well."

Understanding dawned. "Were you planning on asking me, Kristair, or informing me after the fact?" I teased, glancing in wonder at the symbol before meeting his gaze and brushing my thumb over his jaw.

"Didn't think I needed to."

"No, you didn't." I propped myself up, still looking deep into his eyes, and brushed an openmouthed kiss across his lips. "I'll be happy to tell everyone you're mine for the rest of eternity."

A glint appeared in Kristair's dark brown eyes, chasing away his uncertainty. "Maybe it's me laying my claim on you. Ever think about that, my smart-mouthed brat?"

"Nope. See, you may have been the one who started this relationship, but as much as you fight against your own natural instincts and fight against me taking control, you want me to. You crave it." I laid a hard kiss on his mouth, smiling as his lips softened. "And I'm not going to ask either. You're mine. You've always been mine. So if this tattoo represents some kind of marriage ceremony, then let's go. It'll be the first one I paint on you once you're done sticking needles in me."

"Thank you, I think," Kristair said dryly as he picked up the tattoo gun again. I could sense how pleased he was and couldn't help teasing him more. My lover just raised the devil in me.

"Does this make you the wife?"

Kristair's head jerked up and I started laughing. Indignant shouldn't be so sexy on a man, but Kristair did it well. "It's not wise to taunt the man who's tattooing you," he growled.

"You're not going to retaliate that way. Remember, whatever goes on me will end up on you too." I blew him a kiss. "And you've got way too much pride to put something permanently on you that's gonna be embarrassing."

"Doesn't mean I won't retaliate."

I chuckled. "Look forward to it, love."

Kristair brushed his fingers over my skin and shook his head with a wry smile. "I've never worked on someone who heals so fast. At least you won't be miserable tomorrow. Most of the tattoo designs are small, but the one on your side will take some time."

"How long?" I glanced at the clock, almost wishing I'd tossed it out the window earlier. I'd be staring at the damn thing all night.

"A couple of hours. Don't worry, Jacob. We'll be able to get everything done."

It wasn't just that. I wanted to make love to him again too. I bit back an impatient sound as Kristair adjusted another piece of transfer paper. My mind drifted as he continued to work until I found myself thinking of odd moments of my life, things I hadn't remembered in a long time. The taste of my grandmother's pecan pie. The scent of tobacco clinging to my dad's jacket and the sound of my mother humming as she cleaned our trailer or did laundry.

Before I knew it, several more small tattoos were scattered on my chest and Kristair was urging me to lie on my side. "What's happening to me?"

"We're binding who you are to these tattoos. Instead of spacing them out over your lifetime, we're doing it all at once. You're entering into a fugue state to evoke as much as possible. It's normal." Kristair pressed a kiss to my shoulder. "Lift your arm above your head. This one's going to take the longest and will probably be uncomfortable too."

"I'm a big boy." I watched him fiddling with the paper on my side, replaying earlier conversations in my head. "You never really answered me."

"Regarding?" He lifted his head and cocked it a little to the side as his mind touched my thoughts. "Ah, regarding whether or not you'll lose your abilities if the bond is broken?"

"Yeah, that. All you said was it's impossible to go back or something like that. Am I gonna still be Super Jake?"

"I don't know."

I raised my brow and then poked him in the side. "Come on, Kristair. You have an answer for everything, or at least a theory."

"Not this time. My gut instinct says you'll keep some of them, maybe all, but I cannot say for sure. The mind is a very mysterious organ and we only know a little about it. Who knows what may happen? I think that may depend more on you, and what you want, than any laws regarding magic. What it really comes down to is a matter of will. You're very strong-minded, Jacob. If you choose to forget them, then they may be forgotten. If you choose to exercise them, you may keep them. This has never been done before, not to my knowledge, at least."

"I guess there's no real sense worrying about it then," I said as Kristair opened a new bottle of ink. "We're committed either way now." Before he could start inking me again, I half sat up and kissed him. "I love you."

Instead of smiling as I'd expected, his face turned serious. "And I you. I need to reiterate this. I'm not giving up. Despite how it may have seemed when they shortened our time. I didn't want to waste my energy arguing when I could use the decision to wrest a boon from them." I sensed there was more he wanted to say so I remained silent. "And if... when this works, it's because of you."

"Okay, I'll admit I had an excellent idea, but you would've come up with it too or something else, with all your brains."

"That's not why it'll work, though you did come up with an excellent plan." Now Kristair smiled, a soft smile that I hadn't seen on his face before. "We'll win because of who you are, *mo chroí,* and because of your sheer tenacity."

I ran my hand over his scalp then tugged him down for a long, lingering kiss. "I don't care why we win, or how, even if it takes cheating, just as long as we do."

He laughed. "So says the man whose integrity won't let him accept an extra edge for his football games."

"That's different; that's a game. This is my life and there are no rules. Besides, they fucked with us first. I'm more than willing to fuck with them back."

Kristair started on the final tattoo, beginning at the top along my rib cage then working his way down. Once again, I found myself slipping into my memories, even deeper this time. So much so that I had a hard time remembering it wasn't reality. At first I fought them. I only had a few hours left with Kristair, after all. But then they slowly began dragging me under.

It was almost like reliving my life all over again and my sense of time passing disappeared altogether. I lingered on the memories that held Kristair, memorizing how his smile lit up his dark eyes, soothing away his too-serious demeanor. Or how I would get caught up in the swirl of his emotions or confused by how quickly his mind worked when he was sorting out a problem.

Before I knew it, Kristair's voice was pulling me out of my dreamworld, a place I found to be safe and sane and back into the real world where our time together was hanging on by a thread. I blinked up at him. "What time is it?"

"Nearing two." He smoothed back my hair then began cleaning up his supplies, creating room for a neat row on my cluttered desk. "What do you think?"

I glanced down at the tattoo that covered my left side. I'd expected a twin to the one on the right. It was similar in size and design, but with thinner lines and less blocky than the other one. "I like it."

I was surprised to find it was true. When had I crossed the line between putting up with the tattoos to now enjoying the look and feel of them? I couldn't figure out when that had happened, but it seemed significant somehow. I grinned at my lover. "I'm sure Coach won't feel the same."

"I expect you'll survive his wrath and your Ma's too."

"So what now?"

Kristair picked up the wooden bowl and brush, turning back toward me with a smile. "Now we can get into your body-painting fetish."

Nerves struck my stomach all over again. "What if I fuck it up?"

"I told you, you can't," Kristair said, sitting down on the bed. "The key is to relax."

"That's easy for you to say," I grumbled.

Kristair shot me an exasperated look then set the bowl in my hands. "Everything you need is in that thick skull of yours, if only you'd stop fighting it." He gave me a playful bite on my lower lip. "Stop fighting it."

I resisted rolling my eyes. "Fine. Where do I start? Do I meditate or something, chant a mantra?"

"Why don't you start by closing your eyes? Maybe think about how you prepare for a big game, of how you get into that mind-set where no distractions are allowed."

That was actually a pretty good idea. I did as he asked. That was the easy part. I willed away my nerves and worry over time passing and then Kristair spoke again. "Remember the night I did the ritual on you?"

"Oh boy, do I."

He chuckled. "I don't know whether to take that tone as good or bad." I just smiled and kept my eyes closed. The scent of the candles made the memory sharper, drawing me back. "Now remember that night, but from my point of view," Kristair murmured.

The shift was so smooth I barely noticed. I saw myself stretched out naked on the bed, looking up with both uncertainty and wonder in my eyes. I saw my hand, Kristair's hand, stir the blue paint in my little wooden bowl, taking the excess off the brush with the edge of the bowl, and begin to paint.

It all fell into place. Kristair wasn't copying the designs; he was barely looking at them. It was as if his hand had moved of his own volition. When I opened my eyes, I saw that Kristair had stretched out on the bed as I had, gaze steady on my face.

"Well, I suppose that's one way to do it." I always talked to Kristair about faith, so maybe it was time to have a little of my own. I swirled the brush around in the paint, took a deep breath, and bent over my lover. "Does it matter what order we do it in?"

"Not really."

"Good." I started the big one first. That one would take the most time. I'd get it out of the way first and then concentrate on the triquetra last, since that one meant the most to me. This area of Kristair's skin was smooth and free of scars and I resisted the impulse to start kissing every inch of him.

Kristair started laughing. "This kind of thing really does get you fired up, doesn't it? You kept breaking my concentration the last time with your salacious thoughts."

"Salacious? Who uses that word except you? Besides, I did it that night on purpose. This time, what can I say? It's making me think of feasting on you. Nice and slow." I shot him a wicked grin. "Kinda like what you did that one night to me."

"I remember," Kristair said, desire sparking inside him.

"I bet you do." He'd had me begging and cursing at the same time.

"Or maybe, given how possessive you are, you like the idea of us marking each other."

"You might be onto something there. We'll have to experiment another night." I blew some air across the glistening ink, surprised at how fast it dried and seemed to absorb into his skin. "So this language that I have to do the ritual in, what is it?"

"Pictish."

"Well I guess that makes sense, doesn't it?" I scooted down the bed, sliding the brush over his hip, trying to ignore his nakedness. From our first night together, when I really didn't understand what was going on, I'd still been affected by the intimacy and eroticism of the ritual. "It's not the same as the other language you use. The one that's in your head half the time, where you call me *mo chroí* and whisper all those things you don't think I know what they mean."

"No, that's Irish." I frowned and before I could ask the question he answered it for me. "One of the Gaelic languages."

"Aren't they all the same?"

A smile flickered over his lips. "Similar, but no, they're not. What are you trying to uncover?"

"Just passing time," I said and sat back to see how the painting looked before bending back over him to start filling in the outline. "I guess I just realized that, though I know you, I don't know too much about your past. And going through your memories seems like, I dunno, sneaking through your dresser drawers when you're not around or going through your safe deposit box."

"My past would take longer than the few hours we have left to tell."

"True, but what else do we have to do while I'm painting you? And to tell you the truth, it would distract me from wanting to jump your bones."

He laughed. "Ask away then."

"When did you go to Ireland instead of back home? Where was home anyway?" I had a vague idea that it was somewhere in Great Britain, but that was about all.

"Home? It was in what's now Scotland, somewhere around Perth or Stirling, I believe. It's been a very long time." His voice was lost in thought and I made a promise to myself that one day we'd go back and find out exactly where he'd lived. "I did return once, but there was nothing left for me there and staying around seemed pointless, so I left and ended up in Ireland. Only it wasn't called by that name, yet. I was there for a very long time. Longer even than Rome."

"What made you leave?" If Kristair had been restless when we mentioned his first home, he became even more so now. Enough that I raised my head to look at him. "What is it?"

"It's not important. We should be concentrating on other matters tonight instead of spending our energy on the past."

Now my curiosity was really aroused. "You do realize I'm not gonna let it drop now."

"I had hopes."

"They're dying an early death." I brushed against his mind, not so much to pry, because I preferred him telling me himself. I just wanted to see how reluctant he was to talk about it. To my surprise, I found that his reluctance centered around me and my feelings. "Go on; I can deal."

"That is a very bad habit you've picked up, poking around in other people's heads."

"I wonder who I got it from."

"Point taken." Kristair paused, and then made an impatient sound. "If you really must know it was because of another man."

I tamped down on my gut's initial possessive surge, though the look Kristair gave me told me he sensed it. "One of the other ones you did the exchange with?"

"Yes, only he couldn't handle who or what I was. It ended up driving him away." He rubbed his hand over my knee. "I think I only worried once that I'd do the same to you, but you quickly disabused me of the notion."

"I'll admit it took some adjusting." I grinned and gave him a wink. "Well worth it, though."

It didn't take nearly as long to paint the designs on Kristair's skin as it had been to tattoo them on mine, and he hadn't bothered to do any on my back. Soon I got to the last one and paused to kiss Kristair's shoulder, just as he had done to mine.

"No more joking," I said as I began to outline the triquetra. "So this symbolizes that we're married or something like that? Did your people even have marriage ceremonies?"

"Not as elaborate as your modern-day one, though the celebration lasted days longer." Kristair touched the interwoven lines he'd tattooed on me. "It didn't always stand for marriage, but it did stand for two people who shared a deep bond and committed themselves to each other. Sometimes it was husband and wife and sometimes it was an older sibling with a younger one, or two warriors who'd become closer than brothers. The type of bond wasn't as important as the strength of it."

"We do have that." I thought about it as I finished painting the triquetra onto him. No ceremony could make our connection stronger than it was right now. We were such a part of each other that even after the link had been broken the first time, we'd somehow, on instinct, found a way to forge it again. I supposed in the most intimate sense we could already say we were married.

Weird. Then I grinned. It just meant Kristair had no way of getting away from me. I kept what was mine.

"You are the most possessive man I have ever met," Kristair teased as I straightened and set the bowl aside.

"I'll take that as a compliment." I tugged on my earlobe and grimaced, feeling the nerves again now that I was no longer concentrating on what I was doing. "How'd I do?"

"You did just fine. We're almost done now." Kristair took my hands and brought them to either side of his face. "Do you remember the words I spoke that night? Bring them to your mind."

I closed my eyes and the memory became so clear to me. The power in Kristair's eyes, his voice, the electricity in the air, and the strange words that rolled off of his tongue. I sensed Kristair's guiding presence in my mind. "Open your mind, *mo chroí*. Open your eyes and look at me."

When I did, I felt the power of the night weave around us again, only this time it was inside me, and just as when I'd painted the tattoos on Kristair's body, my nervousness vanished. The words of the ritual poured from my lips as if they were ingrained into my bones. The candles flared and wavered, flickering madly before sinking low as the power between us built.

The sense of who I was, the memories, the feelings, the ingrained character, all seemed to well up until it almost formed a distinct second self. I smiled at Kristair, leaning over him until our foreheads were pressed together, and then said the final words. I sensed a part of myself pour into my lover and merge with him. Then exhaustion rolled over Kristair.

Chapter 28

"ARE you okay?" It was weird. I didn't feel any different from how I had before, but then I hadn't last time either. Maybe it was because our psychic bond had already been firmly established before we'd done either ritual. This just kinda made it official.

"I will be. It takes a great deal of energy from the recipient."

"If circumstances weren't what they were, I'd make you take a little nap," I teased, then stretched out next to him. "How's it feel to know every last bad thing I've ever done?"

It was euphoric, realizing that we'd done it. There was no way the Ascended could keep us apart for long. Not now. And we still had time before dawn. I had been so afraid that they'd figure out we were up to something, stop us, and take him from me. But he was still here.

"I don't know. I'll explore your misdeeds another day," Kristair said, reaching for me and pulling me over him. "You wanted to hear me beg earlier. Well, now I am. Right now, I don't want to think about anything, but you. I don't want to feel anything, but you. I want all my senses to be consumed by you. Please, *mo chroí*, whatever you've ever dreamed of doing with me, make it real."

Some people might not consider that begging, but from my lover, it was as good as Kristair going down onto his hands and knees and pleading. I smiled at him and rubbed my lips over his jaw before giving it a rough nip. "That's a very good start."

Shock flickered through Kristair and then a shudder as I entered his mind, letting him fully understand the strength of my conviction. "A start?" he said breathlessly. "I thought I did a rather good job."

"For you, my oh-so-restrained love, it was better than good. I know how hard it is for you to let go of your control, just as I know how much you want me to have it. I want more than what's on the surface. I want the deep unconscious begging, the gut reaction pleading when you can't think anymore. I want you to let loose all of that wild emotion I know you keep locked up inside you and give it to me."

"I don't know if I can." I had to smile at the genuine worry in his dark eyes.

"I do." I wrapped my arms around him, pulled us over onto our sides. I wanted to be so tangled up in him nothing would be able to tear us apart. "Now stop thinking about it, love. Just feel. No more thinking for the rest of the night."

Our mouths met and I could have drowned in his kiss. Those firm lips against my own, his hot tongue and even hotter mouth, the way he tasted, and the heat sizzling along my nerves as we kissed.

I wanted to touch him forever, be touched in return. Calloused, warrior hands whispered over my skin with a gentleness and reverence that came from the most private part of him. I caressed him in return. All that golden skin covered in tattoos, the scars on his shoulder and thigh, and every other inch untouched by needle or blade.

I sank myself into his mind as I claimed his body with my mouth and hands. I stroked his soul with my own and felt the response that came from the deepest heart of him. Still I demanded more.

Kristair shuddered, moaning into my mouth, his arms tightening around me. *"Jacob...."*

"It's okay," I soothed, sliding one hand down his long leg, lifting and spreading him wider. *"I've got you."*

Bit by bit, I chipped away at his restraint and, trembling, he made no move to try to stop me. I knew he wanted to, but he didn't. He just kept saying my name, with desperate hot kisses against my skin and urgent arches of his lean body into mine.

I kept my eyes locked on his face, drinking in every flicker of emotion. Of how velvet-hot his eyes looked instead of cool and reserved. Smiling, I used my mind and touched him inside, the way he'd done with me on the plane, groaning at how sinuously he moved beneath me. And we were only getting started.

"You're beautiful," I murmured, snickering at his incredulity.

"And you talk too much," Kristair replied. His hands cupped my ass, giving it a firm squeeze. "Not to mention that you've picked up some very unsavory habits." He gasped as I used my thoughts to massage his prostate, his eyes darkening to midnight. "Wicked brat."

I chuckled and dragged my tongue down his chest, tormenting his nipple with my teeth. "Once again, you only have yourself to blame."

"Hasn't anyone ever told you that revenge is rude?"

I savored the breathlessness of his voice, the way his heart beat faster inside my chest. "You're not one to talk about revenge. I've seen you in action."

Kristair pressed a kiss to the side of my throat and I couldn't stop the shiver of weakness. It had never been one of my hot spots before I'd met him, but it sure as hell was one now. His teeth scraped against my skin, an almost feral ache welling up. I shivered again. No matter what happened, whether everything went the way we hoped it would or not, I had the sudden intuition that this was the last time he was going to bite me.

"Kristair...."

There was a sharp prick, then the soothing brush of his tongue along my exposed throat. I made a soft sound and trembled as he penetrated me slowly, drawing out the moment. It was when he bit me that Kristair held nothing back. Maybe that was why I liked it so much. His love for me, his need to be in my life, washed over me so completely it swept everything else away.

I was panting by the time he pulled back and kissed me. I tasted my blood on his lips as the fire in my throat eased. For once, I wished I didn't heal so damn fast.

Breaking away with a groan, I reached for the lube and coated my fingers. Kristair's eyes gleamed as he hooked his arms under his knees and spread himself wide open for me. Somehow he made such a vulnerable position seem more like an erotic demand than one of submission.

I stroked one finger down the shadowed cleft, teasing his puckered entrance with the tip. "You are going to make me ask, aren't you, damn you?" Kristair said, with an impatient rock of his hips.

"No, not yet." I pushed the tip of my finger inside him and stopped. It was so rare that I got Kristair to curse that I reveled in it. "You'd just be saying the words then, not meaning them. By the time I'm done with you, you'll be meaning every last one."

"Sounds like a hell of a challenge. Sure you're up to it?"

I pushed my finger all the way into him, stroking just the edge of his spot. "Have you ever known me not to be up to it?" I twisted my finger, teased before easing another one in. "I'm always up to taking you on."

He clenched around my fingers and shivered. "Do it, Jacob."

Raw lust combined with pure heat, need, and love. I shifted through his mind until I found the pressure point I wanted, and then chuckled as he gasped. "What are you doing?"

"Making sure you can't come, love. Not until I'm damn good and ready for you to."

His eyes narrowed and I laughed again as he touched my mind in the same way. "Two can play at that game."

"I play every game to win," I promised. Not that there were going to be any losers this time. I just wanted to come out on top, and I would.

Kristair started to uncoil his body to reach for me, but I shook my head. "Don't move. Leave yourself open just like this."

He made a sound, a half-frustrated moan, but didn't argue. "I'm going to have so much fun with you." I kissed the inside of his thigh, trailing my tongue along all the tender, sensitive areas. My teeth nipped the curve of his ass. I drew his balls into my mouth and lashed them with my tongue. The whole time I continued to torment him with my fingers, stretching him, making him more than ready for me.

"Jacob...."

"Not yet." I swirled my tongue over the head of his cock, tracing it over the slit as my mouth filled with the musky, salty flavor of him, and his thighs trembled. "Not even close."

Kristair moaned again in that rich voice of his. I kissed and nipped, following up the thin path of hair on his stomach and chest. He shivered again as I settled against him, our cocks grinding together. As much as I wanted to thrust into him right then, I made myself wait. Not quite yet. Kristair had to be wild.

"I want to touch you," Kristair said. But he kept his hands on his thighs, still holding himself open as I rocked my hips. I shifted so my cock thrust between his cheeks and rubbed against the fingers I still had buried inside him.

"Ask me." I captured one peaked nipple and gave it a bite. I nipped him again as he bit back a curse, then soothed away the sting with a stroke of my tongue.

"Please, Jacob," he whispered, with an impatient arch of his hips. "Let me touch you."

I smiled and thrust my fingers into him a little harder, craving the little catch in his voice as he panted and twisted, grinding against me. I loved how helpless he was, not able to stop himself from reacting so wantonly. And I loved how he still kept his hands in place, even though I could taste how he hungered to get them on me.

"You may." I was so close to having him right where I'd wanted him. So close.

Surprise widened his eyes, but Kristair didn't waste one moment. Those long legs wrapped around my waist and pulled me close. His hand dug into my hair as he lifted up to steal a torrid kiss. He was so close. There was desperation in the way his tongue battled mine, the way he pressed himself against me, until there was nothing but skin to skin along his entire body.

Yet still he held onto that veneer of self-control.

Once again, I nudged at his mind, silently urging him to let go. I could make him. He'd let me take control, but I so wanted him to give it to me. "*I can't,*" he said in my mind.

"Yes, you can." I pushed a little more, teasing his prostate, kissing him deeper, silently demanding his surrender. The tension in his body built up to a fever pitch. I held nothing back, letting him feel in my mind everything that was in me, everything that I wanted to do to him.

He tore his mouth away from mine, his body riding the edge of an orgasm I refused to release. Kristair's fingers dug into my shoulder and upper back hard enough so I was sure there would be marks the next day. The more marks the better.

His dark eyes were wild, his lips parted as he moaned. Every one of those sweet emotions evident on his face as his control crumbled. It was damned beautiful. I leaned in close to him, and he bit his upper lip as I smiled down at him. "Now beg for real."

A shudder ripped through Kristair as I pressed with my fingers, stroked him with my thoughts, leaving no part of him untouched. "You're evil," he said, and I laughed. He could retaliate if he wanted to but he just kept accepting my torments without even trying to take control.

"Jacob...."

"Yes, love?" I dragged my tongue over his gasping lips then nipped his jaw. He was so damn close. Without warning, I slid down his body again and took the full length of his cock into my mouth, tightening the muscles in my mouth and throat around it.

Kristair shouted, his hands fisting in my hair as he drove his hips up. My mouth was filled with his rigid cock, the taste and scent of him. I groaned and relaxed my throat and when my lover struggled to get his control back, to stop his relentless thrusts, I blocked him.

"I like you like this, Kristair. Out of control, letting your body guide you."

"Jacob... Jacob... please, let me go."

"Never."

I looked up the length of his body as he drove his hips down onto my fingers then back up again into my mouth, holding my head still. I delighted in the sting of his hands hard in my hair. I had pushed him to this.

"Jacob…," he said, his voice harsh with need. I almost gave in to my desire to drive my cock inside of him until we were both spent, but I held on. "Let me go…."

I didn't respond. I didn't have to; Kristair already knew the answer. And with that the last vestige of his control broke and he began to plead. Desperate words falling from his lips, dark eyes begging, lean body writhing for more.

"Jacob, Jacob, Jacob. Fuck me. Let me come, please, Jacob."

I could barely breathe the sound of it was so damn erotic. It made my head swim and, for a moment, I couldn't react, only take it in. Then as Kristair's begging continued, I rose up from him and rolled onto my back, pulling him with me so that he straddled me. I didn't have to say anything. Kristair grasped my cock, guiding it against his entrance, and drove back hard. He cried out, head falling back, eyes closing in ecstasy, throat corded as he began to ride me with abandon.

Kristair had never been so beautifully wanton. Nothing remained hidden. It was so fucking hot I would've come on the spot if only Kristair hadn't taken the same hold on my mind as I now held on his.

I grabbed his hips, driving up hard to meet each rock of his hips. "Fuck, you're so beautiful, Kristair."

He didn't say a word, his elegant features drawn in tension and concentration. He leaned back, the muscles in his stomach and thighs taut. Then he crouched back over me, hands fisting in the sheets for balance, and our eyes locked. The power of the connection jolted through me.

I started stroking his cock as he clenched around my own. It was mindless and ferocious and all consuming. Kristair's pleas continued, half moans and half whispered thoughts. All sense of time and place disappeared as we lost ourselves in each other.

The need to come became painful. Kristair's voice was hoarse. Sweat dampened my body. "Jacob…." He repeated my name again like a prayer and I nodded, wetting my dry lips.

We released our hold on each other's minds at the same time and I sensed his orgasm hit as hard as my own. I wrapped my arms around him, yanking him close. He slid his arms underneath me as I struggled to catch my breath.

"Don't move. Please don't move, *mo chroí*."

"Don't plan to, love." Not until I had to.

WE HELD onto each other, our foreheads together, my hands clasping the back of his head as I breathed in the essence of him. Through Kristair, I sensed those fuckers hovering in the background, watching the scene, watching our goodbye. In that instant I hated them like nothing I ever had before. They watched like some diseased, arrogant spider gloating over our feeble efforts to avoid our parting. I wouldn't let them force Kristair anymore, or to cause him any grief by worrying over me.

I opened my eyes and stared hard up at Kristair. He looked back at me, his dark eyes troubled, anguish stealing over his face, sudden fear striking his heart. "Jacob, I—"

"No. It'll be okay." I buried my own doubts, shoving them deep where he wouldn't be able to sense them through his own turmoil, and gave him a fierce kiss. "Go…. Now."

When Kristair hesitated again, I gave him a mental push. "Go, before I change my mind and insist we take these motherfuckers out."

Kristair nodded and seemed to be at a loss for words. He didn't need to say anything though, because I could sense everything in his soul, mirroring my own. In a hoarse voice he began to speak words in a language long since extinct, words whose meaning were dead to everyone, except the two of us. I didn't pay attention to the meaning, just the timbre as he spoke, locking the rich sound in my memory.

Then the words faltered and I slid my hands gently down his scalp and over his shoulders. "Do it, love."

A new color began to creep in the sky, becoming a shade lighter. I didn't have to look out the window to know. All it took was the sense of the Ascended gathering their will to strike. Kristair's features hardened and his dark eyes flashed.

As the last words of the ritual fell from his lips, his heart in my chest went silent. There was a sudden wrenching sensation and an explosion of pain in my psyche as the room spun and I tumbled into darkness. When I managed to drag my eyes open again, he was gone.

Chapter 29

THE Ascended kept me waiting. And as hard as I tried, I couldn't find a chink in the leash they'd put on me. Not being able to sense Jacob made me restless. Knowing he was waiting made it worse. Not knowing what was going to happen eroded my patience until I was hanging onto it through the sheer effort of my will.

I had done everything they'd demanded and still they kept me apart from them. I should be the same as the rest of the Ascended now, with no invisible shackles holding me back. I should be able to exercise my will to the fullest extent, yet still they blocked me.

They were watching, lingering to see what I would do next. I could play that game very well. I was tempted to explore, to bide my time by sinking into the wonders around me, only it would be too easy to fall into the seductive lure of that life. I knew my weaknesses well. And I suspected, so did the Ascended. In all likelihood they were gambling on my curiosity.

It was hard not to second-guess my decisions. Was I being shortsighted by not accepting the hand that had been dealt me? I kept telling Jacob it wasn't possible to go back, yet wasn't that what I was trying to accomplish? Would I only be making myself less than what I could be?

But that would be assuming that just because I was limited to Earth there was nothing left to learn or explore. No, I refused to believe that. If I did then I would truly become blind. The Ascended, with all their power, forgot, I think, the beauty of the sometimes seemingly insignificant.

Besides, Jacob had faith in me. He was blind sometimes, but I wouldn't betray that faith.

So I waited, left with my constant questions and roundabout thoughts.

How time passed while I was with the Ascended did not concern me. Time ran differently among them. It wasn't linear. Centuries could pass and I was content to wait if that's what it took. What did concern me was that I didn't know how much time had passed for Jacob. Had it been days? Weeks? Had no time passed at all?

Time was fluid for me. Once I regained my powers I could go wherever I wished, when I wished, but I couldn't affect what had already passed for those it affected. I could only observe. Whatever life he had lived without me couldn't be reversed. That was one rule I couldn't break, no matter how much I wanted to be with Jacob.

To do otherwise would be pure selfishness. I had no way of knowing how many ripples I'd cause if I did or how much damage they would do.

And I waited and paced and railed against the silent voices of the other Ascended who never answered my demands.

EVERY Ascended who had ever existed arrived for my hearing. I had to give them credit for intimidation. The immensity of their whole was awe inspiring and a not-so-subtle reminder of what I'd tried to give up. All because of Jacob. Maybe that wasn't entirely fair. I shouldn't lay the blame on him. More so, all because I wasn't willing to give up the bond I'd unknowingly searched for my entire existence.

"Isn't this all a trifle dramatic?" I stood in the midst of them, calm and ready. If they had thought to wear me down with the wait, they were wrong. It had only strengthened my resolve.

"You are arrogant."

They spoke as one, choral voices swelling the air as a single, immutable chord. Still, I swore I could hear my Mistress's voice threaded in amongst them, so I concentrated on her as I answered.

"Shouldn't that be we? We are arrogant. To deny that fact would be a lie. You accuse me of your own flaw… or strength, depending on how you wish to view it."

"So you are saying that you now fully accept being one of the whole? You consider yourself to be one of the Ascended and not look back on your former life with longing? We find that difficult to believe in light of your actions since you've returned. You could've made yourself a part of the whole as you were before, yet you kept yourself separate. You could've shared in our explorations, yet again you held yourself apart."

I paused. Had I miscalculated? I tried to read them, only to find them as inaccessible as ever. Could I have merged with them and regained my powers and only been blocking myself this entire time? Had fear of losing my sense of self blinded me so much? Shaken, I gathered myself together again.

"It doesn't matter what I consider myself, as you've pointed out several times. After all, as you have made clear, I cannot go back, only forward. Nor does it matter if you believe me. I have done as you wished. The link between me and Jacob is broken. What you do now is nothing but a farce. Release me."

"It is not so simple anymore." The choral song turned steely and cold.

"We had an agreement." I tightened my hold on my rising anger. I never would've agreed to break the link if I hadn't believed their word to be binding. "Have you so little control that you think it necessary to trick me into doing your bidding?"

That stung them. It gave me no small measure of satisfaction to break through their calm. The air became heavy with the sharp pressing edge of their pique. "You were to go back for one reason and one reason only." The ethereal voices were stern. "To break the link with your human lover. We did not send you back to make war on the vampires. We did not send you back so you could reveal our secrets to those who had not earned them." The weight of their rising voices became almost too much to bear.

I searched the massed minds of the Ascended for Jacob's friend Tony, trying to find something positive to cling to. Some comfort I could bring back to Jacob. But if he was there, a part of them, I couldn't pick him out. Still the search helped me to cope with the vastness of those standing against me.

"I warned you it would take time and you put limits on me, forcing me to reside in Jacob's mind. He was being targeted by the Syndicate, thus I had no option but to participate in their war. They sought the fight from the beginning, not us. Thus, both you and the Syndicate left me with no other choice."

"And the secrets? You have a ready answer for that as well?"

"Jacob already knew the secrets before I was taken by you in the warehouse. He was linked with my mind at the end. Though he chose not to access that information for a long time, it was still there."

"And Anthony Hodge?" They persisted. "He should not be a member of our ranks, yet he is because of your interference. He is too raw, a lost babe."

Lost among the wolves, in my opinion, and his involvement was the one regret I had. Not only for the pain his passing had caused but because, as a youngling, he would find it as difficult as I had to become one of the Ascended. Who knew how long it would be before his mind could accept what he had become, before his will would become strong enough to handle such power?

"You know I intentionally gave Tony no secrets. I had not realized how deep his friendship with Jacob had gone. I had not trusted their bond when I should have. If I had, I would've recognized the risk. No one regrets more than I what happened to him, but the danger is gone now. Jacob will never give up that information and all those who searched for the secrets have been destroyed." I paused then allowed myself a slight smile. "In that war you chastised me about. The secrets are now secure with him and only him."

"And Kayla? You were not to make contact with your daughter."

"Do not dare to accuse me of breaking that rule." Anger whipped out and I turned the force of it toward them. "Do not dare. I made no effort though it cost me. True, I did not fight Jacob when he wanted to tell her and that may have bent the rules. But it did not happen."

"Only because we took measures to prevent it from happening."

"No, you interfered. Something you keep saying you don't do. You merely observe. It would've made no difference to your existence if Kayla knew there was a part of me still alive. It would not have altered or threatened you in any way. You blocked it merely because you enjoyed exercising your own powers."

The choral voices died down into a sibilant whisper, the thousands of voices talking in layers, the shifting patterns obscuring what they were saying. Whispers that were so very familiar. At one time, I'd thought their sound was a sign of impending insanity. How wrong I had been.

I forced myself to wait and not demand answers and before too long, I sensed their full attention return to me again. "Kristair, it is our judgment that you obeyed the strictures of the agreement. Though you tried to twist out of it, you caused no lasting harm. In truth, we expected you would try some trick. However, you did break the link. You no longer carry your lover's emotional taint." They paused. "Though it is strange, you somehow carry a piece of him with you, in that part of yourself that has been missing."

"We will forever carry a part of each other. Breaking the psychic link and destroying my heart was the deal, not separating our souls. That cannot be broken."

The Ascended gathered closer, crowding around me, and I steeled myself, unwilling to give them the satisfaction of showing any weakness or worry. "Based on the loss of that connection, we will release your full abilities. Though your thoughts are still consumed with him and your feelings for him still color your decisions, obscuring the full measure of what you could be. Still, an agreement is binding and we have no choice but to unblock you and accept you as one of us."

As much as I wanted to rejoice, I was wary instead. This was far too easy. It couldn't be this easy, despite their interrogation.

The air shimmered and Nerissa appeared in front of me, a physical representative of the Ascended. She was terrible and beautiful in her power and I was dwarfed by her immensity.

"We know you, Kristair. You are stubborn and willful. We will excise Jacob from your mind." Horror dawned and I tried to bolt only to find myself frozen as she loomed, blotting out everything but her, as the voices grew to a painful crescendo. "By the time your memory returns he will have ceased to matter. Then you will be one of us."

Chapter 30

POOH Corner was just as crowded as ever, though this time the stares of its denizens didn't faze me. I walked alone up to the bar where Deke stood and he nodded. "Hey, kid. Congrats on being invited to the combine again."

"Thanks, Deke." I grinned; it still gave me a thrill every time I thought about it. The timing and testing sessions brought me one step closer to my dream and kept me too busy to brood after Kristair was taken. In two more months I'd be in front of the NFL officials with all the other hopefuls, and I was gonna blow their minds.

"Why didn't you go last year?" Deke asked, starting to put together a beer order on a tray. Seeing him do something as prosaic as work a barroom tap was a little surreal, but I guess even vamps had to have some downtime from all the fighting and hunting. "School's not your thing. I've seen you play. You could've left it far behind you last year."

"When I was given the scholarship, I made a promise to my mother that I'd finish school." I accepted the beer he handed me. "Thanks, man."

"Mothers...." A sudden grin crossed Deke's grizzled face. "My mother was not someone to cross, but that's a story for another time. Guess you don't dare cross yours either."

"Fuck no. Is he waiting?" I nodded toward the back room.

"Yep. Go right on in."

Ussier glanced up from the video game he was playing as I entered the back, and his gaze took on a teasing glint. "Well, if it isn't Pittsburgh's own star running back."

"You don't look any different. Video games?" I bantered back. "This mean you're done chasing Syndicate goons all over the world?" As I approached, he paused the game and rose, giving me a nod and clapping me on the arm. I think it was the first time he'd ever stood up when I came in.

"If there is anyone left who was once a part of that group, they're keeping it a close, dark secret. Alette and Hugh are still hunting down rumors. They're good at that and it should keep them out of trouble."

"So it's over with?" I sat down in the chair Ussier indicated. I found it a little hard to believe; it was just that weird. They'd harassed me on and off for over a year and though I had healed quickly from the injuries they'd given me, I was still human. Ever since Kristair broke the link, my back would ache after an especially hard day of playing, as a result of Montrose's bullets shattering my spine. And on really cold, raw days I could feel the lingering pain in my shoulders too. I'd live with those scars the rest of my life.

And now that I wasn't carrying around a vampire's heart, the bruises lasted when I got knocked around. That had been a hard wakeup call. I'd wanted to be normal again, and now I was with all of its glory.

"Yeah, Jake, it's over with. Let's not get cocky though. Just concentrate on playing football and leave the supernatural stuff to me. See if you can stay out of trouble."

I laughed and dragged a hand through my hair. "I am planning on a life where my only thrills are the games and the excitement of fame."

"Do you mind if I ask you a question?"

I cocked my head. Ussier didn't ask—he demanded answers—, and that alone was enough to trigger my curiosity. "Shoot."

"You said you carried a part of the old man with you. There were times when I swear I could see his hand in what you were doing. Just how much is he a part of you now?"

There was a twinge in my chest where Kristair's heart had been. I missed it. I hadn't thought I would. Its constant beating at weird times, the not knowing, had driven me crazy, and now I missed it. I really was an ornery bitch.

"More then, than now." I wasn't like Kristair, keeping secrets just for the sake of keeping them. I'd learned my lesson. "For a week or so there, he was with me as much as it was possible to be."

Ussier's brow rose and then after a moment, he nodded. "I'm not surprised. If anybody could come back for one last hurrah it would be that stubborn bastard. Is he gone for good now?"

"Who the hell knows?" I shrugged and then grinned. "Somehow I doubt it. It's just a matter of when."

Sooner rather than later, please. It had already been a very long month. I'd gone home for Thanksgiving alone and told myself that he would be with me for Christmas. Now, I was packing up to see my Ma again and wouldn't get the chance to introduce them if Kristair didn't hurry up and pop up out of the blue in the next two weeks. Still, I held on to my faith. Kristair had promised he'd be home by April. All I could do was be patient.

"Did Kayla know?" I winced at his question, tugging on my earlobe, and Ussier laughed. "That answers the question."

"She does now." And what a loud mess that had been. "She's not so pissed at me as she is at Kristair." Even more so at Nerissa for stealing that moment from her. "She doesn't like people making decisions for her, even if it's to spare her feelings. Gets her back up more than anything else does."

"She's not the only woman to feel that way." The vampire lord gave me a little salute and picked up his game controller. "Stay out of trouble. This time I mean it."

I rose from my chair and shook Ussier's hand again. "No offense, but you don't mind if I'm happy I'll never see you again. At least I hope I won't."

"You won't see me, but I'll see you." He grinned his predator smile.

"Fucker."

"HOW was Louisiana?" Steve asked, holding the door open for me as I kicked snow off my sneakers.

"Hell of a lot warmer than here," I complained. Pittsburgh was balls cold in January, wind whipping up snowdrifts and stinging every bit of exposed skin until it felt raw and abused.

"Want a beer or something stronger?"

I tossed my coat on the hook then followed Steve into the kitchen. "Stronger would kick ass. I swear I'm never going to warm up again."

"Pansy. You'd better hope you get drafted to Miami, bro. Your blood's getting thin." Steve took down two tumblers and poured whiskey into them. "Happy New Year," he said, handing me one.

The whiskey burned all the way down, banishing some of the frozen numbness both from the cold and the emptiness in my soul. "Thanks, man." I raised my glass to him then downed the rest. "It's quiet. Your roommates around?"

"Nope, still on winter break. They'll be trickling in over the week. Kayla's taking a nap upstairs. You'd best stick around 'til she wakes up or you know what she'll do to you when she sees you next."

"Thanks for the heads up. Think she'll feed me if I stay?"

"Don't push your luck." Steve grabbed the whiskey bottle and we went into the living room. The TV was on low, showing one of the playoff games. The Titans were up by six points. A good game was just what I needed to relax.

"So this thing with *chica*, it's finally gotten serious? 'Bout damn time." I liked the thought of Kayla and Steve together more and more. They balanced each other, both with strong personalities that didn't drown the other out.

A quick grin flashed across Steve's face and I realized that I'd never seen quite that expression on him. Oh boy, he had it bad. My smirk must've shown because he punched my arm. "Knock it off. Yeah, it's serious." He paused and took a sip of the whiskey, his eyes on the TV. "She spent Christmas with me and my brother."

I almost choked on my drink, but managed to catch myself in time. For Steve, that was like close to a marriage proposal. He'd never taken a girl to meet his brother. Ever. "Damn, that explains why she didn't run off with me then."

I hadn't liked the idea of her being by herself, but nothing I'd said had made her budge at all. She wouldn't consider spending the holiday in Louisiana. Now I knew why. I chuckled. The thought of them together over the holidays made me feel so much better.

"What's so funny?"

"Nothing. So, how did your brother and Kayla react to each other?" I almost wished I'd seen it.

"He thinks she's a crazy white girl and she thinks he needs to lighten up and get a life."

This time I burst out laughing and Steve joined in with me. "I think Kayla's the only girl you could've brought home that wouldn't be intimidated by him."

"Yeah, he's impressed. He won't say it, but he is."

I poured us some more whiskey. "That's awesome, man. I'm really happy for you."

"I should've known you'd returned."

At the sound of Kayla's voice, I peered over my shoulder and smiled. She leaned against the entrance of the living room, sleep rumpled, her arms crossed and a fake scowl aimed at me.

"Hey there, gorgeous. Don't I get a kiss?"

"You've been drinking whiskey. My lips aren't touching yours." She came over and gave me a hug before Steve pulled her down onto his lap. I rolled my eyes as they kissed and felt a quick, hard knock of emptiness. I wished Kristair were there, just so I could see his face. I'd rag on him big time.

"How come he gets one and I don't?" I complained when they finally broke apart.

"My face isn't as ugly as yours," Steve retorted.

"Now I know you're delusional. Your face scares small babies and grandmas." I turned my smile on Kayla and her lips twitched. "I don't suppose you could find it in your heart to feed me, at least."

"That's why he gets kissed and you don't, hotshot. Do I look like Donna Reed?"

"You wouldn't want me to waste away."

Kayla snickered and pointed to a pile of junk mail circulators on the table. "You're in no danger of wasting away. There's pizza coupons in there. Have at it. Your mom spoils you too much."

"Yeah, she does." I sighed and pulled over the pile. "I wish 'The O' delivered."

"Keep wishing," Steve said. "There's an Italian place around the corner that does and you can get pasta instead of pizza, or both."

"Sounds perfect. I'm starved."

We put in an order and sat back with beer this time instead of whiskey, watching the game and catching up. The only thing missing was Tony lounging on the floor and Kristair curled up next to me. Otherwise, it would have been a perfect afternoon.

"I had the weirdest dream a couple nights ago," I said, without even thinking about it. "Both Tony and Kristair were there. In some big, oh, I don't know how to describe it, like some Roman temple or something." It wasn't the first dream I'd had of Kristair. I'd had many of him waiting and pacing, and figured it was because I missed him. After all, we weren't linked anymore, though sometimes I thought it might be because he carried a piece of my soul with him. I'd often wondered if maybe there was some sort of an echo effect and I really was seeing him. Then I'd convince myself it was just wishful thinking.

Kayla sat up straight, her dimples disappearing. "Was that bitch there too?"

Before I could comment on her odd remark, Steve spoke up. "A big place, kinda like almost how you'd picture judgment day in heaven or something? With rows of people, your boy in the center and Tony sitting up front?"

We exchanged glances, and then all of us began talking at once until Kayla whistled to silence us. "Wait a minute. One dream at a time. Jake, you describe yours first."

I tried to gather my thoughts past the excitement bouncing in my stomach. My head spun and I now wished that I hadn't had the damned whiskey. We'd all had the same dream. Sure, details were different, but the overall story was the same. How the hell was that possible? Kristair had never had a mental link with them. Well, maybe Kayla, but he didn't have any of his powers, unless the Ascended had released them. But if they had, he'd be home.

The room became quiet once we were all done describing our dreams and then Steve got up to grab the food from the delivery man. I wasn't hungry anymore. Kristair was on trial, or had been. At least that's what it had seemed like. And he'd been upset at the end, pissed off, afraid. The details were sketchy like dreams tended to be. I couldn't remember the words they'd spoken or if they'd been spoken at all.

"What does it all mean?" Steve asked. "Have either of you have any other dreams like this of Kristair? Why's he in my head? I'm telling you now: I don't want him in my head."

"Not like this. I mean I've had dreams of him. Of course I have." Some which I knew were products of my imagination because they were all X-rated. But even the dreams I'd had of him waiting and pacing weren't like this. Those were more like quick flashes of consciousness gone as soon as they appeared.

"This is the only one I've had," Kayla said. "You think Kris sent it to us?"

I thought it through before I answered and then shook my head with a sigh. "I'd like to, but I doubt it. It's not his style. One, he was a little bit preoccupied in the dream and two, even if he had the ability to send us the dream, he wouldn't if it was something bad."

"And that whole situation seemed fucked up. Who was that lady at the end?" Kayla growled, her eyes flashing, and Steve held up his hands. "Forget I asked."

"That was Nerissa. She's the one who made Kristair a vampire." She was also Kayla's ancestor, but I thought it wiser to shut up about that. She was never gonna forgive Nerissa for interfering and costing her a chance to talk with Kristair. "I must admit, I don't think Kristair sent the dream either. He does like to keep us in the dark until everything's lined up just how he likes it."

Steve gave my shoulder a hard squeeze, his other arm locked around Kayla's waist. "I'm sorry. I know you both have been waiting."

I shook my head and squared my jaw. "I'm not ready to give up yet. Come on; it has to mean something. If Kristair didn't send the dream, then who did?" I refused to let worry sink into my gut. Not after all this time.

"Whiskey has addled your brains. Kristair wasn't the only one we knew in the dreams." Kayla paused, her head cocked expectantly, then let out an explosive breath. "Tony! For chrissakes, have you two forgotten about him already? You both saw Tony there. He might've been in my dream too, but I don't remember much other than Kris and that bitch. I don't know him as well."

A little thrill of hope raced through me, but Steve was already shaking his head. "You don't know for sure if he was really there. I know you guys think he became one of the Ascended, but he wasn't an Ancient. I mean, I love the dude and all, but Tony with cosmic powers? That's a little frightening. And even if he was one of them, didn't you say it had taken months for Kristair to remember who he was?"

Excited now, I jumped up. "Yeah, but it's been months, and Tony may have been a bit of a doofus, but he's not stupid. And he's our doofus. This is just the kind of thing he would do."

"Why, just answer that, Jake. It doesn't make sense. Why would Tony send the dream? What would it do other than to make you worry?" Steve argued.

"Fuck worrying," I laughed. "Now I know Kristair's going to be home before too long."

Kayla and Steve exchanged a worried glance, but I refused to acknowledge it. Kristair was coming home. I jutted my jaw out.

"How do you know?" Kayla asked. "I mean, I want to believe as much as you do, but it didn't look good for him at the end." She paused and bit her lip and Steve pulled her closer.

"It means we've got a friend up there," I said. "And those bastards are going to underestimate him just the way we did. You'll see."

Chapter 31

As MUCH as I enjoyed all the wonders I'd discovered and my mind being occupied with the wealth of information the universe held, I still found the constant presence of all the other Ascended cloying and irritating. I'd always been a solitary soul and it was a rare occasion when I invited someone into my life. Though, on those occasions, the bond I'd formed had been very tight. I suppose eventually, I'd get used to it, but for now I needed some time to myself.

I slipped away from the other Ascended. We tended to do things as a group and there were some who never left the contemplation of the whole. But there were enough who did go exploring on their own that I wasn't concerned my exit would be commented on by the whole.

As I wandered, I searched within myself for the reason why I was so restless. It wasn't just because I preferred to be alone. I felt incomplete, as if a limb had been hacked off and the phantom pain from it lingered in my soul. To the other Ascended I think I appeared intact, only I knew that somehow I wasn't.

I couldn't reason out what was missing. No amount of introspection yielded the answer so I stopped twisting and turning the problem, and let it be. The answer would come in its own time.

I found myself watching a star, a red giant, wondering how many thousands or millions of years it would take to reach the critical point, for it to explode into a supernova. What would that be like, the slow deterioration, losing energy until suddenly it all burst back into life again for one final massive explosion, lighting up the galaxy? As one of the Ascended, could I make myself one with the star and experience the whole thing?

Before I could contemplate on how I'd accomplish such a feat, another distinct presence appeared beside me, somewhat familiar, though I couldn't say why. He took form, something I had rarely seen once I'd become one of the Ascended.

He looked to be a young man, almost a kid, though appearances were deceiving. My own body, when I'd had one, looked to be only a few years older than his. However, I was thousands of years old. To my surprise, his mind was almost as young as his body. I'd never met an Ascended like him. He was an anomaly, the same as me.

His hair was in need of a cut and his eyes were gray-green, with a mix of humor and eternal wonder. As I took form, out of politeness as well as curiosity, I noticed how different he was. In truth, I preferred being like this, another difference that set me apart, but I figured it was because I was so new to it all.

I don't know how often I'd be reminding myself that I'd adapt.

"Kristair," he greeted with a slight grin. "You're a hard man to track down. I was almost beginning to believe the rest of the Ascended were trying to keep us apart." He took in the giant star, swollen red and huge against the sky. "It's almost like an episode out of *Star Trek*," he murmured. "Or *The Twilight Zone*, take your pick."

"I don't see why they would do that. We are all open to each other." Or were we? Something niggled at my mind then disappeared. "And you are?"

"Tony Hodge, though the name won't mean anything to you."

It sparked something though and when I tried to grasp it, it eluded me once again. "It should, though," I said.

"Yeah, but I didn't come here to talk about that. I came to ask you about your tattoos."

"My tattoos?" I glanced down at my bare chest and the designs that symbolized my life. I'd had them for so long they were as natural to me as thinking. "What about them?"

"They are a link to your past."

It wasn't a question, though what he was trying to get at, I didn't know. "That's one way of looking at it. In truth, the tattoos are meant to provide a link for the future. But in the long run, they have failed. Except for me, there is no one left alive who remembers the Picts. Even then my knowledge is imperfect. The group racial memory, the sum of my people, was never passed down to me. I was taken before I could do the ritual with one of my elders."

"Really? That's kinda interesting. What about that one?" Tony pointed to the outline of a creature on my right shoulder. "What does that one make you think of?"

I stared at the tattoo in confusion, my fingers brushing over the lines that didn't belong there. Memory came to me. An alligator, jaws snapping dangerously close. The air was green, the scent of lush growing and rotting death, the song of a swamp and all its myriad creatures closing in around me.

This was not the land I'd grown up in. Those were not my hands on a boat hook beating off the gator or my own voice shouting a string of vicious curses. "Jake! Holy shit! Will ya look at him?" Someone shouted behind me. A crawfish trap hurtled past my shoulder and struck the gator right on its snout.

Before I could question the oddity of the memory, Tony drew me out by pointing to another tattoo on my right chest, a broad smile on his face. "And that one? What does it bring to mind?"

The image of a man appeared before me, so much bigger than I. Joyous terror filled me as he swung me up high in the air, catching me in large hands before I fell. A trucker hat was perched on his head and his eyes were a light, twinkling blue. "A'gin! A'gin, Daddy!" I demanded.

The memories moved quicker. Police talking to a fair-haired woman whose eyes were red from weeping. The same man in a casket, his skin gray and cold, and me straining up on my toes to peer inside, my jaw clenching tight as someone murmured, "Jake, come sit with me" in the background.

"I don't understand," I said, pulling myself out of the memories.

"You will," Tony promised and pointed to another tattoo. "What about the triquetra? What's it mean?"

"It's the balance of body, mind, and soul."

"No, Kristair. What does it mean to you?"

My soul mate, the other half of my heart. That made even less sense than any of the other tattoos. I had not found someone like that for me, though I'd searched over the long years of my life. I'd had hope once or twice, but that had been so long ago and now it didn't matter.

"You're not making any sense."

"Yes, I am. Just think about it." A faint smile touched his face. "I owe him. Look, tell Jake that he made an awesome touchdown in his last game. Saved Pittsburgh's ass." He shook his head. "How come I'm not surprised?"

"What are you talking about?"

As the memories, which didn't belong to me, continued to roll through my mind, I realized I knew this man as intimately as I knew myself. Jake, Jacob Corvin, *mo chroí, m'anam, mo shaol, mo ghrá*. Only the memories belonged to him alone. I had no personal memory of him. How could that be?

How could I feel so much for someone and not remember?

Tony gave me another one of his impish smiles. "You've got it now. I knew you'd get this far on your own, but for the rest, I'm afraid you'll need help." Before I could ask what he meant, he touched my forehead. "Remember."

My memory came back in a tidal wave of emotion and sensation. Jacob. They'd blocked me from him again and taken away my choice. I straightened in fury as Nerissa appeared beside me. "What have you done?" she said to Tony.

I turned to her, gathering my will, my fury, until it blazed through me. I unburied the wish that I'd hidden in the back of my mind and formed the one single thought that would change everything for me, for the good or the bad.

"Kristair, don't!"

"It's too late." I gave her a tight smile, thought of Jacob and where I wished to be. "I am human."

Epilogue

"DUDE, I don't think I've ever seen anybody dodge and run like you do."

I turned and grinned at Frode Williams, another running back from Ohio State. "Thanks, but you beat me in the weight reps and Quirnio kicked both of our asses in the broad jump."

At least I could be sure that it was all me in the contests and not some souped-up version of me. If I didn't make it, I'd at least have my pride intact. Still, I was pretty damn stoked about my scores.

"Want to grab a beer?" Frode gestured to the hotel bar where a number of other guys were already headed.

"Sure." The idea of going back to an empty hotel room was too unappealing even if it did call to me. It wasn't too late. A couple beers wouldn't slow me down in the morning.

All the stools around the bar were taken up by other college hopefuls and the pool room off to the side teemed with players. The click and clack of balls smacking each other filled the air. We found a little table crowded in the back and gestured for the waitress.

Frode studied the notes he'd made of individual scores, a line forming between his brows. "Looking at this stuff drives me nuts, but I can't seem to stop myself." He took several large swallows of his beer. "What do you think?" He pushed the paper toward me.

I shook my head, ignoring the notes, and pulled out my planner. "I'd rather go with my gut." I crossed out today's date. Sixty-two more days until draft day. Sixty-two more days for Kristair to show up. I'd had a few more dreams about him, but nothing like the one I'd shared with Kayla and Steve. It was beginning to wear on my patience.

"What does your gut tell you?" Frode asked.

"That I have nothing to worry about. Neither should you." I'd never been accused of being humble. It was more than that, though. I'd poured out everything I had in the drills today. It was the best I could do and it was damn good. Now, all I could do was wait. Frode, I bet, was going to obsess over every Web site report until he had an answer one way or another.

Me, I kinda wanted to check out the tests for the linemen tomorrow. It would at least keep me occupied. I shut the planner and took a sip of my own beer.

"I've never met a guy with a planner before, except for maybe my dad."

"Yeah, the guy I was with, am with, he's obsessed with organization. Rubbed off on me, I guess." I set my beer aside and pushed my chair back, too restless to stay still. I'd thought I was in the mood for hanging, but I just wanted to be back in my room. I'd take a shower, maybe see what movies were available and just relax.

My room called to me.

"Hey, don't leave yet." Disappointment flashed across Frode's face. "You haven't finished your beer."

"I guess I'm just more bushed than I thought I was." I laid some money on the table to cover my drink. "I'll see ya tomorrow."

"Want to get together for a workout in the morning?"

I paused, studied the expression on Frode's face, and then smiled and shook my head. "I'm taken. Practically married." There was a time when I would've taken Frode on his unspoken offer and nailed that ass if for no other reason than to release the tension of the day. I smiled again to ease the sting. "See ya."

I made idle chat as some of the other guys stopped me on my way out, not paying too much attention to what I was saying. Mostly congratulations, or good luck, or what my opinion was on the meets today. Eventually, I made it out the door and breathed a sigh of relief as I got onto the elevator.

My room called me with a siren's song, its pull getting more potent as I walked down the hallway. The day must have taken more out of me than I'd realized. Forget the movie. I'd get naked, lose myself in a few memories, and then let them carry me until morning.

As I went to unlock the door, I knew, somehow I just knew, who was waiting for me on the other side. A tremor shook me so hard I almost dropped the key card. Holding my breath, I opened the door, my heart twisting once, hard, as my eyes immediately went to the bed.

Kristair lay in the center, naked, his long legs drawn up and tucked in close to his body, his forehead touching his knees and his arms clasped around them. His chest rose and with each indrawn breath and fell again. And even though it had been several months since I felt his heart beat inside his chest, I knew it was beating for him now.

Really beating like someone who lived.

My throat was so tight that my chest ached. And as much as I wanted to sprint over to the bed, all the power and speed I'd shown earlier in the day for the coaches had deserted me. Instead, I stumbled over to him and fell down on the bed.

He was here. Somehow, he was here and he was breathing, really breathing, not just going through the motions so he could talk. Kristair stirred, his head turning toward me, and his long, sooty lashes fluttered open. After a moment, his dazed eyes focused on me and a slow, brilliant smile crossed his lips, lighting my life with its promise.

"Kristair."

MARGUERITE LABBE has been accused of being eccentric and a shade neurotic, both of which she freely admits to, but her muse has OCD tendencies, so who can blame her? Her husband and son do an excellent job keeping her toeing the line, though. Together with her co-author Fae Sutherland, Marguerite has found a shared passion for beautiful men with smart mouths.

When she's not working hard on writing new material and editing completed work, she spends her time reading novels of all genres, enjoying role-playing games with her equally nutty friends, and trying to plot practical jokes against her son and husband. Her son is learning the tricks too quickly and likes to retaliate. You'd think she'd learn.

Visit Marguerite's web site at http://chasethedream.net/.

DON'T MISS THE OTHER BOOKS OF THE TRIQUETRA